Praise for the Saga of the Skolian Empire

"The latest in the Skolian Empire series, but it can be read as a stand-alone novel. . . . The plot is convincing, well staged and incredibly exciting. Kamoj is like a butterfly emerging from a cocoon of ignorance and degradation. Her relationship with Vyrl blossoms almost immediately and she begins to question her own passivity to Jax's cruelty. Vyrl is a tortured but honorable hero who falls in love with the young Kamoj when he observes her from a distant hillside as she takes a moment away from her responsibilities. Jax isn't entirely dastardly either; his mixed feelings for his former betrothed are sadly pathetic.

"Beautifully written with great characters that demand the reader's attention, *The Quantum Rose* is more than science fiction and romance; it is an excellent novel with twists and turns that kept me riveted. Be prepared to stay up late, you won't want to put this book down." —*Romance Reviews Today*

"A treat. Thought-provoking, entertaining and very, very enjoyable. Asaro begins with interesting scientific and cultural speculation, and then draws in the reader by making the story human and personal for a most satisfying read." —*SF Site*

"A freestanding page-turner as a romance, with a hard science framework." —*Publishers Weekly*

"The writing is strong and the plot and characters engaging, and Asaro walks the line well, holding it all together with a complexity of situations, scientific marvels, and loads of intrigue." —*Locus*

Tor Books by Catherine Asaro

THE SAGA OF THE SKOLIAN EMPIRE
Primary Inversion
Catch the Lightning
The Last Hawk
The Radiant Seas
Ascendant Sun
The Quantum Rose
Spherical Harmonic
The Moon's Shadow*

*forthcoming

The Quantum Rose

Catherine Asaro

TOR®

A TOM DOHERTY ASSOCIATES BOOK
NEW YORK

This is a work of fiction. All the characters and events portrayed in this book are either products of the author's imagination or are used fictitiously.

THE QUANTUM ROSE

Edited by David G. Hartwell

A Tor Book
Published by Tom Doherty Associates, LLC
175 Fifth Avenue
New York, NY 10010

www.tor.com

Tor® is a registered trademark of Tom Doherty Associates, LLC.

ISBN 0-812-56883-4
Library of Congress Catalog Card Number: 00-043027

First edition: December 2000
First mass market edition: February 2002

Printed in the United States of America

0 9 8 7 6 5 4 3 2 1

This book is dedicated to three exceptional people:
the scientists, teachers, and role models
who taught me quantum theory

Alex Dalgarno
Eric Heller
Kate Kirby

Contents

Acknowledgments

I would like to express my gratitude to the readers who gave me input on *The Quantum Rose*. Their comments greatly helped the book. Any errors that remain are mine alone.

To Jeri Smith-Ready and Binnie Syril Braunstein for their thorough readings; to Damon Knight for his invaluable input on GEnie; to Dr. Lee Cafferty for his advice on medical details; to Dr. Richard Drachman of NASA for checking the essay; to the writers who critiqued various scenes: Aly's Writing Group, including Aly Parsons, Simcha Kuritzky, Connie Warner, Al Carroll, Paula Jordon, Michael La Violette, George Williams, and J. G. Huckenpöler; Washington Independent Writers, including Francis and Norm Miller, Martha Midgette, Leslie Haag, and Leslie Cohen; to Ruth's "class," including Ruth Glick (Rebecca York), Randy DuFresne (Elizabeth Ashtree), and Chassie West; and to all the folks who answered my research questions in the GEnie SFRT4.

A special thanks to my editors, Jim Minz and David Hartwell, for their excellent insights and suggestions; to the publisher, Tom Doherty, and to Mary Louise Mooney and all the fine people at Tor and St. Martin's Press who made this book possible; and to my much appreciated agent, Eleanor Wood, of Spectrum Literary Agency.

A most heartfelt thanks to the shining lights of my life, my husband, John Kendall Cannizzo, and my daughter, Cathy, whose constant love and support make it all worthwhile.

1

Ironbridge

First Scattering Channel

Kamoj Quanta Argali, the governor of Argali Province, shot through the water and broke the surface of the river. Basking in the day's beauty, she tilted her face up to the violet sky. The tiny disk of Jul, the sun, was so bright she didn't dare look near it. Curtains of green and gold light shimmered across the heavens in an aurora visible even in the afternoon.

Her bodyguard Lyode stood on the bank, surveying the area. Lyode's true name was a jumble of words from the ancient language Iotaca, which scholars pronounced as *light emitting diode.* No one knew what it meant, though, so they all called her Lyode.

Unease prickled Kamoj. She treaded water, her hair swirling around her body, wrapping her slender waist and then letting go. Her reflection showed a young woman with black curls framing a heart-shaped face. She had dark eyes, as did most people in the province of Argali, though hers were larger than usual, with long lashes that right now sparkled with droplets of water.

Nothing seemed wrong. Reeds as red as pod-plums nodded on the bank, and six-legged lizards scuttled through them, glinting blue and green among the stalks. A few paces behind Lyode, the prismatic forest began. Up the river, in the distant north, the peaks of the Rosequartz Mountains floated like clouds in the haze. She drifted around to the other bank, but saw nothing amiss there either. Tubemoss covered the hills in a turquoise carpet broken by stone outcroppings that gnarled up like the knuckles of a buried giant.

What bothered her wasn't unease exactly, more a troubled anticipation. She supposed she should feel guilty about swimming here, but it was hard to summon that response on such a lovely day. The afternoon hummed with life, golden and cool.

Kamoj sighed. As much as she enjoyed her swim, invigorated by the chill water and air, she did have her position as governor to consider. Swimming naked, even in this secluded area, hardly qualified as dignified. She glided to the bank and clambered out, reeds slapping against her body.

Her bodyguard continued to scan the area. Lyode suddenly stiffened, staring across the water. She reached over her shoulder for the ballbow strapped to her back.

Puzzled, Kamoj glanced back. A cluster of greenglass stags had appeared from behind a hill on the other side of the river, each animal with a rider astride its long back. Sunrays splintered against the green scales that covered the stags. Each stood firm on its six legs, neither stamping nor pawing the air. With their iridescent antlers spread to either side of their heads, they shimmered in the blue-tinged sunshine.

Their riders were all watching her.

Sweet Airys, Kamoj thought, mortified. She ran up the slope to where she had left her clothes in a pile behind Lyode. Her bodyguard was taking a palm-sized marble ball out of a bag on her belt. She slapped it into the targeting tube of her crossbow, which slid inside an accordion cylinder. Drawing back the bow, Lyode sighted on the watchers across the river.

Of course, here in the Argali, Lyode's presence was more an indication of Kamoj's rank than an expectation of danger. Indeed, none of the watchers drew his bow. They looked more intrigued than anything else. One of the younger fellows grinned at Kamoj, his teeth flashing white in the streaming sunshine.

"I can't believe this, " Kamoj muttered. She stopped behind Lyode and scooped up her clothes. Drawing her tunic over her head, she added, "Thashaverlyster."

"What?" Lyode said.

Kamoj jerked down the tunic, covering herself with soft gray cloth as fast as possible. Lyode stayed in front of her, keeping her bow poised to shoot. Kamoj counted five riders across the river, all in copper breeches and blue shirts, with belts edged by feathers from the blue-tailed quetzal.

One man sat a head taller than the rest. Broad-shouldered and long-legged, he wore a midnight-blue cloak with a hood that hid his face. His stag lifted its front two legs and pawed the air, its bi-hooves glinting like glass, though they were a hardier material, hornlike and durable. The man ignored its restless motions, keeping his cowled head turned toward Kamoj.

"That's Havyrl Lionstar," Kamoj repeated as she pulled on her gray leggings. "The tall man on the big greenglass."

"How do you know?" Lyode asked. "His face is covered."

"Who else is that big? Besides, those riders are wearing Lionstar colors." Kamoj watched the group set off, cantering into the blue-green hills. "Hah! You scared them away."

"With five against one? I doubt it." Lyode gave her a dry look. "More likely they left because the show is over."

Kamoj winced. She hoped her uncle didn't hear of this. As the only incorporated man in Argali, Maxard Argali had governed the province for Kamoj in her youth. In the years since she had become an adult, Kamoj had shouldered the responsibility of leading her people and province. But Maxard, her only living kin, remained a valued advisor.

Lionstar's people were the only ones who might reveal her indiscretion, though, and they rarely came to the village. Lionstar had "rented" the Quartz Palace in the mountains for more than a hundred days now, and in that time no one she knew had seen his face. Why he wanted a ruined palace she had no idea, given that he refused all visitors. When his emissaries had inquired about it, she and Maxard had been dismayed by the suggestion that they let a stranger take residence in the honored, albeit disintegrating, home of their ancestors. Kamoj still remembered how her face had heated as she listened to the outlanders explain their leige's "request."

However, no escape had existed from the "rent" Lionstar's people put forth. The law was clear: she and Maxard had to best his challenge or bow to his authority. Impoverished Argali could never match such an offer: shovels and awls forged from fine metals, stacks of firewood, golden bridle bells, dewhoney and molasses, dried rose-leeks, cobberwheat, tri-grains, and reedflour that poured through your fingers like powdered rubies.

So they yielded—and an incensed Maxard had demanded that Lionstar pay a rent of that same worth every fifty days. It was a lien so outrageous, all Argali had feared Lionstar would send his soldiers to "renegotiate."

Instead, the cowled stranger had paid.

With Lyode at her side, Kamoj entered the forest. Walking among the trees, with tubemoss under her bare feet, made her even more aware of her precarious position. Why had he come riding here? Did he also have an interest in her lands? She had invested his rent in machinery and tools for farms in Argali. As much as she disliked depending on a stranger, it was better than seeing her people starve. But she couldn't bear to lose more to him, especially not this forest she loved.

So. She would have to inquire into his activities and see what she could discover.

The beauty of the forest helped soothe her concern. Drapes of moss hung on the trees, and shadow-ferns nodded around their trunks. Argali vines hung everywhere, heavy with the blush-pink roses that gave her home its name. Argali. It meant "vine rose" in Iotaca.

At least, most scholars translated it as rose. One fellow insisted it meant resonance. He also claimed they misspelled Kamoj's middle name, Quanta, an Iotaca word with no known translation. The name *Kamoj* came from the Iotaca word for *bound,* so if this odd scholar was correct, her name meant *Bound Quantum Resonance.* She smiled at the absurdity. *Rose* made more sense, of course.

The vibrant life in the autumnal woods cheered Kamoj. Camouflaged among the roses, puff lizards swelled out their red sacs. A ruffling breeze parted the foliage to let a sunbeam slant through the forest, making the scale-bark on the trees sparkle. Then the ray vanished and the forest returned to its dusky violet shadows. A thornbat whizzed by, wings beating furiously. It homed in on a lizard and stabbed its needled beak into the red sac. As the puff deflated with a whoosh of air, the lizard scrambled away, leaving the disgruntled thornbat to dart on without its prey.

Powdered scales drifted across Kamoj's arm. She wondered why people had no scales. The inconsistency had always puzzled her, since her early childhood. Most everything else on Balumil, the world, had them. Scaled tree roots swollen with moisture churned the soil. The trees grew slowly, converting water into stored energy to use during the long summer droughts and endless winter snows. Unlike people, who fought to survive throughout the grueling year, seasonal plants grew only in the gentler spring and autumn. Their big, hard-scaled seeds lay dormant until the climate was to their liking.

Sorrow brushed Kamoj's thoughts. If only people were as well adapted to survive. Each Long Year they struggled to replenish their population after the endless winter decimated their numbers. Last winter they had lost even more than usual to the blizzards and brutal ices.

Including her parents.

Even after so long, that loss haunted her. She had been a small child when she and Maxard, her mother's brother, became sole heirs to the impoverished remains of a province that had once been proud.

Will Lionstar take what little we have left? She glanced at

Lyode, wondering if her bodyguard shared her concerns. A tall woman with lean muscles, Lyode had the dark eyes and hair common in Argali. Here in the shadows, the vertical slits of her pupils widened until they almost filled her irises. She carried Kamoj's boots dangling from her belt. She and Kamoj had been walking together in comfortable silence.

"Do you know the maize-girls who do chores in the kitchen?" Kamoj asked.

Lyode turned from her scan of the forest and smiled at Kamoj. "You mean the three children? Tall as your elbow?"

"That's right." Kamoj chuckled, thinking of the girls' bright energy and fantastic stories. "They told me, in solemn voices, that Havyrl Lionstar came here in a cursed ship that the wind chased across the sky, and that he can never go home because he's so loathsome the elements refuse to let him sail again." Her smile faded. "Where do these stories come from? Apparently most of Argali believes it. They say he's centuries old, with a metal face so hideous it will give you nightmares."

The older woman spoke quietly. "Legends often have seeds in truth. Not that he's supernatural, but that his behavior makes people fear him."

Kamoj had heard too many tales of Lionstar's erratic behavior to dismiss them. Since he had come to Argali, she had several times seen his wild rides herself, from a distance. He tore across the land like a madman.

Watching her closely, Lyode lightened her voice. "Well, you know, with the maize-girls, who can say? They tried to convince me that Argali is haunted. They think that's why all the light panels have gone dark."

Kamoj gave a soft laugh, relieved to change the subject. "They told me that too. They weren't too specific on who was haunting what, though." Legend claimed the Current had once lit all the houses here in the Northern Lands. But that had been centuries past, even longer in the North Sky Islands, where the Current had died thousands of years ago.

The only reason one light panel worked in Argali House, Kamoj's home, was because her parents had found a few intact fiber-optic threads in the ruins of the Quartz Palace.

The panel intrigued Kamoj as much as it baffled her. It linked to cables that climbed up inside the walls of the house until they reached the few remaining sun-squares on the roof. No one understood the panel, but Lyode's husband, Opter, could make it work. He had no idea why, nor could he fix damaged components, but given undamaged parts he had an uncanny ability to fit them into the panels.

"Hai!" Kamoj winced as a twig stabbed her foot. Lifting her leg, she saw a gouge between her toes welling with blood.

"A good reason to wear your shoes," Lyode said.

"Pah." Kamoj enjoyed walking barefoot, but it did have drawbacks.

A drumming that had been tugging at her awareness finally intruded enough to make her listen. "Those are greenglass stags."

Lyode tilted her head. "On the road to Argali."

Kamoj grinned. "Come on. Let's go look." She started to run, then hopped on her good foot and settled for a limping walk. When they reached the road, they hid behind the trees, listening to the thunder of hooves.

"I'll bet it's Lionstar," Kamoj said.

"Too much noise for only five riders," Lyode said.

Kamoj gave her a conspiratorial look. "Then they're fleeing bandits. We should nab them!"

"And just why," Lyode inquired, "would these nefarious types be fleeing up a road that goes straight to the house of the central authority in this province, hmmm?"

Kamoj laughed. "Stop being so sensible."

Lyode still didn't look concerned. But she slipped out a bowball anyway and readied her bow.

Down the road, the first stags came around a bend. Their riders made a splendid sight. The men wore gold diskmail, ceremonial, too soft for battle, designed to impress. Made from beaten disks, the vests were layered to create an air-tight garment. They never attained that goal, of course. Why anyone would want airtight mail was a mystery to Kamoj, but tradition said to do it that way, so that was how they made the garments.

On rare occasions, stagmen also wore leggings and a hood of mail. Some ancient drawings even showed mail covering the entire body, including gauntlets, knee boots, and a transparent cover for the face. Kamoj thought the face cover must be artistic fancy. She saw no reason for it.

Her uncle's stagmen gleamed today. Under their vests, they wore bell-sleeved shirts as gold as suncorn. Their gold breeches tucked into dark red knee-boots fringed by feathers from the green-tailed quetzal. Twists of red and gold ribbon braided their reins, and bridle bells chimed on their green-glass stags. Sunlight slanted down on the road, drawing sparkles from the dusty air.

Lyode smiled. "Your uncle's retinue makes a handsome sight."

Kamoj didn't answer. Normally she enjoyed watching Maxard's honor guard, all the more so because of her fond-ness for the riders, most of whom she had known all her life. They served Maxard well. His good-natured spirit made everyone like him, which was why a wealthy merchant woman from the North Sky Islands was courting him despite his small corporation. However, today he wasn't with his honor guard. He had sent them to Ironbridge a few days ago, and now they returned with an esteemed guest—someone Kamoj had no desire to see.

The leading stagmen were riding past her hiding place, the bi-hooves of their mounts stirring up scale dust from the road. She recognized the front rider. Gallium Sunsmith. See-ing him made her day brighten. A big, husky man with a friendly face, Gallium worked with his brother Opter in a sunshop, engineering gadgets that ran on light, like the mir-ror-driven pepper mill Opter had invented. Gallium also made a good showing for himself each year in the swordplay exhibition at festival. So when Maxard needed an honor guard, Gallium became a stagman.

Down the road, more of the party came into view. These new riders wore black mail, with dark purple shirts and breeches, and black boots fringed by silver fur. Jax Iron-bridge, the governor of Ironbridge Province, rode in their center. Long-legged and muscular, taller than the other stagmen, he had a handsome face with strong lines, chiseled like granite. Silver streaked his black hair. He sat astride Mistrider, a huge greenglass stag with a rack of cloud-tipped antlers and scales the color of the opal-mists that drifted in the northern mountains.

Kamoj's pleasure in the day faded. Still hidden, she turned away from the road. She leaned against the tree with her arms crossed, staring into the forest while she waited for the riders to pass.

A flight-horn sounded behind her, its call winging through the air. She jumped, then spun around. Apparently she wasn't as well-concealed as she thought; Jax had stopped on the road and was watching her, the curved handle of a horn in his hand.

Kamoj flushed, knowing she had given offense by hiding. Her merger with Jax had been planned for most of her life. He had the largest corporation in the northern provinces, which consisted of Argali, the North Sky Islands, and Ironbridge. Argument existed about the translation of the Iotaca word *corporation*: for lack of a better interpretation, most scholars assumed it meant a man's dowry, the property and wealth he brought into marriage. A corporation as big as Jax's became a political tool, invoking the same law of "Better the offer or yield" as had Lionstar's rent.

Ironbridge, however, had given Argali a choice. Jax made an offer Kamoj and Maxard could have bettered. It would have meant borrowing from even the most impoverished Argali farmers, but besting the amount by one stalk of bi-wheat was all it took. Then they could have declined the marriage offer and repaid the loans. She had been tempted to try. But Argali was her responsibility, and her province needed this merger with flourishing Ironbridge. So she had agreed.

Jax watched her with an impassive gaze. He offered his hand. "I will escort you back to Argali house."

"I thank you for you kind offer, Governor Ironbridge," she said. "But you needn't trouble yourself."

He gave her a cold smile. "I am pleased to see you as well, my love."

Hai! She hadn't meant to further the insult. She stepped forward and took his hand. He lifted her onto the stag with one arm, a feat of strength few other riders could manage even with a child, let alone an adult. He turned her so she ended up sitting sideways on the greenglass, her hips fitted in front of the first boneridge that curved over its back. Jax sat behind her, astride the stag, between its first and second boneridges, his muscular legs pressed against her hips and leg.

The smell of his diskmail wafted over her, rich with oil and sweat. As he bent his head to hers, she drew back in reflex. She immediately regretted her response. Although Jax showed no outward anger, a muscle in his cheek twitched. She tried not to flinch as he took her chin in his hand and pulled her head forward. Then he kissed her, pressing her jaw until it forced her mouth open for his tongue. Despite her efforts, she tensed and almost clamped her mouth shut. He clenched his fist around her upper arm to hold her in place.

A rush of air thrummed past Kamoj, followed by the crack of a bowball hitting a tree and the shimmering sound of falling scales. Jax raised his head. Lyode stood by the road, a second ball knocked in her bow, her weapon aimed at Jax.

The Argali and Ironbridge stagmen had all drawn their bows and trained their weapons on Lyode. They looked acutely uncomfortable. No one wanted to shoot Kamoj's bodyguard. The Argali stagmen had grown up with her, and Gallium was her brother-in-law. Jax had visited Kamoj at least twice each short-year for most of her life, since their betrothal, so the Ironbridge stagmen also knew Lyode well. However, they couldn't ignore that she had just sent a bow-ball hurtling within a few hand-spans of the two governors.

In a chill voice only Kamoj could hear, Jax said, "Your hospitality today continues to amaze me." Turning to Gallium Sunsmith, he spoke in a louder voice. "You. Escort Lyode back to Argali House."

Gallium answered carefully. "It is my honor to serve you, sir. But perhaps Governor Argali would also like to do her best by Ironbridge, by accompanying her bodyguard back."

Kamoj almost swore. She knew Lyode and Gallium meant well, and she valued their loyalty, but she wished they hadn't interfered. It would only earn them Jax's anger. She and Jax had to work this out. Although their merger favored Ironbridge, it gave control to neither party. They would share authority, she focused on Argali and he on Ironbridge. It benefited neither province if their governors couldn't get along.

Perhaps she could still mollify Jax. "Please accept my apologies, Governor Ironbridge. I will discuss Lyode's behavior with her on the walk back. We'll straighten this out."

He reached down and grasped her injured foot, bending her leg at the knee so he could inspect her instep. "Can you walk on this?"

"Yes." The position he was holding her leg in was more uncomfortable than the gouge itself.

"Very well." As he let go, his fingers scraped the gash between her toes. Kamoj stiffened as pain shot through her foot. She didn't think he done it on purpose, but she couldn't be sure.

She slid off the stag, taking care to land on her other foot. As she limped over to Lyode, bi-hooves scuffed behind her. She turned to see the riders thundering away, up the road to Argali.

2

The Offer

Incoming Wave

Jul, the sun, had sunk behind the trees by the time Kamoj and Lyode walked around the last bend of the road, into view of Argali House. Seeing her home, Kamoj's spirits lifted.

Legend claimed the house had once been luminous pearl, all one surface with no seams. According to the temple scholar, who could read bits of the ancient codices, Argali House had been grown in a huge vat of liquid, on a framework of machines called *nanobots,* which were supposedly so tiny you couldn't see them even with a magnifying glass. After these machines completed the house, one was to believe they simply swam away and fell apart.

Kamoj smiled. Absurdities filled the old scrolls. During one of her visits to Ironbridge, about ten years ago, Jax had shown her one in his library. The scroll claimed that Balumil, the world, went around Jul in an "elliptical orbit" and rotated on a tilted axis. This tilt, and their living in the north, was purported to explain why nights were short in summer and long in winter, fifty-five hours of darkness on the longest night of the year, leaving only five hours of sunlight.

She had always thought it strange how her people counted time. One year consisted of four seasons, of course: spring, summer, autumn, winter. They called it the Long Year. A person could be born, reach maturity, wed, and have a baby within one Long Year. For some reason her ancestors considered this a long time: hence the name. Even more inexplicable, they divided the Long Year into twenty equal periods called short-years, five per season. People usually just called those "years." But really, it made no sense. Why call it a short-*year?* The scroll claimed this odd designation came about because the time span came close to a "standard" year.

Standard for what?

Still, she found it more credible than too-little-to-see machines. Whatever the history of Argali House, it was wood and stone now, both the main building and the newer wings that rambled over the cleared land. Huge stacks of firewood stood along one side, stores for winter. Seeing them gave her satisfaction, knowing that preparations for the harsh season were well under way.

Bird-shaped lamps hung from the eaves, rocking in the breezes, their glass tinted in Argali colors—rose, gold, and green. Their radiance created a dam against the purple shadows pooled under the trees. The welcome sight spread its warmth over Kamoj. Here in the road, a fluted post stood like a sentinel. A lantern molded and tinted like a rose hung from a scalloped hook at its top, its glow beckoning them home.

They entered the front courtyard by a gate engraved with vines. Five stone steps ran the length of the house, leading up to a terrace, and five doors were set at even intervals along the front. The center door was larger than the others, stuccoed white and bordered by hieroglyphs in rose, green, and gold, with luminous blue accents.

As they neared the house, Kamoj heard voices. By the time they reached the steps, it resolved into two men arguing.

"That sounds like Ironbridge," Lyode said.

"Maxard too." Kamoj paused, her foot on the first step. Now silence came from within the house.

Above them, the door slammed open. Maxard stood

framed in its archway, a burly man in old farm clothes. His garb startled Kamoj more than his sudden appearance. By now he should have been decked out in ceremonial dress and mail, ready to greet Ironbridge. Yet he looked as if he hadn't even washed up since coming in from the fields.

He spoke to her in a low voice. "You'd better get in here."

Kamoj hurried up the steps. "What happened?"

He didn't answer, just moved aside to let her enter a small foyer paved with white tiles bordered by Argali rose designs.

Boots clattered in the hall beyond. Then Jax swept into the entrance foyer with five stagmen. He paused in mid-stride when he saw Kamoj. He stared at her, caught in a look of fury, and surprise too, as if he hadn't expected to reveal the intensity of his reaction to her. Then he went to Maxard, towering over the younger man.

"We aren't through with this," Jax said.

"The decision is made," Maxard told him.

"Then you are a fool." Jax glanced at Kamoj, his face stiff now with a guarded emotion, one he hid too well for her to identify. In all the years she had known him, he had never shown such a strong response, except in anger. But this was more than rage. Shock? Emotional *pain?* Surely not from Jax, the pillar of Ironbridge. Before she had a chance to speak, he strode out of the house with his stagmen, ignoring Lyode, who stood just outside the door.

Kamoj turned to her uncle. "What's going on?"

He shook his head, his motion strained. Lyode came up the stairs, but when she tried to enter, Maxard braced his hand against the door frame, blocking her way. He spoke with uncharacteristic anger. "What blew into your brain, Lyode? Why did you have to *shoot* at him? Of all days I didn't need Jax Ironbridge angry, this was it."

"He was mistreating Kamoj," Lyode replied.

"So Gallium Sunsmith says." Maxard frowned at Kamoj. "What were you doing running around the woods like a wild animal?"

She would have bristled at the rebuke, except it was too far outside his usual congenial nature to make sense. She always walked in the woods after she finished working in the stables. He often came with her, the two of them discussing projects for Argali or enjoying each other's company.

She spoke quietly. "What is it, Uncle? What's wrong?"

He pushed his hand through his dark hair. "We can meet later in the library. You've several petitioners waiting for you now."

She studied his face, trying to fathom what troubled him. No hints showed. So she nodded, to him and to Lyode. Then she limped into her house.

For her office, Kamoj had chosen a large room on the ground floor. Its tanglebirch paneling glimmered with blue and green highlights in scale patterns. The comfortable old armchairs were upholstered in gold, with a worn pattern of roses. Stained glass lanterns hung on the walls. She didn't sit behind her tanglebirch desk; she had always felt it distanced her from people.

A carafe of water waited on one table, with four finely cut tumblers. Kamoj was pouring herself a drink when the housemaid showed in her first visitors, Lumenjack Donner, a broad-shouldered man with brown eyes, and Photax Prior, a much slimmer man who could juggle light-spheres like no one else in Argali. Both were wearing freshly cleaned homespun clothes and carrying their best hats, with their dark hair uncut but well-brushed for this meeting. They bowed to her.

Kamoj beamed at them, a smile warming her face. She had known both farmers all her life. "My greetings, Goodmen."

Lumenjack's deep voice rumbled. "And to you, Governor."

"Tidings, Gov'ner." Photax's hands moved restlessly on his hat as if he wanted to juggle.

She indicated the armchairs. "Have a seat, please. Would either of you like water?"

Both declined as they settled in the chairs. Kamoj sat in one at right angles to theirs, so she could watch their faces and judge their moods. "What can I do for you today?"

Lumenjack spoke up. "Photax be cheating me, ma'am. I come to ask your help."

"It's a twiddling lie, it is," Photax declared.

Kamoj suspected that if they had agreed to seek an arbitrator, the situation was probably salvageable. "What seems to be the problem?"

Lumenjack crossed his arms, accenting his husky build. "Photax is plowing my land and taking my crops."

"It's my land!" Photax gave Kamoj his most sincere look. "He traded it to me last year when I juggled for his daughter at the festival."

Lumenjack made an incredulous noise. "I wouldn't give you my *land* for throwing pretty gigags in the air." He turned to Kamoj. "I said he could have the crops, just last year, from a strip of my land that borders his."

"You said the land!"

"I meant the crops!"

Photax shot Kamoj a beseeching look. "He be going back on his bargain, Gov'nor."

Kamoj rubbed her chin. "Photax, do you really think such a parcel of land is a fair trade for a juggling show?"

"That's not the point. He made a deal and now he's reneging." Photax glowered at Lumenjack. "You're as crazy as that madman Lionstar." To Kamoj, he added, "Begging your pardon, ma'am. Lionstar rode through my fields yesterday and tore up my bi-grains."

Kamoj didn't like the implications. Lionstar seemed to be stirring from his borrowed palace more often lately. "Did he recompense you for the damage?"

"Nary a bridal bell. He doesn't even stop." Photax gave a theatrical shudder. "He was riding like a man possessed. He's a cursed one, he is."

She doubted it involved any curses. Lionstar's destructive

behavior was problem enough by itself. "I will send a messenger to the palace. If he wrecked your crops, he owes you for them."

Photax looked mollified. "I'd be right obliged if you would do that, Gov'ner."

"That's why you're so set on Lumenjack's land, isn't it? Because you're going to be short this year."

"I can't feed a family by juggling balls," Photax said.

"So if you get your recompense," Lumenjack said, "will you quit trying to steal my land?"

"*Steal?*" Photax bristled at him. "I don't steal. You *gave* it to me!"

"Why would I do something so stupid?" Lumenjack demanded. "What, I'm going to feed my family rocks?"

Photax shifted in his chair, his mobile face showing less confidence now. "I heard you say it. So did my wife and other people."

Lumenjack made an exasperated noise. "If I said the land, instead of last year's crops on the land, it was a mistake."

"You gave your word," Photax repeated.

Kamoj sighed. Technically, if Lumenjack had given his word, he did owe Photax the land. But the mistake was so obvious, she couldn't imagine Photax holding him to it if he hadn't already been in trouble due to Lionstar's rampage. "How about this? Photax, I will see to your compensation for the crop damage. For the disputed land, why don't you and Lumenjack split the yield this year and then call the debt done, with Lumenjack keeping his land. That way, neither of you suffers unduly from the mix-up."

"I don't like giving him half my crops for nothing," Lumenjack grumbled. After a pause, he added, "But I will agree."

Photax moved his hands as if he were feeling the weight of light-spheres. "All right." He stopped his ghost juggling and frowned at Kamoj. "Do you think Lionstar will make good?"

"I can't say." She doubted it, but she didn't want to sound negative. "If he doesn't, Argali House can help you from our yield this year."

"It be right decent of you, Gov'ner."

"I wish I could do more." Her province needed so much. Not for the first time, she wondered if she should hasten her merger with Jax, to ensure Ironbridge support. After what had happened today, though, she dreaded facing his temper.

She talked more with Photax and Lumenjack, catching up on news of their families. They took their leave on better terms than when they had entered, though now they were arguing about whose son could throw a bowball farther.

She next met with the representatives of several committees she had set up: the storage group, which worked to ensure Argali had stocks of grain for the coming winter, when the village would live off crops grown during autumn; the midwives, who discussed childbirth techniques, with the hope that sharing knowledge would decrease Argali's heart-breaking infant mortality rate; and the festival group that planned the harvest celebrations.

The housemaid finally announced her last visitor, Lystral, or *Liquid Crystal,* an older woman who was well-liked in the village. Instead of arriving with her usual good nature, today Lystral stalked into the room. She wasted no time on amenities. "Well, so, Governor, have you done anything about that maniac?"

Standing by her armchair, Kamoj blinked. "Maniac?"

"Lionstar!" Lystral's scowl deepened the lines around her eyes. "That misbegotten demon-spawn of a maddened spirit raised from the dead to bedevil the good folk of this land."

Kamoj held back her smile. Granted, Lionstar was a problem, but she suspected it had more to do with human misdeeds than misbegotten spirits. "What happened?"

"He and a pack of his stagmen stopped at my daughter's house in the country, where my grandchildren were playing. He jumped down at the well, helped himself to water, and broke the chain on the bucket. He's a demonic one, I tell you. No normal man could break that chain—and Lionstar didn't even notice! He scared the little ones so much, they almost jumped from here to the Thermali Coast. Then he just got on his greenglass and rode off. Never even pulled down his cowl. Not that any of us *want* to see his pud-ugly face." She put her fists on her hips. "At least his stagman had the decency to apologize before they went tearing after him."

"I'm sorry he frightened your family, Lystral. I'm sending an emissary to the palace. I will include a protest about his behavior and a statement of the recompense he owes you for fixing the well."

"I be thanking you, ma'am." Lystral shook her head. "I wish he would leave Argali alone."

Kamoj also wished so. However, he had a right to the palace as long as he paid the rent. She just hoped Argali could weather his tenancy.

The centuries had warped the library door-arch beyond simple repair. Kamoj leaned her weight into the door to shove it closed. Inside the library, shelves filled with codices and books covered the walls. The lamp by Maxard's favorite armchair shed light over a table. A codex lay there, a parchment scroll made from the soft inner bark of a sunglass tree and painted with gesso, a smooth plaster. Glyphs covered it, delicate symbols inked in Argali colors. Kamoj could decipher almost none of the symbols. Now that she had taken primary responsibility for Argali, Maxard had more time for his scholarship.

He was learning to read.

Behind her the door scraped open, and she turned to see her uncle. With no preamble, he said, "Come see this."

Puzzled, she went with him to an arched door in the far wall. The storeroom beyond had once held carpentry tools, but those were long gone, sold by her grandparents to buy grain. Maxard fished a skeleton key out of his pocket and opened the moongloss door. Unexpectedly, oil lamps lit the room beyond. Kamoj stared past him—and gasped.

Urns, boxes, chests, huge pots, finely wrought buckets: they crammed the storeroom full to overflowing. Gems filled baskets, heaped like fruits, spilling onto the floor, diamonds that split the light into rainbows, opals as brilliant as green-glass scales, rose-rubies the size of fists, sapphires, topazes, amethysts, star-eyes, jade, turquoise. She walked forward, and her foot kicked an emerald the size of a polestork egg. It rolled across the floor and hit a bar of metal.

Metal. Bars lay in tumbled piles: gold, silver, copper, bronze. Sheets of rolled platinum sat on cornucopias filled with fruits, flowers, and grains. Glazed pots brimmed with vegetables and spice racks hung from the wall. Bracelets, anklets, and necklaces lay everywhere, wrought from gold and studded with jewels. A chain of diamonds lay on top a silver bowl heaped with eider plums. Just as valuable, dried foodstuffs filled cloth bags and woven baskets. Nor had she ever seen so many bolts of rich cloth: glimsilks, brocades, rose-petal satins, gauzy scarves shot through with metallic threads, scale-velvets, plush and sparkling.

And light strings! At first Kamoj thought she mistook the clump on a pile of crystal goblets. But it was real. She picked up the bundle of threads. They sparkled in the lamplight, perfect, no damage at all. This one bundle could repair broken Current threads throughout the village, and it was only one of several in the room.

Turning to Maxard, she spread out her arms, the threads clutched in one fist. "This is—it's—is this *ours?*"

He spoke in a cold voice. "Yes. It's ours."

"But Maxard, why do you look so dour!" A smile broke out on her face. "This could support Argali for years! How did it happen?"

"You tell me." He came over to her. "Just what did he give you out there today?"

He? She lowered her arms. "Who?"

"Havyrl Lionstar."

She would never have guessed Lionstar would see to his debts with such phenomenal generosity. This was so far beyond any expected recompense for Photax and Lystral's family, she couldn't begin to comprehend his intent. "Why did he send it here?"

"You tell me. You're the one who saw him."

Hai! So Maxard had heard about the river. "I didn't know he was watching."

"Watching what?"

"Me swimming."

"Then what?"

Baffled, she said, "Then nothing."

"Nothing?" Incredulity crackled in his voice. "What did you promise him, Kamoj? What sweet words did you whisper to compromise his honor?"

She couldn't imagine any woman having the temerity to try compromising the huge, brooding Lionstar. "What are you talking about?"

"You promised to marry him if he gave you what you wanted, didn't you?"

"What?"

His voice snapped. "Isn't that why he sent this dowry?"

Dowry? Sweet Airys, now what? "That's crazy."

"He must have liked whatever the two of you did."

"We did nothing. You know I would never jeopardize our alliance with Ironbridge."

• Her uncle exhaled. In a quieter voice he said, "Then why did he send this dowry? Why does he insist on a merger with you tomorrow?"

Kamoj felt as if she had stepped into a bizarre skit played out for revelers during a harvest festival. This couldn't be real. "He wants *what?*"

Maxard motioned at the storeroom. "His stagmen brought

it today while I was tying up stalks in the tri-grain field. They spoke as if the arrangement were already made."

It suddenly became all too clear to Kamoj. Lionstar didn't want the ruins of an old palace, the trees in their forest, or Photax's crops.

He wanted Argali. All of it.

Strange though his methods were, they made a grim sort of sense. He had demonstrated superiority in forces; many stagmen served him, over one hundred, far more than Maxard had, more even than Ironbridge. With his damnable "rent" he had established his wealth. He had even laid symbolic claim to her province by living in the Quartz Palace, the ancestral Argali home. Any way they looked at it, he had set himself up as an authority. Today he added the final, albeit unexpected, ingredient—a merger bid so far beyond the pale that the combined resources of all the Northern Lands could never best his offer.

"Gods," Kamoj said. "No wonder Jax is angry." She set down the light threads, the remnants of her good mood vanishing like a doused candle. "There must be a way I can refuse this."

"I've already asked the temple scholar," Maxard said. "And I've looked through the old codices myself. We've found nothing. You know the law. Better the offer or yield."

She stared at him in disbelief. "I'm not going to marry that crazy man."

Maxard brushed back the disarrayed locks of his hair, his forehead furrowed with lines that hadn't shown anywhere near as much yesterday. "Then he will be within his rights to take Argali by force. That was how it was done, Kamoj, in the time of the sky ships." He squinted at her. "I'm not sure my stagmen even know how to fight a war. Argali has never had one, at least not that I know about."

"There must be some way out."

It was a moment before her uncle answered. Then he

spoke with care, as if treading through shards of glass. "The merger could do well for Argali."

Kamoj was sure she must have misheard. "You *want* me to go through with it?"

He spread his hands out from his body. "And what of survival, Governor?"

So. Maxard's words came with sobering force, as he finally spoke aloud what they dealt with implicitly in every discussion about the province. Drought, famine, killing winters, high infant mortality, failing machines no one understood, lost medical knowledge, and overused fields: it all added up to one inescapable fact, the long slow dying of Argali.

The province wouldn't end this Long Year, or next, maybe not even in a century. But their slide into oblivion was relentless. With the Ironbridge merger, they still might struggle, but their chances improved. She and Jax had regularly visited each other to discuss the merger. At worst, Jax would annex her province, making it part of Ironbridge. She would do her best to keep Argali separate, but if she did lose it to him, at least her people would have the protection and support of the strongest province on this continent. Although Jax didn't inspire love among his people, he was a good leader who earned loyalty and respect.

And Lionstar? Yes, he had wealth. That said nothing about his ability to lead. For all she knew he would drive her province into famine and ruin.

"Hai, Maxard." She rubbed her hand over her eyes. "I need to think about all this."

He nodded, the tension of the day showing on his face. "Go on upstairs. I'll send a maize-girl to tend you."

She went stiff, understanding his unspoken implication. "Lyode always tends to me."

"I need her elsewhere tonight."

"*You* need her? Or Jax?" When he didn't answer, her

pulse surged. "I won't have my people flogged." Kamoj headed toward the door. "If you won't tell him, I will." She dreaded confronting Jax, but this time it had to be done.

Maxard grabbed her arm, stopping her. He held up his other hand, a tiny space between his thumb and index finger. "Ironbridge is this close to declaring a rite of battle against us. I've barely thirty stagmen, Kamoj. He has over eighty, all better trained." He dropped her arm. "It would be a massacre. And you know Lyode. She would insist on fighting with them. Will you save Lyode and Gallium from a few lashes so they can die in battle?"

Kamoj shuddered. "Don't say that."

His voice quieted. "With the mood Ironbridge is in now, seeing you will only enrage him. He can't touch you yet, so Gallium and Lyode are the ones he will take out his rage on."

Knowing Maxard was right made it no easier to hear. Kamoj wondered, too, if her uncle realized what else he had just revealed. *He can't touch you yet.* She spoke with difficulty. "And after the merger, when the rages take Ironbridge? Who will pay the price of his anger then?"

Maxard watched her with a strained expression, one that reminded her of the wrenching day he had come to tell her that the village patrol had found the bodies of her parents frozen beneath masses of ice in a late winter storm. She had never forgotten that wounded time of loss.

He spoke now in an aching voice. "Does it occur to you that you might be better off with Lionstar?"

She rubbed her arms as if she were cold. "What have I seen about him to make me think such a thing?"

"Hai, Kami." He started to reach for her, to offer comfort, but she shook her head. She loved him for his concern, but she feared to accept it. Taking shelter from the pain now would only make her responsibilities that much harder to face when that shelter was gone.

Maxard had caught her off-guard with his insight into her relationship with Jax. Her uncle had always claimed he delayed her merger to give her experience at governing, lest Ironbridge be tempted to take advantage of a child bride. Now she wondered if Maxard had a better idea than he let on about the life she faced with Jax. As an adult she had more emotional resources to deal with Jax's temper.

But Maxard hadn't guessed the whole of it. Last year, in Ironbridge, she had enraged Jax when she visited the city outside his fortress without his permission. Nor had that been the first time she bore the brunt of his temper. Most people saw him as the strong, inspired leader who had built Ironbridge into a great power. Kamoj also knew his other side, the Jax who would make Lyode and Gallium pay for defying him. The only difference was that in this case he would have a stagman mete out the punishment rather than taking care of it himself, as he did in private with Kamoj, when he used his hands or riding quirt against her.

In her childhood, he had never touched her in anger, instead using censure or cold silence to reproach behaviors that offended him. But since she had become an adult, his temper had turned physical. She had never told Maxard, knowing it would drive her uncle to break the betrothal no matter what price it cost Argali. She could never set her personal situation before the survival of her people.

Gentle one moment, violent the next, Jax kept her on the edge between love and hatred. She dreaded his rage, savored his wisdom, feared his cruelty, longed for his mercurial tenderness, resented his need to control, and admired his remarkable intellect. But beyond her conflicted emotions, she knew one fact: Argali needed him. Her loyalty and love for her people came first, above all else, including her personal happiness. So she had learned to cope with Jax. The situation wasn't perfect, but it would *work*. Lionstar threatened that careful balance like a plow tearing up their world.

"Can you talk to Jax?" she asked. "Mollify him? Maybe you can keep him from hurting them."

"I'll do what I can." He watched her, his dark eyes filled with concern. "This will work out, Kami."

"Yes. It will." She wished she believed those comforting words.

After she left her uncle, she walked through the house, down halls paneled in tanglebirch, then up to a second floor balcony. At the top of the stairs, she gazed out over the foyer below, treasuring the sight of this home where she had lived all her life—the home she might soon leave. The entrance to the living room arched to the right. A chandelier hung from the room's ceiling like an inverted rose aglow with candles. It reflected in a polished table, drawing blue scale-gleams from the wood. Near the table, a light panel glowed in the wall, the last working one in all the Northern Lands.

Regret and longing for all that her people had lost washed over Kamoj. When that panel failed, a thousand new light threads would do no good. Even Opter Sunsmith couldn't fix a broken panel. The knowledge had been lost long ago, even from the Sunsmith line.

Kamoj walked along the balcony to her room. Candlelight filled the chamber, welcoming her. It glowed on the parquetry floors, worn furniture, and her old doll collection on the table, which she kept in memory of her mother, who had given her the beloved toys. Her bed stood in a corner, each of its four posts a totem of rose blossoms and fruits, ending at the top with a closed bud.

A voice spoke behind her. "Ev'ning, ma'am."

She turned to see Ixima Ironbridge, a young woman with a smudge of flour on one cheek. Jax had sent the Ironbridge maize-girl to Argali last year, so Kamoj could get to know her. That way, whenever Kamoj traveled to Ironbridge, she would bring a familiar face with her, someone who already knew the province and could help Kamoj feel more at home. The thoughtful gesture had both touched and confused Kamoj. How could Jax be so considerate one moment and so harsh the next?

Ixima spoke in her Ironbridge dialect. "Shall I be a'helpin' you change, ma'am?"

"Thank you." Kamoj sat tiredly on her bed.

Ixima slid off the boot and peeled away the sock. Kamoj winced as the cloth ripped away from her toes. The gouge must have bled and then dried her sock to her skin. Lifting her foot, she saw dirt in the cut. "We better clean it."

The maize-girl tilted her head, considering Kamoj's foot. "I donnee see how a'rubbin' it would help. You rest, hai, ma'am? Tomorrow it be feeling better enough to scrub."

Her lack of knowledge troubled Kamoj. Dirty wounds festered. Nor was Ixima the only person she had known to make mistakes on health matters. She thought of asking the healer in the village about setting up a program to educate people. He was already overworked, and she hated to add to his load, but in the long run this might help ease his burden.

"We must treat it now." Kamoj kept her voice kind so Ixima didn't take it as a rebuke.

The maize girl fetched a bowl of warm water and soap. While she cleaned Kamoj's foot, Kamoj leaned against the bed post, struggling to stay awake. After Ixima helped her prepare for sleep, Kamoj settled in bed. The maize-girl darkened the room and left quietly, leaving one candle flickering on the window sill.

Kamoj lay on her back, her hands behind her head, staring at the ceiling. She would always remember the first time she had met Jax, not long after her parents had died. Tall and powerful, his mail gleaming, his handsome face kind, he had knelt to speak to her, bringing his eyes level with her own. He had seemed like an enchanted hero then, a shining savior come to rescue Argali. Over the years she had learned the truth, that under the hero's exterior burned a complicated, violent man whose clenched need to control contaminated his many good qualities.

If she refused the Lionstar merger, it would placate Jax but break the law. If Argali and Ironbridge combined forces, they could raise an army almost equal to that of Lionstar. But if Lionstar attacked, Kamoj would have to send people she loved into a rite of combat. A good chance existed they wouldn't come home. Lionstar might slaughter them; neither Ironbridge nor Argali had ever ridden into battle.

Kamoj knew what she had to do. As she made her decision, she felt as if a door closed. She had no way to predict what would happen in a Lionstar merger, but he had made it clear he could support her province. If she turned him down, the people and realm she loved could suffer, perhaps even die, at his whim.

Never again would Jax raise his hand or whip to her person. Never again would he use the survival of Argali as a weapon against her. It was a bitter victory, given what she had seen of Lionstar, but it was all she had.

3

Lionstar

Second Scattering Channel

Kamoj squinted at the mirror while the threadwoman fussed over her clothes. All this attention disconcerted her. She never dressed this way, in such formal garments. Leggings and a farm tunic were much more her preference, or a farm dress for more festive occasions. However, today was her wedding, and at one's wedding one wore a wedding dress no matter how dour the bride felt about that incipient marital status.

Despite everything, Kamoj treasured this dress. Knowing her mother and grandmother had worn it at their weddings made her feel close to them. Dyed the blush color of an Argali rose, it fit snug around her torso and fell to the floor in drapes of rose-scale satin. Lace bordered the neckline and sleeves, and her hair fell in glossy black curls to her waist. The Argali Jewels glittered at her throat, wrists, and ankles, gold chains designed like vines and inset with ruby roses.

With tugs and taps, the aged threadwoman tightened the dress at the waist and tried to make it stretch over Kamoj's breasts. She cackled at her reluctant model, her eyes almost lost in their nest of lines. "You've no boy's shape, Gov'ner. You be making Lionstar a happy man, I reckon."

Kamoj glowered at her, but the seamstress was saved from her retort by a knock on the door. Kamoj limped across the room in her unfamiliar shoes, heeled slippers sheathed in rose scale-leather. She opened the door to see Lyode.

Her bodyguard beamed. "Hai, Kamoj! You look lovely."

"It's for my wedding." She wondered what Lionstar would do if she showed up in a flour sack. Go away maybe. Then again, he was so odd he might like it.

Her guardian's enthusiasm waned. "Yes. Maxard told me."

Lyode's presence offered a welcome respite from all these wedding preparations. Kamoj dismissed the seamstress, then drew Lyode over to sit with her on the sofa. The older woman started to lean back, then jerked when her shoulders touched the cushions and sat forward again. Watching her, Kamoj felt another surge of anger at Jax, that he inflicted pain on the people she loved because they sought to protect her from his anger.

"You've huge bags under your eyes," Kamoj said.

"I had—a little trouble sleeping last night."

Kamoj wasn't fooled. It dismayed her to see Lyode's discomfort. But Maxard must have mollified Jax to some extent; otherwise Lyode wouldn't be able to move. "I'm so sorry."

The archer laid her hand on Kamoj's arm. "It's isn't your fault."

Isn't it? At times like this Kamoj felt trapped. "How is Gallium?"

Lyode spoke gently. "He's all right, Kami. We both are."

Kamoj crumpled her skirt in her fists. "I hate that all this has happened."

"Hate is a strong word. Give Lionstar a chance."

"I tell myself it will work out for the best. But after all we've heard about him—" She stopped, unable to voice her fears, as if saying them aloud would make real the tales of sorcery and dread that surrounded him.

"You've a kind heart," Lyode said. "He would be blind not to see that."

"Lyode—"

"Yes?"

"About tonight . . ." Although Kamoj knew what happened on a wedding night, it was only as vague concepts. She felt awkward asking advice on such matters even from Lyode. It touched a part of her life that would have given her both anticipation and apprehension even if she had gone into it with a man she knew, loved, and trusted. None of the three applied to Lionstar.

Lyode's face relaxed into the affectionate grin she always took on at the mention of her own husband, Opter. "Don't look so dour. Weddings are good things."

Kamoj smiled. "You look like a besotted fruitwing." When Lyode laughed, Kamoj said, "How will I know what to do?"

"Trust your instincts."

"My instincts tell me to run the other way."

Lyode touched her arm. "Don't judge Lionstar yet. Wait and see."

At sunset the Argali coach rolled into the courtyard, pulled by four greenglass stags and driven by a stagman. Shaped and tinted like a rose, it sat in a chassis of emerald-green leaves. Unlike Argali House, which had only legends attesting to its construction, the coach was inarguably one surface with no seams, glimmering like pearl. Its making was so long in the past, no one remembered how it had been done.

Watching from her bedroom window, Kamoj suddenly wanted to go down to the courtyard and tell them all that she had changed her mind, that they must cancel the wedding. Taking a deep breath, she calmed her thoughts. *You made the best decision you could. Trust your instincts.*

The door opened behind her. Turning, she saw Lyode framed in the archway. Her bodyguard wore a fine white shirt and soft suede trousers, with her ballbow in her hand instead of on her back. Her familiar presence reassured Kamoj.

Lyode's expression was both fond and sad. "It's time to go."

Kamoj crossed the room without a limp. Her foot had gone numb. She had soaked and cleaned the wound again this morning, but it remained swollen. It didn't hurt now, though.

Maxard was waiting at the bottom of the stairs. A swell of pride filled Kamoj. Today no lack of splendor would shame Argali. She wished Maxard's lady in the North Sky Islands were here to see him. His mail gleamed, a gold contrast to his black hair and eyes. He wore a suncorn shirt, wine-red suede breeches, and a belt made from quetzal feathers in Argali colors. Green feathers lined the tops of his gold knee-boots, and a ceremonial sword hung at his side, its scabbard tooled with Argali designs.

As Kamoj descended the stairs, Maxard watched, his face filled with the affection that made her love him so. When she reached him, he said, "You look like a dream." His voice caught. "It seems just yesterday you were a child. How did you grow up so fast?"

"Hai, Maxard." She hugged him. "I don't know." It was true. A few years ago she had been a child. Then she became an adult. Almost nothing separated the two; her adolescence had lasted only a few tendays. It gave her an inexplicable sense of loss. Why should she want a longer time of transition? Most people had no adolescence at all.

She knew the stories, of course, of the rare child who took longer to reach adulthood. Rumor claimed Jax Ironbridge's youth had stretched out far longer than normal. Years after his peers had become adults, he had still been an adolescent, tall and gangly, with only the first signs of his beard. He continued to grow long past the age when most youths reached maturity. Jax came into full adulthood well after most men his age—and by that time he was taller, stronger, and smarter than everyone else.

If only it had made him kinder, too.

With Maxard and Lyode on either side, Kamoj left the house. A group of her childhood friends had gathered in the courtyard, young women with rose vines braided into their black hair. They waved and smiled, and Kamoj waved back, trying to appear in good spirits.

Arrayed around the coach, ten stagmen sat astride their mounts, including Gallium Sunsmith. A smudgebug flittered into the face of one animal and it pranced to the side, crowding Gallium's greenglass. As the first rider pulled back his mount, his elbow bumped Gallium's back. Kamoj saw the grimace of pain Gallium tried to hide, just as Lyode had done on the sofa.

Kamoj's smile faded, lost to thoughts of Jax. He had shadowed so much of her life. She had treasured Gallium for as long as she could remember. The stagman had given her rides when she was a little girl and gave her his unwavering loyalty now.

As she passed him, she looked up. "My gratitude, Goodman Sunsmith. For everything. I won't forget."

His face gentled. "And you, Kami. You be a sight of beauty."

She managed to smile, not wanting to burden him with

her fear. Lyode opened the door of the coach and Maxard entered first, followed by Kamoj. Lyode came last and closed them into the heart of the rose. The driver blew on his flight horn, and its call rang through the evening air. Then they started off, bumping down the road.

Sitting between Lyode and Maxard, Kamoj took each of their hands. Maxard patted her arm and Lyode hugged her, but no one spoke. They needed no words; after so many years, they could speak with the simplest touch. She cherished this time with them. It felt ephemeral. She wished she could put this moment in a locket, a gold heart that would protect it, so she could take it out when the loneliness came and remember these two people who were her only family.

The coach rolled slowly, so the people walking could keep up. Even so, it seemed that far too little time passed before it stopped, bringing an end to their moment together.

The door swung back, leaving Gallium framed in its opening. Beyond him in the gathering dusk, the golden face of the Spectral Temple basked in the rays of the setting sun. Kamoj's retinue of stagmen and friends, and now many other villagers too, waited in the muddy plaza before the temple. It touched her to know that so many had come to see her wed Lionstar, especially given how much they feared him.

Lyode left the coach first. Kamoj gathered her skirts and followed—but froze in the doorway. Across the mud and cobblestones, a larger coach was rolling into view. Made from bronze and black metal, it had the shape of a roaring skylion's head with wind whipping back its feathered mane. Every burnished detail gleamed. The eyes were emeralds as large as fists. A blush spread across Kamoj's face at the imposing sight.

Her groom had arrived.

As soon as the coach stopped, its door opened. Two stagmen came out, decked in copper and dark blue, with cobalt diskmail that glittered in the sun's slanting rays. Sapphires lined the tops of their boots. Kamoj wondered where Lionstar found so many incredible gems. Argali's jewel master had checked and double-checked the ones in his dowry. They were real. Flawless and real.

Then a cowled man stepped down into the plaza.

Lionstar towered over everyone else, easily the largest man in the courtyard. Seeing his unusual height, she wondered if—like Jax—he too had spent years as an adolescent. What if he had other, harsher, similarities to her former betrothed? As always, he wore a blue cloak with a cowl pulled over his head. She wasn't sure she wanted to know what he hid under that shadowed hood. Only black showed inside; either he had a cloth over his face—or he had no face.

Maxard took her arm. "We should go."

His touch startled her into motion. She descended from the coach, onto a flagstone that glinted with mica even in the purple shadows. Her heels clicked as she stepped from stone to stone to avoid the mud.

Even tonight, the sight of the Spectral Temple gave her a thrill. The terraced pyramid stood surrounded by the Argali forest. When rays from the setting sun hit the stairs that ran up its side at just the right angle, it made light ripple down them to the statue of a starlizard's head at the bottom, creating a serpent of radiance and stone. In the front of the temple, a huge starlizard's head opened its mouth in a roar, forming an entrance. When a sunray hit its crystal eyes, arcs of light glistened around its head like the Perihelia spirits, also called Sun Lizards, that guarded the temple.

Kamoj had always loved the sun lizards that appeared in the sky. They made halos on either side of the sun, like pale rainbows, each with a tail of white light. This was their favored time, as tiny Jul descended to the horizon, scantily dressed in wispy clouds. During winter, when ice crystals filled the air, Perihelia and Halo spirits graced the heavens in arcs and rings. They might even form around the head of a favored person's shadow as it stretched across dewy tubemoss at dawn. But she saw no nimbus now, no sign to portend good fortune for this merger.

Lionstar's group reached the temple first. He stopped under the overhang of the sun lizard's fanged mouth and waited, his cowled head turned toward Kamoj. She came up with her retinue and stopped. After they had all stood that way for a moment, she flushed. Didn't he know he should go in first? She shifted her weight, wondering how to balance courtesy with expediency. They couldn't stand here all night.

One of Lionstar's stagmen spoke to him in a low voice. He nodded, then entered the temple with his retinue. Relieved, Kamoj followed with her people. No one spoke. She wondered if Lionstar could even talk. No one she knew had ever heard him say a word.

Inside, light from the sunset trickled through slits high in the walls. Stone benches filled the interior, except for a dais at the far end, which supported a polished stone table. Carvings decorated the table, Argali vine designs, those motifs called *Bessel integrals* in ancient Iotaca.

Kamoj savored the scents in the temple. Rose vines and ferns heaped the table, filling the air with their fragrance, fresh and clean. Around the walls, garlands hung from the statues of several Current spirits: the Airy Rainbows, the Glories, and the Nimbi. In wall slits above the statues, light slanted through faceted windows with water misted between the double panes, creating rainbows. Music graced the air, coming from breezes that blew through fluted chambers on the ceiling, hidden within engravings of the Spherical Harmonic wraiths.

Most days, Kamoj enjoyed the Spectral Temple's beauty. Now it all seemed unreal, its ethereal quality untouched by the far less serene ceremony going on within it. As everyone else sat down on the benches, Kamoj walked to the dais with Maxard at her side and Lionstar preceding them. The priestess, Airysphere Prism, waited by the flower-bedecked table.

Tall and lithe, she had large eyes and shiny black hair that poured to her waist.

After he stepped up onto the dais, Lionstar turned to watch Kamoj approach. At least she assumed he was watching. His cowl hid his face. When she reached him, she saw only darkness within that hood, perhaps a glint of metal. She told herself she was mistaken. Surely a man couldn't have a metal face.

Maxard bowed to him. "Argali welcomes you, Governor Lionstar."

The taller man just nodded. After an awkward silence Maxard flushed, though whether from anger or shame, Kamoj didn't know. Did Lionstar realize the insult in his silence, or did he act out of ignorance? The answer to that question would have told her a great deal about her groom, but she had no way to judge from the unreadable shadows within his cowl.

When the silence became long, Maxard turned and took Kamoj's hands. He spoke tenderly. "May the Current always flow for you, Kami."

She curled her fingers around his. "And for you, dear Uncle."

He lingered a moment more, watching her face. But finally he released her hands. Then he left the dais, going to sit on the front bench with Lyode.

"It is done?" Lionstar asked.

Kamoj almost jumped. His voice rumbled, deep and resonant, with a heavy accent. On the word "is," it vibrated like a stringed instrument.

Airys blinked, the vertical slits of her pupils opened wide in the shadowed temple. "Do you refer to the ceremony?"

"Yes," Lionstar said.

"It hasn't begun." Airys took a scroll from the table and unrolled it. Glyphs covered the parchment in starlight blue ink. She offered it to Lionstar, and he accepted with black-gloved hands.

"Governor Argali," Airys said. "Give me your hand."

As Kamoj extended her arm, Airys said, "In the name of Spectra Luminous I give this man to you." She closed her hand around Kamoj's wrist. "Havyrl Lionstar, give me your hand." When he complied, Airys took a vine from the altar and tied his and Kamoj's wrists together, bedecking them in roses and scale-leaves.

It startled Kamoj to feel the leather of his glove against her skin. Why did he hide himself, even his hands? Surely he must realize it might disquiet his bride. Try as she might, she could find few good reasons for his behavior, unless he really were the proverbial demon, in which case she preferred not to think about the details.

Airys spoke to Lionstar. "You may read the contract now."

Kamoj waited for him to decline. No one ever read the contract at a wedding. Only scholars could read, after all, and only the most gifted knew ancient Iotaca. Most people considered the scroll a fertility prayer. Kamoj had her doubts; Airys had managed to translate a few parts for her, and it sounded more like a legal document than a poem. In any case, the groom always returned the scroll. Then the couple spoke a blessing they composed themselves. Kamoj hadn't prepared anything; what she felt about this merger was better left unsaid. Unless Lionstar had his own poem, which she doubted, they would continue the ceremony without the blessing.

Except they didn't. Lionstar read the scroll.

As his voice rumbled with the Iotaca words, indrawn breaths came from their audience. Kamoj doubted anyone had ever heard the blessing spoken, let alone with such power. Lionstar had a deep voice, with an unfamiliar accent and the burr of a vibrato. His words also sounded slurred. The sounds rolled over her, so unexpected she had trouble absorbing them.

When he finished, the only sounds in the temple were the faint calls of evening birds outside.

Finally he said, "This ceremony, is it done?"

Airys took a breath, as if coming back to herself. "The vows are finished, if that is what you mean."

He gave her the scroll. Then he untied the vine joining his and Kamoj's wrists and draped it around Kamoj's neck, spilling the roses over her breasts. She blushed, jarred by the break with tradition; they weren't supposed to undo the vine until they consummated the marriage. Before she could speak, he took her elbow, turned her around, and headed for the entrance, pulling her with him.

Murmurs came from the watchers, a rustle of clothes, the clink of diskmail. Belatedly Kamoj realized that he had misunderstood; he thought the ceremony was over when it had hardly begun. But the rest was only ritual. They had said the vows. Argali and Lionstar had their corporate merger. Whatever happened now, she had committed herself and her province to this man. She just hoped that future didn't tumble down around them.

They came out into a purple evening. She barely had time to catch her breath before they reached Lionstar's coach. This was happening too fast; she had thought she would have at least a little more time to accept the marriage before she was alone with her new husband.

Then he stopped, looking over her head. She turned to see Maxard coming up behind them, with Lyode and Gallium, their familiar faces a welcome sight.

Lionstar spoke to her uncle. "Good night, sir."

Kamoj wondered what he meant. Was "good night" a greeting or a farewell?

Maxard bowed. Lionstar just nodded, then motioned to his men. As he raised his arm, his cloak parted and revealed his diskmail, a sapphire flash of blue. What metal did he use, to create such a dramatic color?

As one of his stagmen opened the coach door, Lionstar put his hand on Kamoj's arm, ready to pass her inside. Before she even realized what she was doing, she balked, stepping back. She couldn't leave this way, not without making her farewells.

Kamoj went to Lyode and embraced her, taking care with Lyode's back, her head buried against the taller woman's shoulder. Lyode spoke softly. "You're like a daughter to me. You remember that. I will always love you." Her words had the sound of tears.

Kamoj's voice caught. "And I you."

Before she could go to Maxard, Lionstar drew her toward the coach. She almost pulled away again, but then she stopped herself. Antagonizing the man who had just taken over Argali would be a poor start to their merger and could endanger the province. She glanced at Maxard, her eyes misted with tears, and he nodded, moisture glimmering in his as well.

Then Lionstar passed her to his stagmen, who handed her up into the roaring lion. Black moongloss paneled its somber interior and dark leather upholstered the seat. A window showed in the wall across from the door. She turned as Lionstar entered and saw another window in the door behind him. Yet from outside, no panes had shown at all. *It has a reasonable explanation,* she told herself. She only wished she believed that.

A stagman closed the door, and Lionstar sat next to her, his long legs filling the car. His cloak fell open, revealing ceremonial dress much like Maxard's, except in dark sapphire. As the coach rolled forward, Kamoj turned to her window for a final glimpse of her home. But the "glass" had become a blank expanse of wood. Dismayed, she looked toward Lionstar's window, only to find it had vanished as well. With such a dark interior and no lamps, the coach should have been pitch black. But light still filled it. She was having more and more trouble believing that a normal explanation existed for all this.

"Here." Lionstar tapped the ceiling. His voice had a blurred quality.

Puzzled, she looked up. A glowing white strip bordered

the roof of the coach. It resembled a light panel, but one made as thin as a finger and flexible enough to bend. She didn't know whether to be relieved that a reason existed for the light or disquieted by its unusual source.

"That's what you were looking for, wasn't it?" he said. "The light?"

How had he known? "Yes."

"Thought so." He reached into his cloak and brought out a bottle. Curved and slender, it was made from dark blue glass with a gold top. He unscrewed the top, then lifted the bottle into his cowl and tilted back his head. After a moment he lowered his arm and wiped his hand across whatever he had for a face. Then he returned the bottle to his cloak.

A whiff of rum tickled Kamoj's nose. Like a trick picture that changed if she looked at it in a new way, her perception shifted. She thought of his slurred words at the wedding and his actions at Lystral's well. Could *drink* be what made him act that way? That thought wasn't exactly reassuring either, but it was far more palatable than supernatural causes.

Lionstar sighed. As he turned toward her, she caught another glint of silver within his cowl. Then he slid his arms around her waist.

Hai! Kamoj's instincts clamored at her to push him away. *He is your husband,* she told herself. *Sit still.* He had a right to hug his wife. But she couldn't bring herself to return the embrace.

He rubbed the lace on her sleeve, then rolled it between his fingers. His black glove made a dark contrast against the rosy silk. She wondered if he would wear gloves when he made love to her. What if he never pulled off his cowl, even in the bedroom? She felt a blush spreading in her face. Maybe she had better not think about that right now.

Lionstar slid his hand up her torso, under the vine of roses around her neck, and folded his gloved palm around her breast. Kamoj froze, her logic vanishing like the windows in the coach. She didn't *care* if he was her husband; he was still a stranger. As he caressed her breast, she held back the urge to sock him. She wished he would speak or show her some sign that a human person existed in there.

He fondled her for a few moments, but gradually his hand slowed to a stop. Then it fell into her lap. He was leaning on her, his weight making it hard to sit up straight. She peered up at him, wondering what to do.

While she pondered, he gave a snore.

Her new husband, it seemed, had gone to sleep.

Kamoj rubbed her chin. What did one do in such a situation? Perhaps nothing, except thank the Spectral Harmonic spirits for this respite.

With Lionstar leaning against her, though, it was hard to sit straight. So she gave him a nudge. When he made no objection, she pushed him upright. He lay his head back against the seat, his mail-covered chest rising and falling in a deep, even rhythm, his cowl fallen over his face.

Just as Kamoj began to feel grateful for this unexpected reprieve, he tried to lie down. The seat of the coach had too little room for his legs, so he stretched out with his feet on the ground and his head in her lap. Then he went back to snoring.

Kamoj had no idea what to think. Of all the scenarios she had imagined for their ride to the palace, this wasn't one of them. She stared at his head in her lap and the hood lying across his face. Was he truly as hideous as rumor claimed? With one twitch of the cloth, she would know.

Your husband hides his face for a reason. He valued that reason enough to cover it even at his own wedding. If she looked now, she might antagonize him.

But he was asleep.

A torment of curiosity swept over her. She touched the edge of his cowl. No, she couldn't take the chance. She withdrew her hand. He continued to sleep, a soft snore at the end of each breath. How would he know if she looked? Perhaps he would never find out. Then again, he might wake up if she uncovered him.

Finally Kamoj could take it no more. She tugged on his cowl. When he showed no sign of waking, she pulled the cloth more. Still no response. Emboldened, she brushed the hood back from his head—and nearly screamed.

He had no face.

No eyes. No nose. No mouth. Just metal. His head was man-shaped, with the contours of a face, but instead of skin and human features, he had only silver scales.

Kamoj put her hands over her mouth. She could only stare at him, her breath caught in her throat.

"Ah, no," she finally said. "No. Please, no."

So. Now she knew. How she would live with this, she couldn't imagine. Sweet Airys, what about their wedding night? No, she wouldn't think about that.

As her surge of shock calmed, she took in more of his appearance. Another surprise: he had glorious hair. Thick, glossy curls spilled to his shoulders, a mixture of gold, bronze, and copper, with silver at the temples. She had never seen those colors. Some farmers in Ironbridge had yellow hair, but nothing like this multi-hued mane.

It fit his name well. Almost too well, in fact. A remarkable coincidence, that someone named Lionstar happened to have such a leonine mane, like the skylions in the mountains, with their six-legged scaled bodies and feathered manes. Perhaps his ancestors adopted the name because such hair ran in his line. People had done stranger. She was named for a plant, after all, and the Current only knew what Quanta meant.

Kamoj brushed a finger over his curls. He kept on sleeping. At least she thought he slept. How did one tell when a person had no eyes? He gave no evidence he objected to her touch, though. She slid her hand deeper into his curls. Hai. His hair felt as good as it looked.

As she stroked his curls, her fingertips scraped his face. The metal felt smooth. She ran her fingertip down to his jaw and pushed the scales.

His face slipped.

"Ah!" Kamoj jerked away her hand. When he still showed no sign of waking, she peered at the metal. It had indeed moved. She pushed again—and it crumpled, uncovering a stretch of skin.

A mask. He was wearing a *mask*. She hadn't married a man with no face. She laughed with a rush of relief so intense it felt physical, then took a breath to quiet the sound, so she didn't wake him.

Caution told her to stop, but she couldn't now. She had to know what that mask hid. Sliding her finger along its edge, she peeled it off his face. It came away like a silver skin— and she saw the truth.

Human. He was *human*. Different from any man she had ever seen, but a man. A tear rolled down her face.

He was nowhere near as old as rumor claimed, only about forty, perhaps a bit more. He had a handsome face, with high cheekbones and a straight nose. His lashes lay against his cheeks in a lush gold fringe. They glinted like metal but felt soft under her fingertip. His golden skin was warm under her palm. Alive. His lips were full. Sensual. She ran her finger along the lower one, and it yielded to her touch.

His breathing sounded strained, and dark circles showed under his eyes. She also smelled the rum. The mask had helped hide the odor, but now it filled the coach, mixing with the scale dust.

As his breathing grew labored, Kamoj became alarmed. She spread the mask over his face, but no matter how she placed it against his skin, she couldn't get it to stay.

Suddenly he moved, rolling onto his back to stare up at her. He croaked words in a language she didn't understand and clawed at the mask. Dismayed, she pushed it into his hand. Before he could put it on, his body went rigid and he began to choke, his fingers clenched around the crumpled metal skin.

A siren pierced the air, coming from nowhere Kamoj could see. Frantic now, she pried the mask out of his fist and pressed it against his face again. Still it wouldn't stay.

The coach lurched to a stop so fast it threw both her and Lionstar onto the floor. The door slammed open and two stagmen jumped inside. One pulled Kamoj back while the other knelt by Lionstar. The second stagman had another mask in his hand, this one stiff and translucent, with a tube connected to a metal cylinder. He set the mask over Lionstar's face, and a hissing filled the coach.

Kamoj tried to pull away from the stagman holding her, but he wouldn't let go. She looked up and saw him staring at the mask she held. Then he called her a name, one she had never thought anyone would say to her. As she stiffened, a stagmen behind them opened his mouth to chastise the man who insulted her. Then he saw the mask she held and whatever he meant to say died on his lips.

A groan came from the floor. Startled, she turned back and saw Lionstar breathing from the new mask. The stagman gripping her arm relaxed, but not enough to let her pull away.

Lionstar sat up, holding the mask in place. When his man tried to offer assistance, the governor shook his head. So the stagman withdrew, stepping out of the coach. Lionstar stood up, one hand braced against the wall, bending his head so it didn't hit the roof.

He moved his mask aside and spoke to the man holding Kamoj. "Let her go, Azander."

"Sir, she took off your breathing skin," Azander said.

Lionstar waved the mask. "Curiosity's nay murder. Go'n. Drive us home."

"Yes, sir." As Azander backed out of the coach, he gave Kamoj a hard look. She recognized the warning. If she hurt Lionstar, Azander would see that she paid for that act.

They were soon rumbling along the road. Seated next to Kamoj, Lionstar leaned back and closed his eyes, holding the new mask over his face, with the metal cylinder at his side. She rubbed her hands up and down her arms, chilled despite the warmth of the coach. Did he believe she had taken off his other mask out of curiosity? She feared he might suspect what Azander almost said, that his new bride had tried to murder him.

Sitting up straight, Lionstar tugged out his bottle and fumbled with it one-handed. Finally he dropped the mask in his lap and used both hands to open the bottle. He drank deeply, his throat working as he swallowed.

When he finished, he handed Kamoj the empty bottle. "Put top back'n." Then he put his mask over his face again, holding it with one hand.

Kamoj had no idea what to say to him. She replaced the top, wondering if he always drank this much. That could explain why he didn't care that he lived in the ruins of a palace. Holding the bottle in her lap with one hand, she rubbed her eyes with the other, exhausted by the ups and downs of this strange day.

The new mask covered only his mouth and nose, letting her see his eyes. They were large, and a remarkable violet color. They would have been beautiful if they hadn't been so bloodshot. His pupils were even stranger. They were round discs, rather than vertical slits. Although odd, the effect wasn't unpleasant. It had a sense of *rightness* that puzzled Kamoj, an inexplicable familiarity.

Right now those unusual eyes were watching her. Lionstar pulled aside his mask. "Why'd do it?"

She knew what he meant. "I wondered what you looked like."

"You could've just asked."

"I'm sorry. I didn't know it would hurt you."

He nodded, apparently willing to accept the explanation. "Never thought t'set the mask's smart-tech so you couldn't fiddle with it." Seeming satisfied that this bizarre statement made sense, he lay his head back and closed his eyes. After a moment the mask fell into his lap.

"Governor Lionstar." Kamoj shook his shoulder. "Your breathing skin." When he opened his eyes, blinking, she gave him the silver mask. He tried pressing it into place, with no more success than she had managed earlier. He squinted at it, then flipped it over and tried again. This time the mask stayed in place, leaving his face a smooth sheen of silver, with black ovals for eyes.

"S'better," he mumbled. He laid his head back and the ovals closed, taking away that last vestige of humanity.

4

Pacal

Scattering Kernel

They rode for an hour, Lionstar snoring quietly while Kamoj sat in bemused silence. Finally the coach rolled to a stop. Azander opened the door and took in the scene, Lionstar asleep and Kamoj holding the empty bottle. The stagman didn't look surprised.

Leaning inside the coach, Azander shook Lionstar's shoulder. "Prince Havyrl. We be home."

Kamoj blinked at the archaic title. Prince? Of *what?*

Lionstar's eyes opened, black on silver. "What?"

"Home," Azander repeated. "You and your bride."

"Bride?"

"Yes, sir. Your bride."

"What bride?"

Azander tilted his head toward Kamoj. "Governor Argali."

"Oh. Yes. Of course." Lionstar sat up, rubbing his hand through his hair. "See to the stags."

"Yes, sir." Azander backed out of the coach.

Lionstar followed him out into the night, which was lit by a faint radiance. As Kamoj stepped down from the coach, he offered his hand. Taking it, she thought she felt calluses under his glove. That made no sense, though. A man of his power would hardly have the calluses of a farmer.

Then she turned around—and went utterly still.

They were in the courtyard of the Quartz Palace. Gone were the ruins covered by tangled vines, briars, and roses. Now the rose-quartz palace gleamed, restored to its full beauty and more. Long and narrow, with a terrace that stretched its length, it had nine evenly spaced entrances. A tower reached up at each end, topped by gold turrets. Glass lamps shaped like birds hung in the windows and from the eaves, making the walls glow. Above it all, the aurora borealis rippled in the sky, curtains of gold and pink luminance undulating across the heavens.

"Sweet Airys," Kamoj whispered. "It's lovely."

"S'pretty," Lionstar agreed.

He took her elbow and led her toward the steps that went up to the terrace. The double doors in the center entrance swung open and radiance spilled into the night, backlighting three people. She recognized two as villagers from Argali, a man and woman, both dressed in servant's clothes.

The third person came out to meet them. Tall and gaunt, with a craggy face and graying hair wound on top her head, the woman was like no one else Kamoj had ever seen. She wore a form-fitting gray suit made in one piece, with gray knee-boots. A patch on her shoulder showed an exploding star within a triangle.

She met them halfway down the steps. Lionstar nodded to her, and they all walked up the stairs together. Although the woman appeared hale and fit, her breathing was growing labored, as if she had run a race instead of walking a few steps.

At the top of the stairs, Kamoj stopped. A few paces away, a shimmer of light hung in the open doorway.

"S'even nicer inside," Lionstar said, mistaking her hesitation.

No one else seemed bothered by the curtain of light, and Kamoj didn't want to look foolish. So she took a breath and walked with them through the shimmer. It clung to her like a soap bubble, sliding over her face, hair, and clothes.

The entrance foyer was as she recalled, a small room with floor tiles enameled in Argali rose designs. Except now the tiles were whole and the walls smooth, each brick snug with its neighbors, none showing any chinks and cracks.

As Lionstar peeled off his mask, Kamoj tensed. But no one else seemed alarmed. In fact, she had never tasted such pure, rich air. It made her dizzy, almost euphoric.

The tall woman was breathing normally now. She asked Kamoj a question, but Kamoj had trouble understanding her heavy accent. Although the woman spoke Bridge, Kamoj's language, she had the same odd dialect as Lionstar. Also like him, she mixed in words from Iotaca.

The woman tried again. "Are you all right, Governor Argali?"

Kamoj stood up straighter, trying not to feel intimidated by the stranger's unusual height. "Yes."

"She's fine." Lionstar waved his arm at the two Argali servants. "Jus' like them. Fine."

The woman glanced at him, then at the bottle Kamoj still held. She spoke to Lionstar in another language, concern and anger in her voice. Lionstar answered with a scowl, then turned away and took Kamoj's arm. He led her to an archway across the foyer, where another light-curtain hung. Kamoj held her breath as they walked through it, no more sanguine about interior shimmers than exterior ones, but nothing untoward happened this time either.

The air in the Entrance Hall beyond tasted as pure as in the foyer. New panels of sunglass wood covered the walls. She had never seen the paintings that hung there, scenes of the Argali countryside. Lionstar must have commissioned them from the villagers, which meant he was supporting the Argali economy.

Then she saw the other additions. Light panels—light panels!—glowed near the ceiling.

Lionstar was watching her face. " 'S good, yes?"

"Oh, yes." She had never expected this generosity. He didn't even own this building he had restored. Then it occurred to her that maybe it wasn't such generosity after all. He did own the palace now, as well as everything else that had belonged to her family. Including her.

Accompanied by the servants and the tall woman, they went down the Entrance Hall to a gleaming ballroom that stretched out on their right and left. Radiance from its chandeliers reflected off the walls and parquetry floor, yet she saw no candles within the chandeliers, only shimmers of light. The unexpected gift of finding her ancestral home lit with such beauty warmed Kamoj.

They crossed the ballroom to another archway. It opened into the Long Hall, which ran the length of the palace at right angles to the Entrance Hall. Moongloss wood paneled its walls and dark carpet covered the floor. Rose-shaped lamps glowed on the walls. Lionstar set off down the hall, holding Kamoj's arm. The tall woman easily matched his stride, but Kamoj and the servants almost had to run to keep up.

Lionstar didn't stop until they reached a door at the east end of the palace. Then he turned to the others. "You can go. I'll take her up."

The tall woman spoke. "Maybe Kamoj would like to meet the staff. Look at the palace. Have dinner." Dryly she said, "Catch her breath."

"Who?" Lionstar asked.

"Kamoj," the woman said.

"Who's that?" he asked.

This isn't happening, Kamoj thought.

The woman stared at him. "Your *wife.*"

Lionstar turned to her. "Kamoj? Is that your name?"

"Yes." Kamoj didn't know whether to laugh or groan.

" 'S pretty," he said. "Like you."

"She hasn't even had a chance to unpack," the woman said.

"Unpack what?" he asked.

"Her suitcases. Trunks. I don't know." She looked at the servants. "Whatever her belongings came in."

"She donnee have any, Colonel Pacal," the plump woman said.

The tall woman swung back to Lionstar. "Saints above, Vyrl. Didn't you arrange to have her things brought up?"

"If it hasn't been done," he growled, "then do it."

The woman blew out a gust of air. Then she turned to Kamoj and gentled her voice, the way she might speak to a child. "Do you have things you would like? We can send someone down to Argali House in the morning."

"Yes, thank you." Kamoj wasn't sure how to take the woman's tone. "Lyode will know what to send."

"Lyode?" the woman asked. "Is that a person?"

Lionstar scowled. "Dazza, stop interrogating her."

Kamoj wished they would decide what to call one another. Was the tall woman Dazza or Colonel Pacal? Was Lionstar a governor or a prince? The woman called him Vyrl. A shortened version of Havyrl, probably. Perhaps if she thought of him by a nickname, it would make all this seem less intimidating.

Vyrl dismissed the others again, and this time he glared until they left. Then he pushed open the door. The staircase beyond spiraled up inside the tower at this end of the palace. Although the steps had been repaired, the rough stone was otherwise untouched. The only windows were slits high on the walls. No glass showed in them, just the shimmer curtains.

They climbed three flights to a landing. Vyrl opened the door there and escorted her into a spare chamber only a few paces across, its stone walls polished but unadorned. Its inner door opened into a large, austere bedroom.

After all the wonders downstairs, Kamoj wasn't prepared for the stark changes in the suite. She had last seen this room open to the sky, with snow drifted across its broken edges. Now the floor stretched in a smooth expanse of stone. The walls and ceiling were also bare stone, with two crossed swords over the bed. No fire burned in the hearth, yet the room felt warm. Tanglebirch furniture gleamed with blue-green highlights: desk, chairs, and a wardrobe against the far wall. In the left wall, the door to the bathing room was ajar. Near it, the bed stood on the dais, its posters repaired and varnished, its canopy new. Everything was clean, fresh, and devoid of ornamentation.

Staring at the bed, Kamoj felt warmth spread through her body. She tried not to dwell on what would soon happen under those downy covers. She wasn't sure what to think after finding out that her husband, far from being a hideous demon, was very much a human man: vibrant, strapping, comely—and drunk.

" 'S not such a good room for a wedding night, is it?" Vyrl said. "Solar told me this. She says it is 'cold.' "

"Solar?" Kamoj asked.

"One of the housemaids. She said she'd prepare a chamber you might like better."

Vyrl led her to the one place where the austere decor softened, an archway across the room with a curtain of sparkling beads. When he moved aside to let her enter, she hesitated, both charmed and awkward with his offer to let her go in first. Were customs so different in his land? Deciding it would be ruder to refuse his courtesy than to precede him, she walked into the small room.

It touched Kamoj that they had gone to so much trouble for her. This room felt warm in a way that had nothing to do with temperature. Tapestries hung on the walls, and the delicate shutters were open, revealing a stained glass window with a rose in its center. To her right, a comforter lay on the floor, with posts at each of its corners, carved totems like her bed at home. She wondered why they put the bedding on the ground. Then she remembered. This chamber had been a second bathing room. Vyrl's people must have filled the small pool with mattresses for her bed.

"This is all for me?" she asked.

"Can't be for me," Vyrl said. "I'd break those chairs if I sat in 'em."

Kamoj almost laughed, but held back, unsure if he meant it in jest. Jax never joked about himself, a subject he considered of great weight. A few years ago he had teased her, saying that he would build bridges made from iron in her province. She had laughed more out of surprise that he made a joke than because it had been funny.

Watching her, Vyrl smiled. It warmed his whole face and made him look like a farm boy. He slid his arms around her waist. "Ever since yesterday, I've been thinking about you, water sprite. I still can't believe you agreed to this." Then he bent his head and kissed her.

Caught off guard, Kamoj didn't react at first. His lips felt warm against her mouth, a sensual contrast to the masculine power of his body. She put her arms around his waist, trying to relax. The rum smell of his breath made it difficult, though, the way it clogged her nose.

Vyrl lifted his head. "Is it that bad?" He winced. "I am as rude as Dazza suggests. I'll go clean up." Tilting his head toward a wardrobe by the wall, he added, "Will it harm your dress to go there tonight? Tomorrow the housemaids can tend to it."

Kamoj blinked at the rose cabinet. The formerly crumbling antique gleamed now, whole and varnished, even its carvings redone. A mirror bordered by frosted vines hung on one door.

"Camber?" Vyrl asked.

It took her a moment to realize he meant her. "Kamoj," she said. Too late, she realized she had corrected him. With a surge of fear, she started to raise her arm, shielding her face.

Except Vyrl didn't hit her. Instead he reddened. "My sorry. I'm terrible with names." Taking her shoulders, he gave her a resounding kiss. "Don't go away." Then he spun on his booted heel and strode out of the room. The bead curtain swung in his wake, clinking and sparkling.

"Goodness." Kamoj pushed her hand through her hair, mussing the roses that hung around her neck. Then she went to the curtain and peered out. The main bedroom was empty, but water was running in the bathing room. She didn't know what to think. Uncertain how he would react if he knew she was checking out the suite, she slipped off her shoes so she could walk in silence. As she crossed to the entrance, pain stabbed her sole. Confined in her shoe, her foot had gone numb, but now it hurt again.

Under her push, the foyer door swung open as smooth as oil on glass. She padded through the entrance chamber and edged open the outer door.

Guards.

Two stagmen stood on the landing, Azander by the door and another man by the wall. She had often seen the arrangement, with Jax's bodyguards outside his room when he stayed at Argali House. They had always remained in the room when she and Jax visited, though in her case they had served more as chaperones than guards.

Azander looked down at her. "Be there a problem, Gov-'ner?" His accent wasn't as thick as an Ironbridge dialect, but it wasn't pure Argali either.

"Nothing, thank you." She nodded to them, then closed the door, unsure herself what she had wanted. Why did they guard Vyrl in his own bedroom? To ensure *she* did him no harm? That seemed rather silly, given his size and strength compared to hers, especially now that he didn't need his mask. Besides, they were outside and she was here. Perhaps they were there to keep her from leaving.

She returned to her room and undid her dress, letting it

fall into a heap of satin around her feet. It left her standing in nothing more than her wedding silks. Dyed the color of an Argali rose, the translucent, lacy underdress came to her knees. It covered the tops of her rose-silk stockings, which were held up by lace garters with embroidered roses. Lyode claimed such underclothes would evoke pleasant reactions from her groom. Kamoj didn't see why, but she had figured it was worth a try.

She bent down to scoop up her dress—and nearly passed out when she straightened back up. Black spots floated in her vision. The air was too thick, so rich it made her giddy. She swayed, waiting until her head cleared. Then she took a breath and carried her dress to the rose cabinet.

When Kamoj finished putting away her dress, she sat on the bed and sank into its billowy comfort. Self-conscious in her filmy underdress, she crossed her arms over her breasts. It was hard to keep her eyes open. She lay down and let them close. She would rest for a moment. That was all. Just a moment.

5

Stained Glass Moons

Vibrational State

A crash woke Kamoj. She sat bolt upright, her heart pounding. She couldn't fathom her surroundings. Then, as she came more fully awake, she remembered. The Quartz Palace.

Groggy from sleep, she struggled out of bed and went to the window. She pushed open the stained glass panes, hoping the night air would clear her head. Outside, the East Sky Mountains slumbered under their carpet of trees.

Three of Balumil's six moons were visible, offering their moonglow as a good omen. The Elder Brother shone high in the sky, almost full, casting blue light over the world. The Wild Stag made a ragged green shape above the trees. For every four times the Brother crossed the heavens, the Wild Stag only managed three. The Brother always presented a serene face to the world, passing smoothly through his phases. The Wild Stag knew no such civilized behavior. He changed both shape and size as he tumbled through the heavens, varying from an uneven disk to a squashed sausage. They also called him the Chaos or Fractal Moon.

The sight of the familiar sky reassured her. The auroras were quiescent now, letting Balumil's faint ring show. Its gold thread curved across the sky and the gibbous disk of the Shepherd Moon glistened pink above its arc. From the positions of the moons, Kamoj guessed she had slept about seven hours. Dawn was a long time away; in mid-autumn the days split evenly, thirty hours of darkness and thirty of light. She usually slept twice at night, once after sunset and then again before dawn.

A firepuff fly flew against the shimmer in the window and stuck. With a frenzied beating of its scaled wings, it freed itself and trilled off into the night, its golden puff vibrating as it sang. Curious, Kamoj pushed her hand through the shimmer curtain. It stretched along her arm like a film. When she pulled her arm back inside, the shimmer clung to her skin, then returned to its original shape.

So odd. For all the beauty that Vyrl had restored to her ancestral home, he also brought these strange changes. It all captivated her, yes, but it also made her wary. Such beauty might hide unknown dangers. It reminded her of the sleekers that swam in the Glimmerback River. They looked like beautiful scarves waving in the water, but their venom killed when they bit a swimmer.

Kamoj turned back to her chamber. Where was Vyrl? The fountain still gurgled in the bathroom. What if he had passed out and fallen in the water? Azander already suspected her of foul play against her husband, and many people knew she had dreaded this merger. If something happened to Vyrl, she was the obvious suspect.

She limped into the main bedroom. The door to the bathing room stood ajar, but no one answered her knock. She nudged it open, revealing a chamber larger than hers, though still smaller than the main bedroom. A pool filled most of it, tiled in pale blue squares. In its center, the sculpture of a rose opened to the ceiling. She remembered crawling into that bowl as a child and playing with dried leaf-scales that had drifted into it. Now water surged out of the fountain and cascaded down its sides.

A statue stood at the corner of the pool, a quetzal, that bird named for a mythical creature on a mythical world no one had ever seen. The bird was actually a great stone chair, its head raised high, its great wings forming the back, its upper legs as armrests, its middle legs encircling the seat, and its lower legs making the base, along with its glorious feathered tail.

Sprawled in the chair, a naked Vyrl was sound asleep.

Heat spread in Kamoj's face until she felt sure she had turned as rosy as her name. She didn't know whether to stay or leave. She saw what had caused the crash that woke her. Blue shards of glass from a shattered bottle lay scattered around the base of the quetzal. The bottle must have slid out of Vyrl's hand, probably resting on an edge of the statue, gradually slipping, until it fell. His legs were braced against a ridge in the base of the statue, his muscles tense even in sleep. It was all that kept him from sliding into the pool.

Kamoj put her palms against her cheeks, amazed to find her skin cool rather than burning. But she didn't want to leave. Picking her way through the glass, she went to Vyrl.

She couldn't stop staring at him, at his broad shoulders and chest, his narrow hips, his long legs, all well-muscled, his skin flushed with health, his magnificent hair tousled around his face. The lamp light made his gold lashes glitter. For all her attempts to imagine his appearance, it had never occurred to her that he might be beautiful.

Did he always drink this way? She thought of Korl Plowsbane in the village, old before his time, wandering with his bottle. She balked at believing the same of Vyrl. Even if he was like Korl, he couldn't have been drinking that heavily for long. He seemed too healthy.

Still, what she had seen didn't look auspicious. She inhaled, widening her nostrils so their membranes captured every stray scent under the odor of rum. She caught traces of trees and ferns, a hint of sun on scale-leather, even a lingering trace of Vyrl's diskmail. It all mixed with a strong soap smell and another scent harder to define, a masculine smell she liked. Drawn by it, she stepped closer and rubbed the knuckles of his hand where it lay on his thigh. Her fingers trailed along his leg.

"Higher," he said drowsily.

Kamoj snatched back her hand. He was smiling at her, his eyes half open.

Words deserted her. She finally managed to say, "I didn't mean to wake you."

He sat up straighter, rubbing his eyes. "How long have I been in here?"

"A few hours."

"Ah." His gaze wandered over her body. Mortified, Kamoj realized she had nothing on but stockings and a translucent underdress. Then again, given his "clothes," she was overdressed.

Vyrl grinned. "You look beautiful." He slid out of his chair and she jumped back, losing her balance as she stepped on her injured foot. Teetering on the edge of the pool, she flailed her arms.

With unexpected grace, Vyrl lunged out of the chair and caught her around the waist. Bending her over his arm, he leaned down to kiss her. Kamoj stared up at him like a bird caught in his hold.

He blinked at her expression. Then he straightened up, bringing her with him. "Don't you ever smile?"

"Well—yes. Of course."

Vyrl stepped away from the pool. "Maybe we should—ah!" He jerked up his leg, then peered at his foot and pulled a glass shard out of his heel. Blood welled up from the cut. With a grimace, he stuck his foot in the water and swirled it around until the blood washed away. His graceful movements made her think of a greenglass stag.

He smiled. "Either that's a compliment to me or an insult to the greenglass, I'm not sure which."

"How do you do that?" she asked.

"Do what?"

"Know my thoughts."

"I don't." He took her hand. "Come on. Let's go somewhere with less glass."

Too unsettled to pursue this business with the thoughts, she went with him. They picked their way through the shards and returned to the main bedroom. Although Vyrl walked reasonably well, several times he stumbled. When they reached the dais with his bed, he stopped, said, "We should do this right," and hefted her up into his arms.

Hai! The last thing Kamoj wanted was a half-drunk man carrying her up stairs. "It's all right," she said quickly. "I can walk."

He started up the dais. "You hardly weigh a thing."

They made it to the top with no mishaps, but then Vyrl tripped. He took a huge step forward, lunging for the bed, and tossed her across it as he lost his balance. She hit the mattress with a thud, pillows tumbling around her head. Vyrl landed on top her, and her breath wumped out with a muffled "oomph."

"Ah, hell," Vyrl muttered. "My sorry, Chamois."

This time she was too flustered to think of correcting the name. When he slid onto his side and pulled her into his arms, she stuttered, "Maybe you should, uh, call a healer." She knew she was talking too fast, but she couldn't stop. "For your—for your, you know. Your foot."

"My foot?" He gave her a languorous smile. "Why?"

"It's just, mine swelled—Vyrl! What are you doing?"

He moved his hand over her breasts. "Appreciating my beautiful wife." Then he slid down along her body. Closing his mouth around her nipple, he suckled her through the glimsilk of her underdress.

Kamoj flushed, said, "Oh, my," and cleared her throat. Then she sighed and put her hands in his hair, tangling her fingers in his curls. After a while, she murmured, "You're different than I expected."

He came back up, cradling her in his arms. "How is that?"

Too late, she realized how her answer would sound: *I expected that you would be cruel.* She tried to hide the thought, imagining a blanket to cover it. "You're younger."

Vyrl flashed her a wicked grin. "Such sweet words." He reached down and fingered the garter that held up her stocking. Then he sat up and tugged the lacy ring off her leg. Setting it on his palm, he squinted as if it were another life form. "It's pretty. But who'd ever think to make such a thing?"

"I don't know," Kamoj said. Lyode had given it to her.

Vyrl set the ring on the bed. Then he touched her thigh above her stocking. "So soft . . ." He stroked his hand along her leg, pulling down the stocking. "Soft here . . ." Taking her stocking by the toe, he pulled it off through the gold circlet around her ankle. "And soft here—gods, what is that?"

She wished he would go back to showing her what was soft. "What?"

Vyrl peered at her foot. "This is serious." He lay on his back and stretched his arm above his head, reaching across the bed to a nightstand. Seeing his body laid out that way, right next to her, so distracted Kamoj that she barely noticed him press a panel on the stand.

A drowsy voice spoke out of nowhere. "Colonel Pacal here."

"Hai!" Kamoj sat bolt upright and clamped her arms over her breasts, looking around for the owner of the voice.

"I need you up here," Vyrl said to the air.

The woman suddenly sounded awake. "On my way."

"For flaming sakes," Vyrl said. "Don't say it like that."

"Like what?" the woman asked.

Vyrl scowled. "Like 'What has he done to that poor girl?' "

"Is she all right?"

"Her foot is hurt."

"I'll be right there."

"Good." Vyrl pushed the panel again.

After the room had stayed silent for several seconds, Kamoj's agitated pulse began to calm. "Who was that?"

"Dazza." Vyrl drew her back down into his embrace. "My doctor."

"What is a doctor?"

He pulled her arms around his waist. "Healer."

Kamoj liked the solid feel of his body. "But where is she? We're the only ones here."

"She's coming," he murmured, his eyes closing. Then he kissed her.

After several moments of discovering she liked kissing Vyrl far more than she had ever liked it with Jax, Kamoj moved her lips to his ear and spoke shyly. "If someone is coming up here, shouldn't we get dressed?"

"Ai . . ." He sighed. "I guess so."

While Kamoj sat up, pulling her dress into place, Vyrl went to the wardrobe across the room and took out a blue robe with iridescent green and gold highlights. As he put it on, a knock came from the entrance foyer. Tying his sash, he went to the door.

Dazza stood in the foyer, dressed in rumpled trousers and a shirt, her hair tousled as if she had just climbed out of bed. She had something in her hand, Kamoj wasn't sure what. A large book? As the doctor entered the suite, she glanced at Kamoj, at the stocking on the bed, and at Vyrl. Then she reddened. It didn't surprise Kamoj that the colonel looked as if she wished she were someplace else.

"It's her left sole," Vyrl said, walking with Dazza across the room. They came up the dais and he leaned against the bedpost with his arms crossed. Dazza sat on the bed and set down her book.

The doctor's awkwardness vanished as she lifted Kamoj's foot to examine the sole. "Did you treat this cut?"

"I cleaned it and soaked it in water," Kamoj said.

Dazza looked up at her. "If you ever get a cut like this again, debride it right away."

"Debride?" Kamoj didn't recognize the word.

"Clean off the torn skin." Dazza set down Kamoj's foot and opened her "book." Its top lifted like a box, revealing tubes and rectangles inside. She touched a small square and ghost pictures appeared, rotating in the air, each with a different view of a woman's body. Red and blue lines veined one, another showed a skeleton, and a third internal organs.

Kamoj had heard tales of how the ancients made ghosts dance this way, but until now she had never believed them. A thrill of curiosity went through her.

Symbols appeared on a rectangle in the box, flowing across the surface as if they were alive. Studying them, Dazza said, "You're a healthy young woman." She snapped a featherless quill off her box and bent over Kamoj's foot as if she were going to write on the sole.

Kamoj pulled away her leg. "What are you doing?"

"Numbing the area." With a gentle touch, Dazza tugged back her foot. "That way, it won't hurt when I drain the wound."

Although Kamoj found that hard to believe, the pain did recede after Dazza wrote on her sole with the quill. The doctor kept working, but Kamoj couldn't see what she was doing.

"Gods," Vyrl said. "That's a bad one."

Intent on her work, Dazza said, "If we hadn't caught it in time, she could have lost the foot."

Kamoj blanched. No wonder it had hurt so much when Jax jabbed the wound.

"Kimono?" Vyrl said. "Are you all right?"

Dazza made an exasperated noise. "Saints above, Vyrl. Her name is Kamoj. *Kam-oge.*"

He reddened. "My sorry, Kamoj."

"It's all right," Kamoj said, smiling.

Dazza withdrew her quill, catching drops of blood from its tip with her finger. She cleaned Kamoj's foot with a white mesh, then removed a new quill from the box. She pressed a knob on it, and a spray came out of its tip, coating Kamoj's sole.

When Kamoj tensed, Dazza said, "The nanomeds will aid the healing. Then they'll dissolve in your bloodstream."

"Nanny muds?" Kamoj asked.

"Nanomeds. Each has an active moiety linked to a pico-chip—" Dazza stopped, watching Kamoj's face. Then she said, "They're like machines, but so small you can't see them."

"Nanobots," Kamoj said.

"Again?" Dazza asked. "I have trouble with your accent."

"She said nanobots," Vyrl said. "She's speaking Iotic."

Kamoj stared at him. He understood Iotaca? Then again, he had read the contract scroll at their wedding, which was written in pure Iotaca. Maybe he could clear up the mystery of what the blasted thing said.

Dazza, however, also looked puzzled. "Why do you say it that way, as if she used a different language for 'nanobot'? Everything we've said is in Iotic."

Vyrl shook his head. "You and I may be speaking it, but the people here don't. Or not pure Iotic. Their 'Bridge' language is a dialect."

It would never have occurred to Kamoj to describe Bridge as a dialect of Iotaca. The differences seemed too extreme to call them two forms of the same language. Of course, to the people of the Northern Lands *any* change was extreme.

"Nanobot is a word from the temple language," Kamoj said.

"I haven't heard enough of your temple language to be sure," Vyrl said, "but I think it's what we call classical Iotic. That contract I read at the ceremony was written in it. What Dazza and I are speaking now is modern Iotic."

Dazza regarded him with curiosity. "You speak the classics?"

"I learned them when I was a boy," he said.

She looked impressed. "You must have had a good education."

He shrugged. "There were no schools where we lived, so my parents brought in tutors from offworld."

Kamoj wondered what he meant by *offworld*. She too found the result impressive. "I can pronounce phrases in Iotaca, but I don't understand it all. Like *nanobot*. I know the word but not the meaning."

"Do you know what 'molecule' means?" Dazza asked. When Kamoj shook her head, Dazza said, "It's like a tiny machine. A nanobot is designed for a specific duty. The ones that help make us healthy, we call nanomeds. Each has a picochip." She paused, watching Kamoj. "A picochip is like a brain that tells the bot what to do."

Kamoj tried to absorb it. "You put all that in my foot?"

"I did indeed. Three types of nanomed. Two ferry nutrients and structural materials to the wound and help maintain your physiological balance as you heal. The third catalyzes molecular repair processes."

Kamoj still didn't know what it meant, but it sounded splendid. "Well. Good."

"Is she going to be all right?" Vyrl asked.

"She'll be fine by tomorrow." Dazza snapped her quill into her box. "She should stay off that foot for tonight."

Vyrl started to speak, then just smiled. His sleepy-eyed look sent a ripple of sensation through Kamoj, embarrassment mixed with shy arousal. Walking clearly wasn't what he had in mind for tonight.

Closing the lid of her book-box, Dazza looked up at Vyrl. "Did you talk to Azander after you arrived?"

"Not really. Why?"

"He said you were followed by Ironbridge stagmen."

"Ironbridge? Whatever for?"

"Azander seemed to think you would know."

"I've no idea."

His response disquieted Kamoj. Ironbridge was nothing to ignore. What was Jax up to?

Vyrl sat on the bed. "What is it, water sprite? What troubles you about Ironbridge?"

Dazza drew in a sharp breath. Startled, Kamoj glanced at her. The colonel had the look of a healer whose patient had just showed signs of a recovery she had feared would never happen. It made no sense to Kamoj. Vyrl wasn't sick, at least that she could see. Except for the rum. But he wasn't drunk now, and all he had done was ask her about Ironbridge.

He hadn't noticed Dazza's reaction. Intent on Kamoj, he said, "Talk to me."

"It is forbidden," Kamoj said.

"To talk to me?"

"For me to talk of Ironbridge."

"Why?"

"Because you and I have a dowered merger."

"Why does that make a difference?"

She wasn't actually sure why tradition forbade discussing other bid candidates with the winner of a hostile merger. Rules changed when the balance of power tipped so far in favor of one party. "Hostile" was probably the operative word; if she spoke about Ironbridge she could aggravate Vyrl and so bring harm to herself, Argali, and Ironbridge.

"It is forbidden," she repeated.

Vyrl glanced at Dazza with an expression that clearly said: *Can you do something with this?*

Dazza considered her. "If Prince Havyrl gives you permission to speak about Ironbridge, can you do it?"

"She doesn't need my permission to talk," Vyrl said.

Kamoj looked from Vyrl to Dazza, at a loss to understand the hierarchy of authority here.

Dazza tried again. "Can you talk to me about it?"

"No," Kamoj said.

"Who can we ask?"

Who indeed? Maxard, perhaps. He hadn't married Vyrl. He was less likely to incur Vyrl's wrath by talking about Kamoj's relationship with another man.

"My uncle," Kamoj said.

"We can send someone to Argali tomorrow." Vyrl grimaced. "Which'll be forever with how long the nights here last."

Kamoj wondered what he meant. Nights weren't long in autumn, not compared to winter, when snow covered the world and blizzards roared down from the North Sky Islands.

Dazza was watching her. "This is about your customs, isn't it? All of you here, you're afraid of showing disrespect. That's important. Respect. To custom, to authority, and to the land."

Relief settled over Kamoj. "Yes."

Vyrl blinked at the doctor. "Where did you get all that?"

With a scowl, Dazza said, "From talking to your ever-so-patient butler the last time you went riding during one of your binges. I wanted to know why no one stopped you."

"Don't start with me, Dazza."

"Why? Because you happen to be more sober now than you've been in weeks? You're going to kill yourself."

Vyrl ignored the comment. "What did my butler tell you?"

Dazza nodded toward Kamoj. "They all feel that way. I think they're genetically engineered to obey authority. I've never known such a docile, cooperative people."

"They have armies." Vyrl paused. "If you can call thirty farmers who practice swordplay every now and then an army."

Kamoj wondered why he found that strange. An incorporated man's stagmen rode in his honor guard when needed and otherwise worked to support their families. Ironbridge had the only army that trained all year round. Only Jax could afford to pay a good wage in every season.

Given what she had seen with Vyrl, though, it wouldn't surprise her if he had his men training all year too, while he supported them at a higher rate than anyone else without realizing it. His servants and stagmen came from Argali. She and Maxard employed the best in the village, so Vyrl must be drawing from outlying hamlets, which were even more impoverished. By hiring locals instead of his own people, he had been supporting her province even before their merger. Appreciation brushed her thoughts. So far, Lionstar hardly seemed the monster she had feared.

"Their 'wars' are more like arguments," Dazza was saying. "In the rare instances when they do fight, it's a ritualistic ceremony. Ironbridge is the only province with real cavalry or troops, and they're more of a police force. I doubt you could convince these people to defy authority even if you paid them."

Kamoj blinked. What an odd notion. Why would anyone pay them to be defiant?

Vyrl smiled at her. "They wouldn't. It was just a manner of speech." He didn't see Dazza's startled look; by the time he turned back to the colonel, her face had gone back to normal.

"I'll send someone tomorrow to talk to Maxard Argali," he said. "See if we can untangle all this."

"I think that's a good idea." Dazza packed up her book.

She smiled at Kamoj, gratitude on her face. Why? Kamoj saw nothing she had done to make the doctor grateful.

After Dazza left, Vyrl lay back on the bed. The bags under his eyes had darkened again.

"You look tired," Kamoj said.

"Just a headache. I should have asked Dazza for something." His scowl came back. "But then I would have to listen to her harp on 'my drinking.' Tell me she can 'treat' that too. As if I have a problem. It's ridiculous. I have a few drinks, I go to sleep, I'm fine."

Kamoj knew he wasn't fine. She hesitated, unsure what to say. "I can rub your head."

"That would be nice, Kamoj." He paused. "Is that right? Kamoj?"

She smiled, then slid up past his shoulders and drew his head into her lap. "Yes. That's right." As she massaged his temples, he sighed, closing his eyes.

After a while he said, "What you talked about before, our 'dowered merger'—what does that mean, exactly?"

"Merger is perhaps not the best word." It implied a more balanced partnership. She wasn't sure how he would respond to a suggestion of imbalance in their marriage, so she chose a blander description. "Your corporation absorbed Argali."

He opened his eyes. "My what?"

"Your corporation. It was far too big for us to best. I used it to compensate Photax and Lystral's family, but even giving them double the recompense didn't put the slightest dent in what you sent to Argali House."

His forehead furrowed. "Compensate? What do you mean?"

She spoke carefully. "When you trampled Photax's crops and frightened Lystral's grandchildren."

Vyrl sat up, facing her. "I'm sorry. I didn't realize I had caused hardship. I will send apologies."

Her tension eased. "I think they would appreciate that."

"But I still don't understand. I sent you a dowry. I know that's the word. Our anthropologists double-checked. The dowry is the property a man brings to his wife at marriage, right? Drake told me that in your culture, inheritance goes through the female line, and that the women court the men. To get a highborn wife, you need a good dowry." He paused. "So I, uh, got one."

She spoke dryly. "The man is usually more subtle in making his interest known."

"I don't actually remember what I did." He rubbed the back of his neck. "I think I told my stagmen to clear out one of the storerooms and send the contents to Argali House. I almost fell over when they said you had accepted it."

She stared at him, unsure which stunned her more, his manner of instigating the takeover, or what his words implied about the extent of his corporation. "You have *more* in your dowry?"

"Well, yes, you could say that. I could fill up this palace with stores like what I sent you." He studied her face. "I don't understand how the idea of a corporation got mixed up here with a dowry. You make it sound like I bought you."

That was, in fact, how it felt. Kamoj doubted he would appreciate her saying it, though. "It is fine." She tugged on his arm. "Come lie down again."

"I won't argue with that." He stretched out with his head in her lap and closed his eyes again.

As she rubbed his head, she thought what an irony it was that a merger certain to become a legend might have been a whim born of a drinking binge. Would he regret it tomorrow? What if he changed his mind? She had no wish to return to Jax. He might not want her anymore. Even if Jax took her back, she would still be humiliated by the Lionstar rejection. If they both spurned her, then all the years of preparation for the Argali-Ironbridge merger would have been destroyed in a day.

Vyrl spoke in a quiet voice. "My father told me something when I was young. If you plant in the wrong place, you still have to tend the crops."

"Was he a farmer?"

"Yes."

Softly, she asked, "Am I the wrong place?"

"Gods, no." He opened his eyes. "You're sunlight. I was incredibly lucky. What if the beautiful nymph I saw rising out of the river turned out to have a personality like shattered glass? But regardless, it's my responsibility to see this through now." His face gentled. "I would never humiliate you."

The stiffness in her shoulders eased. She also rather liked being compared to sunlight.

His grin flashed. "I'm glad you like it."

"How do you know everything in my mind?"

"I don't." When she gave him a doubting look, he said, "Usually I just pick up emotions. My ability to do even that falls off with distance, roughly as Coulomb's Law."

Coulomb's law? "I don't understand."

"It's complicated."

Her voice cooled. "And I am too slow to understand?"

"Kamoj, no. I didn't mean that. I just don't know how to explain it, except as I learned it."

"Then explain it that way."

He hesitated. "I've an organ in my brain called the Kyle Afferent Body. The KAB. It's too small to see. Certain of its molecules, that is, certain bits of it, undergo quantum transitions when they interact with fields produced by the brains of other people. That means—well, you could say my KAB changes its behavior according to what it picks up. It also must couple strongly to the fields. That's why I don't pick up, say, radio waves. The changes in my KAB make it send pulses to neural structures in my cerebrum, which interpret them as thought." He stopped, watching her. "I'm not doing this very well, am I?"

"I don't know. I don't understand many of your words."

He tried again. "My brain picks up signals from yours and interprets them. It isn't that accurate, so emotions are easier than full thoughts. It only works up close because the signals aren't that strong."

Although the words made more sense this time, it sounded as strange as before. "How can you do that with me?"

"For some reason you're more open to me than most people." His voice warmed. "I felt it that first time I saw you, when you were swimming. You were so beautiful. So alive. So *happy*."

She smiled. "So naked."

Vyrl laughed. "That too."

She went back to massaging his head. After a while his lashes drooped and his breathing deepened. Then he jerked and opened his eyes. When they closed again, he forced them back open. Watching his struggle, Kamoj wondered why it was so important to him to stay awake.

The third time he started to fall asleep, he rolled on his side and pressed his lips against her leg. Distracted, she stopped rubbing his head. He was peeling off her other stocking, kissing her thigh as the silk slid away. A shiver ran along her body, though he was neither touching nor kissing the places that tingled.

After he pulled off her stocking, he slid his hand up her inner thigh. "Your skin is softer than glimsilk." Then he sat up and pulled her into his lap, wrapping his arms around her. Nuzzling her hair, he murmured, "I always thought I liked this room austere. I never realized how cold it is."

She laid her head on his shoulder. "It would look softer in the moonlight."

"Morlin," he said, "turn off the lights."

"Their web contacts aren't complete," a man said.

"Hai!" Kamoj sat up straight and yanked her dress down over her thighs.

Vyrl rubbed his hand down her back. "It's all right. He won't bother us."

"He is here? *Watching?*"

"He's just a computer web. I call him Morlin." Vyrl hesitated. "The name was supposed to be after an ancient Earth wizard, but I think I got it wrong."

"I'm having trouble completing the contacts," Morlin informed them. "The molecular engines that repair fiberoptic cables in this wing stopped replicating centuries ago."

Kamoj pressed her fist against her mouth. Morlin didn't exist, yet he was here.

"I suggest you reconsider trying to use the original web in the palace," he went on. "These problems continue to—"

"Morlin," Vyrl said. Watching Kamoj, he added, "We'll deal with it later."

It was quiet after that. Kamoj's heartbeat gradually slowed to normal. Whatever Morlin was, he apparently answered to Vyrl. As Vyrl explored her body, she relaxed against him and trailed her fingers down his arm. She breathed in his scent, spice-soap mixed with his own natural smell. His calloused hands scraped against her skin.

"Link established," Morlin suddenly said. The lights went out.

"Hai!" Kamoj jerked up her hands to protect herself.

"It's nothing." Vyrl stroked her hair. In a louder voice, he said, "Morlin, shut up."

Kamoj lowered her hands. "Does he obey you?" She had never imagined the palace might have a voice.

"Well, yes, you could say that." Vyrl gave her a curious look. "It's just the old computer web in this building. Parts of it. Some components are too decayed. Their repair bots failed a long time ago."

Kamoj wasn't sure what he meant, but she knew the palace had been in abominable shape when he rented it. That Vyrl had repaired her ancestral home meant more than she knew how to say. She had always longed to do it, but she could hardly use precious resources to fix a building when babies in Argali needed cereal.

"Look," she said, gazing over his shoulder.

Vyrl turned. A ghostly image of the stained glass window in her chamber stretched across the floor here in the main bedroom, laid there by moonlight slanting through her room. Sparkles glistened in the image, from where moonlight hit the bead curtain.

"It's beautiful," he said.

She slid off the bed and reached out to him. Tenderness showed on his face as he took her hand. Together they crossed the room, their fingers intertwined. When they entered her chamber, strings of beads trailed along their arms. The window glowed with light from the Sister Moon.

As Vyrl laid her on her bed, the moonlight cast shadows on his robe, making him look as if he were cut from onyx. His calluses felt nubbly on her skin when he peeled off her underdress. He set it on the floor, then paused, kneeling between her legs, just looking at her.

Too self-conscious to meet his gaze, Kamoj sat up and set her palms on his chest. She took off his robe, shy and unsure, trying to act self-assured. She didn't succeed, but he seemed to like how she touched him anyway. She couldn't look at his face because—she wasn't sure why. If she looked, he would somehow acknowledge her touch, making her too embarrassed to continue.

Kamoj tried to relax. Most women her age were already married, even mothers. Lying down, she reached her arms out to her husband. He stretched out on top of her, supporting his weight on his forearms so he didn't crush her under his body.

Vyrl took their love-making slow, giving her as much time as she needed. Even so, when he finally tried to enter, she tensed up. It was *tearing*—she wanted him to *stop*—

He went still on top of her. "Kamoj—?"

Hai. If she kept this up she would still be a virgin after her wedding night. In a low voice, she said, "It's all right."

Vyrl handled her even more gently after that. The moons shifted in the sky, their light casting a stained glass rose on the floor. He murmured against her ear, saying her name over and over, and right this time. His intensity and rhythm increased, until suddenly he went rigid on top of her. He drew in a sharp breath and blew it out, the stream of air wafting tendrils of her hair around her cheeks.

Then he relaxed, his body settling onto her. He kept murmuring, his voice a soft current of sound against her ear. After a while his words trickled into silence and he lay still, one hand curled around her breast. His breathing deepened, until it came with a faint snore at the end of each breath.

Kamoj blinked. Apparently they were done. Although the experience had been pleasant, after the initial pain, it seemed incomplete. Was this why Lyode extolled marriage? Certainly it was nice, but Kamoj didn't see why it made her usually no-nonsense bodyguard smile like a besotted fruitwing. She wondered if, in her shyness, she had overlooked or missed the important part.

Vyrl felt heavier now that he wasn't supporting his weight. She nudged him until he rolled off and stretched out next to her. Then she turned onto her side, her body spooned into his, her back against his chest. He slid his arm around her waist without a break in the rumble of his sleep.

Kamoj drifted in a doze, like the fever-sleep of a delirium, her body so sensitized that even the air currents seemed to caress her. She felt restless. Incomplete. Sometimes she awoke to find herself touching private places of her body.

When Vyrl shifted, at first she thought he was restive in his sleep. Then he slid his hand down over hers. As she pressed against his palm, he kissed her neck, his teeth playing with her necklace. Whatever he was doing, he knew how to do it well. She felt as if she were trying to climb a peak she couldn't reach. She rose higher and higher—and finally the release came, like a crest with many bumps. It spread to the rest of her body in waves of sensation, until she lost control and cried out.

When she calmed, Vyrl murmured, "Sweet water sprite."

Kamoj wanted to say soft words too, call her husband beloved and other endearments. Yet she didn't feel she knew him well enough. So strange, to be so intimate, yet so unfamiliar at the same time.

Languor settled over her like a downy quilt . . .

Kamoj wasn't sure what woke her. The moonlight had dimmed, both the Sister Moon and Far Moon having finished their voyages across the sky. The sense of drowsy satisfaction had also left the room.

She rolled over. Vyrl was lying on his back, staring at the canopy above them, his gaze fixed, seeing nothing. The tendons in his neck had pulled taut, and his jaw was clenched so hard that the bones stood out against his skin.

"Vyrl?" She pushed up on her elbow. "What's wrong?"

He jerked his head. Then he sat up, his face contorting.

And he screamed.

It shattered the silence. He gasped and screamed again, his fists clenched on his thighs. His face twisted until she hardly recognized him.

Boots pounded in the main bedroom. "Prince Havyrl!" The bead curtain rattled as Azander and the other bodyguard strode into the chamber. Scrambling to her knees, Kamoj yanked on Vyrl's robe, covering herself.

Vyrl showed no hint that he saw any of them. He stared straight ahead and worked his mouth like a man in a nightmare struggling, with horrific futility, to scream again.

Azander knelt and shook Vyrl's shoulders. "Prince Havyrl, wake up! It only be the nightmares. Wake up!"

Vyrl swung his fist so fast, Azander had no time to duck.

He hit Azander in the chin and the bodyguard flew over backward, hitting the floor with a thud.

"Get out!" Vyrl shouted. *"Now."*

Azander stared at him, holding his chin. Then he jumped to his feet, and the two bodyguards left as fast as they had come.

Kamoj slid back, away from Vyrl, until the wall stopped her retreat. Had she been mistaken about her new husband? But no. This was different from Jax's rage. Something was wrong, very wrong. Vyrl leaned forward, his arms wrapped around his stomach, as if he were hurt somehow, not a physical hurt, but something else.

She didn't know how long they sat that way. Finally she moved closer to him. Then she waited. When he neither objected nor showed anger, she came the rest of the way to his side. He turned to her, moisture gleaming under his eyes.

She touched his wet cheek. "What is it?"

"Nothing." He took a breath. "Go back to sleep."

Nothing? He had just split the night with his screams. She wanted to offer comfort, but she feared to anger him, a risk she couldn't take, not when the well-being of Argali depended on his goodwill. So she slipped off his robe and lay down with her eyes closed. She heard him put on the robe, then heard the bed creak and felt the mattress shift.

Kamoj opened her eyes. She was alone. She slipped her underdress over her head and got out of bed. Her footsteps made no sound as she crossed to the curtain. She peered through the beaded strings into the main bedroom.

Vyrl had opened the window above his desk and was sitting in his chair, staring at the night, his body silhouetted against the sky. As she watched, he raised a bottle to his lips. The cloying smell of rum drifted in the air.

Watching, Kamoj knew that whatever troubled him went far deeper than the rum could reach. What had happened to give a man of such power the terrors that haunted his dreams?

6

Binge

Metastable State (1,2)

Early morning light filled Kamoj's room. Jul had yet to rise above the forest, so no rays slanted in the window, which someone had opened while she slept. She lay alone, staring at a tapestry on the wall. It depicted two fierce women in ancient warrior garb engaged in a duel over a youth. They faced off in a forest clearing, one with a bowball cupped in her palm, her arm raised to throw it. Their young man stood leaning against a tree with his muscular arms crossed, looking appropriately dashing. He also looked disconcerted, which Kamoj suspected was closer to the truth of whatever long-past event had inspired the tapestry.

She felt lethargic, unable to face the day. She had watched Vyrl for an hour last night, afraid to intrude on his solitude. Exhaustion finally forced her to choose between sleeping on the floor or returning to bed.

Well, lying here solved nothing. She got up and went into the main bedroom. It was empty of Vyrl, but two trunks stood against the foot of his bed. Her trunks!

Her mood lightening, she ran across to them. The first held her clothes and the second had personal items, including the dolls from her collection. She picked up her favorite rag doll, savoring the familiar feel of its yarn hair against her cheek.

"Governor Argali?"

Startled, Kamoj looked up. A housemaid stood in the doorway of the entrance foyer. She must have been on the landing, waiting for Kamoj to wake up. "I heard you moving about," the woman said. "Would you like help dressing?"

Kamoj reddened, embarrassed to be caught holding a doll. "Not today. But thank you."

"Yes, ma'am." The woman bowed and withdrew.

Putting away her things took several hours. Then Kamoj went to the bathing room. Someone had swept up the glass and opened the window, letting sunshine in and the rum smell out. Bracing herself for the icy mountain water, she slid into the pool. What she found came as even more of a shock: warm water. How? She saw no steaming stones or other heat sources.

Then she remembered her foot. Holding a claw of the quetzal statue, she pulled her leg out of the water. All she saw was healthy pink skin with a slight bruising. That rapid healing impressed her as much as all the other marvels she had seen here.

After her bath, she ran naked to her chamber, racing across the main bedroom. She wasn't sure why she ran. Vyrl had seen her without her clothes, and besides he wasn't here. But she ran anyway. For all she knew, Morlin watched everything.

In her room, she started to take out a tunic. Then she changed her mind and chose a rose-cotton dress instead. It gave her pleasure to think Vyrl might enjoy the dress. It had been years since she had worn it, though, and it no longer fit. Her breasts plumped out the neckline and the skirt barely reached her knees. She pulled up lace from her underdress to cover her breasts and tugged her underskirts down until their ruffles swirled around her knees like a border to the dress. Then she pulled on gray leggings made from Argali wool, followed by her suede farm boots.

After Kamoj dressed, she left the suite and paused on the landing. She was hungry, but she wasn't sure where to find the kitchen. She also had to find Vyrl, to discuss Argali. Theirs was a tricky situation, one with no recorded precedent. The union of two provinces through a dowered merger of two governors was almost unheard of, and she knew of none as one-sided as the Lionstar-Argali merger. She and Jax had agreed to split their time between Argali and Ironbridge. With Vyrl, she had no idea. He could demand control of Argali or leave it to her, tax her province to death, shower it with riches, ruin it, or ignore it.

She descended the stairs, listening to the forest, the wind in the trees and the blue-tailed quetzals calling, even the trill of a gold-tail. Flaring the membranes in her nostrils, she inhaled the forest scents. It wasn't until she reached the bottom that she heard the voices. As she walked down the Long Hall, they resolved into an argument between Vyrl and Dazza.

"I can't," Dazza was saying. "I haven't the equipment."

"Don't treat me like a stupid farm boy," Vyrl answered. "The *Ascendant* has plenty of facilities. It's a damn city."

It sounded as if they were in the entrance foyer of the palace. Kamoj hesitated near the chandeliered ballroom, unsure whether to stay or leave.

"These aren't simple alterations," Dazza told him. "I would have to change your lungs and hemoglobin, redesign the way your body absorbs oxygen and carbon dioxide, and add filters for impurities. Who knows what side effects it would cause? I couldn't even begin until I made a thorough study. Surely you realize the magnitude of what you're asking."

"Contact the *Ascendant*," Vyrl said. "Tell them to send down what you need."

Dazza made a frustrated noise. "The web systems in this building aren't sophisticated enough to run the equipment. If you want me to work on you, we have to do it on the ship."

"No!"

Her voice turned placating. "Vyrl, listen. Why change

your body? Doesn't the respirator let you breathe in comfort?"

"I don't want a metal face."

"You *asked* for metal. It doesn't have to be that way. If it bothers you, we'll redesign the mask."

"The people here don't need respirators." He sounded vexed. "If I'm going to live on this planet, I want to go without anything."

"Why? Is this temporary exile worth such drastic changes?"

Kamoj froze. Temporary exile? Vyrl was going to leave? What did that mean for Argali?

Troubled now, she went through the ballroom and stopped in the archway that opened into the Entrance Hall. Vyrl and Dazza were at the far end of the hall, in front of the foyer. Azander and two other stagmen were standing back from them, trying to accomplish the impossible by being simultaneously attentive to their liege and oblivious to his argument.

"I told you what I wanted," Vyrl told Dazza. "Do it. I'm going riding."

"You're in no condition to ride—"

"Contact the *Ascendant*."

Dazza crossed her arms. "And if I refuse?"

"Don't push me, Colonel."

"Vyrl, stay here," she urged. "Let me give you something to deal with the alcohol. Or let it work out of your system. When you're sober, we'll talk modifications."

"You're not putting more of your bugs in my body." He grimaced. "Those bloody things never die."

"Nanomeds aren't bugs. And meds designed to flush out alcohol do 'die.' They dissolve after a few—"

"No," he said.

She scowled at him. "If I alter your body so you can live on this planet unaided, you'll need even more self-replicating meds than the ones you carry now for health maintenance."

"Fine." With no warning, he spun around and strode up the hall, straight at Kamoj. His sudden attention caught her off guard. She hadn't even realized he knew she was there.

A farmhand must have given him the clothes he wore, an old white shirt, frayed with many washings, and rough pants tucked into scuffed boots. Although Maxard wore old clothes when he worked the farm, it was still the garb of a highborn man. It startled her to see Vyrl, the wealthiest man in the Northern Lands, possibly on all Balumil, dressed like the poorest farmer.

Before she could react or retreat, he reached her. He didn't even stop, just slid his arm around her waist and swung her around, then pulled her with him as he headed back down the hall. His longs legs covered ground so fast she had to run to keep up.

He stopped in front of Dazza. "My wife and I are going riding." Propelling Kamoj ahead of him, he stalked into the foyer. He left her in the middle of the room while he went to the wall, where his cloak hung like a patch of evening sky.

Kamoj pushed her hand through her hair. She could refuse to go. Perhaps she was naive, but she didn't believe he would do anything other than leave her behind. The idea of his going alone bothered her more. Could he ride, as drunk as he seemed right now? Suppose he fell from his stag and broke a limb? Or worse? She didn't know how it worked with his people, but among her own, a man thrown from a greenglass could die alone in the forest before anyone found him. She couldn't bear the thought of his lying alone and hurt, lost in the mountains.

Vyrl smacked his palm on the wall and a block of stone slid aside, revealing a square hole. He pulled out his silver mask. Crumpling it in his hand, he spun around and spoke to someone behind her. "Bring Graypoint out front."

Turning, she saw Azander by the great double doors that opened onto the courtyard. A bruise purpled the stagman's chin where Vyrl had hit him last night. Azander pulled back the heavy bolts on the doors and leaned his weight into one until it slammed open, letting blue sunlight pour into the foyer. Then he walked through the shimmer curtain out into the autumn day.

Dazza spoke from the foyer's inner archway. "Vyrl, at least let Kamoj ride her own stag. She'll be safer."

"Safe from what?" Vyrl swung his cloak over his shoulders, the blue cloth swirling through the air like a swath of twilight sky. "Military witch doctors who want to fill my blood with bugs to stop me from enjoying a drink, but who refuse to fix my body so I can goddamn breathe?"

"Don't go riding," Dazza said. "Wait until you're sober."

Bi-hooves clattered on the flagstones outside. Vyrl strode over to Kamoj and took her arm. Pulling her with him, he stalked through the shimmer, out into the sunlight and down the stairs to the courtyard.

Dazza called from behind them. "Vyrl!"

When he turned to the colonel, Kamoj's hope jumped. Would he change his mind?

Dazza was standing in the palace entrance, behind the shimmer. "Your respirator," she said.

He watched the colonel, the mask crumpled in his fist. Then he whirled around and pulled Kamoj over to where Azander held a stag. Graypoint. The animal was huge and muscled, with gigantic antlers that shaded from emerald at their bases into silver tips. Azander made a stagmount with his hands for Vyrl. Despite the stag's great height, Vyrl swung onto its back with mesmerizing grace. Graypoint pranced sideways, shook his head, and stamped his four front legs. Then he stilled, becoming a statue as he looked down at Kamoj. His eyes, huge and green, were filled with intelligence.

Vyrl motioned to Azander, and the stagman put his hands on Kamoj's waist. Before she had a chance to react, Azander was lifting her up into Vyrl's grasp. Vyrl hauled her up in front of him so she straddled the stag, her flared skirt foaming over her thighs and knees. It happened so fast, it made her dizzy. Or maybe it was the air, so thin after the palace. He held her around the waist with one arm, his mask clutched in his fist, while Graypoint danced under them, agitated with Kamoj's unfamiliar weight.

Suddenly the greenglass reared on his back legs, rising up and up to his full height, his front four legs pawing the air, their scales splintering the light. Clangs filled the courtyard as he crashed his bi-hooves together. He threw back his head and bared his fangs, the opaline teeth glittering like daggers. And then he screamed at the sky.

Kamoj went rigid, terrified she would fly off the greenglass. From this height the fall could break her neck. She grabbed its antlers, their velvety green scales slippery in her hold.

"Vyrl!" Dazza shouted. "Don't do this!"

The greenglass came down, jerking his head until Kamoj released his antlers. Vyrl's labored breath rasped behind her. She twisted around to see him staring at Dazza, his face flushed. As Graypoint danced beneath them, on the verge of rearing again, Vyrl yanked a narrow slab out from his cloak, a rectangle covered with symbols. Extending his arm, he pointed the slab at Dazza. Its reflective surface caught the sunshine and splintered it into shards of light.

"You can forget about having your orbital monitors track me, Colonel. I'm setting up a jamming field—" He pressed a blue light on the slab. "—now."

Dazza paled. "We want you here, Vyrl. What if something happens and we can't locate you?"

"Is that all any of you think about?" he rasped. "What you want?" He thrust the slab back in his cloak and grabbed Kamoj's shoulders. "Look at this. My wife. A farm girl who looks like a virginal sex goddess, and all she asks is a simple life, a husband who doesn't beat her, and the freedom to walk in the woods. Did it ever occur to all your generals, politicians, and strategists that maybe that's all I want? That what I want might actually *matter?* Or are you all too busy plotting how to use your oh-so-valuable prince to give a flaming damn what I think?"

Before Dazza could answer, Vyrl jabbed the stag with his heels and Graypoint leapt forward, racing for the forest. Vyrl held the reins with both hands, his arms around Kamoj. He was gasping, choking as if every breath hurt.

Kamoj wasn't sure how she felt about being called "a virginal sex goddess," she only knew her husband was too drunk to ride. "Vyrl!" she shouted. "Your mask!" The wind carried away her voice. Desperate, she called to him in her mind. *Vyrl! The mask!*

His arm moved and his breathing stopped. Dismayed, she twisted around—and stared into a face of silver scales. Jerking at the sight, she lost her balance. Vyrl caught her as she fell, but in his drunken state he misjudged his strength and almost shoved her off Graypoint in the other direction. She spun around and hung onto the stag's neck while they raced through the iridescent forest.

The path sloped upward. Trees towered on both sides, their branches meeting overhead. Despite the cloudless day, thunder rumbled in the sky. Kamoj shivered, wondering what other strange spirits Vyrl's outburst would call up.

"It's just a shuttle engine," he said against her ear. He slowed Graypoint to a walk and prodded him off the path, into the woods. The stag had calmed, his fire eased by the race. He trotted between the well-spaced trees.

They went deep into the forest, always headed farther up in the mountains. Every now and then an "engine" grumbled overhead. Each time, Vyrl tensed, and each time the engine faded he relaxed again.

Eventually Kamoj said, "Where are we going?"

"Away. Until they find me." He sounded tired. "Actually, they always know where I am. Usually they let me come back on my own." He paused. "Except today I took the jammer. They'll have more trouble this time."

"Jammer?"

"What I pointed at Dazza. It works best against electro-magnetic sensors."

"Lector's senses?" She couldn't follow his winding train of thought.

"It confuses the things they use to find me." His voice slurred. "Neutrinos are hardest t'fool. They go through anything. This jammer now, it's a real beaut. It can even throw off neutrino sensors."

"Oh." Kamoj wondered if the rum made him babble, or if his words had some actual sense.

"What do you think is this Current you all worship?" Vyrl asked. "Electromagnetic radiation. Light. Those threads in your light panels are just optical fibers."

That gave her pause. In Iotaca, *Optical Fiber* was the full name of Lyode's husband, Opter Sunsmith. If their line ran true, their children would inherit the sunsmith talents. Opter's brother, Gallium Phosphide Sunsmith, worked in the sunshop with him. Other provinces had other gifts, such as the Amperman and Ohmston lines in Ironbridge. The Argali temple was dedicated to sun spirits, like the Glories and Airy Rainbows, but Kamoj had always seen them more as guardians than deities.

"Why do you think we worship the Current?" she asked.

"Don't you?"

"The Current just is. Like rain, clouds, and sun."

"Not *like* the sun." he said. "It *is* the sun. Well, not just the sun. But light."

"Of course, Prince Havyrl."

"Don't call me that."

"That?"

"Prince Whatsit. You're my wife. Call me Vyrl."

"Yes, Vyrl."

"Why are you so formal? Last night, I even thought you were afraid—" Suddenly he stopped. "Gods *almighty*. I'm an idiot."

Kamoj didn't know whether to laugh or be shocked. Never in a hundred Long Years would Jax have ever said such a thing about himself.

"You had no choice, did you?" Vyrl said.

"Choice?"

"About the marriage. Bloody flaming hell. I should have seen it before. That wasn't a dowry. It was a *purchase* order." He pulled Graypoint to a halt and dismounted, swinging his leg over the stag's back. He landed on the ground with leonine grace. Graypoint danced sideways, and Kamoj had to grab the bridle to keep from falling.

Standing with his back to her, Vyrl looked normal, a man with a mane of tawny hair. Then he turned and she saw the silver mask. She froze, as unsettled now as the first time she had seen it.

He peeled off the mask. "I hate this thing."

"Vyrl, no. You need to breathe."

"You must hate me."

"Never." Every time she thought she began to understand him, he went off on a rant again.

He crumpled the mask. "You think you have to say that."

Although she meant what she said, his words made her stop to consider. Had Jax asked if she hated him, certainly she would have denied it. Otherwise he would have hit her.

Vyrl was concentrating as if she were a tangle of threads he wanted to unravel. "I'm not going to beat you. Gods, Kamoj, I would never do such a thing."

Kamoj thought he truly meant it. She wanted to trust him, but she didn't know if she could let down her guard.

"I like being with you," she said. "It's just that . . ."

"Yes?"

"I don't understand you."

Vyrl gave a rueful smile. "That makes two of us." He pressed the mask back onto his face, then came over and reached for her. As he helped her off the stag, she put her arms around his neck. He held her with her feet dangling in the air while they hugged. The covering on his face felt cool against her cheek.

"I have a place out here where I go to be alone." He set her down on the ground and took her hand.

Vyrl drew her over to an outcropping of moss-covered slabs half-buried in the ground. Bridle bells clinked as Graypoint followed them. When they stopped, Vyrl rubbed his mount's neck, pressing on the scales in that way greenglass stags liked. Graypoint stood patiently while Vyrl removed the bridle and tended him. He pushed his long snout against Vyrl's palm, nipping at his fingers with fangs that could have torn Vyrl to pieces, had Graypoint wanted. Then the greenglass took off, running in a effortless six-legged lope among the trees.

Vyrl glanced at Kamoj. "Don't worry. He'll come back."

She spoke softly. "I know." Graypoint's behavior told her far more than Vyrl realized. After working all her life in the glasshouses at Argali, she knew stags. Graypoint was wild, never broken or tamed. A gifted stagman might attract the interest of a wild stag, but never one as high-strung and powerful as Graypoint. That the animal freely chose to follow Vyrl impressed her more than all Vyrl's wealth, titles, and palace repairs.

He led her through an opening in the rocks into a cave. It had a roof half again as tall as Vyrl and a floor of packed dirt, with boulders jutting out here and there. He knelt at a platform beside the entrance and ran his fingers over its surface. Despite all the wonders Kamoj had seen, it still startled her when lights appeared within the platform, glowing and winking. A shimmer formed in the entrance of the cave, blending into the rocks on either side.

Vyrl sat back on his heels. "The generator will bring the air to normal. Normal for me, that is."

She stood just inside the entrance. "Why can't you breathe the air?"

"Too much carbon dioxide. Too little oxygen. All the

scale dust." He seemed distracted, either tired or depressed. "The amount of sunlight that reaches Balumil is about half the human standard, and a lot of that is ultraviolet. The carbon dioxide in the atmosphere helps keeps the temperature up." He touched the mask on his face. "This concentrates oxygen and dilutes the carbon dioxide. It also filters out the dust. That gives me asthma." He regarded her, his eyes black ovals. "It would kill me if I breathed it too long."

She tried not to let his metal face disturb her. "But the air doesn't bother me at all."

"Your lungs have filters." Vyrl took off his mask and dropped it on the console. "You also have redesigned hemoglobin, and your circulatory system responds to different partial pressures of oxygen and carbon dioxide." He rubbed the bridge of his nose. "Those slitted cat's eyes of yours let in more light, too. It's why you can see in the dark."

That surprised Kamoj. "You can't?"

"Not as well as you. Human vision can adapt to lower levels of light, but everything here probably looks bluer to me than to you." He massaged the back of his neck. "Your ancestors biosculpted this world, altering the atmosphere and biosphere. Balumil is still a killer for unmodified humans, though, especially during winter and summer. That's why your ancestors wore space suits."

"Space suits?"

"You know those pictures of ancient stagmen in full-body diskmail?" When she nodded, he said, "Those are space suits."

She poked her finger into the shimmer. "And this?"

"It's an airlock. It surrounds the cave." He paused. "I'm not sure how to describe it for you."

"Use your own words. I like to hear them." Now that she knew he wasn't mocking her ignorance, she found a beauty in his words, the promise of knowledge and wonders.

Vyrl thought for a moment. "The curtain is a membrane. We call it a modified lipid bilayer. It contains enzymes. They're like tiny keys. They fit certain molecules. Certain locks." He tapped the platform. "This applies a potential to the membrane. Different potentials activate different keys. When a key opens a lock, it changes the membrane permeability. Right now it holds in air . . . but water can diffuse through." He seemed to bog down in fatigue.

"Are you all right?" Kamoj wished he would let himself sleep.

"I'm fine." He stood up slowly. "The generator recycles our air and sends out floating nanomeds that remove the scale dust."

She thought of the firepuff fly that had stuck to the shimmer. "But we can push through the membrane."

"On this setting, yes. You become part of the seal." He pressed the heels of his hands against his temples. "A pico-web within the membrane remembers its original form, so after you pass, it returns to normal."

"Vyrl, are you sure you are all right?"

"It's just a headache." He pulled a bottle out of his cloak and unscrewed the top. Then he drank deeply, tilting his head back as he swallowed.

Watching him, Kamoj felt at a loss. Her only experience with anyone who drank this much was Korl Plowsbane. Would Vyrl become that way, decimated and dulled, with no family or friends, only the bottle he loved above all else? She had no idea what to do. She had seen how angry he became if Dazza even mentioned it.

He walked across the cave, his boots scuffing up swirls of scale dust. The generator hummed, making its nanomeds clean the air so it wouldn't kill her husband.

Vyrl turned and stood looking at her, broad-shouldered and long-legged, his tawny hair tousled around his face, his shirt only half-laced up the front, the gold hair on his chest curling, his large eyes luminous in the shadows. His appealing appearance only made his next words all the more jolting. "That day at the river—you have no idea. I was so close to going after you. Just one bodyguard you had, to my four stagmen." He raised his hand, palm up. " 'But no,' I thought. 'Do you want her to hate you? What of honor? Decency? All that.' So I courted you. Or I thought I courted you." He took a swallow of rum. Lowering the bottle, he spoke with self-disgust. "Seems I raped you anyway."

"Don't say that." How could he be so empathic and not know the warmth she felt for him? She had never wanted Jax to touch her, but after Vyrl's gentleness last night even the thought of Ironbridge revolted her.

"I *knew*, blast it!" Vyrl said. "I knew you wanted me to stop last night. You even cried it in your mind." He sat on a hip-high boulder and took another swallow of rum. "Self-delusion is remarkable, isn't it? I convinced myself you wanted me."

"You weren't deluding yourself," she said.

"You think you have to tell me that. Because I *bought* you." He let the empty bottle slide out of his hand. It hit a rock and broke into pieces. "You aren't bound to me, Kamoj. You're free." He rubbed his eyes. "I'll have the *Ascendant* move our base to some other place. We'll tell your people—hell, tell them what?" Lowering his hand, he said, "That I went back to my own land and will send for you. Then we'll say I've been killed. That way you'll be free of me without being humiliated."

"Killed?" She couldn't believe his words.

"Imperial law recognizes unions made in the colonies, even the rediscovered ones like this. That means we're married by my law as well as yours." He spoke awkwardly. "I'll have someone arrange divorce papers."

She didn't see how he could speak her language, yet say so much she didn't understand. Enough made sense, though. He meant to dissolve their merger. The realization stabbed like broken glass. With news of Vyrl's "death," Jax could claim the widow. Ironbridge would get everything: Argali, the redone palace, Morlin, all of it.

Kamoj took a breath. Then she went to him and toed aside

the broken bottle. With shy affection, she put her arms around his waist. "Stay with me."

His arms came around her. "You don't have to say that."

"I know." She hesitated, suddenly unsure of herself. "Unless you want to go."

"Gods, no." He stroked her hair. "Are you sure?"

"I'm sure."

"Even after last night?"

"Especially after last night."

"I thought I hurt you."

"Vyrl, no." She tried to recapture her feeling from then, so he would feel it too. Rubbing her cheek on his chest, she inhaled his scent. Then she undid the tie at his waist and folded her hand around him, seeking to give to him now what he had given her last night. As she moved her hand, his breath quickened. He brushed his lips over her head and slid his palm down her waist-length hair.

After a while, he pulled off the scarf she used for a belt and helped her fold it around him. Then she continued, holding him with the scarf now. He suddenly tensed, then jerked, the muscles of his body going rigid as he strained in her hold.

Finally he relaxed. Holding her close, he murmured words from an old Argali harvest song: " 'So soft is her touch on grain full with nectar . . . ' "

Kamoj smiled at his new interpretation of the lyrics. *Sweet lion,* she thought. But she felt too shy to speak the endearment. Looking up, she saw his eyelids droop closed, the metal lashes a glittering contrast to the dark circles under his eyes.

"Let's lie down," she said. "I'm tired." She wasn't really, but Vyrl obviously needed to sleep. Why he fought so hard against it she had no idea, but perhaps he would do for her what he wouldn't do for himself.

Tenderness showed on his drawn face. "All right." He refastened his clothes, then folded her scarf and set it on the rock. Standing up, he swung off his cloak. It swirled through the air in a swath of twilight and settled on the ground. "There you go." As Kamoj sat on it, he watched her like a greenglass stag mesmerized by blue moonlight on the water. " 'S pretty . . . your dress. That color. What d'you call it? Rose? 'S nice the way you fill out—" Then he stopped and flushed. "Ai, Kamoj. I'm rambling. What an idiot you married."

"No, you aren't. Don't say that." She patted the ground. "You lie down. I'll rub your head."

"Won't argue with that." He stretched out on his back and put his head in her lap. As she massaged his temples, his eyes closed. Within moments his breathing had settled into the steady rumble of sleep.

Watching him, Kamoj wondered how to understand this husband of hers. He spoke like a highborn man, dressed like a farmer, carried a title, had a laborer's calluses, moved like a dancer, and had a stagman's gift with greenglasses. The silver in his hair and the lines around his eyes suggested he had reached his forties, yet he had the powerful physique and vigor of a young man. His wide-open emotions and beguiling mischief made him seem boyish.

Beneath all that, though, buried also under his mood swings, drinking, and tormented dreams, he gave off a sense of deep-seated satisfaction, the contentment that came from well-advanced years, not for everyone, but for some. He obviously wasn't happy now, yet she picked up a deeper serenity, the kind it took a lifetime to form.

"Vyrl, what are you?" she asked. Elderly, middle-aged, or young? Prince or farmer? Athlete or stagman? Drunkard or wise man? Brushing back his hair, she decided she would simply try to accept him for himself.

After a while she slid out from under him and lay down. Outside, a quetzal called, and another answered. Branches creaked in the wind. She could imagine the woods, ancient trees nodding together, their heads lifted high above the ground. If she were a bird, she could rise out of the forest and see it rolling in wave upon iridescent wave through the mountains, beneath the limitless violet plain of the sky.

7

Sword and Ballbow

Perturbations

A shudder racked Vyrl's body, waking Kamoj. Deep in his dreams, he made a strangled noise, his face clenched. She pushed up on her elbow and massaged his head until he calmed.

When he was sleeping well again, she went outside and stood gazing at the forest. Morning had passed into early afternoon. Overhead an "engine" rumbled. She wondered if it knew Vyrl was here.

When she returned to the cave, she found him sitting up. Although fatigue still lined his face, he looked more rested.

"Is anyone out there?" he asked.

"I heard an engine. I didn't see anyone, though." She sat cross-legged in front of him. "May I ask you a question?"

"Of course."

"What are you a prince of?"

He shrugged. "Nothing, really. I'm just a citizen of the Skolian Imperialate. It's about nine hundred worlds governed by an elected Assembly."

"You are not a prince?"

"I've the title. But it doesn't mean much in this modern age." He considered her. "Tell me what you know of Balumil's history."

She thought of the stories she had learned as a child. "Long ago the Current gave light and warmth to our houses.

And voices." Like Morlin, she realized. Vyrl had given the Quartz Palace back its voice. "Sailors brought the people here on ships that flew above the sky."

"That fits."

"It does?" She had expected him to smile at their fanciful tales. "How?"

"The Ruby Empire established this colony." He rubbed his shoulder, working out the kinks that came from sleeping on the ground. "That's why I know your language."

It didn't surprise her that their language had remained constant enough for him to understand. Her people never varied anything. Change brought upheaval, upheaval threatened revolution, and revolution was anathema.

Still, it had been a long time. "The sky sailors vanished five thousand years ago."

"That's when the Ruby Empire collapsed." He stretched his arms. "Originally we all came from Earth."

The word had an odd sense of familiarity. "Earth?"

Softly he said, "Home, Kamoj. For all of us. Green hills, blue sky, sweet fresh air."

His words evoked ancient mysteries of her people, strange birds also called quetzals, but without scales, flying in an eggshell blue sky. "If home is a place called Earth, why are we here?"

Dryly he said, "Many people would like to know that." He pushed his hair behind his ear. "About six thousand years ago, around 4000 B.C., an unknown race moved a group of humans from Earth to the world Raylicon. Why? We don't know. Our abductors vanished without so much as a 'Sorry about this.' Knowing star travel existed, my ancestors eventually developed star drives and built the Ruby Empire."

"But it fell."

"It was fragile, built by a people with many gaps in their knowledge. But we did eventually relearn interstellar propulsion, about five centuries ago." Suddenly he laughed. "When Earth's people reached the stars, they went looking for aliens and found us instead, their own siblings, busily building empires. Gave 'em one hell of a shock."

She smiled. "You look quite smug about that." When he chuckled, she asked, "And Balumil was a Ruby Empire world?"

"That's right. We've been reclaiming the old colonies and settling new worlds. We call ourselves the Skolian Imperialate now."

"How are you a prince?"

Vyrl shifted his weight. "My mother descends from the Ruby Dynasty."

"Ruby Dynasty? From the Ruby Empire?"

"That's right. The House of Skolia."

"Skolia is your family name?" When he nodded, she spoke quietly. "You are a great man, to rule nine hundred worlds."

He looked uncomfortable. "My family hasn't ruled anything for thousands of years. I'm just a farmer."

She sensed unspoken subtleties in his words. "Dazza's people hold you prisoner because you have value to them."

"I'm not their prisoner." When she just looked at him, he said, "They have their reasons."

"Good reasons or bad?"

The question seemed to surprise him. "Valid reasons."

"Why?"

"The Ruby Empire had a thriving slave trade. The Ruby Dynasty outlawed it. That's one reason the old empire fell. The merchants went to war against my family." Tiredly he said, "Now it's all started again, worse than before."

She stiffened. "This is why you are a prisoner? Dazza is a slave trader?"

"Good gods, of course not. Dazza Pacal is a colonel in the Pharaoh's army, the oldest branch of Imperial Space Command, the Skolian military."

Relief washed over Kamoj. "So your own people hold you captive."

He shifted his weight. "If you mean, did ISC bring me here, the answer is yes. I wouldn't use the word 'captive.' "

"Then why won't they let you go?"

"The members of my family are Rhon telepaths." At her baffled look, he said, "What I told you about last night. We're the ultimate result of breeding for psions. Our minds can power the very few Ruby machines that still survive. Modern science doesn't yet understand the ancient technology, but my family can use it. The Ruby machines allow us to access universes outside this spacetime, places where the physical laws are different."

She quirked her eyebrow at him. "These odd-sounding things have value?"

"Indeed. It makes instant communication possible. In this universe, the speed of light limits our signals. But not elsewhere." His grin flashed. "We beat the Current, Kamoj. It gives us a speed and precision the Traders can't match." His smile faded. "It's the only reason we survive against them."

That he could beat the Current impressed her. No wonder his clan had such value to his people. "But where is the rest of your family?"

His silence stretched out so long, she wondered if she had offended him. But finally he spoke. "My father came from another of the rediscovered colonies. He was a simple man. A farmer. He was also that one in a trillion, a Ruby psion." Anger leaked into his voice. "We're thoroughbreds, exotic and rare. For reasons our geneticists can't yet unravel, attempts to make us in the lab almost always fail." He shrugged, a gesture all the more eloquent for its attempt to indicate a nonchalance he obviously didn't feel. "But my parents could have children. So the Assembly made them do it."

"Hai, Vyrl." She watched his face, trying to understand the shadow on his mood. "It hurts, yes?"

He didn't answer. Instead he said, "During our last war with the Traders, the Allied Worlds of Earth stayed neutral.

But they gave protective custody to my family." Bitterness edged his words. "Then Earth betrayed us. After the war ground to a stalemate, they refused to release my family. I'm the only one they don't have. ISC keeps me guarded because they fear I will be kidnapped or assassinated otherwise."

Kamoj tried to put it all together. "So your own people hold you prisoner to keep you from being held prisoner by the allies who were supposed to protect you from being taken prisoner or murdered by your enemies."

He gave a rueful laugh. "That about sums it up."

"But why come here?"

"I asked ISC to let me live in an agrarian culture similar to that of my homeworld, Lyshriol." He took her hand. "A place where life revolves around the land and the harvest."

"Then you really are a farmer."

He spoke with a deep satisfaction. "Yes. It's all I've ever wanted to do."

That she understood. Lifting his hand, she kissed his knuckles. He pulled her into his arms, holding her between his legs, and they sat listening to the rustle of the forest.

A twig cracked.

Vyrl swore silently, only his lips moving to form the words. He drew Kamoj to her feet and set his finger against her mouth, warning her to silence. Then he went to the entrance, where he paused to one side, poised, the muscles of his shoulders rigid.

A man stepped through the shimmer. But he wasn't one of Vyrl's guards. Rather, he wore the garb of an Ironbridge stagman. An archer. He had his bow up and aimed at the place where Kamoj and Vyrl had been sitting just seconds ago.

Vyrl didn't wait to see if the man meant to attack or only threaten. Lunging forward, he yanked the bow away from the archer. The stagman responded fast, clenching his fists together and bringing them up under Vyrl's chin. Kamoj tensed, afraid the archer would snap back Vyrl's head and injure his neck. But Vyrl twisted with easy grace, making even the agile stagman look clumsy, and the blow just glanced off his cheek.

Then Vyrl clenched his fist and hit him. Staggering back, the archer hit the wall and knocked his head on the rock. As he slumped to the ground, Vyrl pulled the man's sword out of its sheath with a hiss of metal. He moved back, holding the sword, while the dazed archer blinked up at him.

"Does Ironbridge know you're here?" Vyrl asked.

The stagman rubbed his face. Moving stiffly, he climbed to his feet and brushed off his clothes. Then he turned to Kamoj and said, "Slut."

As Kamoj's mouth fell open, Vyrl said, "Call her that again and you won't have a tongue any more. What's the matter with you?"

The man snorted. "Be quiet, boy."

"Oh." Kamoj finally understood. "Vyrl, he thinks you're a farmhand."

Vyrl regarded him. "Is that true?"

The stagman had the sense to look worried. "Yes."

"I'm Havyrl Lionstar," he growled. "And if you ever call my wife a slut again, then after I cut out your tongue, I'll hang you upside down from a tower of the Quartz Palace and let the bi-hawks peck out your eyes."

Kamoj wondered if he were serious. The stagman stared at him for a full count of five before he remembered himself. Then he dropped to one knee and lowered his head so his hair fell forward, leaving his neck bare. "I have no excuse, Governor Lionstar. Use my sword."

Vyrl made an exasperated noise. "I'm not going to cut off your head. Get up and tell me why you were skulking around my woods."

Moving with obvious, albeit belated, humility, the stagman stood up. "Please accept my most abject—"

"Just answer the question," Vyrl said.

"I was riding to the Quartz Palace, bringing salutations from Ironbridge on your wedding." The man paused. "When

I came by here, I saw the bridle and thought a rider was in trouble. I investigated and heard voices. I recognized the woman." He glanced at Kamoj, then quickly shifted his gaze to Vyrl. "I heard her call you a farmer and your agreement. It seemed that given the, uh, appearance of this matter, I ought to apprehend—I mean—what I thought—"

"I get the idea," Vyrl said. "Why are you here? The road to Ironbridge is on the other side of the palace."

"I was coming from another errand for Governor Ironbridge."

"So." Vyrl motioned toward the entrance. "Outside."

The man obeyed, his back stiff, either with fear or shame. Kamoj didn't believe for one second that Jax had sent "salutations." He was having her watched.

As Vyrl followed the stagman, he motioned to Kamoj. At first she didn't know what he wanted. Then she remembered. The mask. He couldn't do something as simple as walk into the forest without endangering his life.

She retrieved the mask and his cloak. With her arms full of Argalian wool, she stepped out into a breezy afternoon. Vyrl and the stagman were about twenty paces away, Vyrl still holding the sword. He looked as if he was threatening the stagman with the man's own weapon, but as Kamoj came closer she realized he was only giving directions to the road.

It didn't surprise her that Vyrl intended to let him go. The stagman seemed wound up, though. Disbelieving. That didn't surprise her either. Had one of Vyrl's stagmen attacked Jax, the Ironbridge governor would have sent him to prison.

Then, in her side vision, she saw the trees move. *"Vyrl!"* she shouted. "Look out!"

He spun around just as a bowball hurtled toward him, the kind with an arrow embedded in the marble. It slammed against his side, the arrow stabbing deep into his body. Then the weight of the falling ball yanked out the arrow, pulling shreds of muscle with it.

As blood spurted from the wound, Vyrl staggered, and the

stagman lunged for his sword. He almost recovered it; Vyrl's injury slowed him down, and the stagman was well-trained. But Vyrl handled the weapon like an extension of his body. Metal flashed in the dappled forest—and he thrust the blade into the stagman's chest.

"No!" Dropping the cloak, Kamoj ran toward them. A second bowball whistled through the air and hit Vyrl. He was moving, so it missed his heart and slammed into his chest below his shoulder. This time he managed to grab the shaft of the arrow before the falling ball ripped it out of his body. The weight of the ball broke the arrow, leaving its upper end embedded in his muscles.

A great roaring had filled the forest, and the cry of a siren. With shock, Kamoj realized the siren was coming *out* of Vyrl's body. Wind thrashed the trees overhead.

Just as Kamoj reached Vyrl, another ball hurtled between them. Vyrl tried to shove her away, to safety. "Stay back!" He had to shout to be heard above the noise. He sank to his knees, his face contorted with pain. Blood soaked his clothes, and the stagman lay dead at his feet. No, not dead; his wound still pumped blood. But Kamoj recognized mortal injuries; neither Vyrl nor the stagman would live much longer.

Dropping down next to Vyrl, she pressed the mask over his face, trying to make it stay as he gasped for air. Before she had it in place, someone grabbed her arm and yanked her back. Twisting around, she found herself looking up a second Ironbridge stagman, another archer, probably the one who had shot Vyrl. She struggled as he dragged her back, but she couldn't pull free. Frantic, she threw the mask to Vyrl—and saw it hit the ground beyond his reach.

"Let me go!" she yelled at the stagman.

He spoke, but she couldn't hear. The forest was in motion now, come alive, trees parting overhead while the wind roared.

Incredibly, Vyrl made it to his feet and stumbled toward them, his hand clutched on his side, blood running over his fingers. Then he fell, barely managing to put his hand out in time to cushion the impact. His face had gone pale, a mask of death to replace the silver mask that still lay out of reach.

"Let go of me!" Wrestling in archer's grip, Kamoj looked up—

And froze in shock. A gigantic black and gold bird was cutting a swath through the trees, blasting away scales and dirt. The roar of its descent drowned out even the siren coming from Vyrl's body.

As soon as the bird landed, its mouth gaped open. *People* ran out of its throat, Dazza and others in gray uniforms, all sheathed in shimmers that molded to their bodies. Two Lionstar stagmen came also, Azander and another man. The unfamiliar Lionstar man raised his arm and pointed a tube at the Ironbridge archer that held Kamoj.

"Ah—" With a stunned expression, the Ironbridge archer collapsed. The Lionstar man looked startled, as if he hadn't been sure himself what would happen when he did whatever he had done with the tube.

Kamoj ran toward Vyrl, but a shimmer-sheathed stranger caught her and held her back. The other healers were kneeling around Vyrl. As one of them placed a mask over his face, Dazza checked a cylinder connected to the mask by a cord. Two other healers lifted him onto a stretcher.

Impossibly, the stretcher rose off the ground. The healers grabbed its ends and sprinted for the metal bird, with Dazza running alongside. Two more of Vyrl's people put the dying Ironbridge man on another stretcher and followed. The siren from Vyrl's body still rang throughout the trees.

Kamoj struggled in the grip of the healer. "Let me go with him!" When he only tightened his grip, she shouted, *"Let me go!"*

Still running, Dazza glanced back. "Let her come," she called. Then she disappeared into the bird's throat.

The instant the healer released her, Kamoj took off. She had no time to fear the consequences of running into the mouth of a giant metal bird. Its jaw was already closing. She barely managed to race inside before it snapped shut. Two more steps took her through the throat—and into a nightmare.

The bird's stomach was a demon's nest of tubes and metal curves, surfaces that gleamed, light panels, other things she had no names for, looping coils, and projections like clawed hands.

Suddenly the bird lurched. Kamoj lost her balance and slid to one knee, her shoulder hitting the metal "wall" that lined the beast's gut. A roaring filled the air and the bird vibrated around her. As it grumbled and boomed, a great invisible hand shoved her against the wall of its stomach.

The Lionstar stagman who had knocked out the Ironbridge archer knelt on one knee at her side, his presence both a reassurance and an offer of protection. She managed to incline her head in gratitude. He nodded back, his face as pale as a white-skeeted snowlizard. She suspected he had no more love of riding in the innards of giant metal birds than did she.

A few paces away, Vyrl lay on a pallet enmeshed in coils and jointed metal arms. The siren from his body abruptly cut off, leaving a calm broken only by the muted clinks and hissing of the bird's guts. The Ironbridge man lay on another pallet, surrounded by healers. Kamoj couldn't tell what was happening with him, or even if he still lived.

Vyrl, however, was very much alive. He had ripped the mask off his face and was grabbing at a tube Dazza kept trying to press against his arm.

"I won't be put to sleep like some wild animal!" he told her.

"Stop fighting," Dazza said. "It will drive the arrows deeper into your body."

Either he didn't hear or didn't care. He kept struggling while the healers fastened down his limbs with straps. Still he fought, his face flushed as he strained against his bonds. It terrified Kamoj to see him that way, like a man possessed.

"Prince Havyrl, you must hold still," a man said. "We can't get the arrows out." In almost the same instant, Dazza said, "The sedative isn't working," and another man said,

"I'll try Perital." He pressed a tube against Vyrl's arm and Vyrl swore, the tendons in his necks as taut as cords. His eyes rolled back into his head and his body went rigid—no, not rigid, it was *jerking*—

Someone yelled, "What the—?" and a new siren went off. In the same instant, Dazza shouted, "Give me an air-syringe!" while a woman said, "Gods almighty, what kind of neural map is that?"

Vyrl's body spasmed against the restraints, convulsing hard. As Dazza slapped another tube against his arm, someone else said, "I'm reading discharges all over his brain," and another healer shouted, "We have to clear—*damn.* The arrow punctured his lung!"

Kamoj rocked back and forth, agonized. Vyrl was dying and she was helpless to do anything. Even his healers couldn't stop the demon that wracked him like a stick-man of twigs.

"Give him more meds!" Dazza said. "Double-dose the chest wound."

"He's got too many in his body already," a man said.

"Do it!" Dazza ordered.

A woman said, "Pulse and blood pressure dropping below critical levels. Colonel, we're losing him."

"No. Gods, *no.*" Dazza gripped the pallet. "Vyrl, come back! Don't let go. Not *now.* Not after you've come so far."

"The nanomed concentration in his blood is too high," a man said. "They're starting to break down his tissues."

"Clean them out," Dazza said. "Neutralize NOW!"

Vyrl stopped jerking. As his body went limp, a healer said, "Neural inhibition working. Neurons fatiguing." Riding on the tail end of her words, a man said, "His right lung collapsed," and another said, "Med concentration decreasing."

Dazza glanced at a man bent over a panel of lights. "Can we save the lung?"

"The meds got to the puncture site before we flushed," he said. "I've got the pneumothorax under control, and regeneration around the wound is taking."

The colonel nodded. Then she turned to a woman who was studying a collection of ghosts above a silver platform. "What happened to him?" Dazza asked.

"That was a *grand mal* seizure," the woman said. "A generalized tonic-clonic attack, like an epileptic convulsion. I haven't tracked the cause yet."

"There!" a man said. He held up the arrow that had been in Vyrl's chest. When Kamoj saw blood gush out of Vyrl's wound, bile rose in her throat. It wasn't the blood; she had tended injured farm hands with wounds just as serious. But it had never been her husband before, bleeding away his life. His lung had *collapsed*. How could he survive such wounds?

Someone said, "We have the second one," and held up another bloody arrow. Kamoj hadn't realized part of that one had stayed in Vyrl's body. Other healers attached patches to the inside of his elbows while a man pressed a tube against his neck.

"Colonel, I have what caused his seizure." That came from the woman bent over the silver ghosts. "The last sedative, the Perital, interacted with the alcohol in his bloodstream. It set off a reaction in the series-N nanomeds he carries, which acted on the psiamine receptors in his brain. With all those extra neural structures he has up there, it was too much. His neurons started firing like mad and the excitation spread." She glanced at the doctor. "His brain went into overload."

Dazza nodded tiredly. "Log the whole cycle, Lieutenant. Next time we'll know."

A man's voice came out of the air. "Colonel Pacal, shall I take the shuttle up to the *Ascendant?*"

"Yes," Dazza said.

"No," Vyrl whispered.

Dazza leaned over him, tears running down her cheeks. "Gods alive, Vyrl, don't you ever stop arguing?"

He opened his eyes. "Never want . . . see that medical bay again."

"We need its equipment."

"Everything you need . . . at palace."

She laid her palm on his forehead. "I'll feel better with you on the ship."

"Won't go back there."

"Jak Tager can meet us at the docking bay—"

"No! Told you. Don't *need* him."

"Vyrl, I'm sorry. But I want you on the cruiser."

His eyes closed. "Then the hell with you."

"Doctor-Colonel," Kamoj said.

Dazza looked up. "Kamoj? Are you hurt?"

"No, ma'am." She tried to keep her voice calm, so Dazza would listen to her, but it made her words come out stilted. "If you break the spirit of a greenglass, you can still force it to serve you. But it will serve neither willingly nor well. Break the king of the stags and the entire herd dies."

"What the hell?" a healer said.

"She's just a kid," another said. "She's probably scared."

"It's not fear." Dazza was watching Kamoj. "I know what she means." She pushed her hand through the silver tendrils of her hair. Then she said, "Major, change of orders. Take us to the palace."

The disembodied voice answered. "Will do, ma'am."

Kamoj closed her eyes with relief. When she opened them, Azander was watching her from the other side of the bird, where he stood against a curved wall. He nodded as if to thank her for intervening on Vyrl's behalf. Then he dropped his gaze to indicate respect. She swallowed, grateful he saw her as an ally now instead of an enemy.

"Colonel Pacal." One of the healers working on the Iron-bridge man spoke. "We've a problem."

"What's wrong?" Dazza asked.

"We're having trouble replicating this man's erythrocytes. We need a transfusion from someone native to this biosphere."

"Do you have a compatible donor listed in the files?" Dazza asked.

"We aren't sure." The healer glanced at Azander. "Can you try? You're the closest match."

Azander nodded, seeming to understand the odd words. As he knelt by the Ironbridge soldier, the healers attached tubes to his arms that went to their various machines. Silent and tense, they concentrated on their displays, their faces furrowed as they studied the flickering ghosts.

Suddenly one said, "It's good."

With obvious relief, they made more adjustments to their boxes, then used the tubes to connect Azander with the dying stagman. Soon red liquid was moving through the tubes. Azander remained still, like a statue, staring at the flowing liquid, his face pale. With a jolt, Kamoj realized his *blood* was in those tubes.

Finally a healer said, "We have replication." Others worked on the tubes, and Azander's blood stopped flowing. Soon they had him free of their machines.

"Will your patient survive?" Dazza asked.

"It looks like it," one of the healers said.

Kamoj stared at them. Who were these people, that they could give life to a man who for all intents and purposes was already dead?

Turning to Vyrl, she saw he had succumbed to the sleep makers. Or she thought he had. Then he mumbled.

Dazza leaned closer. "Again?"

"Kamoj," he said.

"She's here," Dazza said. "We're going to the palace."

"Good . . ." Vyrl's breathing eased into sleep.

Kamoj bit her lip. He was so pale. But she saw no blood, neither on his body nor spilled onto the bird's guts. In fact, she couldn't see his wounds at all. Where ragged gashes had rent his body, new skin showed now. Then she realized the "skin" was a bandage.

"Colonel." The voice came out of the air. "We're coming into the palace."

Dazza glanced at the healers around the Ironbridge man. "As soon as we have Prince Havyrl off the shuttle, take your patient to the *Ascendant*. I don't want him anywhere near the palace until we figure out why the two of them were trying to kill each other."

An odd sensation came over Kamoj, as if she were falling. The bird jolted, and its dull thunder stopped. The mouth gaped open with a whoosh of air, and sunshine poured into the stomach.

With the Lionstar stagman at her side, Kamoj walked through the bird's throat. Incredibly, they came out onto the courtyard in front of the palace. The stagman glanced at her, the disquiet on his face mirroring what she felt. Only moments ago they had been in the forest.

The healers brought Vyrl out on the floating stretcher, with a silver sheet over his body. Servants threw open the doors of the palace, and the healers strode inside.

8

Above the Sky

Phase Shift

Kamoj slept sitting up, leaning against the headboard of the bed. Vyrl lay next to her, either asleep or unconscious. Each time she awoke, she saw Dazza in an armchair by the nightstand, watching Vyrl, dozing, or studying images in her book-box.

Sometimes the colonel spoke to the nightstand. Different voices answered, most in unfamiliar languages, though a few used the odd Bridge dialect spoken by Vyrl. Dazza discussed Azander's *para-medic* training with one, saying she wanted more of the household staff to learn it. Another voice told her the Ironbridge stagman was recovering on the *Ascendant*. Later someone said a delegation from the *Ascendant* had gone to Ironbridge to speak to Jax.

From what Kamoj gathered, Vyrl's people were holding the second Ironbridge archer in Argali, until they decided what to do about his shooting Vyrl. Apparently the Lionstar stagman had knocked him out with a sleep weapon. Kamoj didn't understand how a tube could carry sleep or how a person could throw that sleep at other people, but nevertheless, it had happened.

She was drowsing when a rustle of sheets woke her. She opened her eyes to see Vyrl jerking, restless with his dreams. Dazza sat sleeping in her chair, but when Vyrl groaned she snapped awake. The doctor took one look at him, then removed a black tube from her case. She stood up, leaning over Vyrl as she brought the tube to his neck.

"Wait," Kamoj said. "He hates that."

Dazza didn't look happy about it herself. "I know. But if he jerks like that, it could tear open his wounds."

Vyrl's fingers curled into claws. His breathing sounded ragged, and his forehead contorted as if he were in pain.

"There might be another way." Kamoj slid the pillow out from under his head and put herself in its place, sitting cross-legged with his head in her lap, his curls spread across her legs in red-gold profusion. Then she massaged his head. As she worked, his face relaxed and his breath slowed to an even rhythm.

"Well, I'll take a launch off a lily-pad," Dazza said.

Kamoj looked up at her. "Ma'am?"

Smiling, Dazza said, "It seems you're effective alternative medicine."

Kamoj hesitated. "May I ask a question?"

"Of course."

"That sound Vyrl's body was making today, when he was hurt. How did it do that?"

"He has an implant. If he's in trouble, it sets off alarms, including the siren. It also activates a neutrino beacon. That's how we found him." Dazza considered her. "May I ask a question?"

It felt odd to have the doctor request permission to seek information. Kamoj had no idea what position "colonel" occupied in the hierarchy of things, but Dazza clearly ranked high among Vyrl's people.

"I will answer to the best of my ability," Kamoj said.

"Why did Vyrl try to kill the Ironbridge man?"

"Because he tried to kill Vyrl."

"The Ironbridge soldiers claim they acted in self-defense." Dazza settled back into her chair. "We've done scans on them. They're both telling the truth as they see it."

"Didn't know who I was," Vyrl mumbled. He opened his eyes, his gaze bleary.

Dazza leaned forward. "How are you feeling?"

"Lousy." His lashes drooped over his eyes. "Flaming sedatives."

"I'm sorry. I had to do what I thought necessary." With the look of someone who already knew what response she was going to get, Dazza added, "That's why I've posted Jagernauts as your bodyguards. You will have two with you at all times. Right now they're on the landing outside this suite."

His eyes snapped open. "Damn it, Colonel. I'm tired of privacy being a luxury I'm forbidden."

She crossed her arms and glowered. "What did you expect? That ISC would stand by while you steal state-of-the-art special operations gear, ride off in a drunken rage, and almost get yourself killed?"

Vyrl scowled at her.

In a quieter voice, Dazza said, "Why would an Ironbridge archer try to kill you?"

"Because of what he saw." Vyrl rubbed his temple, his motions slower than usual. "It probably looked like I was threatening the other man with his own sword. And I had Kamoj. The archer was defending his partner and Kamoj's honor. Or else he thought like the first one, that Kamoj was committing adultery with me."

"With her own husband?"

"Interesting concept, yes?" Vyrl hesitated. "The stagman . . . ?"

"He'll live," Dazza said. As relief sped across Vyrl's face, she added, "You damn near killed him. Why did you stab him? He was just trying to recover his weapon."

"Why do you think? Someone shot me. Then this one lunged at me. I reacted in reflex."

"I hadn't realized you knew how to use a sword."

He shrugged. "I learned on Lyshriol."

"You trained with swords on your home planet?"

"All highborn boys do there. It's part of the culture."

"It just seems so—" She squinted at him. "Barbaric."

Vyrl snorted. "What, if I crisped him with a laser carbine, that would be civilized? Hell, we could be really civilized and drop an antimatter bomb on Ironbridge."

Dazza didn't answer, and Kamoj could tell Vyrl's words bothered her. She had been prepared to hate Dazza after what Vyrl had told her this afternoon. Instead she kept remembering Dazza's tears, so uncharacteristic for the craggy colonel, as she treated Vyrl's injuries.

"What I don't understand," Vyrl said, "is why Ironbridge stagmen are prowling around my woods."

Dazza glanced at Kamoj. "Would you feel more comfortable if I told him?"

Kamoj nodded, wondering what Dazza knew.

"Told me what?" Vyrl asked.

"We sent people down to talk with Maxard Argali," she said. "It seems your bride was betrothed to Jax Ironbridge."

Vyrl stared up at Kamoj. Mortified, she averted her eyes.

"Their marriage was arranged years ago," Dazza said. "Apparently Ironbridge is quite fond of her."

Kamoj almost gagged. If Jax was fond of her, she would hate to see how he treated people he didn't like.

Vyrl spoke gently. "Look at me, water sprite." When she met his gaze, he said, "I'm sorry. I should have realized a woman such as yourself would already be spoken for."

She wished she could disappear into the woodwork. Vyrl glanced at Dazza and tilted his head toward the door.

"Uh—ah, yes, well." The colonel stood up. "I have to check in with the *Ascendant*. I'll look in on you later."

When Kamoj and Vyrl were alone, he said, "I truly am sorry. I figured there might be others, but I assumed if something was serious, you would refuse my offer. It didn't occur to me that you would have no choice." After a moment he added, "Or maybe I didn't want it to occur to me."

"You established your bid legally. No one could match it." Kamoj didn't know what else to tell him. Although for her this marriage had turned out far better than she could have hoped, she feared it would cause great political damage. Together she and Jax represented most of the Northern Lands. It would have been better for them to meet with Vyrl's people as a team, two governors united in a merger. Jax was the strongest leader in this region, and Vyrl had pulverized any hope of good will with him. For herself, she was glad of her marriage, but for her people she had many doubts. She just hoped it didn't become a crisis.

"I don't get it," Vyrl said. "How did the concepts of slavery and a dowry get mixed up together here?"

"Slavery?" She brought her thoughts back to the present. "What do you mean?"

"Don't you hear what you're saying? I outbid him for you." Although Vyrl still had his eyes closed, he sounded wide awake now. "That's wrong. On top of which, it was a woman who had already given her word to another man."

Dryly he added, "A woman younger than most of my grand-daughters."

Granddaughters? *Older* than she? Surely she heard wrong.

Then again, Jax looked about Vyrl's age and he had illegitimate children everywhere, even grandchildren. That, she realized, was what bothered her. Not that Vyrl had children but how he came about them. With Jax, she had almost managed to convince herself that she didn't care what he did; with Vyrl, an agony of jealousy rose in her.

"What's wrong?" he asked.

She stopped massaging his head. "Nothing."

His lashes lifted and he looked up at her. "Something about my children. Their mother?"

Kamoj tried to sound disinterested. "Men can marry only one woman here. Perhaps in your Imperial court it is different."

He gave a startled laugh. "Concubines and court intrigue? Gods, Kamoj, that isn't me. I may have more titles than I know what to do with, but I'm still a farm boy from nowhere. All I ever wanted was my wife, my family, and my land."

Relief washed over her. "Then you are widowed?"

"I married my childhood sweetheart when we were kids." With difficulty, he added, "Ten years ago she took a fall in the Backbone Mountains. She died instantly."

"Hai," Kamoj murmured. "I'm sorry."

"It was a long time ago." His voice softened. "We had many good years, twelve beautiful children, over forty grandchildren, and gods know how many great-grandchildren." He scratched his chin. "I get mixed up which of the new ones are grandchildren and which are great-grand. There's even a few great-greats in there."

She stared at him. "But you are so *young*."

"People marry young where I come from. I was fourteen." He laughed. "When I told Dazza that, she nearly went through the wall. Legal age in the overarching culture of Imperial Skolia is twenty-five, and the average number of children for a couple is two. By the time I was 'legal,' I had six children."

It didn't sound odd to Kamoj. In her experience, people married young and had as many children as possible, with the hope that at least some would survive until adulthood, and perhaps, if the family was lucky, even prosper.

But the numbers still didn't fit. She struggled to work it out. Although she was better at mathematics than most people, she usually had wires with beads to do problems like this one. No matter how she looked at it, she kept coming up with the same impossible results.

Finally she said, "Even if your children married as young as you did, I don't see how you could have so many descendants, especially great-grandchildren and great-greats."

"Why? I'm almost sixty-nine."

Her mouth fell open. "What? No. That can't be."

"It's true." His wicked grin flashed. "But if you want to tell me how young I look, I won't object."

She smiled. "You can angle for compliments all you wish, my handsome husband. But I still don't understand. How can you look so young?"

"Good genes and exercise, I suppose. Also, the nanomeds in my body do cellular repairs, enough to delay aging." His confident expression shifted into uncertainty. "Did you mean what you said this afternoon about wanting to stay with me?"

"Yes."

"Even though you could have your betrothed back if we arranged for me to 'die?' "

Kamoj faltered. "Jax Ironbridge is a—" The word slug tempted her, but she held it back. No more appropriate word came, though. The contrast between Vyrl and Jax made her resent Jax even more. She kept imagining a slug making its way through the mud.

The mischief came back to Vyrl's voice. "You can compare my competition to all the slimy creatures you want."

"I would never speak ill of Ironbridge's good name."

"Your tact is laudable." He closed his eyes. "I like your worm images better, though."

She stroked his forehead. "Lionstar Province has no worms."

A guilty look passed over his face. "I don't really have a province on this planet."

"Of course you do."

"I do?"

"Argali and our villages." She thought of Azander. "Your stagmen come from outlying hamlets, yes?"

"That's right."

"Most of those hamlets were originally part of the North Sky Islands. But they've become unattached." It appalled Kamoj. Rather than trying to support villages so distant and so impoverished, past governors of the Islands had ignored them, until finally, after many generations, the villages lost all association with their former province—and with that, their last hope of survival. "If their stagmen are your sworn liegemen, then you are also now the authority in their villages."

He opened his eyes. "What does that mean, exactly?"

"A union such as ours is a merger. A business arrangement. In marrying me, you agreed to help support my people."

"In other words, responsibilities come with power."

She took a breath, knowing they had reached an crossroads. Which way would he go? "Yes. They do."

"Such as?"

"Food. Work. Tools. Shelter." Softly she said, "Survival."

Vyrl considered her. Then he reached out and pressed a turquoise stone on the nightstand.

A voice floated into the air. "Colonel Pacal here."

"Dazza, when is Morlin coming back up?" Vyrl asked.

"I'm not sure. The techs are replacing the fiberoptics. Is there a problem?"

"No. I just need some information."

"Maybe I can help."

He scowled. "Yes, but Morlin never argues with me."

Dazza spoke dryly. "What are you about to do that you think will start an argument?"

"Do you remember our decision to minimize interactions with the native culture here?"

"Yes."

"Well, we may have a problem."

Now she sounded wary. "What problem?"

He cleared his throat. "It seems that by marrying Kamoj, I've set myself up as a sort of sovereign in Argali."

Dazza made an exasperated noise. "That's hardly what I call 'minimizing interactions.' "

"I want to send some techs to the villages."

"Why? The villages have no tech for techs to work on."

"That's the point. These people have a killing winter coming. We can heat their houses."

After a moment, Dazza said, "I'll assign a group to it."

"Discreetly, though. I don't want to scare anyone." Vyrl rubbed his chin, thinking. "Dress them in native clothes and send some of my stagmen with them."

"All right."

"Some houses here are old enough to have web systems—"

"Vyrl." Her voice had a warning note. "Don't push it."

He tried a new tack. "Can you go down to Argali too?"

"Me? Why?"

"To see if they need medical help."

Her tone turned incredulous. "In case you forgot, I'm an ISC colonel. I can't just drop my work."

"Oh. Yes. Of course." He waited.

The silence stretched out. Finally Dazza said, "I have some residents on the *Ascendant* who are just out of medical school. They could benefit from the experience."

He smiled. "Good."

Grudgingly she added, "We should send agriculturists too."

"We already have one." His voice grew animated. "Dazza, listen. I've been working on quad-grains. Give me a few years and I could engineer crops and livestock to increase production here tenfold."

"We don't have a few years."

"Just think about it."

She exhaled. "All right."

"Good." Vyrl yawned and stretched his arms. Then he turned his head until his lips touched Kamoj's inner thigh.

Kamoj spoke softly. "Thank you, beautiful lion."

"Vyrl?" Dazza asked.

"I'm sleeping," he mumbled.

"Ah," the colonel said. "Good night, Governor Argali."

Kamoj blinked at the phrase. "Good night?" When no answer came, she said, "Dazza?" The nightstand stayed quiet.

So she stroked Vyrl's hair and watched the stars in the patch of sky visible through the window across the room. Could he truly warm their houses in winter? Heal their ills? Help them grow ten times as much food? It was remarkable how, when life seemed to reach its worst, things could turn around this way. Surely all would be well now.

Surely Vyrl wouldn't drink anymore.

"Water sprite, wake up."

Kamoj moved, then groaned. It felt like thornbats prickled her legs, where she had folded them under her body. She didn't remember sliding out from under Vyrl, but she was sitting next to him now, leaning sideways against the headboard, her hands tucked between her knees. Moonlight poured over the bed.

Vyrl lay watching her. "I need you to do something for me."

She smiled, imagining his hands on her body. "Anything."

"In the second drawer of my desk. Bring me the bottle there."

Her good mood vanished. "You don't need that."

"I can't sleep."

"Dazza could give you—"

"No!"

"But—"

"I don't need Dazza's damn sedatives."

She swallowed. "I can't get you the bottle."

"Why not?" His voice hardened. "You have two legs. You can walk the ten steps it would take to reach the desk."

"The rum hurts you."

"After two days you claim to know me well enough to dictate what is and isn't good for me?"

"Vyrl, no. That's not what I meant."

"Then get it for me." His voice softened. "Just for tonight. To help me sleep."

"I can't. I-I'm sorry."

His warmth disappeared. "Then get out of my bed."

"But I—"

"Get out."

Stunned, Kamoj slid off the bed. As she ran across the room, her bare feet slapped the stone. Inside her chamber, she dropped onto her bed. Moonlight shone through the window, creating a swath of pale colors across the floor. Her heart beat hard, driven more by his harsh words than her short run.

A grunt came from the master bedroom, followed by the rustle of blankets. Kamoj froze, listening.

A gasp, labored but brief.

Silence.

Was he having trouble breathing? It was hard to believe he had suffered a collapsed lung only this afternoon. She started to get up, then hesitated. *Get out*, he had said. If she walked in and he was fine, she would feel like a fool.

The crash of shattering glass broke the silence. She jumped up and ran back to his bedroom.

Vyrl was kneeling by his desk, wearing only his sleep trousers, his chest bare except for the bandages, his arms wrapped around his body. Shards of broken glass covered the floor, glinting in the moonlight. A pool of rum was spreading under the desk.

Kamoj knelt in front of him. Tears showed on his cheeks, just as she had seen them last night after his nightmare. She wanted to take him in her arms, but she held back, unsure what he needed now. She wondered if his waking helped at all, or if his night terrors recognized no boundaries between sleep and reality.

He pulled a strand of her hair away from her lips. His words came with difficulty, low and deep. "Touch me. Let me feel you. See you. Smell you."

"Always." She reached out to him. "Whenever you want."

He only touched her hand, just the barest brush of his fingers over hers. Then he took hold of his desk and pulled himself to his feet. The window above the desk looked south, over the Lower Sky Hills that fell away to the plains. Staring at the mountains, he spoke in a distant voice. "I've a younger brother. Kelric."

She stood up next to him, trying to fathom his mood. "A little brother?"

"Little?" He gave a short laugh. "He's huge. Joined ISC."

"Is he here now?"

"No. He's a prisoner of war."

"Ah, Vyrl, I'm sorry."

"I have a lot of brothers." His reply had a dulled sound, like glass clouded with ice damage. "Althor. I always looked up to him. He joined ISC too. As a Jagernaut."

"Jagernaut?"

"A psibernetically enhanced starfighter pilot. Like Kelric. Like those new bodyguards Colonel Pacal gave me."

"Althor is a soldier too?"

"Was." In a wooden voice, he said, "ISC gave him a beautiful funeral."

She wanted to hold him, to offer comfort, but she could almost feel the emotional shield he had raised. "Vyrl, I'm so sorry."

He kept on, as if unable to stop. "There's my sister. Soz. We were closest in age, out of ten children." He turned to Kamoj. "You look a little like her."

"She is also a soldier? Like Dazza?"

"Soz commanded ISC. Dazza served under her."

"Where is she now?"

He swallowed. "Blown to dust."

"Vyrl, I—I'm sorry." If only she knew something better to say.

"Sorry?" His words came like leaded rain. "My brother Eldrin is still alive. The Traders captured him. You know what they do when they catch one of us? No, never mind. You don't want to know. My aunt and her son, they're gone. Prisoners, maybe. Dead, probably. Then there is Kurj, my uncle. War leader before Soz. For decades." In a low voice he said, "She took over after the Traders killed him."

"I'm terribly sorry." It sounded useless, saying that over and over. She had lost only her parents and that had torn apart her world. She couldn't imagine what it would be like to lose so many.

Vyrl walked away, across the room, bathed in the pale light pouring in the window from the Far Moon and aurora borealis. He climbed the dais and turned to face her. "I'm a good farmer. You want crops with bigger yields? Bi-hoxen that can better survive your winters? I can work it out. That's what I wrote my doctorate on, the application of genetic engineering to crop and livestock development. I've had Morlin running DNA simulations here."

"I don't understand what you're trying to tell me."

"Farming." He stood in the moonlight like a statue, the planes of his chest stark in the colorless radiance that filled the room. "I've always loved it. You know where I got that? From my father. He loved the land. And he loved us. His children." His voice broke. "At least I was there when he died."

Ah, no. Kamoj went to him, joining him on the dais. She spoke softly. "How did it happen?"

Vyrl rubbed his palm over his cheek, seeming surprised to find tears there. "Old age. Old wounds." He dropped his hand. "My father spent his last days with his family, in our ancestral house on our home world of Lyshriol. The Allied military let us have that much."

"Allied?"

"The Allied Worlds of Earth." Bitterness edged his voice. "They were holding him and my mother on Earth. When they realized he was dying, they were 'kind' enough to let him return to Lyshriol, to see the rest of us. Of course, Earth now controls the entire planet where we live."

"Earth? I don't understand."

"I told you this afternoon. Our 'allies' betrayed us. They won't let my family go." He took a breath. "Earth believes that without my family to power the Ruby machines, ISC won't risk another war. They fear that otherwise my people and the Traders will destroy civilization, the way they destroyed the Ruby Empire five thousand years ago."

Kamoj felt the holes where he had left out pieces of his story. "If you were their prisoner, how are you here now?"

"None of my family could get offworld."

"But you're here."

He looked away, out the window across the room. "Do you know what my father's dying wish was? His gruesome dying wish? That they launch his coffin into orbit around Lyshriol."

"Orbit?"

"Above the sky."

"Like the moons?"

"Like the moons. He wanted to be a moon."

"But why? If he valued the land—"

"He loved it. The land. The harvest. The seasons." Moisture glimmered in his eyes, reflecting the cool glow of the moons. "Going into orbit terrified him."

She tried to understand what lay beneath his words. "But you said he asked to go there."

"He let our jailers think he wanted it." Vyrl turned back to her. "We held his true funeral in secret, to do what he told my mother he really wished. We cremated his body and spread the ashes over his land." A muscle in his cheek jerked. "Then my family took his coffin to the starport."

"Why, if he wasn't in it?"

"The Allieds didn't know that. There was a body, one their sensors registered as his."

She felt as if her heart stopped. "No."

He went on, inexorable. "Our family physician on Lyshriol was an ISC agent. He installed an intravenous system inside the coffin to feed me. Made the coffin vacuum tight. So I could breathe. Put in a web system to deceive probes. I weigh more than my father, so he streamlined everything. Same for the computer web in it, not because of weight, but to minimize the risk of detection. It didn't even have a voice mod for conversation. He didn't want to use drugs in an unmonitored environment, but finally he agreed to sedate me, so I wouldn't get claustrophobic." His voice cracked. "It would only be for one day, after all."

"They buried you *alive?*"

Flatly he said, "My mother made a heartbroken plea to our jailers. She told them she couldn't bear to think of her husband in that cold wasteland. In compassion for the beautiful bereaved widow, they agreed to let an ISC ship recover his casket from space. To honor his wishes, it would spend one day in orbit. Then ISC would make the pick up." He drew in a deep breath. "By the time I awoke from sedation, I would be safe on the *Ascendant*."

Relief poured over Kamoj. "It was a trick! To get you away from your enemies. And it worked."

"Yes. It worked." His head twitched. "With just one little glitch."

"Glitch?"

"An Allied bureaucrat stalled the pick up." In a too-soft voice, he said, "No one told my family. The Allieds didn't want to upset them. But minutes after the launch, someone somewhere along the line changed his mind and said they wouldn't give up the body."

A chill ran through Kamoj. "No."

"Don't look so grim." Ghostly light silvered his face. "Negotiations to recover the body began even before I woke up."

"You woke up *inside* the coffin?"

He spoke numbly. "Yes."

Kamoj tried to imagine it, buried alive, with only a box separating you from the sky and stars, knowing something had gone terribly wrong, that you were *here* when you should have been there, safe and free. "Sweet Airys, no."

"Do you know what 'sensory deprivation' means? No sound. No sight. No taste. No smell. No weight. After a while I couldn't even feel the inside of the coffin. And my mind—I couldn't—as a telepath, I need to be close to people to pick up anything. My mind opened up, searching for anyone. *Anything.* I was wide open and there was *nothing.*"

"How long?" she whispered.

The brittle edge of his voice broke. "Thirty-one days. When the team on the *Ascendant* finally got me out, I was screaming, raving insane."

Kamoj had no idea what to say. No words would take away this horror, no touch heal it.

"Don't look so dismayed." Anger roughened his tone. "They took care of me. Treated me. Hell, it even helped. To a point." Then his head jerked. "Except the psiber centers in my brain went dead. ISC got their precious Ruby psion, but they broke him in the process. Turned me into a crippled telepath." He shuddered. "When I sleep, my mind opens up like in the coffin. But this isn't space. People are all around. So I go into telepathic overload. But if they isolate me and I can't pick up anything, I start to scream again." He watched her with a hollow gaze. "Every time Dazza sedates me, all I can think is that I'll wake up in that coffin."

"There must be a cure—something—"

"The rum deadens my brain. It lets me sleep."

She took his hands, trying to reach through the invisible shield he used to protect himself. "Surely some other solution exists. Can't Dazza and her people help you?"

His words hardened. "They can all go to hell."

"But—"

"Two people on the *Ascendant* knew my father's body wasn't in that coffin: the special operations officer assigned to the mission and General Ashman, the ship's commander. They could have ended it any time by revealing that I was out there. ISC would have lost me back to the Allieds, but I would have been free from that nightmare." His fists clenched around her fingers. "They wanted me any way they could get me, and to the hell with my sanity."

"Hai, Vyrl. I truly am sorry. I know that won't make it better, but I am."

His crushing grip eased. "I've started to pick up thoughts again with you. You're wide open to me, water sprite. I felt it that day I saw you in the river."

Kamoj finally understood the expression on Dazza's face last night. Joy. Hope. Elation. All signs of a healer whose patient had begun a recovery she feared would never happen. She had realized Vyrl was picking up his bride's thoughts.

Vyrl climbed over the footboard onto the bed, drawing her with him. They lay together in billowy covers soft from many washings and fragrant with the scent of spice-soap.

She touched his damp cheek. "We have a saying in Argali: 'Tears wash clean the debris of the heart.' "

"I'm not crying." Another tear slid down his cheek. "I never cry. Only children do that."

Kamoj thought of all the tears she had held back over the years. "Maybe children know better than we."

His voice caught. "Ai, water sprite. Something inside me is breaking. I don't know what, only that it's thawing."

"Like ice on a lake in spring."

He pulled her into his arms. "Be my spring, Kamoj."

As they made love, a low-lying cloud seeped in the window. Night curled around them, quiet and foggy. Afterward they lay together, drowsing, Vyrl's lips touching her hair, an island of warmth in the night's growing chill.

9

Blue Glass Tears

Resonance

Vyrl stirred next to Kamoj. "Look," he said. "The Lion came up."

Kamoj opened her eyes. The fog in the room reached as high as his desk, but their view of the window remained clear, like a portal above of sea of mist. The constellation of the Lion stalked across the sky, frozen in mid-stride, his head thrown back, his mane flowing in a wind of stars.

"See the star in his front paw?" Vyrl said.

"The yellow one?"

"Yes. That's a sun of my home world. It's why we made up the name Lionstar."

"Lionstar isn't your real name?"

He gave her a guilty look. "It isn't even close."

"What are you called?"

"A lot of nonsense."

"Tell me. Your titles, too."

"You don't really want to hear it."

"But I do," she assured him. "All of it."

"All right. But I warned you." With a grimace, he said,

"Prince Havyrl Torcellei Valdor kya Skolia, Sixth Heir to the Ruby Throne, once removed from the line of Pharaoh, born of the Rhon, Fourth Heir to the Web Key, Fifth Heir to the Assembly Key, and Fifth Heir to the Imperator."

Kamoj blinked. "So many names. What is Pharaoh?"

"It was the hereditary title of the Ruby Empire queens. Now sons as well as daughters are in the line of succession." He rubbed his chin. "The word Pharaoh derives from an ancient Earth civilization, but that culture isn't old enough to explain how our ancestors had the title six thousand years ago. Our customs had also diverged a great deal from any cultures that might have been our roots in Northern Africa, Southern Asia, or Mesoamerica. That kind of change takes time to evolve. That's why scholars think our people were moved in time as well as space."

"It's very mysterious." Kamoj had always enjoyed tales of ancient empires.

He touched her cheek. "And your name?"

"Kamoj Quanta Argali, Governor of Argali." It didn't sound nearly so impressive as his.

"Quanta?" He smiled. "You're a bound quantum resonance."

It relieved her to see his spirits lighten, even if his words were strange. "You also think my name means resonance?"

"Argali refers to a Breit-Wigner scattering resonance. It comes from the Iotic word *akil tz'i.*" He paused. "Actually *akil tz'i* originally meant leash. It's used now for resonance. Some people say it derives from a Mayan language, but no one really knows."

Kamoj had never heard of "Mayan," but she had no doubts about her own language. "Argali means vine rose."

"Not really. It just got mixed up with another Iotic word, *akil tz'usub,* which means vine runner."

Just like that, he took away her entire name and gave her a new one. "What is 'Mayan?' "

He rested his weight on his elbow, his head on his hand.

"My people have tried to determine our origins by comparing our languages to those on Earth. Classical Iotic is similar to Tzotzil Mayan. *Balumil* may derive from the Mayan word for world, and *Jul* from the one for puncture. But other words suggest we originated in the Near East or Mediterranean. Probably we're a mixture of races. No matter how you look at it, though, it makes no sense, unless the starfarers that took our ancestors from Earth also moved them in time. Our history on Raylicon starts six thousand years ago, and back then no culture on Earth resembled that of our ancestors."

"Then how can you be sure about the language?" She thought of his odd words. "Scattering resonance? What does it mean?"

"It's like when you roll bowballs on a table and they bounce off each other." He touched her shoulder. "Particles do that too."

"Particles? You mean dust?" she asked, dubious.

"Much smaller. And they can change state."

"What is 'change state?' "

"Deform, spin, that sort of thing. A resonance is when one ball captures another."

She gave him a skeptical look. "Vyrl, I have never heard of bowballs capturing each other."

He laughed. "Just try to imagine it. The balls don't bounce apart right away. After they collide, they stick together for a while. That's the resonance."

"Why would my name mean such a thing?"

"I don't know. What are some other Argali names?"

She thought about it. "Sable for women. Maxard for men."

"Maxard could refer to a maximum. What is your uncle's full name?"

"Maxard Osil Argali."

"Osil means life." He considered. "Maximum resonance lifetime?"

Kamoj didn't see what sense that made either. "And Sable?"

"I can't say for that one. It just means black, doesn't it?"

"It is a contraction of *Metastable State.*"

Vyrl stared at her. "Metastable state means resonance!" He looked inordinately pleased with this odd statement. "You're all named after *scattering* processes. Wait until I tell Drake."

"Drake?"

"The anthropologist on the *Ascendant.* He's been trying to make sense out of the name 'Jax.' "

Kamoj stiffened. "What about Jax?"

"It's actually an acronym. Jks."

"Yes. I know. But Jax is easier to say."

"Jks. They're *quantum numbers.* For a free particle. J is angular momentum, k is energy, s is spin." He snapped his fingers. "Jax Ironbridge is a free particle! Actually, he's one term in the partial wave expansion for a free-particle plane wave."

"Good for him," Kamoj said dourly.

His smile faded. "My sorry. That was insensitive."

Free particle indeed. All she knew about Jax was that she no longer had to suffer a pendulum of emotions, swinging between fear of his temper and relief for his tenderness. Which was fine with her.

After that they lay in silence, their heads together. Kamoj was almost asleep when Vyrl made a choked sound.

She opened her eyes. "Are you all right?"

He wiped sweat from his forehead. "Yes."

"Shall I get Dazza?"

"No." He pressed the heels of his hands against his temples. "I'll be fine."

"I can rub your head."

He glanced at her. "Yes. Thank you."

Kamoj sat up and took his head into her lap. As she massaged him, his eyes twitched beneath his closed lids. After a few moments he said, "Maybe you better not."

"There must be something I can do."

"Get me another bottle. From the kitchen. That one I broke is the last I had up here."

"Please don't—"

His face went stiff, like the precursor to an explosion.

"Wait." Kamoj couldn't bear the thought of his rejecting her again, a second time in one night. But how could she do what he asked? Perhaps if she went downstairs, she might find someone to give her advice. "I'll go to the kitchen."

The tension in his muscles eased. "Thank you, Kamoj."

She put on her underdress and a robe, then left their bed. As she went to the entrance, she wondered what she would find on the landing outside. Vyrl's new bodyguards, stagmen from the *Ascendant*.

She eased open the outer door, trying to project confidence she didn't feel. Moonlight filtered onto the landing from a window slit in the stairwell. Two men loomed outside, huge figures, bigger even than Vyrl. They wore black jackets, trousers, and knee boots. Metal bands gleamed on their upper arms, and the leather guards on their wrists glinted with metallic ribbing. Each also had a black bulk on his hip, neither sword nor dagger, but something with a handle and snout.

Then Kamoj realized one of the stagmen was a stagwoman. Massive and muscled, she stood taller than most men of Balumil. How did Vyrl's people grow so big?

Both guards were watching her. From their intrigued looks, one would have thought she was some rare, exotic flower instead of an ordinary farm girl.

The man spoke in accented Iotaca. "Can we help you, Governor Argali?"

"I need to go to the kitchen." Kamoj wanted to sound firm and assured, like a governor, but instead her voice came out in a soft lilt, her words like gleams of moonglow in the night.

The stagman smiled down at her. "Tell Morlin what you need. Then you won't have to walk there in this cold."

"Isn't Morlin gone?"

"Most of the system is down. But you can use the intercom to page someone in the kitchen."

"I don't wish to bother anyone. But thank you." Self-conscious, she nodded to them as she would to her uncle's stagmen. Then she started down the stairs. To her relief, neither giant tried to accompany her.

No lamps or candles lit the stairwell, but moonlight slanted in through the window slits, white light, which meant more than one moon was up, and probably the aurora as well. She reached the Long Hall on the first floor without seeing anyone. A few lamps burned in the corridor, and light slanted out of only three rooms along its length.

The first lit room was empty. In the second, a housemaid was cleaning the floor. Kamoj found Dazza in the third. The colonel was sitting on a sofa, reading a metal book with glowing hieroglyphs floating above its surface.

Dazza looked up as she entered. "Good evening."

Kamoj hesitated inside the doorway. "My greetings, Colonel Pacal."

"Did you want to talk to me?" When Kamoj nodded, Dazza closed her book and motioned to a chair by the sofa. "Please. Be comfortable."

Kamoj came in and sat on the edge of the chair.

The colonel smiled. "What is it, child?"

Child? Kamoj stiffened and said nothing.

After a moment Dazza asked, "Have I offended you?"

Kamoj made herself relax. She hadn't come here to bristle at people. "I need your help, ma'am."

"What can I do for you?"

"It's about rum."

Dazza pushed her hand through her hair, mussing the gray tendrils. "Is it the rum? Or someone who drinks it?"

Kamoj twisted her hands in her lap. "He wants me to bring him more."

"Don't do it. Please."

"He will send me away."

"He won't."

"He says he will."

"He doesn't mean it."

"How can you know?"

Dazza's face gentled. "I do believe he's already in love with you."

"He can't be," Kamoj stated matter-of-factly. "We hardly know each other."

"Apparently it can happen this way with telepaths." Dazza set her book on the couch. "Psions have more neural structures in their brains than other people. Vyrl, especially. He feels everything more. Add in that emotional artistic temperament of his and you get real fire."

That surprised Kamoj. Rather than emotional, she would have described Vyrl as capable of deep emotions, which wasn't the same thing. She liked the way he expressed himself, open and warm, full of dash. She wondered, too, what Dazza meant by artistic temperament.

"Why do you say 'fire?' " she asked.

The colonel smiled. "They used to call it 'love at first sight.' That turned out to be a misnomer, though. It's more 'at first thought.' "

Wryly Kamoj said, "We have such a saying. 'Love under the Wild Moon.' It is because this love makes your life chaos."

Dazza gave a rueful laugh. "Yes, I can see that."

"But why do you say 'at first thought?' "

"It has to do with what we call neuroscience," Dazza said. "The study of the brain. The fields produced by his brain couple to an unusually large degree with yours. His mind interprets that in a pleasant way." When Kamoj shook her head, Dazza tried again. "The process of thinking creates fields in your brain. You can't see them, but they can affect what is nearby."

"Like a magnet?"

The doctor gave her a surprised look. "Not exactly, but

yes, that's the idea. The fields your cerebrum produces are more varied and less intense."

"And Vyrl reacts to mine?"

Dazza nodded. "When people are near one another, the fields interact. Usually the effect is minor, even negligible. But every now and then two people hit a resonance. Combine that with a strong physical attraction and you can get intense emotion in a remarkably short time. Over the long term, it can create an exceptional bond." She gave a wry smile. "Poets call it a love 'deeper than the sea' or 'wider than the sky.' 'Quantum resonance' may sound less romantic, but it's more accurate."

Kamoj absorbed that. It sounded like Dazza meant Vyrl's actions were more than a drunken whim, that something special about she, Kamoj, had drawn him to her. It unsettled her to discover just how much she wanted that to be true.

"He is also important to me," she said. "But each time it seems he will be all right, he wants to drink again. I had thought he would stop."

Softly Dazza said, "I wish it worked that way."

"Can you help?"

"I can treat his withdrawal symptoms. And his craving. But I can't make him want to quit." Lines of concern furrowed her forehead. "I'm trying to reach him. But in the end it must be his choice."

"Can't you give him something to make him stop?"

"Not in good conscience. I could inject nanomeds that interact with the alcohol, either to negate its effect or make him sick. But if I force him to quit that way, it won't stick. All I would achieve is to make him resent us even more than he does now." With a grimace, she added, "Besides which, if I did it without his consent, I would be breaking the law and endangering ISC relations with the Ruby Dynasty."

Kamoj nodded. She and Maxard had often needed to juggle politics with expediency for the sake of Argali. "Vyrl doesn't seem like someone who would drink so much."

"Apparently he never did prior to—" She stopped, then said, "to a sickness he suffered."

"He told me about the coffin."

"He *told* you?" When Kamoj nodded, the colonel said, "He's refused to speak of it with anyone else."

Kamoj's hope surged. "If he can talk to me, can't he stop drinking too?"

Dazza shook her head. "It's not that easy. His body expects it now. Stopping will make him sick."

"You can help him with that."

"Yes. But he thinks he can't survive without it."

"He can."

"Vyrl doesn't believe it." Dazza spoke quietly. "I wish I could make him see. Few people could survive what happened the way he has. It's even more remarkable because his being a psion amplified the experience, gods only know how much. Something had to give. I hate what the alcohol is doing to him, but it could have been a lot worse. He hasn't tried to commit suicide. And incredibly, despite everything, he came through it with his mind and personality intact."

"He thinks the rum does that for him."

"Please, Kamoj. Don't give it to him."

She twisted her hands together. "He gets so angry."

"I know. But you must refuse."

"This is easy for you to say. You don't share his bed."

The colonel blinked. "Well, no. I've my own husband."

Kamoj doubted Dazza had ever suffered the humiliation of being banned from her bridal bed. "I am the one who must live with him."

Dazza spoke with care. "No one will force you to stay in this marriage if you desire otherwise."

"Your ISC wishes Vyrl and I didn't wed, don't they?"

It was a moment before Dazza answered. "It is true that the marriage complicates an already complicated situation."

Kamoj forced out the question she wanted to avoid. "You will all leave here, yes?"

"Yes. Probably soon."

"What happens to me then?"

"The choice to come or stay is yours."

"Is it?" She made a conscious effort to keep her voice even. "Vyrl has set himself up as the authority in Argali. If he leaves, it will bring great shame to my province." And to her. "Especially given the way he became governor."

"Surely a way exists to let you save face."

Kamoj stared at her. "More must be saved than 'face.' Argali is *dying*. Why do you think I was betrothed to Ironbridge? Lionstar humiliated Ironbridge, and if Vyrl leaves, he humiliates Argali as well. What happens then to my people? My province? And what about the Argali line? Unless I am pregnant when Vyrl leaves, I will have no heir. If I am pregnant and alone, my uncle will feel honor-bound to stay as guardian to the child, as he did for me. If I leave with Vyrl, Maxard will stay to govern Argali. Either way, Maxard cannot marry his lady in the North Sky Islands, the one who has been courting him all these years, because her duties require she live there. Both Argali and the Argali bloodline, one of the oldest on Balumil, will end."

Dazza spoke with care. "I greatly regret any difficulty my people have caused for yours. But be assured, Vyrl would never leave you without the full resources of his title and name. And Kamoj, he *can* return here for visits."

"You think politics will play attendance on visits?" *Or loneliness?* Kamoj couldn't keep the bitterness out of her voice. "Perhaps it doesn't matter. If Vyrl goes, Ironbridge will seek his place. Vyrl could return to find his wife taken."

Dazza spoke firmly. "We would never let it happen—unless it is what you want. Don't you understand your position? You are a Ruby consort. Do you have any idea what that means?"

Flatly Kamoj said, "No."

Dazza paused at the blunt response. "Your marriage gives you the highest standing a person can have among my people. ISC would never strand you, your family, or your province."

"But it puts Argali in a constant state of hostility with Ironbridge." Kamoj spoke softly. "Vyrl is like a beautiful song that breaks your heart, so strong and deep. I would listen to that song forever, if I could. But will it mean I can no longer hear my own people's music?"

The doctor's craggy face took on a kindhearted aspect she seemed to show very few people. "I wish I had an answer for you."

"Colonel Pacal?" The voice came from behind them.

Dazza looked up. "Yes?"

Kamoj turned to see the *Ascendant* stagwoman towering in the doorway. The guard said, "Prince Havyrl wants to know what happened to his wife."

"Hai." Kamoj stood up. "I will be right there."

"Governor Argali," Dazza said. When Kamoj turned, the colonel said, "One more moment, if you don't mind."

Kamoj sat down. "Yes, ma'am?"

Dazza took a breath. "I may be letting my hope run away from me. But I do believe Vyrl wants to quit drinking. If he can just make it one day without the rum, it's a start. Don't bring it to him. Please."

Kamoj pushed back the disarrayed tendrils curling around her face. "I will do my best."

Dazza spoke gently. "And if he isn't ready to stop, don't blame yourself."

Kamoj nodded to her. Then she stood and went to Vyrl's bodyguard. After the woman bowed, she accompanied Kamoj back to the tower.

Kamoj reentered the suite to find Vyrl sitting on the edge of the bed. He watched as she crossed the misty room and climbed the dais to him.

"Where is the bottle?" he asked.

She stopped in front of him. "I didn't get it."

"Who were you talking to down there? Dazza?" When

Kamoj flushed, his voice tightened. "Your laws say you're supposed to obey me, don't they? So get it for me."

"You don't mean that."

"Don't tell me what I mean." He started to get off the bed. "I'll go myself."

"Vyrl, no." Kamoj pushed him back. "You were almost killed today. You shouldn't be up at all." She took his hands. "Listen. I'll rub your head. We can hold each other. Every time you want a drink, we'll make love. So many better ways exist to sooth your demons than soaking them in rum."

Despite the strain that showed in the lines of his face and the set of his shoulders, his mouth quirked in a smile. "I like your cures a lot better than the ones Dazza comes up with. But I don't need this 'cure,' water sprite. It does more damage than good. If Dazza told you otherwise, she's wrong."

Kamoj raised his hands and bit gently at his knuckles. "Please."

Instead of answering, he said, "Men do that where I come from." He kissed her knuckles, pressing his teeth against them. "Like this."

"Only women do it here."

He pulled her between his legs, holding her around the waist. "Women this, men that. All these 'rules' exist and they're different everywhere. Do you know what I think? That under all those rules, people love the same. They find their way to each other no matter what."

She put her arms around him. "I can't bear to see you hurt yourself."

"I just need a drink. It helps. Not hurts."

"It's drowning you."

"That's nonsense. Did Dazza pressure you to do this?"

"No one pressured me." She willed him to believe her. "I know what I see."

"Now you're a medical expert?"

"I don't need to be."

He brushed her hair back from her face. "If you won't get it for me, I'll go myself."

"Vyrl, please. It's destroying you."

"How would you know?"

"You almost *died* today. Because of the rum."

It was a moment before he answered. "I never used to drink. I don't like the taste."

"Not even now?"

"Not even now."

"Then don't drink it."

His anger flared. "I can stop if I want."

"Then why don't you?"

"I don't want to."

"So why do you care that you never used to drink?"

"I don't care."

"Then why bring it up?"

"Damn it, Kamoj, let it go."

Softly she said, "I wish I could make your night-demons vanish." She heard the ache in her voice. "But I can't. Neither can the rum. I don't want you to send me away. But I can't do what you want."

He swallowed. "Don't sound like this."

"Like this?"

"Like your heart is breaking."

Her voice caught. "Please. Just one night."

Vyrl pulled her into an embrace, with her head on his shoulder. She wasn't sure if he offered affection or couldn't bear to look at her. For a long time they held each other, he sitting, she standing. Gradually she began to hope it would happen, that tonight he would turn from his blue bottle.

He drew back to look at her. "Very well."

Her hope surged. "Yes?"

"I'll send one of my bodyguards for it."

"No."

"If you wanted to be a good wife, you would help me."

"I won't help you kill yourself." She grasped his hands again. "You've already made it more than halfway through the night. You only have a few more hours."

His face was set. "If you won't help, I don't want you here."

She felt as if he had slapped her. But she forced out the words. "All right." She let go of him. "I will have my things sent back to Argali. I can leave in the morning."

A muscle in his cheek twitched. Then he turned and stabbed his finger at a jade leaf on the nightstand. Defeat washed over Kamoj, made worse by the way her hope had built.

A voice came into the air. "Doctor Pacal here."

Kamoj froze, watching Vyrl. He had an odd startled look, as if he had surprised himself.

After several moments Dazza said, "Vyrl? Is that you?"

"Yes. Never mind. I'm sorry I bothered you."

"Are you all right? Do you have any pain?"

"No."

"You're sure?"

"Yes."

"Vyrl—"

"I'm fine."

"I can come up."

"No."

"Are you certain?"

"Yes. Good night."

"Call me if you need anything."

"I will."

After a while Vyrl said, "Are you still there?"

"Yes," Dazza said.

"I don't . . . I mean, I'm fine. But I—" He fell silent. Kamoj wondered if Dazza was waiting with the same held breath as she, afraid to speak for fear of saying the wrong thing.

Finally he said, "You can treat withdrawal symptoms from alcohol, can't you?"

Dazza spoke quietly. "Yes. I can help."

"Can you come up here?"

In an infinitely gentle voice she said, "I'm on my way."

Vyrl touched the leaf again. After a moment he turned to Kamoj. "Just for the rest of tonight."

Tears pooled in her eyes. "Yes. Tonight." In the morning they would deal with tomorrow, and when the time came, with the day after that, each day on its own.

10

Dragon's Breath

Rearrangement Channel

The buzz of a bottle-beetle blended with forest sounds, the call of quetzals, and the blowing wind. The translucent radiance of dawn filled the room. Kamoj's mind gradually sorted out what had awoken her. Someone had said her name.

Turning her head, she saw Vyrl sitting on the bed, dressed in a work shirt and old pants, his hair mussed as if he had been out in the wind.

He leaned over her, his hands on either side of her shoulders, and gave her a long kiss. Then he said, "You're all rumpled and warm under there."

She smiled drowsily. "How long have you been up?"

"A few hours. I had trouble sleeping."

"Did Dazza's medicine help?"

"Some." He winced. "I feel like a stardock crane hit me in the head, though."

Kamoj touched his cheek. It was the only way she knew

to express how much it meant to see him sober this morning. She feared if she spoke of it, she would disrupt his precarious equilibrium. So instead she asked, "What have you been doing?"

"I was down in the old throne room."

"Throne room?"

"Downstairs," Vyrl said. "The hall on the other end of the palace. We haven't finished restoring it yet."

It sounded like he meant the Hall of Audiences. "What are you going to do with it?"

He started to answer, then stopped. Finally he said, "I'm not sure. I was deciding how to resurface the floor."

"The floor?" Kamoj wondered what he was trying to tell her. She tried to hold back her yawn, but it came anyway. It had taken her hours to fall asleep last night, and her fitful dreams had kept her restless.

"Go on and sleep," Vyrl said. "It's barely sunrise." He took a purple glass vial out of his pocket and removed its gold stopper. "I told Dazza you were up all night. She says you can take this if you want, to help you rest."

Grateful, Kamoj drank the potion. It had a pleasant taste, like wind-spices. "What will you do?"

"I have to talk to Drake."

She handed him the empty vial. "Who is that?"

"Drake Brockson. The chief anthropologist on the *Ascendant*. I asked him to put together a summary of his studies on this world."

"What does he say?"

Vyrl hesitated. "He thinks the original population here was breeding stock."

"You mean our animals?" She pulled the covers around her neck, content in their warmth. "Bi-hawks have two stomachs."

"The animals weren't the primary subjects."

"What was?"

Another pause. "People."

"Bi-people," she mumbled drowsily. "Some people have double stomachs, you know. They can go longer without eating."

Vyrl didn't answer right away, and she had just about fallen asleep when he spoke. "Yes. That was the intent."

"Intent?"

"Are you sure you want to know?"

"Hmmmm . . ." Just having Vyrl nearby soothed her. Perhaps Dazza was right, that she and Vyrl had some invisible effect on each other. "Yes . . ."

After a short silence, he said, "Drake thinks your ancestors were engineered to be the ideal slaves."

What? She opened her eyes. "How can he say such a thing?"

"Everything points to it."

"Points how?"

Vyrl spoke quietly. "Your people's docility, your drive to please authority, your reluctance to engage in battle or rebellion, your physical beauty and heightened sexual response, your ability to work for long hours in excruciating conditions of climate, atmosphere, poverty, and lack of food—it all fits the models."

She pushed up on her elbow. "It can't be."

"Even your names support it."

"Our names?"

"Each line has its talent. Ironbridge produces electrical wizards, like the Ohmstons. Argali has sunsmiths." Ire crackled in his voice. "Your names are *labels*. By building your expertise into the brain, your creators avoided having to educate you. They designed you to have trouble learning anything else. Smart slaves are dangerous."

It made more sense than Kamoj wanted to admit. "And my name? Resonance?" When he hesitated, she said, "I want to know."

He touched the jeweled chain around her neck. Rubies and gold. "Human nature prefers freedom. In slaves, that urge must be constrained. Drake believes the Argali line began as an experiment to create humans less resistant to bondage. The 'resonance' is an allegory. Your creators sought to increase the lifetime of a metastable bound state. They wanted people they could hold captive for as long as possible."

Kamoj clenched the quilt in her hands. "That's horrible."

"Yes."

"And Jax?"

"He probably descends from the owners. The free state. It's unlikely they all managed to leave here when the Ruby Empire collapsed."

Pah. Knowing Jax's ancestors had probably bred hers to work themselves into exhaustion made Kamoj that much more determined to fall back asleep. Then it occurred to her that Vyrl had invoked more of their ownership customs than Jax ever did.

He stared at her. "I don't own you."

"Our laws say you do," she told him. "If a man's corporation is larger than the woman can match, she becomes his property. It isn't only marriages. We couldn't match your rent, so we had to give you the palace."

"A corporation isn't a dowry."

"It isn't?"

"The word corporation derives from classical Iotic." He paused as if searching for words. "It means a group that, as a body, has the powers, privileges, and liabilities of an individual. Corporations can buy, sell, and inherit property."

"As you bought me."

"I would never consider you my property."

Although he had already given her good reason to believe he felt as he claimed, she still hadn't been sure. Even now, she spoke with care. "It is almost unheard of for a man to offer a governor a dowry she can't match. With such a merger, his authority extends to her entire province. It is the only way, besides inheriting the title, that a person can become governor. That you were already a leader makes it unprecedented as far as I know."

He shook his head. "You're the leader of Argali. I'll help if I can, but you're the one qualified for the job."

She took a breath. "Would you sign a contract to verify that arrangement?"

"Of course."

Kamoj wondered if he had any idea just how much his answer meant to her. Jax's refusal to sign such a contract was one reason she had agreed with her uncle about the need to delay the Argali-Ironbridge merger. "I will have a judge prepare the documents."

"All right." He hesitated. "I'll be down at the Ridge."

"You mean the palace tri-grain fields?"

"Yes." Shifting his weight, he added, "I told Jak Tager I would talk to him."

Kamoj remembered the name. Dazza had spoken of Tager during their ride in the giant metal bird. "Is he a doctor?"

"Psychiatrist. A healer of emotions." The rigid set of his muscles pulled his work shirt tight across his shoulders. "It can't hurt just to show him a few crop variations I'm working on. I don't have to talk to him again if I don't want to."

"I'm glad, Vyrl." She felt a curious sense of release, as if his words had lifted a weight she carried. She let her eyes close. Whatever Dazza had put in that vial, it was settling over her like a blanket.

"Kamoj?"

She raised her lids halfway. "Yes?"

"This morning I went riding with my bodyguards. We saw some people practicing folk dances in the village."

"They were probably rehearsing for the harvest festival."

"Some were men."

She yawned. "That's right. Men do the Reel of the Greenglass Stags. They stamp their boots a lot in that one. In the

Sun Lizard's March they spin torches in the air." Her lashes dropped over her eyes again. "They do partner dances with the women, too."

"Then it is accepted for men to dance here?"

"Yes, certainly," she mumbled. "Why do you ask . . . ?"

"I just wondered." Leaning over, he gave her one of his warm kisses. "Sleep well, water sprite."

Then his footsteps receded across the room.

Faint voices threaded into her slumber.

". . . Kamoj awake?" Dazza asked in a low voice. It sounded like she was standing across the room, perhaps near Vyrl's desk.

"No, she's sleeping," Vyrl said. "She took the sedative you prescribed."

Kamoj tried to raise her head, to let them know she could hear, but a curious lethargy kept her half-asleep, unable to move. Perhaps her body was responding to Dazza's potion in a manner different than expected.

"How did she handle the news about her ancestry?" Dazza asked.

"Better than I did when I learned it about myself."

Himself? Surely she must have heard wrong.

"The irony kills me," he said.

"Irony?" Dazza asked. "How do you mean?"

Vyrl spoke dryly. "Five thousand years ago, my family ruled an empire. It fell in wars over the slave trade. Five hundred years ago the descendants of those traders bred the descendants of my family into the ultimate slaves. If my grandmother hadn't escaped, they would still own us." His hair rustled the way it did when he raked his hand through the curls. "I love the way Kamoj holds my head in her lap. But how can I ever enjoy it again, knowing what I do now, that she was engineered for it, that she would offer that comfort even if she *hated* me?"

That's not true, Kamoj thought. Giving such succor to Jax

had never brought her joy, only a bittersweet relief that it helped keep his temper at bay. She gave freely to Vyrl, with pleasure, and that made all the difference. She wanted to tell him, but she couldn't seem to finish waking up.

"She wouldn't touch you the way she does unless she cared for you," Dazza said.

Vyrl sighed. "I wish I understood her better."

"Her uncle has been letting us read the codices in his library." Dazza sounded thoughtful. "The fall of the Ruby Empire stranded their ancestors here. They had no idea how to run things, supposedly no ability even for independent thought. Yet here they are, still going when many of the old colonies have long crumbled into ruin." The colonel paused. "Argali genes must have unexpected strengths. Traits that Kamoj's people instinctively selected for over the generations. She descends from five millennia of survivors."

"She's a wonder," Vyrl said.

"You and she are a lot alike, you know."

His voice lightened. "Good gods. Is that a compliment?"

Dazza made a sound that resembled *hmmph* and Vyrl laughed. But then his bantering tone faded. "I don't understand why she stayed with Ironbridge. He must elicit her inbred responses."

"That would be the easiest answer. And certainly it's part of it. But the situation is far more complicated. Her province needed him. She put her people's well-being ahead of her own."

"We could have helped her."

"Like we've helped already?" Dazza exhaled. "We've interfered worse than oil on fire with these people, Vyrl. Have you considered what will happen when we set up formal relations here? We've antagonized a major leader, possibly beyond repair. Now what? Do we force their compliance? That will go over just great in the Assembly. The Moderate Party already considers ISC a bunch of conquering warmongers. This mess won't help."

After a long silence, he said, "I know."

Dazza spoke in a quieter voice. "I realize her ambivalence toward Ironbridge is hard for you. But they've a long history. From what I understand, he wasn't always violent. Erratic positive reinforcement can be powerfully effective. The more he withheld his love, the more it must have relieved her when he finally gave it. Of course it threw her off balance. She was under constant stress, trapped in the situation."

Vyrl was pacing now, his tread steady on the floor. "I hate that he got away with it. Don't people see the truth about him?"

"They see a strong leader. He apparently has a gift for organization and politics, and a keen intellect. I'm sure Kamoj saw that side of him, too."

Vyrl stopped pacing. "She hates him."

"She hates his cruelty. Not him."

"Damn it, Dazza, it's the same thing."

"No. It isn't." She sounded frustrated. "You want this in black and white, but nothing will make it that way. It's shades of gray. We want to believe that all she needs to do is choose what we consider best and she'll be fine. What else is there to think? That for all our power, we can still make this situation even worse if we aren't careful? It's possible, Vyrl."

His voice turned cold. "If it were me, I'd kill the bastard."

"Ah, Vyrl. Don't even say it." Her words had a crystalline quality in the clear night air. "Kamoj nurtures. I think she finds real joy in giving to those she cares for. You. Her uncle. Argali. It *defines* her world view. I hate to think what it would do to her if she caused Ironbridge to come to harm, someone she feels she should love but in some ways hates."

"She deserves a hell of a lot better."

"Many people would have broken under the strain she's lived with. That she has retained her strength of character and capacity to love speaks volumes about her extraordinary nature."

Softly Vyrl said, "I don't want her to leave."

"Neither do I," Dazza murmured.

Their voices faded as they left the room. Kamoj lay curled under the blankets, tears on her cheeks. Why did it have to hurt so much, trying to make the right choices?

A smell of burning scales woke Kamoj. The early morning sunlight had a dirty cast to it. Flaring her nostrils, she almost gagged on the stench. She slid out of bed and ran to the south-facing window.

The East Sky Mountains towered to the left of the palace in peaks carpeted with prismatic forest. Before her, the Lower Sky Mountains spread out in cultivated fields, then fell away in wooded hills to the distant flatlands, where villages dotted the aqua-blue plains and rivers crossed the land in silver threads. To the west, the Argali Mountains descended in great wrinkles until, out of sight, they reached the village of Argali.

The mountains were roaring with flame.

Fires blazed in the Lower Sky and Argali Mountains. Billows of smoke rose from peak after rolling peak, and tongues of dragon's breath threatened the flatlands. With horror, Kamoj realized that if the outlying hamlets of Argali weren't already burning, they would be soon—and then Argali itself.

The floor under her feet vibrated. As she grabbed the desk for support, a giant bird of gold and black metal roared over the tower, shaking the palace with its passage. It arrowed south, to where other birds wheeled over the fires, their metal plumage glittering in the sunlight. One released a purple cloud that billowed across the flames. The burning orange tongues cowered, beaten back, then flared anew, relentless in their advance.

Sweet Airys. Why had no one woken her? Kamoj wanted

to race down the tower. She had to get out there and help. Where was Vyrl? She had no doubt his first thought had been to join the fire-lines, but the *Ascendant* might have ordered his return to its fortress above the sky, forcing him to safety regardless of what he wanted. Their attention would be focused on him now.

She ran into her chamber, to the rose cabinet with her clothes. As she paused to open it, she saw herself in the mirror, a young woman in a translucent underdress, her nipples outlined against the pink silk and a wild mane of black curls rippling to her hips. Rubies and gold glittered at her neck, wrists, and ankles. She gritted her teeth. Collar and cuffs? Was that the origin of these treasured heirlooms? It made her heart ache, knowing she would never see her wedding jewels with the same warmth again.

Metal clinked on stone in the other room.

"Vyrl?" She returned to the main bedroom. It was still empty, though. She checked the landing outside, leaving the foyer doors open, but found no one there either.

Inside the suite, metal scraped on stone.

Puzzled, Kamoj went back inside. Still she saw no one. She walked to the window—

And froze.

An iron tri-hook gripped the sill like a huge dragon's claw, piercing the shimmer curtain. As Kamoj watched, a hand came up and slapped onto the wood. Then a woman pulled herself into view, a husky archer in Ironbridge colors. She hauled herself up onto the sill in one smooth motion.

Kamoj wasted no time on questions: she spun around and *ran.* As she raced onto the landing, boots thudded on the floor in the suite. She sped down the tower stairs, her bare feet slapping the steps. Why hadn't Morlin warned her of the intruder? Was he "down," whatever that meant?

At the bottom of the stairs, the door to the Long Hall was jammed open by the body of an elderly butler who had probably been coming to warn her about the fires. Seeing the gash in his head, she dropped to his side. Mercifully, he still breathed, unconscious but alive.

The sounds of pursuit grew louder, boots pounding on stone in the stairwell. Kamoj scrambled over the butler and ran down the Long Hall. She couldn't outfight or outrun the archer, who had both height and body mass over her, but Kamoj knew these mountains far better than Jax's people. As soon as she made it outside, she could lose her pursuer in the forest.

Bodies lay in the hall ahead, two maize-girls, bound and gagged. For an instant Kamoj feared they were dead. Then she realized no point existed in tying or silencing dead people. She hated knowing she would have to leave them for now, until she could bring help, but she had no seconds to spare—

Far up the corridor, an Ironbridge stagman stepped out of a doorway.

"No!" Kamoj skidded to a stop. Whirling around, she saw the archer striding toward her from the other direction, the woman's long legs covering ground fast. Kamoj ran straight at her, trying to reach the nearest doorway before the archer reached her. She made it and dashed into a sitting room filled with gold and white furniture. Bronzed sunlight poured through its floor-to-ceiling windows, the promise of escape. She sprinted toward them—

Someone caught her around the waist. As Kamoj yelled, the archer swung her around, lifting her feet off the floor. Half-carrying, half-dragging Kamoj, the woman strode back into the Long Hall, where the stagman met them. When Kamoj tried to shout for help, the stagman shoved a sponge in her mouth. He tied a gag around her head, while the archer pinned her arms. Terrified now, Kamoj thrashed in the archer's grip. Her captors each grabbed one of her upper arms and took off, forcing her to run between them or be dragged.

Then they were outside, racing across the courtyard. A cart waited for them, hitched to four blueglass bi-hoxen, bulky six-legged mammoths with sunlight sparking off their scales. Kamoj wanted to cry out in protest, but she could barely even get her breath with the gag in her mouth.

The stagman climbed onto the driver's seat, a plank of wood set across the front. Kamoj caught only a glimpse of him as she fought the archer, her desperation giving her a strength she didn't usually possess. The woman hefted Kamoj into the back of the cart, between two rolls of carpet, by a coil of rope. As she vaulted in after Kamoj, the cart jolted into motion. Kamoj tried to scramble out, but the archer shoved her down on her back.

The stagman jerked his head around, the reins of the bi-hoxen gripped in his hands. "Tera, keep her still."

The archer, Tera apparently, just grunted as she and Kamoj struggled. Kamoj raked her fingernails across Tera's arm, drawing blood. Then Tera flipped her onto her stomach and pulled her arms behind her back. Kneeling on Kamoj's legs, she bound Kamoj's wrists together with the rope. Kamoj tried to scream for help, but she could only make a muffled grunt.

The bi-hoxen plodded on, oblivious to the tumult, pulling the cart up into the North Sky Mountains.

Ancient trees towered over the path, clogged with moss and Argali vines. Kamoj thought the brooding forest made a fitting backdrop for her dread. Black-scaled thornbats hissed among the foliage, searching for puffs to skewer. Their cries echoed in the hoary woods. Except for on occasional Argali rose, the trees hunkered in dark hues, their scaled iridescence subdued by the weather. A misty drizzle was falling, mixed with fog that glinted from the scale dust suspended in it.

Bound and gagged, Kamoj sat in the cart, shivering from the cold. Tera sat next to her, as she had throughout the ride, silent and alert. Seeing Kamoj shake, she unrolled one of the carpets and wrapped it around her captive's shoulders. The cart rolled on, jolting up the narrow path, crushing vines and roses under its wheels.

Kamoj glanced at the boda-bag on Tera's belt. She had

neither eaten nor drunk anything since yesterday, and she felt hollow with hunger and thirst.

Tera watched her watching the boda-bag. The archer spoke with such a strong Ironbridge dialect that Kamoj could barely understand her. It sounded like, "Be you still o'piece, move I yer quieter?"

Kamoj nodded yes, hoping she had guessed the right meaning: *will you be quiet if I take off the gag?*

Tera removed the cloth and pulled the sponge out of Kamoj's mouth. Then she took off her boda-bag and unscrewed the top. Tilting its narrowed end to Kamoj's lips, she squeezed the bag, making wine squirt into Kamoj's mouth. As much as Kamoj disliked the harsh mead brewed in Ironbridge, she disliked her searing thirst even more. She sucked the vessel dry.

As Tera lowered the bag, Kamoj said, "Will you untie me?" Her arms ached, adding to her sense of vulnerability.

The driver answered, what sounded like, "Maybe a'can," to which Tera responded, "Lector, we cannee risk her a'run." Kamoj wasn't sure if *Lector* was an oath or the driver's name; either way, it came from a contraction of *Electromotive Force*. Legends painted Lector as a great hero who converted humans into energy. Why converting people into energy was heroic, Kamoj had no clue, but the name was popular in Ironbridge.

"I won't try to run," Kamoj said. She almost meant it; she had no idea where they were now, besides which she would be even colder wandering in the woods than sitting here under a carpet. But it didn't matter. She would try anything to escape. Better to face a freezing forest than the colder ice of Jax's fury.

She didn't fool Tera, though. The archer made no move to untie her. "Out there you be peat for Argali vines," she told Kamoj.

"Look," Lector said. "That wild greenglass again. I'd spend a Long Year to catch that beaut."

Kamoj looked and saw a huge stag keeping pace with them, half-hidden in the trees. She doubted Lector would have success with this greenglass. Graypoint would never allow anyone but Vyrl to ride him. And it was Graypoint following them, she was certain. But why? The Current only knew what the animal had thought yesterday when a giant metal bird took away Vyrl. Had Graypoint been pacing the woods since then, undecided whether or not to return to the Quartz Palace?

Tera was watching her. "The animal follows you." She grinned, showing teeth turned brown from chewing cabarque leaves. "We caught us a forest nymph guarded by the king of stags, heh?" Her smile faded. "Or else we caught a witch."

"Donnee talk of Argali that way," Lector said.

Tera answered something about, "vile business" and "Lionstar," to which Lector nodded his agreement.

Their words came as an unwelcome reminder to Kamoj of Vyrl's dismal reputation. No one had trusted him before, and now he had trampled their customs. All in the Northern Lands would have the same thought: if a stranger could overthrow Argali and humiliate Ironbridge, no one was safe.

Kamoj shuddered, thinking of a time in Ironbridge when Jax had met with a group of farmers whom he wanted to build a road. They came with reluctance, wary of the unfamiliar project, but Jax fired them with such enthusiasm that they started that night. She had no doubt he could have marshaled the people's fear and anger now until they clamored to augment his army, including archers like Tera who usually served on a highborn woman's bodyguard. He would have left enough forces to protect Ironbridge and taken the rest with him. While Vyrl rode on Ironbridge, Jax was up here, high in the mountains, sealing his plans for Argali.

As the bi-hoxen plodded onward, Kamoj brooded. So much had happened in the past few days, it was hard to absorb. She would never have expected Jax to go this far. The thought of facing him now chilled her in a way that had nothing to do with the wintry air.

Would the *Ascendant* help Vyrl look for her? *Could* they find her? She had no sense of how far their advanced powers went. Either Lector or Tera would go back and hide the tracks of this cart. Probably Tera. Although her name derived from the Volterra line in Argali, the Volterra penchant for travel had long ago spread its name across all the Northern Lands. Volterras had a knack for solving problems that involved a preferred direction. They made good trackers.

Groggy from hunger and drunk from mead, Kamoj fell into a daze, watching trees pass by. The cart finally rolled into a high mountain clearing. Saturated in mist, a camp lay before them, black tents with purple tassels hanging from the edges of their sloping roofs. Stagmen moved about the clearing, cutting wood, mending clothes, cleaning weapons, and tending campfires. They wore fur-lined boots and clothes, protection against the sleet that drizzled from the overcast sky.

When Tera tugged the carpet off Kamoj, a blast of freezing air cut through her underdress. Kamoj inhaled sharply, holding back a cry of protest. Then Tera pulled her out of the cart. Kamoj's bare feet hit the iced ground and she gasped. With her hands tied behind her back, she lost her balance and fell against the cart. Tears smarted in her eyes.

Lector came around the cart and lifted her into his arms. He set off into the camp, carrying her with one arm under her knees and the other around her back. She gritted her teeth against the stares of the encamped army. Her rose-hued dress was the only bright color in the clearing, and glimsilk glowed on overcast days. It was like a beacon drawing attention to her loss of status.

Lector stopped at a large violet pavilion with black tassels hanging from its fringed roof. He nodded to the two stagmen posted outside its entrance. The taller man acknowledged him, his glance flicking to Kamoj, then darting away again, as if he feared Jax might see him stare even here, outside. Then he went inside the tent. Kamoj was shivering uncontrollably, her dress frozen in the sleeting rain.

The flap lifted, releasing a puff of warm air. The stagman looked out at them. "He meets with an advisor now. He be calling you when they finish."

Kamoj stared at him, desperate now to enter the tent. Did Jax mean to freeze her?

"Sweet Airys, man," Lector said. "She cannee survive this cold."

Another stagman appeared at the entrance and pulled the flap further aside, releasing more warm air. "You may come now."

As Lector carried Kamoj inside, warmth closed around her. She closed her eyes, hating herself for the gratitude she felt. Did Jax plan these things, or did he just have an inborn instinct for controlling people?

Silk panels hung on the walls, Ironbridge colors, violet, silver, and black. Dark rugs covered on the ground and a bed made up with purple velvet stood in one corner. On the floor, braziers with iron grates gave out heat that rippled in waves, distorting the air above the scrolled grills.

"Over there," a man said. *That* voice Kamoj knew. Jax. He was sitting with a judge at a table across the tent. He turned back to his meeting without even acknowledging her. She wanted to hate him, but all she could feel now was relief. The anger would come, she had no doubt.

Lector set her on a pile of furred blankets next to a brazier. As he covered her with the furs, she craned her neck to look back at Jax. Unexpectedly, this time he was watching her. When he realized she had caught him doing it, he flushed and turned back to his advisor, who was struggling to decipher a map.

Do I upset you that much? she wondered.

Heat from the brazier warmed Kamoj, melting the ice on

her clothes. She began to feel again: rivulets of water ran down her skin, Lector's jacket scratched her arms, and waterproofed fur rubbed her thighs. Closing her eyes, she soaked in the warmth. She knew she was passing out, but she didn't care. She let darkness carry her into oblivion.

11

Iron Rose

Metastable State (1,3)

In the drowsy contentment of first waking, Kamoj reached for Vyrl. She found only empty air. Opening her eyes, she looked up—at Jax Ironbridge.

Her serenity vanished. She was lying on Jax's bed, her arms no longer bound. The tent was empty except for the two of them. It was also dark: the only light came from the dimly glowing braziers. She had no idea how long she had slept, but night had fallen outside.

Jax was sitting on the edge of the bed, leaning on one hand while he watched her. His hair hung around his face, straight and black, with streaks of gray. He wore a governor's clothes, rich and well-tailored: a violet shirt, black suede pants, and black knee boots edged with silver fur. A small bridge embroidered in silver threads decorated the collar of his shirt.

"How long have you been there?" she asked, still groggy, trying to gather a sense of her situation.

"A while." He brushed her hair away from her eyes. "You looked so pretty sleeping. An Argali rose."

Argali. *Argali.* The memory flooded back and she jerked away from him. "You *burned* it."

His smile vanished. "Perhaps next time you will think before you humiliate Ironbridge."

Kamoj pulled herself into a sitting position. Nausea rolled over her, more from the knowledge of what had happened than from her physical condition. "How could you do it?"

Jax watched her with an intent focus. "If your former husband has any wits about him, he will evacuate the villages in time."

Former? "Lionstar and Argali have a merger."

A muscle in his cheek twitched. "It's being dissolved."

"You can't do that."

"Of course I can." He trailed his finger across her lips. "I have a gift for you."

The change in subject disoriented Kamoj. "What?"

"I had intended it as a wedding gift." He paused. "But I will give it to you tonight, even if we won't sign the contracts until tomorrow."

The words made no sense. "I know of no contracts."

His voice hardened. "I learned a great deal from the *Ascendant* delegation that came to Ironbridge. This Drake Brockson, the man they call an anthropologist—he and I talked a long time. He has concerns about what he calls 'our native sovereignty.' Lionstar's actions disturb him."

Although Kamoj knew the judges of her own people would side with Jax in this, the *Ascendant* remained a cipher. She suspected that at least some of Vyrl's people, if not all, thought everyone would be better off without the mess created by her marriage to their liege. Would they continue to help with the fires? She couldn't bear Argali in flames.

Jax stood up, the dim light casting shadows across his body as if he were a living statue. He had Vyrl's height and well-built form, but the resemblance ended there. Where Vyrl was tawny, alive like the land in autumn, Jax evoked stone.

A tanglebirch chest stood at the foot of the bed, carved with bridges and rivers. Jax went to it and took out a black lacquered box. Straightening up, he regarded her with an unexpected fondness. "Ten years ago I traveled with some of my stagmen to the Thermali Coast, where the ships come in." He came back and sat on the bed again. "I got this from a merchant who sailed from another continent." Setting the box in her hands, he added, "I've kept it for you."

Given the circumstances, how could she accept a gift from Jax? But refusing him might incite his anger. Acutely aware of him watching her, she lifted the lid. Inside, a porcelain egg lay nestled in a bed of gold velvet, with silver filigree curling over it like lace.

She spoke awkwardly. "It's lovely. But I can't accept—"

He touched his finger to her lips. "Look inside."

Still she hesitated. Then his mouth tightened, and she recognized the warning signs. So she undid the latch and opened the egg. Gold velvet lined the interior, cradling a sparkling cluster of jewelry—two earrings and a long necklace, all made in the Argali design, gold vines inlaid with ruby roses. "Sweet Airys," she whispered. "They're beautiful."

"I thought so." Jax picked up the earrings. Holding back her hair, he inserted them in her ears with an expertise that suggested a long practice of putting jewels on women. It reminded her of how much it had hurt over the years every time she had heard rumors of his dalliances. Yet had he even suspected that she looked with desire at another man, he would have beaten her.

The rubies dangled against her neck, their tiny bells making soft chimes. He held up the chain next, letting its rubies glitter in the dim light. "Kamoj, you've truly a lovely stone as your namesake."

She swallowed. "You are kind to offer me such a necklace. But I can't accept—"

"It's not for your neck." He laid his palm against her waist. "It goes here. Actually, with a waist as small as yours, it will rest on your hips. Women in Thermali wear them under their clothes. It's very pretty."

"Oh." She didn't want to hear how he knew what women in Thermali wore under their clothes.

Jax set the egg and box on the floor. He let the chain slide through his hand, until it pooled on the velvet spread in a shimmer of gold and rubies. Then he went back to the chest. This time he took out a braided cord made from glittering scale-hemp, with tassels on each end. It resembled the old farm belts Kamoj often wore, except this one was designed for beauty. Threads of beaten gold and bronze wove through the braid, and jewel dust powdered its surface.

Jax stood by the chest, watching her with a shuttered gaze. "I had this made when you and I were betrothed."

She had no idea how to respond. Never in a decade of Long Years would she have imagined Jax indulging in the sentimentality of these beautiful gifts. "You are too generous."

"Am I?" He returned to the bed and sat next to her again. Taking her hands in his, he wound the belt around her wrists. Then, with a jerk, he tightened the cord. "Am I, pretty rose?"

Kamoj flinched as the cord bit into her skin. "Jax, don't."

"Why?" He twisted the belt tighter. "Is what I have for you not good enough, now you've had his wealth to play with?"

"I didn't mean that." She struggled to stay calm. "What are you doing?"

"Giving presents to my love." His words had a clenched sound, as if he hid pain under anger. "To the woman who humiliated me the moment a richer man made her a better offer."

"You *know* I had no choice."

"You had a choice. You could have said *no*." Incredibly, his voice shook. "You think it was hard for you, being carried through my camp like an unwilling bondsgirl? How do you think it was for me, having you walk away like that, knowing you were going to another man's bed after I had waited almost your entire life for you? It happened so cursed *fast.* One moment I was looking forward to seeing you and the next you were gone."

Kamoj stared at him, stunned by the depth of his reaction. "I—I'm sorry."

"It doesn't matter. You're mine again." Gritting his teeth, he added, "Except he had you first."

"Jax, please—"

"Please, *what?*"

Then he slapped her hard across the face.

"No!" With her face burning from the blow, Kamoj tried to lift her arms, to protect herself. "Don't!"

Jax held her wrists down with the corded belt. "How could you betray me that way?" He hit her again. "*How*, Kamoj?"

"Jax, no! *Stop.* Please."

He reached down to the silver metalwork on his boot and pulled a knife out of a hidden sheath there. "Whether it happens again is up to you."

"What are you doing?" She tried to pull away from him, but he held her in place by the cord around her wrists. With methodical strokes he freed her wrists—by slicing up the belt, shredding the gift until it was no more than a pile of glittering threads.

Kamoj's pulse was racing now. "Jax—"

"No." The blade glinted as he lifted it in front of her. Then he cut the shoulder straps of her underdress. "I will hear no more."

Staring at the knife, she swallowed and remained silent. Jax laid her on the bed, stretching her out on her back. His blade felt like ice as he cut away the remains of her underdress. She let herself see only the tent overhead. Its cloth shook with falling snow. A tassel hung from its highest point, bobbing back and forth. She focused on it, trying to numb her mind to the blowing snow of Jax's touch.

After he pulled away the last scraps of her dress, he took the gold chain with its ruby roses and fastened it around her hips. Then he lay on top of her, his body settling into hers, his hips pushing apart her thighs. His hair brushed her face, the scent of his astringent shampoo strong in the air, mixed with the tang of his sweat.

Kamoj built a dome of ice in her mind, a place where she could hide in numbing cold. When Jax unfastened his belt, she retreated to the harbor of her ice fortress. He pressed against her, and she blanketed her thoughts with snow. The tearing, the pain—that happened to someone else. His clothes scratched her skin as he moved, the buckle of his loosened belt rubbing her thigh, back and forth. She retreated into ice.

When he finished, he lay still, his breathing slowing to a normal pace. Eventually he rolled off her. He sat up on the edge of the bed, his booted feet planted on the ground, his elbows on his knees while he stared across the tent, lost in thought. The dim light from the braziers left his face in shadows. Then he undressed and laid his clothes in a neat pile on the nightstand. Numbly, Kamoj wondered if he always removed his clothes afterward instead of before, or if this was another of the mental games he played with her emotions. She sheltered herself in a frozen retreat.

When he saw her watching him, he smiled, his handsome face a deception that hid the violence beneath. "Curious?" His voice had quieted, his rage spent with his passion. He pulled down the covers under Kamoj and slid into bed with her, then drew the soap-scented velvet over them both. She felt an absurd relief that the blankets were Argalian wool and the sheets spice-cotton, instead of exotic silks, as if their normalcy could muffle the impact of what had happened.

That was when she started to shake. She couldn't stop the tremors that wracked her body. Why, she didn't know. It was over. Done. Yet now her protective numbness cracked open, and she shook like a vine during a storm.

"It's all right," Jax murmured, pulling her into his arms. "It's all right." He stroked her hair with an absent caress. "Perhaps Lionstar did me a favor."

"A favor?" Her voice sounded hollow.

"I got you two years earlier than I expected." Jax turned her onto her side, with her back spooned against his front, a bitter parody of her wedding night. He drifted to sleep with his thumb hooked in the chain around her hips.

Kamoj wished she could cry, but the tears had frozen.

"Something is wrong!" Jax said. "She won't wake up."

Another voice said, "She's tired, Governor Ironbridge."

Kamoj opened her eyes. Sunlight filtered through the tent. Jax stood by the bed, looking as if he had thrown on the first clothes he found, a purple shirt, black pants, and black boots. He hadn't even fastened his shirt, leaving it open to the icy air. Had her inability to wake rattled him that much? She recognized the stocky man with him: Elixson, an Ironbridge healer.

"When did she last eat?" Elixson asked.

"Yesterday morning?" Jax asked. "I don't know."

Elixson stared at him. "That's at least sixty hours. Probably longer, I would guess. She needs food."

Jax frowned at him. "I've gone longer without eating and not even noticed."

"Sir, she only has one stomach. She needs sleep too. If you keep her up all ni—"

"Your opinions are noted," Jax said sharply.

The healer reddened, apparently realizing he had intruded too far on private matters. "Yes, sir."

"You may go."

Elixson bowed, then headed for the entrance. As he was lifting the flap, Jax said, "Healer."

Elixson turned back to him. "Yes, sir?"

Jax pushed at his disheveled hair. "What should I give her to eat?"

Relief washed over Elixson's face. "Bland foods, for now. And tea. Anything more exotic could make her sick."

"Very well. Go tell the cook."

After Elixson left, Jax sat on the bed next to Kamoj. When he saw her looking at him, his entire face changed, his tension easing into concern. Whatever the reason, his mood had softened. She had never understood him. He offered violence one moment and tenderness the next, yet never saw the contradiction. Over the years, trying to meet his expectations had worn her down, until at times she would have done almost anything to achieve the fleeting release of his mercurial kindness.

Then Vyrl had come, offering love but breaking the future into pieces. As much as she longed for him, she feared he and his people would bring Argali to ruin much the way a stagman might brush away a firepuff fly without realizing he had crushed it in the process. She loved Argali with her heart and her soul, but for her entire life, its relentless dying had pressed on her, until she thought she would break beneath the weight.

"Kamoj, sweet rose," he murmured. "I'm sorry if I caused you pain."

You're always sorry after the hurting. Until the next time. She spoke in a low voice. "I've known you all my life. After Maxard and Lyode, you have been closer to me than any other person. But I hate how you hurt me, Jax." Her voice caught. "I hate it so much."

"I never wanted to. But you left me no choice." He watched her with his dark eyes. "You betrayed everything we had built. Did you think I would just walk away?"

She wanted to deny his words. But his anger had calmed now, and she knew her silence could keep it at bay. If they spoke, he would weave his vision of her inadequacies, putting just enough truth in his words to make her doubt her own worth, even the soundness of her mind.

So she said only, "I'm sorry."

"Let us not have angry words." He brushed a curl of her hair out of her eyes. "How do you feel?"

"Hungry."

"When did you last eat?"

It felt like forever. "The day before yesterday."

"When did you last brush your hair?"

Her hair? What was wrong with her hair? "I don't know."

"Rest as long as you need. The cook will send breakfast." He kissed her, then stood up. "I'll be back this afternoon."

Kamoj wanted to stay awake. Sleeping made her feel more vulnerable. Undefended. But she fell into slumber even before he put on his cloak. She woke when a bondsgirl left her a tray with food by the bed. She ate the grain, rolls, and soup, then went back to sleep.

Cramps woke her the next time. Curled under the covers, she held her stomach, willing the pain away, until finally it subsided. Tears gathered in her eyes but she held them back. Then she sought sleep again, where nothing hurt.

When next she awoke, the light had dimmed and the roof sagged, heavy with snow. The braziers had gone dark. The air on her cheeks felt cold, but under the covers she stayed warm.

She rolled over—and saw Jax asleep on top the covers. His presence didn't surprise her; most people slept in the early afternoon. But his cloak had fallen open and he wore only thin clothes. He still hadn't laced his shirt, leaving his chest exposed to the chill air. Did cold never bother him? Such people existed, those almost unaffected by the killing climate. Vyrl claimed they had been bred for it, to better serve their owners. That suggested part of Jax's heritage came from slaves. No wonder Vyrl's people dreaded these *Traders* they fought, if Jax was a watered down version of them.

Like a spirit called forth by her thoughts, he opened his eyes. For a moment he simply watched her. Emotions washed across his face: relief, desire, happiness.

Do I make you glad? she wondered. She didn't know where to put that knowledge. It was like a glass ball with beautiful designs inside that twisted into harsh patterns when she turned it the wrong way.

Jax didn't speak. Instead, he got off the bed, drowsily rubbing his eyes. Once again he went to the chest at the foot of the bed. This time he pulled out an armload of clothes.

Kamoj sat up, self-conscious, holding the covers to hide her body. The thought of him seeing her naked had the same effect as if he had come into her home unasked, like a burglar.

With undisguised satisfaction, Jax draped the clothes on the mound her legs made in the bed. The scent of spice-soap and new cloth wafted around her, fresh and clean. It made her even more aware of how she felt neither.

"I need a bath," she said.

"If you would like." He went to the entrance and spoke to someone outside, then waited by the flap.

Soon a bondsgirl appeared, carrying a vat of steaming water and a tray of soap, with silver ring-towels hanging on her arm. After the girl left, Kamoj looked at Jax, wishing he would leave too.

He returned to the bed and sat next to her. "What's wrong?"

"Can you—?" She stopped. Would he hit her if she asked him to go? "I'm cold."

Jax touched her arm. "You've ice-bumps." He slopped one of the smaller ring-towels in the steaming water, then wrung it out and pressed it against her face.

Warmth spread its relief through Kamoj's skin. She closed her eyes, wishing she would wake to find herself at the Quartz Palace, or home at Argali before any of this had happened. But then Jax pulled the blankets away from her, letting chill air flow across her bare skin.

She crossed her arms over her torso. "You don't have to wash me."

"I know." He lathered the cloth with soap. "But I like it. I always imagined doing this on our wedding night, the two of us in the pool at Ironbridge House."

Kamoj bit her lip, washed with guilt. Their wedding night. She would never have guessed he would make such affectionate plans.

Jax washed all of her, from her face to her feet, his hands lingering on her body. Then he dried her with a large ring-towel. He took a scrap of black silk from the clothes, an underdress unlike any she ever wore, all ties and lace, with a corset top that pushed up her breasts and whittled her waist. He tied the corset so tight, she could barely breathe. Next he chose a velvet dress dyed the same dark purple as his shirt. It covered her from neck to wrists to knees. The flared skirt swirled around her legs, but the torso and sleeves fit so tight she couldn't raise her arms. He finished with gray leggings made from Argali wool, then smoothed her hip chain into place over the wool and pulled down her skirt.

Leaning back on his hands, he surveyed his work. "You're beautiful, Kamoj. Ironbridge colors suit you."

She gritted her teeth. He treated her like a doll. Better this, though, than his violence.

He gave her a pair of knee boots, purple suede lined with silver fur. After she put them on, he pulled her to her feet and drew her into an embrace, folding his cloak around her body. It came to just under her eyes, like a veil of Argalian wool. As always when his mood eased this way, she felt intense relief mixed with an emotion harder to define. Hate? Or love? It hurt so much. But no one had ever promised their lives would be pleasant. She ached with her separation from Vyrl, but her bond with him seemed unreal now, too fragile to survive.

A chime came from outside, a mallet hitting a small gong. Jax raised his voice. "What is it?"

One of his stagmen stepped inside the tent. "The panel be here, sir."

Jax motioned Kamoj toward the bed. "You can sit there."

Panel? Uneasy, Kamoj sat on the edge of the bed and folded her hands in her lap. The stagman brought in two people. She recognized the man, an Ironbridge judge, one of Jax's advisors. The woman wore the robe of an Ironbridge priestess. Although the designs embroidered on its sleeves and hem resembled spindly hieroglyphs, the codices named them with different words. *Circuit diagrams.*

Jax, the judge, and the priestess sat at a wooden table across the tent. Parchment crackled as the judge brought out his scrolls. Kamoj felt dizzy from fatigue and hunger, and barely able to breathe in the tight clothes, but she struggled to concentrate on their words. If she remained silent, they might reveal more.

They first considered the legal situation Jax faced. No precedent existed for a merger being so precipitously lost after so many years of investment. It was inconceivable—until it happened. They meant to draft legislation to make sure it never happened again. As much as Kamoj saw that her people needed these laws to prevent such disruptions in their lives, it made none of this any easier.

They spoke of the *Ascendant* at length. Apparently its minions believed their laws applied to her people. Yet neither Jax nor his advisors feared reprisals. In fact, they seemed to consider the *Ascendant* an ally, albeit a wary one. For some reason its legal people wanted to know if Kamoj had consented to sleep with Vyrl. As far as Kamoj was concerned, her marital bed was none of the *Ascendant*'s business. They should worry about the economic disaster Vyrl had spurred in the Northern Lands by yanking Argali out of its merger with Ironbridge, all the while planning to leave her province and her people.

When Jax began to tap his riding quirt against his palm, she recognized the sign of his anger. Nor was it directed only against Vyrl. Jax had no grounds to censure Maxard for bowing to Lionstar, so instead he and his advisors spoke of other matters, making Maxard sound incompetent, unfit for any form of authority. They started on Lyode next, calling her morals into question, and talked of taking her away from her husband so she couldn't have children.

Kamoj knew how much Maxard valued having a position he could use to help the land, people, and province he loved.

In that, she and her uncle were alike. Lyode and Opter longed for children and planned on a large family. She understood Jax's message: unless she cooperated, the people she loved would suffer.

When they moved on to Vyrl, she almost gagged. They planned to claim he raped her in a drunken fit. The *Ascendant*'s people had translated the contract scroll Vyrl read at the wedding. It was indeed a merger contract, with gibberish about commercial licenses, zoning ordinances, business insurance, and property. Vyrl apparently could be held to its terms, which included provisions to negate a merger made through coercion.

Jax and his advisors all signed the document that annulled the Argali-Lionstar merger. When the judge said the *Ascendant* required Kamoj sign as well, Jax penned her name. Then they wrote out the terms for an Argali-Ironbridge merger and signed that contract as well. Finally the judge rolled up the scrolls and put them in his valise. They all stood and talked a bit more, speculation about when the riders sent to Argali would return with news of the fires. Then Jax dismissed them.

When Kamoj and Jax were alone, he came over and smiled at her. "It is done, Kami rose. Ironbridge and Argali are merged."

Softly she said, "I heard." She had known all her life this day would come, but she had never expected it like this, stripped of her authority and freedom, with Argali in flames. Had Jax deceived her all these years? Perhaps. But she suspected this moment would have been far different had the *Ascendant* never shaken up their lives. Did they have any idea of the damage they had caused? No, that wasn't right. Jax was responsible for his cruelty. Not them.

Jax rummaged in the chest yet again. This time he brought out a silver brush with rose bristles. He sat next to her, relaxed now, as if penning his claim to her lands, her heritage, and her body had eased his clenched temper.

He showed her the brush. "When you and I were be-trothed, Maxard gave me a small inheritance your mother asked you be gifted with on your wedding day. This was part of it." He rubbed a curl of her hair between his fingers. "Shall I brush it for you?"

She stared at her hands in her lap. "All right."

Jax spent a long time working out her tangles, handling her tresses with deft care. Then he brushed her hair in long, slow strokes, from the crown of her head to her hips. After a while he slid his arms around her waist and kissed her neck. "Ah, Kami. I know I'm not an easy man. But I do truly love you."

Her voice caught. "Why does loving have to create so much pain?"

"If only they hadn't come." He laid his head against hers. "If only they had stayed away from Balumil."

Outside, the gong chimed. Jax grumbled under his breath, then called, "What is it?"

"A rider came back from Argali," a voice answered. "He says it be urgent that he speak with you."

"It had better be urgent," Jax muttered. He went to the entrance and pulled aside the flap. "Come in."

An Ironbridge stagman entered and bowed. He glanced at Kamoj sitting on the bed, then looked quickly back at Jax. "My apologies for disturbing you, Governor. But I thought you should know. They've doused the fires. Lionstar be riding up here now."

"The fires are out already?" Jax asked. "*All* of them?"

"Aye, sir. It be the metal birds. They spray a liquid that swallows flames."

Jax's frown deepened. "How did Lionstar find us? Tera hid the trail."

"He rides that wild greenglass. The spirit animal."

That caught Kamoj off guard. Graypoint had fetched Vyrl? She had never heard of a greenglass doing such a thing.

"How many men does he have with him?" Jax asked.

"Seventeen stagmen. The rest ride to Ironbridge." The man squinted at Jax. "A woman be with him too."

"Really?" Jax smiled slightly. "A bondsgirl?"

"I don't think so. An older woman. Gray and craggy. Not at all pretty."

Jax nodded. "You've done well. Get my mount and have sixty stagmen ready to ride."

After the man left, Jax turned to Kamoj. "So. He comes. Sooner than we expected, but still too late."

"You're taking sixty men against seventeen?" Kamoj knew the *Ascendant* would never let Vyrl risk his life, but she couldn't rid her mind of the image: Vyrl in agony from an arrow or sword thrust, bleeding to death.

"Sixty stagmen and you." Jax used a deceptively soft voice. "Make no mistake, Kamoj. You will let Havyrl Valdoria see that you are my dutiful and willing wife. If ever I believe you are even thinking otherwise, you will regret it at great length." He shifted the quirt in his hand. "And if you ever try to go back to him, I will do more than burn Argali. You will watch Maxard and Lyode die."

12

The Right of Inquiry

Three-Particle State

Kamoj stared at Jax. Suddenly cold, she wrapped her arms around her body. "I'll do whatever you want. Just don't hurt anyone."

"That is up to you." He took off his cloak and threw it on

a chair, then went to another chest and took out his sword belt. She wondered what good he thought a sword would do against the *Ascendant*'s defenses. Not that it mattered. Jax had already defeated Vyrl using the *Ascendant*'s own laws.

If only she had refused the Lionstar merger. Vyrl's people would never have let him attack Argali, even if it would have occurred to him, which she doubted now. But how could she have known? Every one of his actions had sent a message in the ways of her people, carrying threats.

Jax took her to the entrance. As he lifted the tent flap, Kamoj tensed. They both had on only flimsy clothes, and his shirt was still unlaced, open to the air.

"Don't you need your cloak?" she asked.

He drew her forward. "It will only get in the way."

Outside, the sky pressed down like a lid of pewter. Kamoj winced as freezing air blasted them. The camp was busy with people. At one fire, a bondsgirl poured a steaming drink for a stagman, her smile shy and her gaze averted as he closed his hands around hers on the mug. Her yellow hair suggested she came from one of Ironbridge's poorer districts.

Kamoj's parents had forbidden the Argali army to use bondservants, and Kamoj and Maxard maintained that ban. Although in theory both Jax and the governor of the North Sky Islands allowed it, only Ironbridge could afford them. The indenture usually lasted only a few years, but that didn't change its basic nature. After what Vyrl had told her, Kamoj understood better where the practice originated and why it made her uncomfortable. When left to their freedom and their starvation, the slaves had fallen back on the only ways they knew. They enslaved one another.

Across the clearing, a group of greenglass stags stamped their feet while stagmen tended them. By the time she and Jax reached the group, Kamoj was shaking from the cold, her breath coming in puffs of icy white condensation. A boy brought a huge stag forward, Jax's mount Mistrider. The animal shook his head, his antlers glinting like glass, his opaline scales ghostly in the mist. He stared down at Jax with green eyes slitted by vertical black pupils. Mistrider's wariness made Kamoj wonder how often he had felt his master's quirt through his supple hide of jeweled scales.

Using a stool called a stagmount, Jax swung onto Mistrider. The greenglass stamped and snorted, coming so close to Kamoj that she jumped back. When Jax motioned, she made herself step up on the stool. He helped her onto the stag, far above the ground, settling himself between the front and middle boneridges so Kamoj could straddle the animal in front of him. Mistrider picked up her tension, prancing beneath her as he grew more agitated.

Suddenly the stag reared, his front and middle legs pawing the air. His bi-hooves crashed together and rang like discordant symbols. With Mistrider all the way up on his powerful back legs, Kamoj and Jax were high in the air, more than the combined height of two tall men. She gasped and clutched the stag's scaled horns, the only "handles" available.

Jax yanked her hands away from the antlers, keeping his other arm gripped around her waist. "Never grab a stag that way!"

Mistrider came down, his bi-hooves pounding the frozen ground. Before Kamoj could catch her breath, the animal reared again, his head thrown back, his fangs barred. He screamed at the sky, a long, high cry that pierced the muted day. Then he smashed his bi-hooves together until the forest rang with their clangs and Kamoj feared they would shatter. She couldn't look down, couldn't move, could barely even breathe.

Jax kept his arm around her, holding his reins with the same hand, his grip the only tether that kept her from flying off the animal. With his free hand, he snapped his whip against Mistrider's flank. "Hai!" he shouted. "Be still!"

The stag came down and danced furiously to the side, invading the area around four other animals. They skitted away, stamping their feet and keening in quieter versions of the scream Mistrider had used to challenge the clouds.

The call of a flight-horn winged into the sky. Another horn answered, then a third. Moving together, the group headed into the forest, the animals falling into the intricate, complex rhythm of their six-legged trot. The riders took the traditional formation, half in front of Jax, half in back. Ever restless with tradition, Jax prodded Mistrider to the head of the company.

Kamoj drew in a shaky breath. As they penetrated deeper into the woods, the noises of the camp faded. The mist suffocated sound, curling around the ancient trees. Drops of water clung to the needles. Scale dust glittered everywhere, in the air, in the mist, on the plants. Vines hung in great loops, draped over branches and twisted around trunks and fallen logs. Scaled ferns grew among the trees, their lacy heads nodding under the shifting weight of the tiny budlizards that clung to the underside of their leaves, a motion all the more eerie because no wind disturbed the woods.

Kamoj saw the other riders before she heard them. She caught glimpses of stags and diskmail among the trees. Jax called out and the Ironbridge company halted, fanning out in a semicircle several rows deep, with Jax at its center.

Like mystical beings forming out of the mist, the Lionstar company emerged from the white shroud and stopped twenty paces away, greenglass stags mingled with scale-trees. Vyrl's towering bodyguards flanked him, clad in black, from their boots to their heavy jackets. Both Jagernauts rode stags huge enough to support their bulk. They sat on their mounts with an ease that unsettled Kamoj, another indication of how Vyrl's people so easily bent her way of life to theirs. Dazza and Azander rode on either side of the bodyguards, and Vyrl's other stagmen fanned out from them in a much smaller semicircle than the one formed by Jax's men.

Neither Vyrl nor his people wore breathing masks. Light

sheathed their bodies instead, like the shimmer curtains. Vyrl's clothes were gray with soot, and his hair fell in disordered curls to his shoulders.

Seeing him made Kamoj hurt inside. Her vision blurred in a haze of fatigue and hunger. She fought her constricting clothes for each breath and clenched her teeth against the cold. Vyrl was watching her, his face strained as if he were struggling to hear a distant song in the trees. She tried to make her thoughts placid so he wouldn't feel them.

Azander spoke. "Lionstar acknowledges Ironbridge."

The stagman on Jax's right answered. "Ironbridge acknowledges Lionstar."

"Lionstar invokes the Right of Inquiry," Azander said.

Behind Kamoj, Jax's hair rustled as he nodded his agreement to the Inquiry. His arm tightened around her waist and he shifted the quirt until its tip rested on her thigh. She understood the warning; she would know his quirt later if she provoked his anger now.

"Proceed with the Inquiry," Jax's stagman said.

Vyrl spoke to her. "Kamoj, was it really your choice to go with Ironbridge?"

"Do not presume to speak to my wife," Jax said.

"She isn't your wife," Vyrl said.

"The papers were signed this afternoon," Jax said. "Your contract is annulled."

Vyrl stared at him. "You can't annul an Imperial contract."

"Perhaps you should read your own laws. A merger made through coercion is not legally binding."

"She wants to stay with me," Vyrl said. "She told me."

"You have witnesses to this?" Jax asked.

Vyrl looked at her. "Tell them."

I can't. Kamoj tried to take a breath, but the boning of her underdress cut into her ribs. *Hear me. Understand.* "I must stay with Ironbridge."

"You have your answer," Jax said.

Vyrl clenched Graypoint's reins. "That's because you have her too terrified to tell the truth."

"If you came to this Inquiry to throw insults," Jax said, "I don't see much point in continuing."

Dazza spoke quietly. "Vyrl, perhaps we should—"

"I won't leave without her," Vyrl said.

"We can discuss this more privately."

"No.

"Vyrl—"

"I said no."

Dazza pushed back her hair, the shimmer on her hands merging with that on her head. "All right. Kamoj told me herself. Her marriage to you puts her in an almost impossible position. If she signed an annulment, then given the circumstances surrounding your merger with her, no Imperial court will honor your claim to Argali."

"I'm not 'claiming Argali,' damn it. I want my wife back."

"Legal won't see it that way," Dazza said.

"They'll do whatever I tell them."

Her voice cooled. "Yes, you could use your titles to take what you want. But this isn't as simple as you would like to believe. Listen to Kamoj. You would be forcing the courts into breaking laws meant to protect cultures such as this from exactly this sort of mistreatment. I suggest you think long and hard about the consequences. Once it's done you can't reverse the damage. And believe me, Vyrl, the political fallout of abusing your position that way would be ugly."

Vyrl stared at her. "I'm not the one breaking laws." He turned back to Kamoj. "I know you don't want to stay with him. Tell them, Kamoj."

She could still hear Jax's words: *I will do more than burn Argali to the ground. You will watch Maxard and Lyode die.* Maxard, Lyode, Gallium, Opter, Argali, her people, her province: what she did now would affect the future of all she loved. She struggled to project feelings of contentment, but her mind kept replaying the nightmare of last night: Jax's hands on her breasts, or pinning her arms to the mattress, or kneading her thighs like a night-cat preparing a place to sleep.

"You *bastard!*" Vyrl's voice exploded, and Graypoint danced under him, on the verge of rearing.

Jax spoke mildly. "Is something wrong with you, Lionstar?"

Graypoint tried to move toward Kamoj, but one of Vyrl's bodyguards grabbed the reins, his hands a blur. Kamoj wasn't sure what had happened. Surely a person couldn't move that fast. Vyrl swore at him, and the guard's hand dropped to a tube hanging on his belt, one of the weapons that threw sleep.

Kamoj saw two Ironbridge stagmen exchange glances. If Vyrl kept acting this way, Jax wouldn't need to discredit him. Vyrl would do it all by himself.

Dazza, however, was listening. "What did you think you picked up?"

Vyrl spoke tightly. "He comes from the same stock that produced the Traders. Think about it."

She glanced at the Jagernauts. "Did you get anything?"

The man said, "There's so much hostility between Prince Havyrl and Governor Ironbridge, it swamps everything else."

The stagwoman nodded. "Governor Argali is frightened. But I'm not sure who she fears, us or Ironbridge. She is also angry at us."

Jax spoke in a cool voice. "As strangers here, you may not realize the insult you give with this discussion." He stopped for a well-timed pause, then touched Kamoj's hair in reassurance. "Of course this causes my wife concern, particularly given what she has recently endured."

Vyrl ignored him. "You don't have to stay with him, Kamoj. We'll protect you."

But he would leave Argali to ruin. She kept her mind numb.

"Damn it," Vyrl said. "You aren't bound to him. You have free will."

"Stop harassing my wife." Jax took a deep breath, like a man pushed beyond reason, yet struggling to remain calm. Then he spoke in a kind voice to Kamoj. "I am sorry. But there seems only one way to resolve this. I must ask you to speak." He paused. "To the *Ascendant* woman."

He wanted her to talk to Dazza? That made no sense.

The colonel responded in a careful voice. "Kamoj, did you sign the Ironbridge contract of your own free will?"

"I can't write," Kamoj said. "Jax signed it for me."

"That's not legally binding," Vyrl said.

"Did you understand the documents?" Dazza asked her.

"Yes," Kamoj said. The shorter she made her answers, the less chance she had of provoking Jax.

"Did you object to the signing?"

"No."

"Were you coerced?" Dazza asked. "Threatened? Did you at any time express the wish to return to Prince Havyrl?"

"No." Kamoj answered only the last question. Did they actually believe she would acknowledge such threats in front of the person who had made them and sixty of his armed soldiers? Jax had more than three times as many stagmen here as Vyrl.

"She's too frightened to say anything," Vyrl said.

Jax spoke coldly. "Lionstar, if you persist in violating the procedures of this Inquiry, Ironbridge will withdraw."

"No." Dazza studied Kamoj's face. "Would you like to speak with me in private?"

Suddenly Kamoj understood why Jax wanted her to talk to Dazza. Although she knew the colonel outranked everyone, the others must see her as an enigma. Women with authority had bodyguards. If a woman formed a merger with an incorporated man, he offered the services of his honor guard as part of his dowry, but only after they were married. By coming alone with Vyrl and his stagmen, Dazza put herself on the level of a bondsgirl. When Jax let her question Kamoj, he undermined Vyrl's authority by taking the Right of Inquiry from him and giving it to someone perceived as having no authority at all.

"Kamoj can speak to whoever she wants," Vyrl said. "You don't own her."

"Of course I own her," Jax said. "The contracts are signed, and this time for a dowry beyond the ability of Argali to match."

As soon as Jax spoke, Kamoj knew he had finally made a mistake. It wasn't only Vyrl who reacted; Dazza and the Jagernauts also stiffened.

"This world is a member of the Skolian Imperialate," Vyrl said. "We may not have instituted formal assimilation procedures yet, but you are under our umbrella. Slavery in any form is illegal according to our laws. If you signed a contract that makes Kamoj your property, you're in trouble."

Jax's hand clenched on his quirt. "You can't ride in here and demand we change customs thousands of years old because it suits your purposes. According to your own people, your laws require your government to work with ours in finding resolutions to societal clashes without destroying our cultural sovereignty. Perhaps it has escaped your notice, Lionstar, but I am the government here." Malice edged his voice. "The moment you married Kamoj in one of our temples, according to our ceremonies, with that obscene dowry you sent her, you became her owner. It would appear you too are 'in trouble.'"

"She isn't anyone's property," Vyrl said.

Kamoj couldn't bear to listen any longer. She knew Jax. Beneath his control, his anger was growing. Argali would suffer his retaliation.

"Jax, I want to leave," she said.

His voice softened. "Of course." In a louder voice he said, "Ironbridge invokes a Close."

"I'm not leaving without Kamoj," Vyrl said.

Dazza spoke quietly. "If she doesn't want to go with you, do you really intend to force it?"

Vyrl regarded Kamoj. "We can protect you from him. Just say the word. You *have* options you don't understand." His voice caught. "I can offer you the stars. All he offers is a lifetime of fear and pain. Come with me."

"Answer him, Kamoj." Jax moved his quirt against her leg.

"I am the dutiful and willing wife of Ironbridge," she said. Was that enough? Would they leave her alone now? Did the people she loved have to *die* before they would listen?

"We can protect you," Vyrl said. "All you have to do is *ask*."

And after you desert Argali? she thought. He wanted her to go with him, but he planned to leave Balumil. No matter how much they might wish otherwise, it didn't change that implacable truth.

She hid her thoughts, imagining them submerged in a lake. "I will stay with my husband. Governor Ironbridge."

"No." Vyrl was gripping Graypoint's reins so hard, his knuckles had turned white. *"No."*

"She gave you your answer," Jax said. "What else did you expect? That being forced to spend a few days with a stranger, a man whose only interest was in assaulting her, would supersede a lifetime of dedicated companionship?"

"She never wanted to marry you," Vyrl said.

"Are you stupid?" Jax asked. "She told you what you wanted to hear. It is you that she fears, Lionstar."

Vyrl watched Kamoj. "Is that true?"

Jax stroked her hair as if to comfort her. "It's all right. Answer him. Then we can go home."

"Yes," she lied. "It's true."

Vyrl stared at her. Then his expression closed on itself. Quietly he said, "Good-bye, Kamoj."

Good-bye. The word echoed in her mind. *Good-bye.*

Vyrl motioned and his party reformed around him. When

he pulled on Graypoint's reins, the stag danced toward Kamoj. It shook its head, once, twice, three times. She recognized the pattern. Many a greenglass went through that dance with his young, herding them where he thought it best they go.

Vyrl rubbed Graypoint's shoulders and pulled the reins again. The stag kept trying to dance toward Kamoj. The third time Vyrl pulled, Graypoint relented and turned with the rest of the company, heading into the woods.

Good-bye. He was going. Forever. When Graypoint receded into the mist, pain broke into Kamoj's deadened thoughts, as jagged as shards of crystal. Vyrl's pain. Her own.

Behind her, Jax's muscles relaxed. He leaned his forehead against the back of her head and whispered, "It's over, pretty rose. We can go home now. Finally." His relief felt almost tangible. He straightened up and pulled on Mistrider's reins, bringing the stag around.

Kamoj swallowed. Home. It was done. She and Vyrl had bounced off each other and hurtled away.

Unshed tears burned in her eyes. She had lost Vyrl and their dreams. They would never share their lives or watch their children grow. If she bore his child, it would call Jax father—

If Jax let the child live.

And that was when Kamoj finally snapped. She had no idea if it was desperation or her first true act of free will; she only knew that she broke inside. Leaning to the side, she strained to see around Jax. Her body protested every move: bile rose in her throat, pinpricks danced on her skin, pain thrummed in her head.

Then she shouted, *"Vyrl! Don't go!"*

13

The Burrow

Capture Amplitude

Jax swore and yanked Kamoj back in front of him. A roaring filled her head. Spurred by Jax's quirt, Mistrider ran through the trees like fog blown by the wind. Jax called to Lector, and the stagman pulled alongside, their mounts running side by side.

"Take her to the burrow," Jax said. He passed Kamoj over to Lector's stag without even slowing down, a difficult move while both animals were in flight, but one they managed with practiced ease. Numb with shock, Kamoj slid onto the stag in front of Lector and clung to its neck. Jax wheeled Mistrider around and took off, vanishing into the mist and the darkening night.

Lector rode hard through the trees. When Kamoj trembled with the cold, he pulled his cloak around her. What had possessed her to call out for Vyrl? Jax had sixty stagmen, plus forty more in camp. Ironbridge would slaughter Lionstar. But Vyrl's people had their *Ascendant* weapons. They might slaughter Ironbridge. Either way, people would die. She couldn't bear being the cause. Her cry for help had come from a place so deep, she didn't know how she could have stopped its escape. Now she and the people she loved had to deal with the consequences.

When the fading light turned the mist a darkling pearl

color, Lector slowed his stag, letting it find its own way. Finally he stopped. As he jumped down, his cloak swirled away and icy air clapped around Kamoj.

He eased her off the greenglass, sliding her to stand on the ground. "We cannee ride any longer. It be too dark."

She tried to nod, but the day's drizzle had turned to snow, and she was shaking too hard. Watching her, Lector removed his cloak and wrapped it around her. Then he tapped his stag with a signal to wait. The greenglass bared its teeth, its breath curling out its nostrils, heavy with a spiced musk odor as it condensed in the fog. Kamoj wished she could blend into the mist and vanish as easily as those white plumes.

Lector led her forward into the darkness. The scents of the wet forest permeated the air, eddying and flowing around them. Even after Kamoj contracted the membranes in her nose, she was swimming in a sea of smells.

She pulled the cloak tighter. "We need shelter."

Lector leaned down. "Eh?"

"Shelter." Her teeth clattered from the cold. "We need shelter."

"Aye." He guided her around an upended tree with moss hanging from its roots. They approached the looming shadow of a hillside, until its darkness folded around them. When Kamoj stretched out her arms, her hands brushed dirt walls laced with roots.

"You best wait here," Lector said.

She stopped, listening to the tread of his boots. A spark jumped in the air about ten paces away. Then a sphere of light appeared, with Lector at its center, holding a lamp. They were in a burrow with earthen walls held together by networked roots. The wavering light threw shadows on the walls, revealing bags of food in one corner and a blanket.

"It inna so bad, heh?" he asked.

"Lector, let me go," she said.

"I cannee do that, Gov'nor Argali."

"What if I just left?"

"I would have to stop you, ma'am. I'm sorry. I be liege to Ironbridge. I cannee fail him."

Kamoj hadn't really expected otherwise. She doubted she could have survived in the forest anyway, on this freezing night, dressed as she was, having eaten only one meal in over two days.

Lector set the lamp on a ledge formed by a tree root. Then he took the blanket from the corner and spread it on the ground. "For you, Gov'nor."

"Thank you." She sank onto the blanket, grateful for the solidity of the ground. "Are you cold?"

He settled himself on a large boulder near the entrance. "Eh?"

"Cold." She offered him the cloak. "Aren't you cold?"

"Please keep it, ma'am. Cold never much bothered me."

Like Jax. Unlike Jax, however, Lector seemed to notice when it bothered others. Grateful for a bulwark against the icy air, she wrapped herself in the cloak again. But nothing could lessen the chill of knowing she had endangered Vyrl's life. She felt trapped.

Lector stretched out his legs and leaned against the wall. "I can tell you what makes ice on my spine. The magics in these woods. You be better off without Lionstar. That demon prince would trap your soul."

She shifted the cloak. "I don't think it's magic, Lector. It just looks that way. And Lionstar is no demon."

"Eh?" He leaned forward. "Who is the demon?"

Her voice caught. "Me. I caused these problems."

"Why do you say that? You hanna done nothing." He spoke kindly. "This madness will end. You will see."

She swallowed. "It is thoughtful of you to say that."

"I've a daughter your age. When I look at you—" He shook his head. "It be a father's nightmare."

The sound of dirt skittering across leaves came through

the entrance, followed by the tread of boots. Lector stood up and drew his sword.

"Step and call," a woman said.

"Come," Lector said. Sheathing his sword, he stepped aside to let Tera and a stagman enter, followed by a taller man.

Jax.

The Ironbridge governor glanced around, his gaze scraping past Kamoj as she rose to her feet. To Lector he said, "Did you have any trouble?"

"None at all, sir."

"Good." Jax lowered his muscular body onto a boulder. The soldiers sat then, too, Lector on the boulder across the burrow and the others on the ground. With five people crowded into the small space, Kamoj stayed on her feet, pressed against the earthen wall.

Jax regarded Lector. "I need your council."

The stagman sat up a straighter. "It be my honor."

"I must decide a course of action," Jax said. "Everything has changed now."

"What happened, sir?" Lector asked.

"Lionstar insisted I let him speak to Governor Argali." Jax made an incredulous noise. "Seventeen stagmen and one old hag, and he threatens me. When I gave the order to my archers to fire, it was like ordering the slaughter of bi-hoxen."

Kamoj dug her fingers into the wall. The question *Is he dead?* hung in the air like a mist-o'-mime.

"What did they do?" Lector asked.

Jax leaned forward. "One of Lionstar's bodyguards drew his weapon so fast it made a blur. An essence came out of it and made sparks in the air. The tree he aimed at exploded in a burst of orange light. Lionstar's other bodyguard swept her weapon through an arc and more trees exploded." He grimaced. "As fast as an archer can knock a ball, his guards could have killed my entire company."

"It be sorcery," Lector said. "I feel it in these woods."

"It just looks like sorcery." Jax considered Lector, then the others. "Do any of you read?"

Hai! Kamoj wanted to shake him. How could he talk about reading now? Was Vyrl alive or dead?

"I can read and write my name," Lector said. "My wife's name too, and our children. I know a few other words."

The other stagman spread his hands. "I cannee read at all."

"I be knowing my name," Tera said.

Jax looked disappointed, but not surprised. Kamoj wondered what it was like for a man with his intellect to live in a place where almost none of the population could even read, let alone offer an educated discussion. He was a study in contradictions, a brilliant leader who guided his province with great vision yet made life a nightmare for those in his personal sphere who might otherwise love him.

"A codex in my library describes weapons similar to those used by the *Ascendant* minions," Jax said. "They rely on something called 'particle physics.' The source of the orange light is a sub-electronic particle called an abiton, the antiparticle of a biton. Whatever that means. It has a rest energy of 1.9 eV and a charge of 5.95 raised to the negative 25th power. And this charge is called *Coulomb*. It's the same as the name in the Amperman line, I'm sure of it. The gun uses a magnet of 0.0001 Tesla and its accelerator needs a radius of five centimeters." He held up his hand, his thumb and forefinger a short distance apart. "This is a centimeter."

The others remained silent, watching him as if his words were an incantation.

"If his people have these weapons," Jax said, "they may well have other devices described in the old codices."

"It be a bad omen," Lector said.

"Is it? Or a promise of the future? I would like to see more of these wonders." Jax rubbed his chin. "Then there is Lionstar's language. He speaks pure classical Iotic."

"You mean Iotaca?" Lector asked.

Who cares what they speak? Kamoj thought. *Tell us what happened.*

"That's right," Jax said. "The temple language."

"But no one understands it any more," Lector said.

Jax shrugged. "That's only because the ancient glyphs are different from those we use now. The temple priestess has a different accent than Lionstar. I have trouble understanding the priestess, but Lionstar is easy."

"I cannee understand him at all," Lector said.

"Your dialect is more removed from Iotic," Jax answered. "Classical Iotic was the language of the highborn here, in the days before the Current died. Lionstar probably inherited it the same way I did, as a nobleman descended from an ancient line." He paused. "But I don't think it's the native tongue of his people. Petrin told me that on the *Ascendant*, the crew spoke a language he didn't understand."

Petrin? It took Kamoj a moment to figure out he meant the Ironbridge stagman Vyrl had stabbed, the man the metal bird had taken to the *Ascendant*.

"Yet they all speak Iotaca to Lionstar," Lector said.

"He is their liege," Jax pointed out.

"He does seem to have authority."

Kamoj began to relax. If Vyrl had died, surely Jax would have said something by now.

"It's more than his authority," Jax said. "He's *valuable* to them, beyond being their prince. His people would kill every one of us to protect him, if it became necessary. And how do they move so fast? What do they have inside their bodies that lets them do that?"

"It be a bad affair," Lector said. "Like that old sorceress who rides with him."

"They don't use sorcery. Just knowledge we've forgotten." Longing showed on Jax's face. "What must their armies be like? It stretches the mind to imagine it."

"I cannee imagine it, sir."

"We had better try. We have to know what we're fighting." Jax glanced at Kamoj. Although she averted her gaze, it wasn't before she saw his pain, the vulnerability toward her that he strained to hide whenever it escaped his defenses.

"None of Lionstar's party were close enough to decipher my wife's outburst," Jax said. When she looked up, he was talking to Lector again. "But it has spurred the *Ascendant*'s people to investigate. They are bringing an 'Arbiter' tomorrow to resume the Inquiry. If we don't cooperate, they threaten to use force."

Lector frowned. "If they be so powerful, why do they hesitate with this 'force'?"

"They don't want to exacerbate the situation," Jax rubbed his chin. "Apparently I'm a leader they expect to deal with when they institute 'formal assimilation procedures' here."

"I donnee understand that," Lector said.

Dryly Jax said, "Nor do I." He fell silent and the stagmen waited. Finally he said, "Well, Lector, what do you think?"

"Sir?"

"Give me your opinion on the situation."

"You must never give in to Lionstar. It would weaken your authority."

"My thought also." Jax blew out a gust of air. "But by the Current, man, how do I maintain authority here?"

"I donnee know, sir. But you must."

Disappointment flickered across Jax's face. Although he glanced at the others, he didn't seek their counsel. It didn't surprise Kamoj. What could they say? He was so far beyond them in intellect and education that his asking for their advice was like Vyrl asking her how to sail a skyship.

Finally he said, "My wife and I will remain here tonight, in case Lionstar violates the truce his people set up and tries to find her. I will need the three of you on watch outside."

"It be our honor," Lector said.

Jax nodded, then dismissed them. After the soldiers left, Jax continued to sit on the boulder, staring at the ground, his face pensive with his thoughts. Finally he looked at Kamoj. "Come here."

She walked over to him. Even wrapped in Argalian wool she still shivered.

"Why are you wearing Lector's cloak?" he asked.

"I was cold. He gave it to me."

"Delicate Kamoj." Bitterness edged his voice. "Pretty delicate rose. I truly am a fool, because I still love you."

"Jax—"

"No." He shook his head. "Tomorrow you will be asked to sign the merger and annulment contracts before witnesses, with an X since you can't write your name." He regarded her steadily. "You will do this, Kamoj. I will tolerate no more betrayals."

She swallowed, afraid to voice her question yet needing the answer. "And if I refuse?"

Softly he said, "Then I will kill you. I will see you dead before I let these conquerors take what belongs to me."

14

The Price of Silence

Steepest Descent

A voice pulled Kamoj awake. For the past few hours, she and Jax had been sitting against a wall of the burrow, dozing. She couldn't truly sleep. Her hunger and thirst had grown even worse. The mere act of breathing had become a battle against the constriction of her clothes. The cold felt as if it permeated to her bones.

Jax slept fitfully. He had neither cloak nor jacket, and he still hadn't laced his shirt. Frost lined the hairs on his chest. His quirt, sword, and leather sword-belt lay at his feet.

"Governor Ironbridge," the voice repeated. A stagman stood within the shadows by the burrow entrance.

Jax stirred, then sat forward, rubbing his eyes. "Lector? Come here, man. What is it?"

Lector came over and knelt by him. "You had the right of it, sir. Lionstar attacked the camp. There was fighting."

"I don't suppose Lionstar is dead by any chance?"

"No, sir. No one died."

Jax rubbed the back of his neck. "What is the situation?"

"We did as you said and made use of the spelled box the *Ascendant*'s minions gave you."

"Did anyone answer?"

"Indeed," Lector said. "The *Ascendant* sent a metal bird. It took Lionstar and left ten of those large stagman who wear black. They be at the camp now."

"Ten?" Jax tensed. "As conquerors or protectors?"

"We donnee know. They say nothing."

Jax considered him. "I want you to send a message to the *Ascendant*. Tell them I've changed my mind about this Arbiter of theirs, that I will go with their first choice after all."

"Sir?"

"They chose a woman. I refused." Jax pushed back his hair. "This is the message: 'His honor, the Governor of Ironbridge, accepts the *Ascendant*'s first choice of Arbiter. Although he has discomfort with this, as women don't serve as judges here, his wife says she would feel more comfortable talking to a woman.' "

Kamoj stiffened. She had never said that. She had no desire to talk to anyone. She just wanted this to be over and done.

After Lector left, Jax drew Kamoj into his arms, pulling Lector's cloak around them both. He spoke against her hair. "You are so warm under here."

She wondered how his body worked, that he thought her warm when she felt so cold. If only he had a kindness to match his physical strength and prodigious intellect.

"This is why he attacked my camp," Jax said. "He knows I'm alone with you." His voice sounded strained. "How does he do it, Kamoj? How can he see what is in your heart so much better than I?"

"He feels emotions." It stunned her that Jax revealed such vulnerability. Did he know his pain filled his voice?

"His bodyguards feel them also, don't they?" Jax asked. "To a lesser extent."

"I think so."

Anger honed his words. "Shall we give him more emotions to feel at the Inquiry?" He rubbed his hand over her breast. "The feelings of a man and his wife together?"

"Jax—"

" 'Jax,' *what?*" He clenched his hand, bruising her skin. "A lifetime we've built together. Then in one day you throw it all to a stranger who invades our land, steals our loved ones, mocks our ways, and plunders our dreams." His voice hardened. "You pushed me too far, calling for him. I can't let it pass."

Sweet Airys, no. As he reached for his belt, Kamoj tried to shield herself with her hands. Her tight sleeves stopped her from lifting her arms, but it soon didn't matter. Jax wanted no clothes separating her from his anger. He showed her the ways of his belt, its every texture. Then he held her in his arms and showed her the ways of himself, giving her memories meant to torment Vyrl as much as please himself.

Later, when he had fallen asleep, she tried to blank the pain from her mind. To forget. If only she could forget.

The Ironbridge camp took form out of the morning's misty light. Stagmen were everywhere: Ironbridge in violet and silver, Lionstar in copper and blue, *Ascendant* in black.

Kamoj rode on Mistrider in front of Jax. Lector and Tera rode their own mounts, flanking them. She could imagine how they looked, emerging out of the prismatic mist, other-worldly and antediluvian on their greenglass stags. The small size of their party accented their vulnerability to Vyrl's people, helpless natives come to face a rampaging skyship prince. She wondered if Jax had planned it that way.

Exhaustion shrouded her mind. In the last three days she had eaten once and slept only a few hours. The chill pene-trated her bones. She fought to bring air into her lungs, and her body ached with each breath.

Kamoj had made her decision. She had tried to look at the greater scheme of her world and beyond, to think past the daze in her mind and her deep-seated fear of Jax. If Vyrl's people separated her from Jax, she knew now that he would never rest in his drive to exact revenge and reclaim what he considered his possession—her. It would never end until she appeased Jax or he died.

She had to consider whether the *Ascendant* could guard her people, every moment of every day, from now until the day Jax passed from this life. In that question, she saw a grim future for her province, its existence constrained by the need for protection from the very same outsiders who had created the situation that threatened Argali in the first place. It made no difference how great the *Ascendant*'s power. Their formidable weapons could never stop the true danger, the destruction of the gentle way of life her people cherished. The welfare of too many people rested on the honed edge between the *Ascendant*'s attentions and Jax's unrelenting vengeance.

However, Vyrl's people could help hers, by teaching them better food production, health care, housing, and more. If she stayed with Vyrl and his goodwill toward her continued, he could do a great deal for her province—but at the price of hostility between Argali and Ironbridge. If she stayed with Ironbridge, she and Jax could negotiate for that aid as representatives for a united Northern Lands—but it left her with Jax. Vyrl's people seemed inclined to help their rediscovered colonies. From what she had overheard Dazza tell Vyrl, it sounded like they might be even more willing in this case, to compensate for the upheaval they had caused.

With Ironbridge, her well-being depended on Jax's goodwill, but the Northern Lands benefited. With Vyrl, the well-being of the Northern Lands depended on his goodwill, but she benefited. Jax had a deep, abiding connection to Balumil, whereas Vyrl would soon leave. If she stayed with Vyrl, his departure would weaken an already troubled situation. If she stayed with Jax, then Vyrl's departure would be better for everyone concerned.

And, too, the events off Balumil had more import than this one world. She had picked up enough to realize it could cause a crisis for Vyrl's people if the difficult situation here hobbled their actions elsewhere.

None of the solutions was ideal. All had problems. But on balance, the Argali-Ironbridge merger seemed better for everyone—except herself. And if she bore Vyrl's child? That too had an answer, one even more painful. She would give Vyrl the child to raise. If he never returned to Balumil, she would send it to him. To lose her child that way would tear her apart, perhaps more than she could bear, but it was better than the alternatives.

She had her answers. And if she mourned them, at least she had done her best to choose well. Vyrl wanted her to believe she had other options, but she saw none. After all that had happened, this seemed the path she must take.

Twelve soldiers waited outside Jax's pavilion, four each for Ironbridge, Lionstar, and the *Ascendant*. As Jax rode to the tent, three boys ran to meet them, staghands in breeches and heavy furs. After Jax and Kamoj dismounted, the boys led away their mounts. The Ironbridge and Lionstar stagmen bowed, and the *Ascendant* soldiers watched Kamoj with an unsettling intensity. Were they trying to know her emotions?

The privacy of her mind was her last refuge. She didn't want them there.

I am a lake, she thought. *A flat lake. No ripples.*

An Ironbridge man spoke. "The Inquiry awaits inside."

Jax nodded. Kamoj wondered how he had arranged to have Vyrl's people wait for him. A morass of conflicting authorities surrounded them here, complex and intricate.

Flanked by stagmen, they entered the pavilion. Braziers warmed the tent, and the sudden heat made Kamoj queasy. The Inquiry members waited at the table where Jax had signed the contracts yesterday. His priestess and judge were already there. Two *Ascendant* strangers also waited: a man of average height, with brown hair and the manner of a clerk; and an older woman with dark eyes, an aquiline nose, black hair streaked with gray, and a spare, lean build. Shimmers covered the strangers. They dressed like Dazza, in gray jumpsuits having no ornamentation except the exploding sun insignia on one shoulder. Only they and Kamoj carried no weapons; all the stagmen wore swords, and the *Ascendant* soldiers had snouted weapons on their belts.

Everyone at the table stood up as Jax entered. Then a rustle came from behind them. Turning, Kamoj saw eight soldiers enter the tent, four *Ascendant* and four Lionstar.

A man with iron-gray hair walked among them.

He towered over the stagmen, massive in build, with a face of granite-hewn lines. He also wore the gray uniform, but his had gold ribbing on the sleeves. His presence riveted attention. Kamoj needed no introduction to tell her that this man carried authority. The force of his personality filled the tent.

Vyrl came next, flanked by bodyguards, two large Jagernauts who seemed to be holding him prisoner as much as protecting him. Seeing him, her heart raced. Neither he nor Jax spoke; instead, the two rulers stared at each other, their hostility almost thick enough to touch.

Vyrl had no weapons, ceremonial clothes, or diskmail.

Kamoj had never seen garb such as he wore: gray trousers with a crease down each leg and cuff at the bottom; a white sweater that would have looked normal except for its high, folded neck; and shoes with no visible seams. The fabric of his trousers was so fine she couldn't see the weave. She knew no one who could sew such a flawless garment.

At the table, the *Ascendant* woman spoke. "It would be best if the weapons remained outside the tent."

There was a shifting of feet, hands sliding on hilts, the crackling of braziers. Kamoj waited for Jax to refuse. If he or his stagmen gave up their weapons, Ironbridge relinquished what share of authority it had so far managed to retain.

Incredibly, Jax removed his sword belt and handed it to one of his stagman, then nodded for his men to remove theirs. After an awkward silence, Vyrl told the Lionstar stagmen to disarm. The man of power from the *Ascendant* watched with an intent gaze that Kamoj suspected missed nothing. When he glanced at the two Jagernauts guarding Vyrl, they gave slight nods, acknowledging his unspoken order. The other twelve soldiers left the tent, but Vyrl's bodyguards remained.

Jax considered the Jagernauts and the bulky black weapons on their belts, the "antiparticle guns." Then he looked around at the *Ascendant*'s other minions, his accusation obvious without his uttering a word.

The *Ascendant* woman at the table spoke. "Given the conditions of Prince Havyrl's arrest, the Jagernauts cannot remove their guns while standing guard on him."

At the word "arrest," satisfaction flickered on Jax's face. He made no further dispute. It surprised Kamoj, given his intent to establish authority. That was done with behaviors that displayed the expectation of obedience. But then, such methods would do little good here, given the superiority of the *Ascendant*'s people in everything from weapons to physical size to clothing. This battle would be fought in more subtle ways.

She suspected Jax had hidden a knife somewhere on his body. It made no difference that one knife was nothing against "antiparticle guns"; the symbolism was what mattered to him.

So everyone stood, waiting. Then Vyrl sat down across the table from Kamoj. She eased into her chair, trying to hide how much her body hurt. The *Ascendant* man of power sat next, followed by everyone else. A rustle came from the tent entrance and the twelve soldiers reentered, all unarmed now.

A new person walked with the soldiers. Dazza Pacal. As she sat at the table, the Ironbridge judge frowned and glanced at Jax. Yet again, Jax made no protest. Instead he nodded to the colonel as if it were perfectly natural for her to attend an inquiry that concerned his personal life and had nothing to do with her. Of all people, he was the last Kamoj would have expected to show such flexibility.

Lean and hawklike, the unfamiliar *Ascendant* woman looked around the table. She had a crisp aura of authority. "I am Major Cara Tulain." She nodded to the man of power. "General Hamilton Ashman."

Kamoj froze. Ashman. *Ashman.* He commanded the *Ascendant.* This was the man who had made the decision to leave Vyrl buried alive above the sky.

"I will serve as Arbiter for these proceedings," Major Tulain continued. "Is this acceptable to all parties?"

Jax spoke in a quiet voice. "Ironbridge accepts."

"Yes," Vyrl said.

The Arbiter waited. When the silence became awkward, she said, "Governor Argali?"

Kamoj tensed. Now what?

"Major Tulain." Jax regarded her evenly. "A governor in Kamoj's position, that is, in a merger that both she and I represent, can choose to listen rather than speak at a proceeding such as this. I will represent us both."

"In other words, she won't talk unless he lets her." Vyrl's voice grated. "As her owner."

Jax tried to look patient. Tulain glanced at Vyrl, then back at Jax. "Is that true?"

"Prince Havyrl chooses to see our lives through the filter of his experiences," Jax said. "Although this is understandable, given his condition, it makes no sense to confuse our customs with those of the people you are at war with, a people we have no connection to at all."

"Confuse hell," Vyrl said.

Tulain gave him a warning glance. Then she spoke to Jax. "Your willingness to adapt to our procedures for the benefit of Governor Argali has been noted and appreciated. However, we can't proceed with this hearing unless she participates." She turned to Kamoj. "If you wish to speak to any of us in private first, we can arrange that as well."

Jax spoke softly to her. "Please. Feel free to speak."

Kamoj knew she was too tired, hungry, thirsty, and in too much pain. Jax knew it too. If she said something he didn't like, she would pay for it later. She had made her decision. Prolonging this would only open her up to Jax's wrath.

"I appreciate your offer," she told the major. "But I need no secluded consultation. I have no secrets from my people." She nodded to Jax. "I wish Governor Ironbridge to represent us."

"I object," Vyrl said.

"She has the right to make the request," Tulain said.

"What's wrong with all of you?" Vyrl said. "Can't you tell she's afraid of him?"

"Perhaps it isn't me that she fears," Jax said.

"Like hell," Vyrl said.

The Arbiter held up her hand. To Kamoj, she said, "In this Inquiry you are under the protection of Imperial Space Command. No one can force you to do anything you don't want." Gently she added, "Do you understand what I'm saying?"

"Yes," Kamoj said. Why did they talk to her as if she was a child? Couldn't they see she was an adult?

"All you have to do is ask," Tulain said. "But the request must come from you."

"I understand." Kamoj didn't want their protection. The price was too high.

"Do you still wish Governor Ironbridge to speak for you?" Tulain asked.

"Yes."

Vyrl made a frustrated noise. "Major, she doesn't trust us."

Tulain considered Kamoj. "We *can* protect you. We won't let anyone hurt you." She paused. "That includes Prince Havyrl as well as your husband."

"He's not her blasted husband," Vyrl said.

Tulain turned to him. "Perhaps it would be better if we addressed that question through proper Inquiry procedures."

Vyrl scowled, but said nothing more. Ashman watched them with piercing concentration, letting his minions probe while he analyzed. Kamoj suspected that he was, by far, the most dangerous person in the room.

Tulain's assistant set a black book-box on the table, then opened it to reveal a sheaf of parchments. Tulain lifted the top paper. "The question," she said, "is whether or not these contracts were willingly signed by Kamoj Argali. Her signature is in your hand, Governor Ironbridge."

"Kamoj can neither read nor write," Jax said.

"Is she aware of what you signed for her?"

"Of course. She was here when we discussed it."

"Prince Havyrl contends you coerced her agreement."

"Prince Havyrl is mistaken."

As the questions continued, the scene blurred for Kamoj. She could think only of food and sleep. But the Inquiry ground on. They covered every detail of her life since the day Vyrl had seen her in the river. The picture that formed was twisted around, yet nothing was false. She *had* said she dreaded the Lionstar-Argali merger. She *had* removed Vyrl's mask in the coach. He *hadn't* known her name, or even remembered he was married.

Then came the statements from the palace staff. Vyrl's servants went far beyond the expected fealty. Again and again they expressed their devotion to him. They spoke of humane working conditions, of wages that allowed them to climb out of poverty, of Vyrl's talent with grains and livestock, his innovation with crop rotation, his cleverness in using tiny flying lizards to aid crops. All described his kindness. Although Jax sat quietly, Kamoj felt his growing anger. He had never expected this.

But every statement stumbled when it came to Vyrl's drinking, his moods, his tormented nights. With his marriage to Kamoj, the stumbles became lurches.

Tulain read the comments of the housemaid who had come to help Kamoj the morning after her wedding. " 'She looked so scared,' " the maid said. " 'So vulnerable. And she be clutching a doll. A *doll*. Like a little girl. I know his Highness be a good man, I know it truly. But this—I don't know what to say.' "

In the silence that followed, Jax said, "Kamoj and I weren't to marry for at least two more years."

"Under the laws of our people," Tulain said, "she can't marry for another seven. That's about eight of your short-years."

"What?" Vyrl sat forward. "What are you talking about?"

Jax snorted. "Perhaps you need to learn your own laws, Lionstar."

Vyrl ignored him, his attention on Tulain. "She can choose to marry for life when she's twenty-five."

"That's right," Tulain said.

"But she's older than that."

Thank you, Kamoj thought. Although he was wrong about her age, at least he treated her like an adult.

Everyone else just looked at him. Finally Dazza said, "Vyrl, Kamoj is eighteen."

"That's impossible," he said. "Look at her. *Talk* to her. She's a grown woman."

"Her people were engineered for accelerated physical maturation," Dazza said. "To increase their useful years as slaves. That trait manifests in Kamoj. She reached adulthood years ago. As Argali's ruler, she's also had to shoulder more responsibilities than many adults twice her age. And in this culture people marry young. Kamoj is actually considered old for a bride. But legally she *is* a child."

Vyrl sat back in his chair. Watching him, Kamoj felt his defeat. He knew how he looked. He glanced at her and flushed, as if he believed she too thought him a monster. If she unveiled her mind, maybe he would sense her true feelings for him. He never seemed to catch her emotions fully, though, only in pieces, and what she felt now, more than anything else, was exhaustion.

After an awkward silence, Tulain picked up a blue paper and glanced at Vyrl. "This is a transcript of your conversation with Colonel Pacal when you took Governor Argali riding." She scanned it, then read, " 'Look at this. My wife. A farm girl who looks like a virginal sex goddess, and all she asks is a simple life, a husband who doesn't beat her, and the freedom to walk in the woods.' "

When Jax stiffened, Kamoj didn't think he was acting. Vyrl's words probably did offend him, though not for the same reasons everyone else looked uncomfortable. Jax considered it his right to beat her.

"It's not the way it sounds," Vyrl said. "I was drunk."

"It also says your stagman Azander had a bruise on his face where you hit him." Tulain considered him. "What exactly did you mean by 'a husband who doesn't beat her?' "

"Gods, Major, I was in the middle of a convulsion when I hit Azander. If you want to know what I meant, ask him." He stabbed his finger in the air, at Jax. "He thinks it's his right to hit her. In bed, no less."

Jax rose out of his chair. "You will not speak of my wife in this manner."

Vyrl stood up. "She's not your wife."

"Gentleman, sit down," Ashman said.

Jax exhaled. Then he nodded to Ashman. "My apologies, General." He sat down, leaving Vyrl standing. After an awkward moment, Vyrl sat down as well.

Kamoj hated this. Jax was making Vyrl look worse and worse. Neither Tulain nor Ashman seemed disposed to speak in Vyrl's defense, and she didn't dare. Dazza, however, could. Kamoj stared across the table at her, sending a silent plea.

Dazza blinked at her. Then she turned to the Arbiter. "Major Tulain, a fairly easy way exists to establish the truth of at least some accusations being made or implied by both parties in this disagreement."

"Go on," Tulain said.

"I can examine Kamoj," Dazza said. "If she's been mistreated, I'll know. And I can probably tell by whom."

Jax tensed. "My wife has suffered enough indignities at the hands of you people. I will tolerate no more."

Vyrl leaned forward. "Are you afraid of what they'll find?"

"Why don't we ask Governor Argali?" Tulain said.

Kamoj gritted her teeth. She didn't want anyone touching her. The idea of being "examined" was revolting. All she had wanted was for Dazza to speak in Vyrl's defense, so he didn't come out of these proceedings looking like a monster.

"Why can't you all leave her alone?" Jax said. "Hasn't she endured enough?"

Tulain regarded Kamoj. "Governor Argali, no one will force you to be examined. But you have the right. If it shows you've been mistreated, it could change the nature of this hearing."

"Change it how?" Kamoj asked.

"At the moment," Tulain said, "the only evidence supporting Prince Havyrl's contention that Governor Ironbridge used coercion is that the servants at the palace were bound, gagged, and unconscious. Governor Ironbridge claims his people restrained them because they interfered when you wanted to leave. The palace's web system was inoperative, and we weren't monitoring the palace at that moment. We had our attention on the fires and Prince Havyrl."

They were all watching her now: general, colonel, major. Too many titles. The priestess frowned and the Ironbridge judge's face had gone hard.

"I've chosen to stay with Ironbridge," Kamoj said.

Vyrl spoke in a soft voice. "Kamoj, last night you shouted for me. Why? If you wanted to stay with him, why did you call me back?"

"You misheard," Jax said.

"Everyone heard her," Vyrl told him.

The Arbiter spoke. "Prince Havyrl, you are the only one who thinks he understood her actual words."

"Damn it!" Vyrl hit the table with his fist. "I heard it because she *said* it."

Jax sighed. "What my wife shouted was an oath. I'm sorry this is so hard for you to accept, Lionstar. You heard what your overwrought mind wanted to hear, not what she said."

As Vyrl stood, his face flushed, the Arbiter said, "Prince Havyrl, please. Sit down. Your outbursts help nothing."

Vyrl clenched his fist. But then he sat down. Kamoj couldn't focus on his face. The room was dimming around her.

The Ironbridge judge spoke. "Governor Argali has stated her wish to remain faithful to her husband. What more do you people require before you stop tormenting her? The only reason this Inquiry exists is because Havyrl Lionstar refuses to believe the truth. He is the one who took her to his bed without her consent."

Diskmail clinked, and Azander appeared at the table. The Arbiter glanced at him, then at the people seated around the table. When no one objected, Tulain spoke to Azander. "Yes?"

"I be sorry to interrupt," Azander said. "I wish to make a testimony."

Jax blinked. So did everyone else. Kamoj wondered what Azander was doing.

"What do you wish to say?" Tulain asked.

"When Prince Havyrl be near to dying in the large metal bird, Governor Argali spoke for him. She convinced them to take him home instead of to the *Ascendant*."

Tulain nodded. "Yes, we have that in your testimony."

"It not be said proper on that parchment you read before," Azander said. "It mattered to Governor Argali that he be well treated. The caring for him, she has it."

Dazza spoke to the Arbiter. "I know what he's saying, Cara. And he's right. I've seen it too. Kamoj has worked miracles with Prince Havyrl, reached him when none of us could come close. His well-being genuinely seems to matter to her."

"Of course it matters to her," Jax said. "Kamoj cares about everyone. It is one of the many reasons her people respond so well to her." His voice tightened. "That Lionstar took advantage of this doesn't excuse his behavior."

Vyrl stiffened, but this time he controlled himself. None of the others seemed to know how to respond. Nor did Kamoj. She had never known Jax saw her that way. He let her think he found her lacking, keeping her on the edge between trying to please him and doubting herself.

Ashman regarded Vyrl. "Did you know she was like that?"

"Not when I married her," Vyrl said.

The two of them kept looking at each other, fighting their own private war, which Kamoj suspected had started long before she met Vyrl. Finally Vyrl stood up. His guards tensed, and several Ironbridge stagmen dropped their hands to their belts, reaching for swords they no longer carried. Vyrl ignored them all and walked away, stopping only when he reached a brazier across the width of the tent.

He turned to Ashman. "Imperial Space Command went to great lengths to get me, lengths so extreme it boggles the mind. Why? Because I'm a great leader? A vital member of ISC? A brilliant strategist? No. Because I'm a Ruby telepath. So why do you doubt me now when I tell you what that *thing*—" He pointed at Jax, "—is doing to Kamoj?"

"Because you've been in a telepathic catatonia for months," Ashman said.

Dazza spoke quietly. "Vyrl, she's the first person you've responded to since you came on board the *Ascendant*. How can *you* be sure of your reactions?"

Vyrl lowered his arm. "I'm sure." He regarded Dazza. "You know how it can affect a person to endure severe mistreatment. Look at hostages or POWs. Keep at it long enough and you can make them 'choose' to do whatever you want. He's had years to set the foundations and he's working with someone genetically engineered to respond to his influence. Can't you see what he's doing to her?"

"You're the only one who has picked up anything about abuse either yesterday or today." Dazza motioned at his bodyguards. "They haven't."

"They aren't Ruby telepaths."

Ashman glanced at the Jagernauts, who had moved to stand near Vyrl. "What are you getting from her?"

"Fatigue," the first man said. "She wants this Inquiry to end."

The second man nodded. "She resents ISC presence here."

That's right, Kamoj thought. Sweet Airys, but she needed to sleep. She stood up slowly, aware of everyone in the room. The world went gray and tilted sideways. She planted her hands on the table to stop herself from falling. Leaning forward, she said, "I invoke a close to these proceedings."

"Kamoj?" Vyrl asked. "What's wrong?" As he started toward her, the others at the table rose to their feet.

In the same instant that Ashman said, "Leave her alone, Valdoria," Tulain asked, "Governor Argali, do you need help?" and Dazza said, "Give her room!"

Kamoj stared at them. It occurred to her that if she didn't eat soon, she was going to die.

15

Consent

Three Particle Scattering

The table was slipping past Kamoj. Jax caught her as she lost her balance. Sagging against him, she heard voices, something about Elixson.

"Keep that hag away from her!" Jax said.

"Ironbridge, don't be a fool," Vyrl answered. "Colonel Pacal is a healer, better than any you have here in camp. Let us help her."

"Don't touch her, none of you."

As Jax lifted Kamoj into his arms, darkness encroached on her thoughts. Her body ached. Then the fresh smell of his bed enfolded her. Someone had washed the covers. She flinched, trying not to remember the last time she had lain here. It made her want to curl in on herself. Jax was a blur above her, wavering in a dark fog. She strained to see, but the mist thickened until it enveloped everything.

A change came in the pitch of voices. Struggling, she pulled her mind back into focus. Jax and Vyrl were standing a few paces apart now, their voices rising in volume.

"—think you can take whatever you want," Jax said harshly.

"That problem is yours, Ironbridge, not mine." Vyrl stepped forward, his fists clenching at his sides.

"Don't threaten me." Jax put his hands against Vyrl's shoulders and shoved him away.

They went at each other then, grappling like wrestlers. As they fought, locked together, Vyrl closed his hands around Jax's throat. Jax stumbled back and fell across the Inquiry table with a crash, knocking over a lantern.

The Jagernauts were also moving. One grabbed Vyrl and the other Jax, both straining to hold their enraged captives. They yanked Vyrl and Jax apart, one Jagernaut gripping Vyrl by the arms, the other holding Jax.

Vyrl swore, fighting his guard's iron grip. For an instant Jax looked too stunned to respond. Then he tried to jerk his arms away from the giant who had caught him, a move he could easily have managed with a stagman, had one of his soldiers been stupid enough to try restraining him. It made no difference to the Jagernaut. Only when Jax quit fighting did the *Ascendant* man let him go.

"You have no right." Kamoj wasn't sure who she meant: Jax, the *Ascendant,* or all of them. Jax had gone too far, and Vyrl's people wanted to rescue her from a crisis they created. She tried to get up, but her body wouldn't respond.

The bed creaked. Then someone lifted her head into his lap. She rolled onto her back and saw Jax's face above her. Just as she had often massaged his temples, so now he did the same for her. Kneeling behind her, he held her head on his legs and gave her comfort with an inborn rhythm designed into his genes. She didn't miss the bitter irony, that he responded to the pain he had caused, as a descendant of the owners, by giving her the succor he was bred to provide as one of the owned.

A bruise purpled his face where Vyrl had hit him, and a ragged hole gaped in the shoulder of his shirt. Vyrl stood at the end of the bed, flanked by his gargantuan bodyguards with their antiparticle weapons.

Jax raised his gaze to Ashman. "Why don't you all go back to your starships and leave us alone?"

The general spoke. "You will have to let my doctor examine Governor Argali."

"No," Jax said.

Kamoj swallowed. "Jax, I don't feel well."

He stroked her hair. "Elixson can take care of you."

"She needs food," Elixson said.

"I fed her," Jax said. "Right after you and I spoke."

Elixson stared at him. "Sir, the Current has gifted you with an endurance well beyond normal folk, that you can go a day and more without food, walk through sleet and never notice, or ride for days without rest. Your wife is a hearty young woman, but compared to you, anyone is fragile. You must learn to account for that. She has to eat four times a day, at least two of them full meals. She must sleep at night and wear warm clothes when she is exposed to the weather."

Dazza spoke in a voice as chill as the day outside. "Governor Ironbridge, exposure and starvation are considered methods of coercion."

"You don't call what you people are doing coercion?" Jax looked around at them. "Sending Argali a corporation I could never match even if I worked at it my entire life? Playing with the future of the Northern Lands as if it were nothing? Attacking my camp during a 'truce.' Threatening us with your soldiers and your weapons and your 'assimilation?' "

"None of that justifies your actions toward Kamoj."

You let me freeze on purpose, Kamoj thought, her anger like ice. Jax had felt attacked by Vyrl's people, with good reason, but he responded by trying to control *her.* She doubted he would admit it to himself; his lack of sensitivity to the needs of others came from his inability to appreciate the extent of his physical enhancements. But she found it easy to believe he also instinctively used the cold, the lack of food, even her discomfort in breathing to control her in a situation he felt had gone beyond his power to contain.

"I need time," Kamoj said. Her depleted condition affected her ability to think. She heard the rustle of camp outside, the snort of a greenglass, the shuffle of boots. She felt as if her mind were dissociating from her body.

Dazza pulled off the belt she wore. Or no, not the entire belt, but a part of it. When she ran her hand along the strip, it changed into a flexible tube.

The colonel spoke to Jax. "This fires a needle that contains a drug. It won't harm you, but it will put you to sleep almost immediately."

Several Ironbridge stagman started toward her. As soon as they moved, Ashman motioned to Vyrl's bodyguards and they also stepped forward.

Jax shook his head at his stagmen, a sign for them to back off. Relief flickered on their faces. Kamoj knew they would have defended Jax if he hadn't stopped them, but they had little chance against the Jagernauts.

Jax spoke to Dazza, his words bitter. "So you too lied about having no weapons. Why is it that I have no surprise at this deception?"

She didn't answer, only raised her sleep tube. Jax jerked a piece of metal-work off his boot—and slapped his knife against Kamoj's throat. "The only way you will have her," he told Vyrl, "is as a corpse."

Everyone went still. Then Dazza spoke carefully. "Don't hurt her."

"Kamoj, sit up," Jax said.

Somehow she pulled herself up on her knees. She moved with caution, not only to avoid provoking Jax, but also because she feared to set off the Jagernauts. Even with their unusual speed, they couldn't reach Jax before he stabbed her. But they would get him soon after—and then Vyrl would take Jax's life. He had said as much to Dazza: *If it were me, I'd kill the bastard.*

At times in the past, Kamoj had wished Jax dead. Her own capacity to hate shook her almost as much as his cruelty. Would she cause his murder now? She could never live with that knowledge, that to escape Jax, she had become like him.

If she survived.

He held her between his legs so they were both kneeling, she with her back against his chest. The flat of his blade chilled her neck. When he shifted position, the razor edge nicked her skin. Vyrl stood at the foot of the bed, watching, his face strained, his fist clenched. His bodyguards stood on either side of him, their hands on their guns, their posture making them look like barely contained weapons ready to explode. They glanced at Ashman, but he gave his head a slight shake. *No.*

Major Tulain spoke. "What do you want us to do, Governor Ironbridge?"

"Where is Baldarin?" Jax asked.

"Who is Baldarin?"

"The Ironbridge archer who shot Prince Havyrl," Jax said. "Your people were holding him in Argali pending the decision on whether or not to 'press charges.' Where is he now?"

"He's still in Argali," Tulain said.

"What about the fires?" Jax asked. "Didn't you evacuate him with everyone else?"

"Argali didn't burn," Tulain said. "Only one outlying village was lost. We put out the other fires."

Jax expelled an incredulous breath. "It is truly amazing, what you people do. Stop fire in its tracks, fly above the sky, heal mortal wounds in a day. We are nothing to you, just a bunch of barbaric ex-slaves." His voice hardened. "I want to know what this means, 'pressing charges.' "

"It is part of our laws," Tulain said. "If Prince Havyrl chooses to press charges against the archer, the man will go on trial for attempted murder."

Kamoj felt Jax turn toward Vyrl. "Are you going to 'press charges?' "

"No," Vyrl said. "He can go free. Whatever you want."

"Good." Jax turned back to the Arbiter. "I, however, would like to press charges."

Tulain tensed. "Against who? And for what?"

"Against Prince Havyrl Torcellei Valdoria," Jax told her.

"For the attempted murder of my stagmen last night, when he attacked this camp during a truce. I also want to file suit with your civil authorities to protest the way Prince Havyrl and your ISC have treated my people." He pointed at the table. "I want the evidence from this Inquiry made part of the record."

"Your testimony is being recorded," Tulain said. "So your charges are in the official record."

"That's not good enough." Jax motioned at Vyrl. "You all would do anything to protect him. Without some guarantee, my comments will never make it past this tent."

General Ashman had his full concentration on Jax. No hint of his thoughts showed on his face, only an impassive focus that disquieted Kamoj far more than would have anger or chill regard.

"You have our guarantee of due process," Tulain said.

Jax snorted. "As I had your guarantee of a truce last night?"

"We're recording this Inquiry," she said. "We will provide you with copies of that record and a web system to verify them, as well as equipment to contact whomever you wish to represent your case."

"It's not enough," Jax said. "I have no way to stop you from setting your machines to break after you have what you want."

"What is it you would have us do?" Tulain asked.

"When your people returned my stagman to Ironbridge," Jax said, "a delegation came with him, including a man called Drake Brockson. He told me that he is part of an organization that represents worlds like ours in the Imperial Assembly, to ensure we aren't mistreated. I want you to contact him. I want his representation."

"Professor Brockson is an anthropologist, not a legal counsel," Tulain answered. "He can't represent you."

"Then he will find me someone who can," Jax said.

Ashman spoke. "No."

Vyrl swung around to him. "What?"

"I will not submit to threats," the general said.

"Damn it, Ashman," Vyrl said. "He's not bluffing. He'll kill Kamoj."

"The answer is no."

Jax moved the knife on Kamoj's neck. "You have fifteen seconds to contact Brockson."

Tulain stared at him. "You would kill your own wife? The woman you've fought this entire conflict for? Doesn't that defeat your whole purpose?"

"Nine seconds," Jax said.

"If she dies," Tulain said, "you have nothing."

"Seven seconds."

"Are you willing to give up everything?" Tulain asked. "Your realms, title, freedom, possibly your life?"

Jax turned the blade so its edge lay against a large vein in Kamoj's neck. "One second."

"Ashman, do it!" Vyrl's voice snapped out. *"Now."*

Jax paused, rigid against Kamoj's back. Ashman and Vyrl stared at each other, locked in a battle that Kamoj knew had started before they came to her land. Who was the authority, the imprisoned prince of an ancient dynasty that supposedly no longer ruled, or a leader in the military that had served that dynasty and now controlled an empire?

Still watching Vyrl, Ashman spoke in a harsh voice. "Major Tulain, contact Brockson. Have the transcript of this Inquiry transmitted to him."

Kamoj almost sagged with relief. Jax turned the knife, setting the flat of the blade against her neck.

Tulain contacted the *Ascendant* using her aide's bookbox. Watching her "upload files," Kamoj felt a hazy detachment, as if she were an observer in a distant place. The knife made a bar of ice against her throat. No one spoke. No one moved.

The blow came from the side.

Kamoj glimpsed the unfamiliar Jagernaut in her side vision when he eased under the edge of the tent. Jax must have also seen him. It happened exactly as she had feared; in the instant that the Jagernaut lunged across the open area to the bed, Jax hurtled himself backward, his arms locked around Kamoj. Even with enhanced speed, the Jagernaut couldn't reach them fast enough; instead of catching Jax, his hand closed around Jax's sleeve and ripped it off his shirt. The man also fired a sleep weapon, but with Jax already moving, the shot missed.

"Liar," Jax spat at Ashman, stabbing his knife at Kamoj's heart—

"*NO!*" Vyrl shouted. In the same instant, Tulain said, "Wait! Brockson is transmitting his reply."

Jax froze, the tip of his knife touching Kamoj's chest. "And?"

A man's voice came into the air. "Governor Ironbridge, this is Drake Brockson. I will take your case and find you legal representation."

Kamoj saw Ashman's sour look. Apparently Brockson's word was good.

Jax must have seen it as well. He spoke wearily. "Good." Then he let go of the knife.

The blade fell down Kamoj's front and onto the bed. Holding her around the waist, Jax sagged forward, resting his head against hers. "I'm sorry," he said in a low voice. "If it makes a difference, I couldn't have done it. I could never have killed you."

He held onto her, rocking back and forth, a ritualistic motion Kamoj knew well, having often lapsed into it herself. Dazza watched them with a strange expression, as if what she saw was breaking her heart. She raised her sleep tube and the expected hiss came. Although Jax stiffened, he made no protest. When Kamoj felt his weight slump against her, she knew he had passed out.

Ashman turned to Vyrl. "You said he wasn't bluffing."

"I wasn't sure," Vyrl said. "I couldn't take the chance."

"Damn it, Valdoria." Ashman looked as if he wanted to

throttle Vyrl. "With Brockson on the case we can't keep it quiet. Do you have any idea of the political repercussions this mess will create?"

"What would you have me do?" Vyrl demanded. "You said it yourself. I've been in a telepathic catatonia. I couldn't be sure he wouldn't kill her."

Dazed, moving on instinct now, with almost no conscious thought, Kamoj extracted herself from Jax and slid behind him. Then she laid his head on her knees, just as he had done earlier with hers. When she began to massage his temples, everyone stopped talking and stared at them.

Vyrl looked as if his heart were tearing in two. He came forward. "Kamoj, you don't have to do that."

Kamoj cradled Jax's head, her thoughts ragged. Her fatigue had gone beyond definition, and she felt a hunger so great it hollowed her.

As Vyrl knelt on the bed, Dazza warned, "Leave her be."

Vyrl shook his head. "She needs—"

"Valdoria, don't be an idiot," Ashman said. "Touch that girl again without her consent, and I'll throw you in the brig myself."

Vyrl looked ready to punch Ashman. But he stood up, moving away from Kamoj. Ashman's words echoed in her mind. *Consent. Consent. Consent.*

"Governor Argali needs to eat," Elixson said.

"Can you get her something?" Dazza asked. "Plain broth, if you have some."

Elixson spoke to a stagman and the soldier left, the entrance flaps swinging back and forth after he was gone, back and forth, back and forth . . .

Kamoj swayed. Her arm was growing numb from supporting Jax's head. She shifted, easing him into a new position.

"Gods, no," Dazza whispered.

One of the Jagernauts spoke in a stunned voice. "She must have incredible mental control. I never detected her pain."

Confused by their words, Kamoj tried to focus on Dazza. The colonel was staring at her arm. Looking down, Kamoj saw that when she had moved Jax's head, it had dragged the sleeve of her dress up past her elbow. There, for all to see, was her shame, the bruises and welts that covered her skin.

Vyrl turned to Ashman. "Now do you believe me?"

Dazza sat on the bed and spoke with care. "Kamoj, let us help you."

"It isn't over yet," Kamoj said.

"I won't touch either you or Governor Ironbridge without your permission," Dazza said. "But if you let me, I can treat those wounds." She swallowed. "And any others you have."

"And then?"

"Come with us, Kamoj. Please."

To her own ears, Kamoj's voice sounded as if it came from far away. "Nothing will be solved. Jax will still be angry, even more bent on revenge. Vyrl will still leave. Argali will still be in danger. The people I love will still forfeit their lives."

"We'll leave soldiers here," Dazza said. "As many as you need, even if we have to put armed garrisons in every province."

"Don't you see?" Kamoj asked. "We'll be your wards. It makes us like infants. Nor have we ever had a garrison. We have lived without needing one for five thousand years."

"I am truly sorry." Dazza watched her with that unbearable compassion. "At least let me help you now. Let me heal you."

"It will hurt." Kamoj didn't mean only the physical pain, but also that which went deep into the identity of her land. The world was changing in ways that none of them could stop.

"I can numb your wounds," Dazza said. "What I did with your foot the other night. You won't feel anything."

Kamoj swallowed. "Yes. Do that."

"We need to separate you from Governor Ironbridge."

"No."

"We won't hurt him."

"What will you do?"

"He's just sleeping," Dazza said. "We'll leave him here with his healer. He'll wake soon enough."

Kamoj turned to Vyrl. "You must not kill Jax."

"I don't want to kill him," Vyrl said, though his expression suggested otherwise. He sat on the bed, ignoring Dazza's warning look, and spoke to Kamoj in a low voice. "If I could take the pain of all this on myself, I would do it in a second. I can't change what's already happened. But I can promise I will do my best to see it never happens again."

Kamoj wanted to believe him. But the Inquiry had revealed another painful truth. Vyrl's people would never step back from Balumil, not even if she stayed with Jax. They wouldn't just help warm houses and increase crops, then leave her people alone. No matter what choice she made, the Northern Lands would never be the same. On the day that Vyrl's people had come here, Balumil had changed forever. She could mourn the loss of their way of life, but she could no more stop the changes than she could bring the *Ascendant* down out of the sky.

No best path existed. She understood too little about Vyrl's people to find one.

What, then, could she do?

Her history with Jax spanned her life. The traits designed into her ancestors were meant to drive her, to make her cleave to him now, to never question, change, or upset the balance, to respond only with unwavering loyalty to the one who claimed her body and her soul as his possession.

Kamoj thought: *No.*

Moving with care, she set Jax's head on the bed. She slid closer to Vyrl and nausea swept over her. She waited for it to subside, then moved another hand span. The nausea surged. She was aware of people watching her, but she didn't care. Right now she could deal only with this journey of hand spans.

After an eon of starts and stops, she reached Vyrl. Looking up into his face, she said, "I want to go with you." She reached for him. "Take me home."

Vyrl took her into his arms. No one spoke. No one told him to let her go. No one said a word.

Tears ran down her face as she held him, her head buried against his shoulder. She made no sound as she cried.

And so she defied five thousand years of conditioning.

16

Moongloss

Predissociation

Moonlight silvered the bedroom, flowing through the window above the desk. Kamoj had discovered she couldn't lie down in a bed when they returned to the palace; just the thought made her ill. Although she let Dazza examine her, she wanted no one else to touch her, not even Vyrl. But she couldn't bear the idea of being alone, either. Even knowing General Ashman had moved in a "regiment" of the Pharaoh's Army to protect Argali, she still felt painfully vulnerable.

So Dazza settled into her armchair by the nightstand, this time to keep a vigil over Kamoj. Vyrl also stayed, but he and Kamoj sat against the headboard of the bed, she curled on her side with her legs drawn up, the two of them separated by several handspans, both fully dressed, he still wearing his *slacks* and *turtleneck,* she in a farm tunic and leggings. The room's warmth and the potions Dazza had given her lulled her into a doze . . .

Voices woke her. "—won't let you leave the palace," the colonel was saying.

"Why?" Vyrl asked. "Where do they think I'll go?"

"Nowhere," Dazza said. "It's a house arrest. Ashman let you come down here because it's better for Kamoj. But if you leave the palace, he'll order your return to the *Ascendant*."

"What, so he can 'throw me in the brig himself?' "

Dazza spoke quietly. "He acts in the best interest of the people. Your people."

It was a moment before Vyrl answered. "I know. But that doesn't make it any easier."

"If we could settle this mess with Ironbridge, Ashman would be a lot happier."

"Ironbridge doesn't want to settle. He wants to punish me." His voice grated. "He's a real piece of work. You would think after five thousand years the owner genes would have disappeared here."

"Why? Genes aren't altruistic."

Kamoj opened her eyes just enough to see Dazza. "But you know," the colonel was saying, "about forty-five percent of his DNA traces to slave stock. In some ways he's the ultimate product of the breeding program, even more so than Kamoj. That's why his physical makeup is different from hers. Can you imagine the metabolism he must have? He also has a triple stomach. How does it fit in his body? I would love to examine him. His DNA is like nothing I've seen."

"How do you know his DNA so well?" Vyrl asked.

After an awkward pause, Dazza said, "From Kamoj."

Vyrl swore. "I can't believe she's letting him get away with it. How can she insist we don't use the evidence against him?"

Dazza's answer chilled Kamoj. "She and Governor Ironbridge love each other."

Vyrl stiffened. "Love, hell."

"They have a fifteen-year history. You can't expect her to

undergo a complete change of attitude in a few days." Dazza regarded him steadily. "I'm not saying she doesn't also hate him. That's what makes this so difficult for her."

Kamoj didn't know how to fit Dazza's words into the confused pain inside her heart. She wanted to forget what had happened with Jax.

"Why isn't she angry?" Vyrl clenched his fist on his leg. "Why am I the only one who wants that bastard drawn and quartered?"

"She *is* angry," Dazza said. "What do you expect her to do? She's been in this situation almost her entire life with no out, at least not in her view. She probably felt she had to repress her anger for the survival of her people. She's not going to show it in ways you expect. She might turn it inward, become moody or withdrawn. Or she may lash out at you."

"Me?" Vyrl blinked. "Why me?"

"Because you're here." Dazza's voice gentled. "And because she trusts you. She knows you won't strike back."

I don't want to hurt anymore, Kamoj thought.

"How should I respond?" Vyrl asked.

"Just be yourself. Doctor Tager is going to work with her, but she'll still need time." Dazza sighed. "Gods know, I wish she would press charges."

Although Kamoj had no wish to "work" with anyone, it meant a great deal to her to know that Vyrl wanted to help. She opened her eyes all the way. "Maybe Jax would bargain."

Vyrl turned with a start. "You're awake."

"How are you feeling?" Dazza asked her.

"Better." Kamoj considered the colonel. "If I threaten to 'press charges' against Jax, he won't know I'm bluffing. He might reduce his complaint." It would infuriate him to discover that an Inquiry could investigate what he had done with her. To lose face that way, in front of his people, was something she doubted he would tolerate.

She just hoped he didn't call her bluff.

* * *

Rain drummed like the fingers of an impatient giant against the stained glass window in Kamoj's chamber. Lightning flashed, followed by thunder. After two days back here, she could lie in bed at night again, though she had retreated to her own chamber rather than sleep with Vyrl. But she hated thunderstorms, even more so now than before.

The next time the thunder crashed, she jumped out of bed. The beads in the archway clacked when she ran through them. In the main bedroom, rain pattered against the shimmer in the window, turning into a fine spray when it diffused through the curtain. As she raced across the room, her white nightgown rippling, lightning slashed the night. Thunder came almost on top of it, like a giant clapping his hands around her head. She cried out, then ran up the dais and scrambled into Vyrl's bed. She yanked the covers up until only her eyes showed.

"Hmmm." Vyrl rolled over, half asleep. He started to slide his arms around her, then hesitated.

"It's all right." Although Kamoj tensed when he embraced her, she appreciated his solidity.

"It's good to have you back," he said.

"I don't like thunder. But I can't—you and I . . ." She flushed, unable to continue.

"Kamoj, it's all right." He regarded her with a sleepy gaze. "We won't do anything you aren't comfortable with."

She wondered how he and Jax could be so different. Despite the inarticulate nature of her attempts yesterday to explain how she had felt trapped by the situation with Ironbridge, Vyrl had seemed to understand.

He leaned his head against hers. "Sometimes it seems like honor and responsibility have no link at all to personal happiness."

"Hai, Vyrl." It unsettled her when he picked up her mood so well. "I regret the hurt it caused you."

"I'm glad those were the reasons you turned from me. I had feared . . ."

She waited, then said, "Yes?"

He spoke with difficulty. "That you annulled our marriage because you found out I was crazy."

"It isn't annulled. And you're not crazy."

"Damaged, then."

"Nothing is wrong with you."

He touched her cheek. "Don't look at me with blinders. Just because I haven't had a drink in a few days doesn't mean I no longer have a problem."

"Your problems are on the outside. Under them, you're a good person." In that way, he was the reverse of Jax.

Vyrl murmured in a voice she almost couldn't hear. Then she realized he had said **thank you,** not in words but in her mind. It didn't alarm her, though. It felt natural.

She spoke softly. "Your people take longer than mine to grow up, don't they?"

"Yes. Your bodies pass through childhood faster."

She could tell he was leaving out something. "But?" When he hesitated, she said, "Please. I want to know."

"You lose a child's learning capacity sooner." He frowned. "That was probably the intent. It's why your people have trouble with education."

Disappointment washed over her. "You mean I can never learn to read?"

He nuzzled her ear. "I think you could learn anything you set your mind to."

The touch of his lips on her skin had a drowsy quality, as if he wasn't completely awake. Kamoj made a conscious effort to relax in his arms. She needed to believe he would still want her when she was ready to be his wife again. Surely she could try one kiss. She tilted up her face, but he only pressed his lips against her forehead.

What was wrong? Did he no longer desire her after what had happened?

Her thought must have been stronger than she realized. Opening his eyes, he said, "Kamoj, no. What happened—

that doesn't matter to me. I just don't want to push you too fast." He squinted at her. "And you are so very young."

She almost laughed then, both from relief and at his words. "You, who married at fourteen, think I'm young?"

He gave her a guilty look. "Lily and I ran away. Our parents were furious when they caught us."

"But they let you stay married."

"It was easier to convince them after the fact. And by then, well . . . Lily was pregnant."

"That didn't take long," she said dryly.

He reddened. "It never seemed to."

"Wasn't it illegal for you to marry?"

"Actually, no. In the Hinterland colonies, local law supersedes Imperial law if the bride and groom are both natives." He shifted her in his arms. "It has to work that way, if the colonies are going to survive. Where I grew up, we have no minimum age."

It made sense to Kamoj. "We don't have one here either."

"I'm not a Balumil citizen, though. But you probably qualify as an emancipated minor. We'll have to fill out a lot of forms, but the legal people on the *Ascendant* say we should be all right." His expression became uncertain. "That is, if you want to stay married."

"I do." She spoke with quiet confidence. "I don't care how your legal people measure age. I neither think nor love like a child."

His voice softened. "And can you?"

"Can I?"

"Love. Me."

Whatever her other fears, she knew that answer. "Hai, Vyrl. Always."

He pulled her closer. "I also, water sprite. For you."

She closed her eyes, content in this cocoon of safety. Thunder rumbled, more distant now, its threat receding until the next storm.

* * *

Kamoj found Dazza standing in the early morning sunshine that slanted through a glass door in the gold and ivory sitting room. The colonel gave her a friendly nod. "Are you looking for Vyrl? He's working out in the old throne room."

"Actually . . . I had a question." Kamoj made herself ask. "You will leave Balumil soon, yes?"

Dazza didn't try to put her off. "Yes. I'm afraid so. But you could come with us."

"I must stay here. Argali is my responsibility."

"Can't your uncle govern in your place for awhile?"

"How long?"

Dazza started to respond, stopped, then said, "The truth? I don't know."

Kamoj wanted her to understand. "I was a toddler when my parents died. Maxard took care of Argali for most of my life. His lady in the North Sky Islands has waited many years for him, but she won't do so forever. He cannot go to her if he must take over Argali again, and she cannot come here because she governs one of the smaller islands."

Dazza's forehead furrowed. "I thought Governor Seaward ruled the Islands."

"Yes. But each also has its own governor, who answers to Seaward. Maxard's lady is also a merchant, so she travels among the islands a great deal." Kamoj pushed back her hair. "It would be wrong for me to thrust Argali back on Maxard. He spent too many years doing for me and our people, putting the province ahead of his happiness."

Although Dazza smiled, she looked sad. "That seems to be an Argali trait."

"When do you go?"

"Two days. But you won't be on your own. We're leaving the regiment here to protect Argali." Her voice quieted. "We misjudged before. I'm sorry. Ironbridge won't hurt you again."

Already it had started, what she feared, the soldiers and the changes. She didn't want to think about Jax. The hurt was too deep. She wouldn't shame herself by shedding tears in front of Dazza. Instead she gave a formal nod. "Thank you."

"Kamoj—" Dazza had that look again, as if her heart were breaking.

Kamoj just shook her head. She left the streaming sunshine and returned to the Long Hall with its moongloss walls.

The Hall of Audiences was at the west end of the palace. In past millennia, tapestries had hung there, vivid in gold, rose, and green threads. Glass sconces molded into leaf clusters had glowed with candles on the walls. On the dais at the far end, a great chair had stood, inset with Argali gems. The governor sat there when her people sought an audience.

The hall had long ago fallen into ruin. Vyrl's people had cleaned out the debris, leaving the room burnished and bare. They had started to lay a new yellowbirch floor, but had only finished about half the room. For some reason mirrors covered two of the walls.

A clank came from one wall. Looking down its length, Kamoj saw Vyrl lying on his back on a bench, raising and lowering a bar with metal slabs attached to it. Sweat drenched his pants and pullover shirt.

Kamoj worried about his exertions. A few days ago he had been near death. For all the incredible deeds of the *Ascendant* healers, surely he must take more care with himself.

The machine clanged as he lowered the weights. For a moment he lay with his arm over his eyes. Then he got off the bench and sat on the floor, facing away from her. With mesmerizing ease, he did a perfect split and put his head on his knee.

Oh, my. Kamoj had often watched people stretch. Dancers at the harvest festival always warmed up before they performed. But she had never seen anyone accomplish it so well. The knot inside her heart eased, letting a pleasant flush spread in her body. Such a finely made man, this husband of hers.

But then he stopped. Drawing up his legs, he rested his arms on his knees and stared off into space.

Drawn like a firepuff fly to a rose vine, Kamoj walked down the hall. When she was a few paces away, Vyrl spun around, his body tensing. He relaxed when he saw her.

"Good morning," he said.

"My greetings." She stopped, suddenly shy. "May I talk to you?"

"Of course. You don't have to ask." He sat on the bench and beckoned for her to join him.

Sitting down, she stared at her hands. Then she made herself look at him. "Dazza says you're leaving soon."

His smile faded. "Yes. I'm afraid so." He started to reach for her, then stopped and winced. "Just what you need. Hugs from a man soaked in sweat."

She managed a smile. "Better that than none at all."

"I will come back. I swear it."

"Of course." She couldn't help but feel that once he left, he would be like a dream that vanished, never to return.

"I mean it." He took a circle-towel off a post on the weight machine and dried his chest. "I've already completed the application forms to let me live on Balumil." He wiped his face with the towel. "Right now it's a technicality, since I'm in ISC custody. But I'll need documents for permanent residence."

Her hope surged. "You will live here?"

"When I can, yes."

She was afraid to hope, afraid she had misheard. "I thought General Ashman wouldn't let you stay."

He considered her for awhile, until she wondered if she had somehow misspoken. Then he said, "I shouldn't talk about this. But I want you to understand why I have to go. Ashman's people have been planning a mission to free my home world, Lyshriol, from Earth's occupation. They're ready to move now and they need me to make it work."

That caught her off guard. "You could be hurt!"

"The danger is more that I will lose my freedom back to Earth's forces."

"I would never see you again."

He took her hand. "Come with me."

"I can't." But Kamoj no longer felt certain of that decision. After all that had happened, one fact had become clear; she needed to know more about the Skolians, not surface qualities, but the in-depth knowledge of their lives and cultures that would help her lead Argali through this time of upheaval.

"I just hate being separated from you," he said.

"Vyrl . . . what if ISC won't let you come back?"

He spoke tightly. "They can't hold me for the rest of my life, controlling where I go and what I do."

"What of your family? Your farm. Your children." She thought of the many generations that called him patriarch. "Your kin all live on Lyshriol."

He regarded her with a tender-hearted gaze. "My children are all grown, with families of their own. But Argali needs you."

Kamoj squeezed his hand, understanding the gift he offered. She felt the depth of his love for his family and knew how hard it would be for him to leave Lyshriol. "I will miss you."

"And I you." He tried to smile. "It won't be for long."

Not for long. If only those words were more than an elusive dream.

The "robot" invaded the suite, rolling on its tread, agleam with bronze planes and curves. It had no head, just a boxy body. Although it stood only half as tall as Kamoj, it was much wider. After Vyrl's stagmen loaded his bags onto its platform, it rolled across the suite. As Kamoj watched in perplexed fascination, the robot extended a jointed limb and opened the door. Then it left the suite. She followed, accompanied by a bemused Azander.

On the landing, the robot grew legs. They unfolded from

under its body, and it rose up on them until it was as tall as a large man. Then it proceeded to walk down the stairs.

Kamoj and Azander blinked at each other. "Do you think it's alive?" she asked.

He scratched his chin. "I cannee say that I know, ma'am."

They went after the robot, listening to the clank of its feet on the stone. Kamoj wondered what Vyrl fed it.

When they reached the bottom of the stairs, they saw the robot in the Long Hall rolling blithely along, its legs folded up and hidden under its body again. It turned into the ballroom and vanished from sight.

Kamoj and Azander pursued the robot and came out of the palace into streaming blue sunshine. They found it sitting in the courtyard. Across the flagstones, a giant metal bird crouched on the ground. It had neither wings nor legs, though, only the gold and black planes of its body. One of Vyrl's bodyguards stood next to the craft.

Sheathed in shimmers, men and women worked in the courtyard, directing robots, talking, or doing things that made no sense to Kamoj. An oval suddenly opened on the bird, creating a doorway. Kamoj swallowed, as unsettled now by the strange behavior of these metal creatures as on the first day she had seen one.

Vyrl walked out through the oval, accompanied by his other bodyguard. She saw the difference immediately; today Vyrl wore neither cloak nor mask. Instead, a shimmer molded to his body, almost transparent. He had on suede trousers, knee-boots edged with blue quetzal feathers, and a white shirt with belled sleeves and thong laces up the front. She recognized the style; many highborn men in the Northern Lands wore such clothes. But the extraordinary cloth! Faint rainbows glimmered around his shirt, haloing his upper body. A diamond chain circled his neck and splintered sunlight into rainbow sparks. The ring on his left hand sparkled with a star sapphire.

Kamoj wanted to run over and throw her arms around

him, but she thought it might add to the image his people had of her as a child. So she walked, trying to appear dignified, with Azander at her side.

Vyrl smiled as they came up to him. "Good morning."

She gazed up at him, suitably dazzled. "You look nice."

He gave her a rueful look. "I didn't want to leave you with an image of me in a metal face or old farm clothes."

It touched Kamoj that it mattered to him. She had worn a dress for him, with lace at its hems and embroidery on the rose velvet. She traced her finger over his sleeve. The rainbows vanished when she covered the cloth. "How does it do that?"

He took her hand in his. "It's holographic. That means it makes images."

"It's remarkable." She glanced at his neck. "I've never seen a chain made that way before."

"My father gave it to me when I was a child." He unclasped the chain, then lifted her hand and poured the chain into it.

Stunned, she realized the links were solid diamond with no seams. "Don't the diamonds fracture when the jeweler tries to form the links?"

He shook his head. "The crystals are synthetic, made by nanobots. These diamond structures are called jizate. Your carriage was made in a similar way, but with a pearl composite, which is harder to do."

So it was true about the carriage. She gave him back the chain. "It's gorgeous." Shyly she added, "Especially on you."

He grinned as he refastened it around his neck. "I'll have to wear it more often, then." But his teasing had a strained quality.

Dazza walked out of the metal bird. Seeing Vyrl and Kamoj, she came over to them. "We're almost ready. If you would like some time . . . ?"

"Thirty minutes?" Vyrl asked.

Dazza nodded. "We'll wait."

Kamoj and Vyrl walked to the forest beyond the courtyard. His two bodyguards also came, but they stayed a few paces away, one in front, one behind, giving Kamoj and Vyrl a degree of privacy.

They followed a path that wound into the mountains. The dirt glinted with crushed scales, and shafts of light cut through the trees, making the dusty air glitter. As they walked, holding hands, the bustling noise from the courtyard faded. Quetzal hoots echoed in the forest and trillflies hummed. Kamoj even heard warble-angels, those graceful fliers with music-box cords in their throats that played a bittersweet harmony. Knowing she might never see Vyrl again, she wanted to save this memory, as she might wrap a treasure in gold velvet and store it in a rose-box.

Eventually they left the path. The canopy of scale leaves blocked the blue-tinged sunlight, so almost no underbrush grew here. Turquoise moss and Argali rose vines draped the widely-spaced trees. When they found a shelf of rock in a hill, they sat together. Their bodyguards took up discreet positions, not too close, not too far.

Vyrl still didn't speak. Instead he cupped her cheeks and bent his head. His lips touched hers, glossy with the shimmer membrane on his body. Then the membrane shifted, making a seal with her skin. So they kissed, sheathed in a glistening halo.

Eventually they stopped and hugged each other. With her cheek against his, feeling the shimmer on his skin, she was more aware that his people were strangers here, even less adapted to Balumil than her own.

After a while Vyrl drew back. He took off his sapphire ring and slid it onto her finger. "My grandfather gave this to my grandmother. She bequeathed it to my father, he gave it to my mother, and she gave it to me." He folded her small hand in his large grip. "Now I give it to you."

"It's beautiful, Vyrl. But are you sure?" She thought it must mean even more to him, after his father's death.

"I trust it into your care." He squeezed her hand. "Someday you can give it to our child."

Her voice caught. "I will do that." She didn't ask if they could have children. Too many other painful questions came with that thought.

So they sat together, holding each other one last time in the prismatic forest.

The palace felt empty. Kamoj wandered the halls, aware of *Ascendant* soldiers here and there, tall in their black uniforms. They bowed when she encountered them.

Across from the Hall of Audiences, the *Ascendant*'s people had set up "consoles" in the Games Room, where centuries ago denizens of the palace had challenged each other to games or contests. Now strange alabaster forms filled the room, with colored lights on their surfaces and ghosts rotating in the air above them. Morlin's heart existed here, though she wasn't sure what that meant.

As she stood in the archway of the Games Room, the people working inside glanced at her, their curiosity obvious. She seemed to fascinate them. Self-conscious, she left and headed down the Long Hall. She sought privacy in an alcove, then stopped when she heard a man and a woman talking in the adjacent sitting room. As she turned to go, the woman said her name:

". . . Kamoj Argali has a lovely sound."

Kamoj froze, disconcerted.

"A fitting name for a lovely woman," the man said.

"What will their children look like, heh?" The woman chuckled. "Neither she nor Prince Havyrl are bodysculpted, either. They come by their good looks naturally."

The man spoke quietly. "They were bred for it."

The woman's voice turned uneasy. "I wouldn't talk that way about a Ruby prince, Jak."

"It's a fact," Jak said. "Prince Havyrl knows."

The woman was silent for a moment. Then she asked, "Do you think Governor Argali is a telepath?"

"Not a telepath. But an empath, yes."

"She seems . . . I don't know. Shell-shocked."

"She's been through a great deal."

"Are you going to take her as a patient?"

Jak sighed. "I wish she would let me. But she shies away. She's like a beautiful wild animal that's injured and doesn't know why she hurts."

Unwanted tears threatened Kamoj's eyes. She slipped away and escaped their conversation.

You're mine again. Gritting his teeth, Jax added, *Except he had you first.*

Then he hit her.

No! She struck at him, struggling, *struggling*—

Kamoj sat bolt upright, her heart pounding. Ghostly light from the stained glass window filled her chamber. She wiped her palm across her face, smearing tears.

Too troubled by her dream to sleep, she pulled on her robe. Then she went into the main bedroom. Vyrl's bed stood empty on the dais. She wrapped her arms around her torso, trying to find warmth against a chill that came from within her.

Restless now, she went downstairs. She passed a few servants cleaning rooms, but no one she could talk to without breaking unspoken rules of protocol. When she had tried earlier, it had made them uncomfortable. She couldn't talk to Vyrl's people either; they treated her more like an exotic flower than a person.

Light spilled out of the Games Room. Kamoj stood in the archway, watching the people work. Some were ensconced in chairs that looked more like machines than places to sit. Silver meshes enclosed their bodies and hoods hid their faces. She wondered if the machines communed with them.

Closer to the door, a woman without a visor was studying ghost images above her console. She smiled at Kamoj. "Good morning, Governor Argali."

Morning? It was the middle of the night. Kamoj had discovered that even when the *Ascendant* people spoke her language, they didn't always share the same concepts. But she appreciated the friendly overature. "My greetings, ma'am."

The woman tilted her head. "May I ask a question?"

"You may." It pleased Kamoj that the *Ascendant* woman had observed the proper protocol for seeking information from a governor.

The woman leaned back in her chair. "Why did your ancestors abandon this building? It's charming."

"We couldn't afford the upkeep of both Argali House and the palace. We would have had to take resources from Argali that it couldn't give us."

"You don't tax Argali to pay for the palace?"

"Well, no. Of course not." Kamoj couldn't imagine such a thing.

The woman sighed. "Would that the rest of our leaders followed your example."

Kamoj wondered if the woman was ridiculing her. They both knew Balumil had little to offer Vyrl's people. She gave a formal nod. "I will leave you to work."

The woman seemed puzzled. "If I gave offense, please accept my apologies."

That blunt acknowledgment of their awkward interaction startled Kamoj. She felt exposed. "No need to apologize, Goodwoman—" She stopped, flustered. She had no idea what name to add. So she gave another nod and then departed before anyone else could speak to her.

Kamoj slept in Vyrl's bed, hoping to feel closer to him. Instead she felt cold. After awhile she got up, donned her robe, and went to the window near the desk. Four pastel moons shone low in the sky, all crescents, some thick, some thin.

A knock came from the entrance. She turned with a start. Who would disturb her now, when most people were taking their second sleep of the night?

Kamoj opened the outer door to find yet another stranger.

A Jagernaut. He towered on the landing, a giant in black, with broad shoulders, a rugged face, and dark curls.

"I'm sorry to disturb you, ma'am." He sounded as self-conscious as she felt. "I'm afraid we've a bit of a situation below."

"What is the problem?" she asked.

"An envoy from Ironbridge has arrived. He refuses to speak to anyone but you." The Jagernaut frowned. "You don't have to talk with him. I'll deliver any message you wish to send."

She pulled her robe tighter. "Why would he deliver his message in the middle of the night?"

"We don't know." A gleam came into his eyes. "If you wish, I will interrogate him."

Kamoj blinked, disconcerted by his flinty tone. "That won't be necessary." A note of fear crept into her voice despite her efforts to project calm maturity. "Will you stay with me while I speak to him?"

"Most certainly, ma'am. You needn't worry."

So she went with him to a sitting room off the Long Hall downstairs. Another Jagernaut waited at the door, a man with yellow hair. Across the room, the Ironbridge stagman stood by the glass doors. Blue moonlight poured through the panes and turned him into a ghostly figure.

As Kamoj came up to him, the stagman gave a stiff bow. She didn't ask the Jagernauts to light the lamps. Cold moonglow fit Ironbridge matters better than golden radiance.

"You have a message?" She kept her voice cool. Anyone who demanded an audience at this hour forfeited the usual courtesies.

He withdrew a scroll from his bag and gave it to her. "I believe this explains the matter."

Puzzled, Kamoj opened the scroll. Written in a bold hand, glyphs covered the parchment. In the moonlight, the ink appeared silver, but she knew it included other hues. Purple. Black. Ironbridge colors.

She recognized a few of the glyphs. The arched bridge meant Ironbridge, and the rose framed by curling vines was Argali. The rearing greenglass stag referred to a nobleman's honor guard. The rest were a mystery.

She looked up. "You may give the message."

The stagman regarded her, his eyes black. "I donnee know what it says, Gov'nor. I woulda never be a'looking at private letters."

Kamoj's stomach clenched. The insult bit deep. Messengers always memorized their letters. By sending only the parchment, with no oral recitation, Jax gave her a deliberate affront. To find out what the scroll said, she would need Airysphere Prism from the Spectral Temple. She couldn't summon the priestess until tomorrow. It would be well into the new day then, and many people would hear what had happened. So much time and effort, all because she couldn't read.

The dark-haired Jagernaut spoke at her elbow. "Governor Argali, may I have the honor of reading the scroll for you?"

His question was so unusual that it took her a moment to absorb. Then she remembered: most of Vyrl's people could read.

Kamoj turned to him with gratitude. "Thank you, Goodman." She had no name yet to add to the title, but she hoped he understood the honor she meant. He had just negated the humiliation Jax intended. As she gave him the scroll, the Jagernaut with the yellow hair moved closer, keeping watch on the messenger.

The dark-haired Jagernaut studied the codex. "It's an invoice of some kind."

"Invoice?" Kamoj didn't recognize the word.

"A statement of money and goods you owe Ironbridge." He scanned the scroll. "The Ironbridge jewels? Something about your debt to a corporation. It says 'Ironbridge requires payment in kind.' "

Heat flamed in her face. Of course. Jax wanted his dowry back. It was only right. But *payment in kind* meant he expected it in the exact same form he had given it. He knew it was impossible. She still had the Ironbridge heirlooms, and he had his lands and holdings, but she had invested the metals and gems to support Argali farms. She could recover some of the gold bridles, but it meant buying them back from their purchasers. As for the foodstuffs, firewood, wines, and other perishables, they were long gone.

With dismay, Kamoj saw what would happen. She would send alternate wealth in place of the vanished items. Jax would refuse the replacements. He had the right. No judge in the Northern Lands would begrudge him that response, given the circumstances. They would have to negotiate. He could draw the process out for years. It would humiliate Argali and shame Vyrl. It didn't matter that as Vyrl's consort, she had the wealth to repay Jax a hundred times over. She didn't have the *right* payment. It would make her look mercenary; she had used Jax's dowry and then chosen Vyrl.

Kamoj turned to the messenger, wishing protocol allowed her to banish him from the palace. She spoke with frost. "Tomorrow you may return to Ironbridge and inform your lord that the debt will be repaid in full."

"As you wish, so I will do." He bowed, his face shadowed. When he straightened, she saw the smoldering anger he tried to hide and knew he understood exactly what message he carried. He had no sympathy for Lionstar.

As the yellow-haired Jagernaut escorted the messenger out of the room, Kamoj walked to the window and stared at the mountains.

"Governor Argali?" The dark-haired Jagernaut spoke behind her. "Would you like this?"

She turned to see him offering the scroll. With stiff fingers, she accepted it. She wanted to dash it to the floor or rip it up. Taking a breath, she set it on a table by the window.

He spoke in a kind voice. "Can I help?"

She looked up at him, self-conscious in his presence because of his muscular build and great height. No wonder they all saw her as a child. Next to them, she probably appeared half-grown.

"Thank you for your gracious offer," she said. "But I am fine." Why did he look like that, as if he hurt for her? Then she remembered. Jagernauts were like Vyrl. Empaths.

Softly she said, "How can you bear it?"

A smile tempered his strong features. "What do you mean?"

"Being both a soldier and an empath. Doesn't it tear you apart?"

He didn't answer at first. Then he said, "We take our title, Jagernaut, from our ships, the Jags. They're single-pilot starfighters. As a Jagernaut, I meld with my ship's Evolving Intelligence brain."

She tried to imagine what he described. "You join your mind to your ship. To become a better fighter?"

"Yes. That's why we must be psions." His next words came with difficulty. "You're right, it can hurt to be both a Jag pilot and an empath. It's hard for me to talk about, Your Highness. I'm sorry."

"I understand." She hesitated. "May I ask your name?"

"Certainly. Secondary Antonyo Lopezani."

"Antonyo Lopezani." She liked the way it rolled on her tongue. "It is a beautiful name, Goodman Lopezani. Like a song. But why Secondary?"

He seemed to relax. "It's my rank. We start as Quaternaries. Most reach Tertiary and retire. Some become Secondary. A very few reach Primary."

Kamoj gave him an approving look. "Then, sir, you must be an accomplished stagman."

He grinned. "I guess you could say that." Now his face showed kindness. "Are you sure I can't help you in any way?"

"Tomorrow, perhaps. I need a—" She stopped, uncertain of the correct word. "A liaison? Someone who can help me integrate my position among your people with my position as governor."

"I can arrange for that." Concern shaded his voice. "We didn't wish to push you today."

Kamoj wanted to tell them she wasn't as fragile as her namesake, the vine-rose. But they meant well. Besides, apparently her name had nothing to do with roses. Long dead strangers had chosen it for the invisible chains they hoped would hold her people forever. She longed to tear apart those bonds, but they were so intertwined with her personality, she wasn't even sure how to find them.

Antonyo escorted her back to her suite, walking at her side. His presence comforted. After her abduction from this very hall, her home, the center of a place where she should have been safe, she felt as if no haven existed anywhere.

Inside the main bedroom, she laid her robe across the foot of Vyrl's bed. Then she slid under the covers and curled into a ball. Her tears came softly in the night, lonely and silent.

17

Mists of the Heart

Transition (B → A)

It will take a while to install heating units in all of Argali's houses," Lieutenant Endar finished. "But we should have it done before the winter comes."

Kamoj nodded, seated behind her desk in the Ivory Suite. She had chosen this room as her office because of its many glass doors, with their curved gold handles and gold filigree. They let in copious amounts of light, giving her a sense of optimism. The room had a high ceiling and white walls with gilded trim. She also liked the desk. Its wide expanse formed a bulwark, making her feel more prepared to face the *Ascendant* minions.

Lieutenant Endar had showed up as her liaison. He looked hardly more than a boy, but he seemed sure of himself. He wasn't as tall as the other Skolians, and he had black hair and dark eyes, like her people. It put her more at ease. She also appreciated that he neither condescended to her nor spoke over her head.

As it turned out, he didn't come from the *Ascendant*. It had already "left orbit," though Kamoj wasn't sure what that meant. Although she had never seen any of Balumil's seas, she could envision a great body of water stretching to the horizon. But a sea of space? How did one imagine such a thing? She wondered if it had swells and seaweed.

"The heating units will be a blessing to my people," she told Endar. "Last winter we lost so many to the cold."

He regarded her with an earnest gaze. "That won't happen again, ma'am."

His manner touched Kamoj. He gave the impression that he genuinely cared about Argali. "Spring and fall are times of life. We have many children in those seasons and our population grows again. But so many of our people—" She swallowed, thinking of her parents. "So many die when the weather becomes harsh."

He spoke quietly. "We can change that."

She took a deep breath. "These 'techs' who will do the work—where do they come from, if the *Ascendant* is gone?"

"We've several ships still in orbit."

Curious, she asked, "Which is yours?"

"One of the frigates. *Aniece's Bounty*."

"Aniece? What is that?"

He beamed at her. "Ma'am, Aniece is one of your husband's sisters."

She smiled at his enthusiasm. "Do they name many ships after his family?"

"A few." He leaned forward. "I do believe an Imperial dreadnought has the name *Havyrl's Valor*."

"Goodness." Kamoj thought it a fine name. She wondered what dreadnought meant, though. She didn't ask, not wanting to appear provincial.

A voice came from the doorway. "Governor Argali?"

Looking up, she saw Antonyo. "My greetings."

"You've a visitor." He moved aside to let a man enter.

"Maxard!" Kamoj jumped up and sped around the desk. They met in the middle of the room. She threw her arms around him, and he gathered her into an embrace.

"Ah, Kamoj." His voice caught. "Thank the Current you are all right."

"Maxard, I—" Then she could say no more, for fear it would unleash her tears. He felt sturdy in her arms, a haven.

"Will you come walk with me?" he asked.

"Yes. I would like that." She looked back at her new liaison, who was standing by his chair now. "Lieutenant Endar, perhaps we can continue this later."

"Yes. Of course." He bowed to Maxard. Then he withdrew, leaving them alone. Or no, not alone. Antonyo remained by the door, discreet and vigilant.

Kamoj and Maxard left the Ivory Suite through a glass door across from the Long Hall entrance. Antonyo followed, staying back a few paces, a tall shadow.

They came out in back of the palace. Where not long ago this land had been overgrown with weeds and briars, now it rolled away in well-tended gardens. They followed a path of golden bricks aglitter with scale dust. Clouds scudded across the sky, white puffs with blue, green, and rose glints. The aurora rippled in sheets, and the lavender chip of moon hung near the horizon.

Maxard sat with her on a crescent-shaped bench. He ran his hand over the Argali engravings in the stone. "This is new."

"Vyrl commissioned a sculptor in the village to make it."

She traced the vines. "I do believe he means well by Argali."

Her uncle scowled. "His people wouldn't let me see you yesterday. Said they had to 'clear me with security' first. What is that? They still won't let Lyode up, and they won't let either of us go anywhere without a bodyguard."

"Ah, Maxard, I'm sorry. They're worried for us." She took his hands. "They regret what happened with Jax. I think their leaders had hoped I would leave Vyrl. So now they feel guilty."

"They should." Concern washed across his face. "Are you well, Kami? You looked so alone behind that big desk."

"I'm fine. But thank you for your care."

He squeezed her fingers. "The *Ascendant* stagman said you have heard from Ironbridge."

"Last night." Kamoj told him what had happened.

Maxard swore. "He knows we can't make payment in kind."

"I have an idea." She paused to consider. "The fire damage to the villages will take much repair, yes?"

"Very much. The *Ascendant* minions say they will help."

"Skolians."

"Skolians?"

"It's what they call themselves," Kamoj explained. "We can't keep calling them *Ascendant* minions. The *Ascendant* isn't even here any more." She thought back to what Antonyo had told her this morning. "They think they have proof that the fires were set. If that is true, it could give us a stronger position in the negotiations with Ironbridge."

Maxard raised his eyebrows. "I can't imagine Jax would have done anything to implicate himself."

Kamoj still remembered how Dazza had examined her when they returned to the palace. The doctor had known a lot of what Jax had done without Kamoj revealing anything. "It is amazing how smart these Skolians are. They're almost certain their proof implicates Jax's agents. Even if they can't prove anything against Jax, he is responsible for the actions of his people."

He nodded slowly, thinking. "It could help."

They discussed strategies, then talked about Argali and how they would work with the liaison. Afterward they spoke of Maxard's merchant lady, who was due for a visit. With an ache, Kamoj realized her uncle would soon marry and leave Argali, going to his wife's home in the North Sky Islands.

So they sat in the slanting sunlight as Jul sank into the mountains. Their shadows stretched out to the fields of split-head grain. Gilded light lay across the land, as ephemeral as it was beautiful, the last of the dying day, foretelling the night.

Cold air wafted against Kamoj's cheek. A night fog had seeped in the window, filtering through the shimmer curtain. Clouds filled the lower half of the room, surrounding the dais and bed in white billows.

She dreamed that Vyrl took form out of the mist. As his body coalesced, a tear slid down her face. "I miss you," she whispered.

He walked toward her, his upper body visible, the rest hidden by clouds. When he sat on the bed, he looked so real it made her ache. Then he gathered her into his arms.

"Is it really you?" she asked.

He held her close. "It's me. They brought me back."

"But why?" The dream seemed so real, it taunted her with the promises it would leave unfulfilled when she awoke. "What happened?"

He answered in a distant voice, as if he were mist curling over the East Sky Mountains. "Space affected me more than they expected. It was like before. In the coffin."

Her voice caught. "I'm sorry. But I'm glad you're here." To have him in her dreams was better than never at all.

He stroked her hair, cradling her head against his shoulder. "My brother Althor always told me that I admitted my feelings too freely. But I can't help it. I missed you so flaming much. I couldn't bear to lose you, too, not after everyone else I've lost."

"You can stay here."

"We must still carry out this mission."

"What will you do?"

Vyrl took a breath. "Come with me, Kamoj. Come on the *Ascendant*. When I'm with you, the nightmares have less power."

What could she say? She no longer had any good answers. It seemed unfair that even her dreams had to end this way. "Vyrl . . ."

"I'm sorry. I shouldn't pressure you. They can use one of their other plans, without me."

Other plans? She drew back to look at him. "How could they do this to you, if they had other options?"

He regarded her steadily. "Because with my help, they might retake Lyshriol without combat."

"How?"

"I can't talk about it. I'm sorry."

Kamoj felt as if the bed were sinking beneath them into the swirling billows. What if people died because he couldn't carry out his part? The guilt would eat away at him.

"Water sprite, don't worry." Mist curled over the bed and around his body, until he became more phantasm than man.

Vyrl undressed and slid under the covers, then drew her into his arms. Kamoj wanted to respond, but she couldn't. He didn't pressure her, neither for lovemaking nor to leave Balumil.

So they lay together, in the dreaming mist.

Kamoj awoke alone. No sign of Vyrl showed: no clothes, no strands of hair, not even a wrinkle in the sheets. He had never been there last night. She lay for awhile, too saddened to make herself rise. Outside, clouds scudded across a night sky.

Finally she got up and dressed in her tunic and leggings.

She left the suite and descended the tower. Cold air gusted through the window slits.

Most of the palace still slumbered. As Kamoj walked down the Long Hall, she glimpsed a maize-girl carrying a tub of flour downstairs to the kitchen. Antonyo walked several paces behind Kamoj, respecting her unspoken wish for privacy.

She wandered to the west tower. It looked much the same as the one she had just left. Stairs spiraled around inside and breezes gusted through window slits. Unlike the east tower, this one had a second-floor landing. She opened its door and walked out onto a balcony above the Hall of Audiences.

The original balcony had rotted centuries ago. For a long time this had only been empty space. She vaguely recalled her parents boarding up the door. She had only glimpses of them now in her memory. She recalled how a cascade of black curls had tumbled down her mother's back. Kamoj resembled her, except she was curved where her mother had been lithe. Her father had been a stocky man, with glossy black hair, brown eyes, and an impressive honor guard of stagmen. She remembered him resplendent in Argali colors and diskmail, his radiant smile making Argali House come alive.

Hai. If only she could have known them.

She looked around, wondering what her parents would think of this fine yellowbirch balcony. She walked to the front and rested her hands on the rail. Moonlight filled the hall below, flowing through floor-to-ceiling windows on the west wall. Mirrors lined the south and east walls, and a wooden bar ran along them at waist level, held in gold brackets. The floor was finished now, all yellowbirch.

Music started to play.

Kamoj nearly fell over the rail. The music continued, blithely unaware that it was impossible. She peered into the empty hall. The musicians must be clustered under the balcony. They had flutes, horns, strings, drums, and instruments she didn't recognize. Their music wound through the air, melodic and mournful, with a steady beat that made her feet want to move.

Then Vyrl walked into view.

Kamoj put her hand over her mouth. He *had* come home. She wanted to call his name, run down to him, stay to admire him, laugh, and cry. Caught among all the alternatives, she ended up just gazing at him.

He wore a knit pullover and knit pants, workout clothes, all black. Standing still, he tilted his head as he listened to the music. Then he frowned and walked out of sight under the balcony again. The music stopped. Just like that. How? Kamoj knew of no musicians who could go from playing such a complex piece to utter silence in one second. If nothing else, they usually talked after they stopped.

The musicians started up again, this time playing a faster tune with a powerful, mesmerizing beat. She could hardly keep her feet still. If she hadn't been so stunned by Vyrl's presence, she might have started dancing.

He walked out into the hall again. She started to call him— —and then he moved.

Kamoj's mouth almost fell open. This was her husband? He became a dream, like magic. He spun on one foot, his other raised to his knee and pulled tight to his body. Then he stretched his leg out in a kick that went above his head. At the same time, he laid out his body in an arched-back stretch. His arms extended in long lines, one in front, the other to the side. The kick pulled him through space with his body parallel to the floor and his head back. He snapped upright, spun again, and exploded out from the turn with a great leap through the air.

Kamoj had seen many people dance during festival. None came close to this, not even the best in Argali. This was so far advanced of any folk dance she knew that calling them the same art was like saying shale and diamond were both rocks.

As she watched his muscles move under his sweat-soaked clothes, arousal tingled through her body. Had other women seen him dance? "Sensual" hardly began to describe it. Although she had never been prone to jealousy, it surged in her now. She reminded herself she was the one he had chosen for his wife. But their link felt ephemeral now, dissolving in the impossible demands of their lives.

Subdued by that image, she withdrew from the balcony. She started up the tower, then sighed and sat on the steps. Resting against the stone wall, she thought about Argali. What she had feared would happen had come to pass. Argali and Ironbridge were now in a state of open hostility. But one difference existed to the scenario she had foreseen; Vyrl's people could offer far greater protection than she had realized. She mourned the need for their presence, but at least they kept her province safe. Skolian stagmen were everywhere, more than she could ever have imagined.

So many new concepts. How could she make good decisions about Argali when she didn't understand her husband's people? She questioned now her belief that she must stay here no matter what happened. A bigger principle was at work, one she needed to grasp. Change. How did one understand it? If she couldn't find an answer to that question, her people might well suffer more than if she left Balumil for a time.

And if it turned out she could never return? It seemed that no matter which way she turned, unpalatable choices faced her. But perhaps the time had come to do what she had never imagined for herself—take risks.

Still lost in thought, Kamoj rose to her feet and climbed the tower. The third-floor landing looked the same as the one outside the suite she shared with Vyrl. From what she remembered, this suite had a smaller bedroom, with one bath and no entrance foyer. She pushed open the stone door—and froze.

Inside, Dazza was sitting at a desk, her elbows resting on its top, her head in her hands. A white sleeping gown covered her from neck to mid-calf.

"What the—?" The colonel lifted her head. "I didn't hear you knock."

Kamoj reddened. "I didn't. I'm sorry. I didn't know anyone was using these rooms."

"No need to apologize." Dazza managed a tired smile, crinkling the lines around her eyes. They looked deeper this morning. She hadn't yet braided her hair, and it rippled down her back. She indicated an armchair by her desk. "Join me?"

"Thank you." Kamoj came over and settled in the chair. "Are you all right?"

Dazza didn't respond at first. Then she said, "I had such hope. But now . . ."

"Is it Vyrl?"

After a moment Dazza said, "Yes."

"He said he had trouble on the *Ascendant*."

"A relapse." Dazza pulled her hair away from her face. "We pushed him too hard, too fast. We nearly lost him."

Lost him? That sounded more serious than what Vyrl had told her. "Your ISC should never have made him do this."

"I hate what happened to Vyrl. But I would hate even more a universe controlled by Traders. We would all be captives—you, me, everyone." Grimly she added, "Vyrl's family are the prizes they want most of all."

Kamoj thought of Jax multiplied many times. She couldn't bear to think of such a person owning Vyrl. "I can't fathom why people would want to hurt other people that way."

Dazza's face gentled. "That's because you're one of the kindest, most nurturing people I've ever met."

Kamoj grimaced. "In other words, I'm weak."

"No you aren't. Strength of character doesn't require aggression."

She wound her fist in her tunic, bunching up the gray cloth. "I couldn't stop *him*." Even now, remembering the things Jax had done, she felt like a greenglass doe caught in the path of an avalanche, staring upward as the mountain came down. She wanted to beat against a barrier she could neither see nor define.

"You're angry." Dazza made it a statement.

With an effort, Kamoj relaxed her fist. "No."

"You've a *right* to be angry."

Kamoj wanted to tell her to mind her business. Instead she said, "Did you know Vyrl can dance?"

"Kamoj—" The colonel started to say more, but then she let it go. In a softer voice, she added, "Yes, I know."

"It's spectacular."

"He *showed* you?"

Kamoj hesitated. "I spied from the balcony."

"Did he know?"

"I don't think so."

Relief washed over Dazza's face. "That's probably for the best. Gods only know how he would react. He's ornery enough about being watched even in normal times."

"He shouldn't be."

"What was he working on?"

Kamoj described the music, then moved her torso and arms to show how Vyrl had moved. She had never felt clumsy before, but trying to copy him made her feel like a clod.

"Ah, yes." Dazza beamed. "That one is gorgeous."

The unfamiliar jealousy surged in Kamoj. "He lets you watch him?"

"I saw without his knowing, like you did." Dazza winced. "I had no idea how he much he hated being watched until I told him. He refused to speak to me for a week."

"That seems a bit extreme."

"Ah, well." Dazza gave her a rueful smile. "No one has ever accused Vyrl of being moderate."

"Doesn't he like to perform?"

"Never." Dazza shook her head. "He *should* perform. He has it all: technical brilliance, artistic expression, and a certain, uh, quality, I'm not sure what to call it . . ."

Dryly Kamoj said, "Sexy?"

The colonel reddened. "I believe that would be the correct term."

"Why doesn't he want anyone to see?"

"Men don't dance where he grew up. Only women."

That certainly sounded strange. "Then why did he learn?"

"His mother was a dancer." Dazza leaned back in her chair. "He told me once that his earliest memories were of watching her work out in the studio. He loved it. She comes from a culture with no taboos against men dancing, so she started teaching him when he was five. Eventually she brought in private tutors."

"It is a foolish custom his people have, to constrain such a talented person. And now he hasn't even his home and family to compensate for what he gives up." Kamoj glared at Dazza. "All for this war you fight."

Dazza showed no inclination to argue the point. Instead she spoke tiredly. "For all our achievements, we can't seem to cure our urge to fight."

"I have no urge to fight."

"That's another reason you and Vyrl suit so well." The doctor leaned her elbow on the arm of her chair. "Many of his siblings entered the military. His half-brother Kurj led ISC for decades, and Vyrl's sister Sauscony took over after Kurj died. His brother Althor was next in line."

Softly Kamoj said, "Until they all died."

"Yes."

That was all Dazza said, but her mood came across with such strength, it seemed tangible to Kamoj. She *felt* what Dazza felt, even a sense of her thoughts. Dazza had served under Vyrl's siblings. She admired them. Vyrl was a conundrum; brother to her late commanders, like them in many ways, yet preferring life as a farmer rather than a fighter; an artist rather than a warrior, a man more of emotion than logic. It made Dazza fiercely protective of him, not only because he was her liege, but also because she felt a debt of honor to his family. For all that Vyrl bemused her, she liked him, maybe even loved him as a sister would love her brother.

Kamoj spoke. "If people die because he couldn't go on the mission to Lyshriol, Vyrl will never forgive himself."

Dazza answered quietly. "No. He won't."

"Is it true what he thinks, that if I went with him, he could complete the mission?"

"No one knows for certain. But yes, I think his chances would improve."

Kamoj crumpled her tunic in her hands. "I talked to my uncle yesterday. He offered to stay on in Argali for awhile."

Dazza watched her closely. "How do you feel about that?"

"Not good." She pushed her hand through her hair. "No good solution exists to any of this."

"Do you know what you will do?"

"I've had time to set up the important programs for Argali. We're going to install heating and cooling boxes in the houses, teach our farmers Vyrl's improved methods of agriculture, and make a medical clinic in the village. I've also set up a committee to deal with—" She searched for the foreign word. "With the *regiment,* the Skolian forces stationed in Argali."

"That sounds like good work."

"I told Maxard he should marry." Kamoj took a breath, then forged ahead before she could change her mind. "But if I talked to him again, I think he would agree to look after Argali for a time."

Dazza went very still. "And your people?"

"I thought before that it would be best if I stayed." She rubbed her thumb over the ring Vyrl had given her. "But what is best in the bigger scheme of things? I no longer know."

The colonel spoke with care, as if she feared Kamoj would retreat if anyone came on too strong. "Are you saying you might consider coming with us on the Ascendant?"

Kamoj took a breath. "Yes." She knew she was taking an irrevocable step, not only for herself, but for Balumil. If she did this, it would be a message that they had lost their childhood, that the time had come to leave the womb of their world and look to the bigger universe.

"Do you think you could you handle it?" Dazza asked.

"I don't know." Then she added, "No matter what I choose, there will be difficulties for my people. I can only use my best judgment."

In a quiet voice, Dazza said, "That is all any of us can do."

18

Ascendance

Spherical Wave

Maxard studied the large bronze and copper bird crouched in the courtyard. Then he turned to Kamoj. "Are you sure?"

"I'm sure." She took his hands. "I will come home again." *Or never stop trying.*

"Lord Maxard?" Vyrl's voice came from behind them.

Maxard dropped her hands and spun around, suddenly taut. Vyrl had come up to them, his blue cloak swirling in the chill autumn wind. It relieved Kamoj that he sheathed his body in a shimmer rather than using the mask; it might put Maxard more at ease. She wondered why Vyrl no longer hid his face. Maybe it spoke to how he felt about himself now. But she wasn't sure. She knew the rum still bothered him. Although he no longer drank it, she didn't think he had lost the craving.

Maxard bowed, his face guarded. "My honor at your presence, Prince Havyrl."

Vyrl spoke quietly. "I'll bring her back to you."

Maxard nodded, but Kamoj could tell he doubted Vyrl. Although in many ways Vyrl remained a stranger to Kamoj, she had a certain trust in him, one Maxard had no reason to share. The way Vyrl towered over them didn't help. She knew now that his size came from his longer adolescence and an inherited tendency to height, but that made him no less imposing.

She gave Maxard her most radiant smile. "Uncle, you and Vyrl should talk some time about crops. Do you know, Vyrl has spent his life studying agriculture? It's incredible what he does with the grain fields here."

Maxard raised his eyebrows. He knew she was trying to find common ground for him and Vyrl. But he gave it a try. To Vyrl he said, "I hadn't realized you were a farmer."

"All my life. Like my father." Vyrl's response had a shadowed quality. Kamoj knew it came from grief, but it made him sound dark.

Vyrl glanced at her. Then he turned back to Maxard and tried a more agreeable look. "It would be a pleasure to talk. When Kamoj and I return, perhaps you and your fiancée will join us for dinner?"

Kamoj beamed. "Yes! You must come to dinner, Maxard." The Bridge language had no translation for *fiancée*, but Kamoj suspected Vyrl meant betrothed. "And bring Sable, please."

"We will, thank you." Maxard tried to smile at her. "Now you must come back. You would be a terrible hostess, Kami, to invite us to dinner and then not show up."

She started to reach for him, to offer reassurance with a hug, as they had done a thousand times since her childhood. But Maxard stiffened, his gaze flicking to Vyrl, and made no move toward her.

Vyrl glanced from Kamoj to Maxard. Then he said, "I should make sure our belongings were properly stowed on the shuttle."

Kamoj could have kissed him for understanding, except she knew it would embarrass him. "I will come in a moment."

Vyrl nodded. Then he headed for the bird, walking straight at it as if he didn't realize he was about to hit a solid wall. Kamoj almost called out to him, but then an oval opened in its side. After he walked into the bird, the oval vanished, leaving an unbroken surface.

"Goodness," Kamoj said.

"Does he do that often?" Maxard asked.

"They do a lot of strange things." She turned back to him with a wan smile. "It takes some time to become accustomed."

"Are you?" He watched her with concern. "Does it please you, the way this turned out?"

No, she thought. *It is a great mess.* But she was glad for one part. "I care for him, Maxard. He's different, but a good man. He intends well by Argali."

"I hope so." He motioned at the metal bird. "It is so strange for you to leave. Life has a rhythm, an order. This breaks it."

She thought of what Vyrl had told her, that her people had been bred to seek order, never asking questions or making changes. "Maybe we need to shake up the order."

"Why?"

"I'm not sure. But it might be a good thing. Like you learning to read."

His face relaxed. "That is good, yes. You must learn too."

"I hope to." Her voice softened with regret. "I am sorry how this turned out. But if all goes well, you won't have to stay in Argali long."

"You must stop apologizing to me." This time he didn't hesitate to take her into his arms. They embraced in the slanting sunlight. "Take care of yourself," he added gruffly.

"And you." Her voice caught as they separated. "Give my love to Lyode."

"I will." He glanced over her shoulder. "I think you have to go."

Kamoj looked to see Vyrl standing in the entrance of the bird. She said a last farewell to Maxard, then went to the bird. Her heart jumped as she entered. She was taking an irreversible step; from this moment until she returned, she would be a part of Skolian life.

The bird had three rows of seats, all blue. The walls curved around, luminous and white. Vyrl's bodyguards were already there, Antonyo Lopezani and a husky woman named Secondary Ko. The entrance to the bird faded, leaving a smooth surface. Kamoj brushed her finger over it. How did Vyrl act so normal with all these strange happenings?

He was watching her face. "It's just a molecular airlock, like in my cave. This one is impermeable to everything." With a smile, he added, "Including us."

"I guess so." Kamoj meant to speak lightly, but her voice had a tremor. She was nervous, yes, but excited, too. She would soon embark on a great journey, travel above the sky and cross seas of space, the first of her people to leave Balumil in ages. Although she had vague ideas of how the ancients had sent skyboats into the heavens, those stories were little more to her than childhood fables. They had survived intact over the millennia only because a few people, like Jax, could still read the ancient codices.

They sat in the middle row, with Antonyo in front of them and Ko in back. The chairs folded around their bodies. Kamoj almost asked if the seats were alive, then decided she didn't want to know. She could only absorb so much strangeness at once.

"When does the bird go into the sky?" she asked.

"Bird?" Vyrl asked.

"This skyboat."

"It won't be long. It's a ship, though. Not a boat. Actually, we call it a shuttle."

A woman's voice came out of the air. "Prince Havyrl, would you like me to turn on the holoscreens back there?"

Kamoj congratulated herself on not jumping at the disembodied voice. Vyrl answered the air with formality. "That will not be necessary, Lieutenant."

"Very well, Your Highness. Please prepare for lift off."

"Thank you." Vyrl turned to Kamoj. "You'll feel pressed into your seat. That's normal. It won't last long."

She managed a nod. A rumbling started within the bird. She felt fine, other than the tickling in her throat that often came when she was excited.

Suddenly an invisible vise clamped her body. She tried to gasp, but no sound came. The pressure grew worse, until she wanted to groan. Then the chair readjusted around her body, easing her discomfort. She began to breathe more easily and even managed a glance at Vyrl. The back of his seat had extended up to support his head. His face looked odd, as if an unseen membrane were pushing against his skin.

"How are you doing?" he asked, his voice slow.

"All right." Kamoj couldn't let go enough to say more.

Mercifully, the pressure finally stopped. Then she felt light-headed, as if she could float to the ceiling, or however one referred to the roof in a metal bird called a shuttle. "I feel so light."

"You are." Then Vyrl said, "Secondary Lopezani, are you linked to the EI?"

"Yes, sir." As Antonyo turned, the top of his seat lowered so he could see them. He glanced at Kamoj, his face friendly, but he didn't address her. His reticence reminded her of Maxard. It puzzled her. Antonyo had never seemed to fear Vyrl before.

"How many g's are we accelerating at?" Vyrl asked.

"About forty-five percent of Balumil's gravity," Antonyo said.

Vyrl nodded to him. "Thank you."

"It is my honor, Your Highness."

So formal. Kamoj realized it wasn't fear, but social position. An invisible wall enclosed Vyrl, separating him from everyone else. Dazza's interaction with him wasn't typical, but even during their arguments, she treated him with deference. His servants showed a respect verging on awe. It unsettled Kamoj. Her own people treated her with respect, but she never felt the distance with them that existed between Vyrl and most everyone else.

As Antonyo turned to the front again, Vyrl spoke to Kamoj. "The gravity you feel right now comes from our acceleration, and it's less than what you experience on Balumil."

"Gravity?"

"How much Balumil pulls on you."

"Oh, Vyrl." She smiled at the absurd image that evoked, of Balumil with big arms. "Worlds don't pull on people."

His grin flashed. "They do indeed, water sprite."

"You're teasing me."

"I would never do such a thing."

"Hah!" Kamoj pretended to glower at him. "Sometimes I think you're just a misbehaved boy, oh Sir Exalted Prince."

He gave a rumbling laugh. Then Kamoj had another jolt. She *felt* Antonyo's amusement at their words, and his surprise too, that Vyrl relaxed so easily with her. Although Kamoj had always been sensitive to people's moods, it had never been this intense. Her proximity to Vyrl seemed to increase the effect.

"It is true about the gravity, though," Vyrl said. "On Balumil, it's about one hundred twenty percent the human norm. Lyshriol, my world, is similar. That's another reason ISC chose Balumil as a temporary home for me, despite my height. It's like my world."

"Your height?" Kamoj wasn't sure she had heard that right.

"It gives me more weight to carry. My mother's people are big by any standard, but her father came from a low gravity world where it didn't matter. On Lyshriol, I'm big enough to cause problems. My knees bother me when I—" He stopped as if catching himself. "When I exercise."

"When you dance?" Kamoj had already decided she wouldn't hide what she had seen.

Vyrl stared at her, his face suddenly unreadable. "You came into the Hall of Audiences this morning."

"Yes. I didn't mean to intrude." Her enthusiasm spilled over. "Vyrl, it was wonderful! Incredible."

"It's just exercise." He shrugged. "Some people run, some people swim. I do this. It keeps me in good shape."

Kamoj could tell it meant more to him than exercise. She didn't push, though. She didn't want him to stop talking to her.

The pilot's voice came into the air. "We're on approach to the *Ascendant*. Please prepare for docking."

"Boarding" the *Ascendant* felt unreal. They exited the shuttle into a white chamber shaped like a sphere. "Decon," Vyrl called it. And they *floated*, all of them, she, Vyrl, their bodyguards, and the pilot, a thin woman with auburn hair. It flustered Kamoj, but it was fun too. She wondered what it would be like to make love here. When Vyrl grinned at her, a blush heated her face. Having an empath for a husband could be embarrassing.

The low-level nausea that had bedeviled her on the shuttle was growing worse. She took a breath, trying to calm her queasy stomach. They left decon and floated through a white tunnel to an odd carriage—an "elevator." The walls inside were a vibrant blue that glowed without the help of candles, like a lake in the North Sky Islands where glancing sunlight made the water radiant.

The seats in the elevator adjusted for their comfort, but the Jagernauts never relaxed. Their constant vigilance impressed Kamoj. She was glad for their presence, especially Antonyo. The muscular Ko intrigued her; she had never seen so formidable a woman. Antonyo had told her that he and Ko had served as "fighter pilots" for years and then took "desk" jobs. Kamoj had only a hazy idea about fighter pilots or how desks came into it, but it was obvious the Jagernauts commanded respect. When she learned that Ko had once been a bodyguard for Vyrl's mother, it reminded her that another formidable event waited in her future: meeting her mother-in-law.

Kamoj found Vyrl's description of the *Ascendant* hard to imagine. She wasn't even sure she believed it. This skycraft apparently had no sails, nor any shape she associated with a ship. Instead, it was a huge rotating cylinder with a counter-rotating bridge at one end and "thrusters" at the other. Vyrl called it a floating city. She tried to envision a city bobbing above the sky. What did one find up there? A great deal of purple air, perhaps.

After they entered the carriage, a slight pressure pushed them. At first she drifted to the side. Then her weight began to return, until she felt almost normal, though still lighter than on Balumil. Nausea continued to bother her, but it didn't become any worse.

Finally the doors slid open and they left the elevator. Her steps felt too springy, as if she had forgotten how to walk. Wide-open space surrounded them. *This was a ship?* Everything gleamed, luminous, and slanted at odd angles. The white platform under their feet curved away to either side. Overwhelmed by the unfamiliar shapes and surfaces, unable to absorb it all, she narrowed her focus to the area in front of them—

And saw General Ashman.

He stood about ten paces away with a group of people, all in gray uniforms. As the group came forward, Ashman smiled at Kamoj, which produced an unfamiliar but not unpleasant expression on his rock-hewn face. Then he stopped before Vyrl and bowed. "My greetings at your honored presence, Prince Havyrl." He wasn't smiling anymore. "You bring distinction with your attendance."

Vyrl answered wryly. "It pleases us to attend the *Ascendant*."

Kamoj glanced from Vyrl to Ashmar. Apparently Skolians were just as adept as her people at using ostentatious words to disguise how they really felt.

Then she caught sight of Dazza in Ashman's retinue. The colonel was watching her with a puzzled expression. Kamoj realized she had been staring straight at the older woman. She nodded a belated greeting, hoping Dazza understood. It was hard to assimilate this all at once.

As Vyrl and Ashman exchanged formalities, Kamoj felt the fluxes of power between them. She might be out of her depth here, but she knew politics, and it was in high form now. This was Ashman's province. He commanded. However, if he pressed Vyrl too hard, he would lose face with his people, perhaps even authority.

They left the platform, following a pathway that curved to the ground, Ashman walking with Vyrl, Dazza with Kamoj, and the others spread around them. Kamoj began to absorb more of her surroundings. They *were* in a city, albeit one with no plants or animals. The buildings evoked alabaster and precious metals. In the distance, a wall rose from the ground to the roof. Or was that a sky? It arched far above their heads, shedding light. She wanted to pour out her excitement and confusion to Dazza, but she held back, afraid it would sound undignified.

Looking over her shoulder, she searched for the carriage. Instead, she saw an even greater wonder: a gigantic column rose up from the ground until it pierced the sky. "Sweet Airys, what is that?"

"A spoke of the ship," Dazza said. "It's like a big, hollow pipe. The elevator came down in it."

Kamoj wondered why the elevator hadn't dropped like a rock. She tried to envision a spoked ship turning in the sky. It seemed like it ought to fall down to the planet.

They soon reached the "wall" she had seen—and then they entered it. Inside, they followed oddly rounded corridors with colorful images and strange devices on their walls. The onslaught of impressions blurred for Kamoj. She still felt nauseated. The light was too bright. Too yellow. It was hard to walk; she seemed to mistime each step and lift her foot too high.

Dazza described the ship as they walked, helping to distract Kamoj, though she didn't recognize all the words. Bat-tlecruisers were navel vessels used by the Imperial Fleet, the largest branch of ISC and the one most involved in space warfare. A ship like the *Ascendant* provided anti-spacecraft defense and communications control, guarded spacecraft car-riers, supported planetary landings, and served as a flagship.

However, Ashman and his crew weren't navy. They served in the Pharaoh's Army, the oldest branch of the Sko-lian military. Established during the Ruby Empire, the army claimed five millennia of service to Vyrl's family. Although it was primarily concerned with planetary warfare, it also maintained deep space divisions. As the ancient guardians of the Ruby Dynasty, the Pharaoh's Army had been the military branch of choice for this expedition.

Suddenly the corridor they were following opened into a spacious hall. Crescent-shaped tables and too many people filled the place. Panels on the walls stretched from the floor to the ceiling. *Living* panels. One showed an ocean with waves rushing onto a red beach. In another, slender plants swayed in a breeze that didn't exist in this room. Yet another had yellow mountains with streaks of red, their peaks oddly jagged, as if wind, sun, and snow had never softened their contours.

Kamoj struggled to take it all in. Dazza was guiding her to a table on a dais at one end of the room. Vyrl and Ashman were already there, waiting. With a jolt, Kamoj understood. This was some sort of reception. They were going to *eat*. Who could think about food now? Her nausea surged.

"No," she said in a low voice.

Dazza took her elbow in support. "Can you hang on a few more moments?"

Kamoj didn't answer. She feared she would say some-thing foolish, or do something even less charming, like throw up.

When they reached Vyrl and Ashman, Dazza spoke to the general. "Kamoj should leave. This is too much. I think she has space sickness, and this lower gravity isn't helping."

Vyrl glanced at Ashman. "I can take her to my suite."

The general nodded, watching Kamoj with concern. "Yes, of course."

Kamoj felt Ashman's consternation; it would be awkward if both she and Vyrl walked out on a ceremony meant to honor them, but the general didn't want her to suffer either. She wet her lips. "Vyrl, you stay." To Dazza, she said, "Can you take me? Then Vyrl and I won't both be leaving."

Vyrl spoke softly. "Thank you, Kamoj."

She managed a wan smile. The air seemed even stranger here than in the palace: too rich, too metallic, too dry.

Dazza took her out through an archway hidden behind the dais. They followed more tunnels, smaller ones than before. The walls leaned over her, so bright. Too bright. No wonder Ashman always looked stern. He probably had a headache from all these glaring lights.

Entrances shimmered open in front of them, the "molecular airlocks" Skolians seemed so fond of. Kamoj assumed the walls reformed behind her. She didn't look, fearing any extra movement would upset her precarious truce with her stomach. Here she was, surrounded by wonders, and it was all she could do to keep from bestowing her last meal on the *Ascendant*.

They ended up in a room with a decor that suggested austere wealth. She couldn't focus, but she had an impression of gold, bronze, and copper, with flashes of sapphire. The furniture was made from a golden wood, the only she had seen on the *Ascendant*, which had no trees. As much as anything else, that told her they had reached a place of significance.

Kamoj sighed. The gold rug looked soft and billowy, like a cloud lit by the sunset. It reminded her of the pillow-strewn tea room in Argali House that she often used for her afternoon rest. Coming to the *Ascendant*, she had missed the daytime sleep period. She sat on the rug, then lay down and closed her eyes, flooded with a relief so intense it felt like physical pleasure.

"Kamoj?" Dazza knelt next to her. "Would you like to use the bed?"

"No." Kamoj didn't try to open her eyes. "This is fine."

"Did they give you meds for the space sickness?"

Space sickness? How odd. She couldn't imagine catching a disease from the sky. "No medicine."

Dazza laid her hand on her shoulder. "The problem, my stoic Governor, is that you don't know how to complain."

"Never complain," Kamoj mumbled, already half-asleep.

"I know. We'll have to work on that."

"Don't want to," Kamoj informed her. Then she let go, and fell like a stone into a deep, welcome pool.

"You were smart to skip that food," Vyrl said.

Kamoj opened her eyes into darkness. No moonlight slanted in the window above Vyrl's desk. It made no sense. Even if no moons were up, the aurora still ought to shed light. Right now she could barely see Vyrl lying next to her. The mattress felt strange, too, buoyant somehow, as if it were full of air instead of stuffing.

"Are you feeling better?" Vyrl asked.

She squinted at him. "Better than what?"

"Dazza told me you passed out."

With a rush, it came back to her: the *Ascendant,* the reception, Dazza taking her away. Pah. She had done exactly what she had tried to avoid, acting like a naive girl instead of an experienced governor.

"I did not pass out," she said with dignity. "I went to sleep."

Vyrl's smile flashed in the darkness. "Well, after you went to sleep, Dazza carried you in here, gave you some meds for the space sickness, and put you to bed."

"I was fine where I was," she grumbled. A pang of longing for home hit her. She hoped all was well with Argali. Now that she felt better, though, she wished she could have stayed at the reception. She had come here to learn. "My regrets, if my leaving caused offense."

"They understood. You can join us tomorrow. Our 'day' cycle here is about one third a Balumil day." In a louder voice he said, "Andorian, lights to five percent."

The room brightened from dark to dim, revealing a chamber half the size of Vyrl's bedroom in the palace. She still couldn't distinguish much, just glints of the bronze and sapphire hues Vyrl seemed to favor. "Is this your *Ascendant* suite?"

"That's right. My quarters."

"I couldn't absorb it all before."

He didn't look surprised. "Dazza thinks you're like a computer code with great complexity but only a few input lines. Give you too much data and the program stops."

She blinked. "This bizarre comment has meaning?"

He laughed softly. "Imagine a large, complicated container with many cavities. It can hold a lot of water, but it only has a small opening to take in liquid. Give it too much too fast and it overflows. That happened to you today."

"Ah. Yes." Now she understood. "It is an Argali trait. Maxard is that way too." She paused, studying Vyrl's face. The dark bags under his eyes worried her. "You should go to sleep. You can explain self-defying soft-wear tomorrow."

For some reason he chuckled. But he didn't argue. "If you need anything, ask Andorian."

"He is like Morlin?"

"Yes. Andorian works better, though." Vyrl yawned. "However, Andorian isn't a 'he.'"

"He is a *she?*" Kamoj had no intention of letting Vyrl share quarters with an invisible woman.

He gave her a sleepy smile. "You're jealous of my computer."

"I am not."

His lashes drooped. "Andorian is the Lyshriol deity of the intellect. It has both a male and female aspect. I programmed this node to sound female, but if it bothers you I can change it." Drowsily he added, "I'll make it neither male nor female."

Neither? That intrigued Kamoj. "Yes. Do that."

"Andorian, androgynize," Vyrl mumbled.

Kamoj waited, but Andorian remained silent. She supposed he—she—didn't need to respond. She watched Vyrl fall asleep. It had been an exciting day, overwhelming, strange but never boring. She was glad for privacy now. Relief flowed over her, unexpectedly arousing in its intensity. What had Vyrl said? Her people were designed for heightened sexual response. What she felt wasn't sexual exactly, but she knew her appetite would flare if Vyrl touched her. She had never much desired anyone before Vyrl, but then, Jax had been her only choice. Just being near Vyrl intensified her responses to everything.

Despite her response to him, it relieved her that he had fallen asleep. Although she no longer flinched at his touch, she didn't feel ready yet to make love to him. She was too restless to sleep, though. Her clothes lay on a nearby table. She got up and dressed, then left the bedroom through an archway. She thought the chamber beyond was where Dazza had brought her earlier, but it was hard to tell in the dim light.

"Andorian?" she asked.

"Good evening, Governor Argali," a pleasant voice said, neither man nor woman, but somewhere between.

"Good evening." She hoped that was the proper response.

"May I make a suggestion?"

"Certainly." She turned in a circle, trying to find the source of the voice.

"If I solidify the archway to the bedroom, it will keep our conversation from waking Prince Havyrl. Also, I could then turn on the lights to let you look around."

"Yes. Do that." She decided to think of Andorian as "he."

The archway shimmered and filled with a wall. As Andorian brought up the lights, Kamoj gazed at the arch, impressed. It looked like a giant keyhole. The sides rose in gold pillars that ended in flat tops high above her head. From there, the arch curved out and around, then came to a point, making a fire-onion shape. A stained-glass window filled the onion.

Then she realized it wasn't glass, but a pane made out of gem crystals. It showed a man and woman, both in wind-blown robes, his emerald, hers ruby. The man had amethyst eyes and dark ruby hair streaked with gold. The woman's hair swirled to her hips, a mane of amber, gold, copper, and bronze. She looked like a Spherical Harmonic angel. Two topaz suns shone behind them and lapis lazuli clouds drifted in an amethyst sky.

"That's lovely," Kamoj said. Then it occurred to her that Andorian probably had no idea what she meant.

Apparently he was more perceptive than she gave him credit for. Before she could explain herself, he said, "The man in the gem-picture is Vyrl's father. The woman is his mother."

Kamoj studied the artwork. "I see the resemblance."

"Would you like to see more images of his home?"

"Oh, yes!"

"Look around. We call these holos."

Kamoj found it easier now to appreciate her surroundings. An elegant blue divan rested against one wall, and blue chairs stood around the room. The holo panels stretched from floor to ceiling and alternated with panels of gold. One panel showed an endless field of silver-green grass beneath a lavender sky. The sky had two suns, both the wrong color, gold rather than piercing blue-white. In the next panel, the field blended into a forest of sorts. The "leaves" were translucent blue disks on glassy violet or red stems. The effect was lovely, a glimmering forest of soap bubbles. The third panel showed the bubble forest giving way to mountains capped by light blue snow. Odd. Could a world have blue water?

"This is Vyrl's home?" she asked.

"That's right," Andorian said. "It's on the planet Lyshriol. You're looking at Dalvador, the region where he grew up."

"It's so full of sunshine."

"The climate does tend to be warm. The weather doesn't change much."

"Does it really have two suns?"

"Yes. The planetary system isn't natural."

"Why not?"

"With the way the suns perturb its orbit," Andorian said, "Lyshriol couldn't have formed in this system. It was probably brought in from somewhere else."

Perturb. The word had an eerie familiarity. "Do you mean the suns pull the planet?"

"Essentially. By the time it becomes a problem, though, we should know how to correct it."

"You can't now?"

"I'm afraid planet moving is beyond our present technology." Andorian sounded apologetic. Then enthusiasm suffused his voice. "But the Ruby Empire performed great feats of astronomical engineering. They also terraformed Lyshriol."

Kamoj smiled at his zeal. "Terraformed?"

"Made it more agreeable for people."

"I wish we could do that for Balumil."

"It takes a long time." Andorian paused. "However, Balumil is close enough to human-habitable for a milder process called biosculpting. Your ancestors used it. They altered or introduced much of the flora and fauna."

"That's what Vyrl said." Kamoj realized the holo images were alive. The silvery grass rippled and the bubble forest swayed. A winged creature soared over the blue-capped mountains. "Lyshriol looks so idyllic."

"It is indeed."

Andorian struck Kamoj as more human than Morlin. She had assumed computers were disembodied spirits that came to inhabit consoles when humans summoned them, but now she wondered. She needed to learn more about these Skolians. "Can I look around this skyship?"

"No one has told me to keep you here." Andorian's voice

lightened. "It might surprise members of the crew to see you up and about, but then, surprising humans can be amusing."

Kamoj grinned at the unseen EI. "I like your sense of humor."

"Thank you. I appreciate that. Prince Havyrl finds it annoying. He often growls at me."

She laughed. "I'll bet."

"You may use this exit to leave." Across the room, the wall within another graceful archway shimmered and vanished. "Enjoy yourself."

"I will." Her answer was part bravado and part anticipation.

The circular chamber outside Vyrl's suite had a strange beauty, dreamlike in quality, as if she were still asleep. She admired its bronze walls, the domed ceiling, and the floor patterned in copper and gold tiles. She wondered where Vyrl's people found such quantities of the precious metals. Perhaps they made them, the way they made their magnificent jewels. A bench with cushions circled the chamber. On the opposite wall, a holo showed two suns rising over the bubble forest.

Another arch graced the wall to her right. Kamoj hesitated, then took a deep breath and went toward it. The wall there shimmered away and she walked under the arch.

Vertigo swept over her. This place had no up or down! The ceiling, walls, and floor of the corridor were all the same. Every surface had hand grips, just like in the decon chamber. But she had *floated* there. Right now she weighed the same as she had since coming off the elevator. If the *Ascendant* stopped rotating, would she float? She grasped one of the grips, reminding herself that *down* was under her feet and *up* over her head.

When she had her equilibrium, she ventured forward. Round holos glowed to her left and right, above her, and in the floor, all showing the moving swell of blue-green waves, reminding her of pictures she had seen of portholes in ships that sailed the Thermali Sea. When she walked across the holos, waves lapped her ankles with ghostly translucence. This all seemed a floating dream, silent and blissful, in a time out of reality.

Then a scream shattered the silence.

19

Star Visions

Travel Time

Another scream came, then a choked cry.

Vyrl.

Kamoj ran back to the bronze room, then stopped in the archway, disoriented. The entrance to Vyrl's suite was still on her left, but a new arch had appeared across the chamber. A man in a green jumpsuit ran through it. As he sprinted into Vyrl's rooms, he called to her in an unfamiliar language.

Then Vyrl screamed again.

Kamoj ran into his suite. The archway to the bedroom was open. She sped through it, but then a tall woman with red hair caught her, holding her back. Grappling with her, Kamoj managed to twist around so she could see the room, but that was as far as she could escape. The woman gripped her tight around the waist, pinning Kamoj's arms to her sides.

Three other *Ascendant* people were there, the man in green and a man and a woman in the silver jumpsuits of healers. The woman was tall and muscular, her yellow hair piled on her head, and the man was even huskier, with powerful arms and a massive build. Both were laboring to hold down Vyrl.

Kamoj stared at her husband in shock. Only moments ago he had been relaxed in a deep sleep. Now he fought like a madman, his face pulled into a grimace, his gaze unseeing. With his large size and strength, he could injure even people as strong as these healers, yet no one made a move to sedate him.

Kamoj also struggled in the grip of her captor. "Let me *go*."

The woman didn't relent. "You can't go over there," she said in accented Bridge. "He'll tear you apart."

The man in green was studying a palm-sized square he held in his hand. As small ghost images of Vyrl formed above it, the man said, "Give him Perital."

The man straining to pin Vyrl's legs managed to get out a few words. "The meds upset him . . . let him ride this one out."

Vyrl fought with single-minded ferocity. His body had gone rigid, the tendons in his neck and arms standing out, his sleep trousers pulled taut over the locked muscles of his legs. The fingers of his hands jerked like claws. In his wild gaze and frantic struggles, she saw no sign of the gentle man she called husband.

Vyrl suddenly succeeded in shoving away the woman with yellow hair. She grunted as she flew off the bed. With only one person holding him, Vyrl had the advantage. He got hold of the other healer, the man in the silver jumpsuit, and heaved him off the other side of the bed. The man hit the floor with a sickening thud, and a loud crack snapped in the air.

As the yellow-haired woman scrambled to her feet, the man in the green jumpsuit dropped his palm-square. Working together, they tried to restrain Vyrl again. Vyrl swung his fist at the man's face, a blow that would have cracked bones if the man hadn't dodged.

The healer Vyrl had thrown off the bed sat up slowly, his forehead furrowed. Wincing, he held his arm against his chest. It looked broken. Kamoj wondered if he regretted his advice not to sedate Vyrl. With his good hand, he pulled off part of his belt. It reformed in his grip, turning into a flexible strip embedded with glowing threads. As he wrapped it around his arm, the belt made itself into a sling. Seeing his face relax, Kamoj thought the belt must somehow be giving him a potion for the pain. He stood up, still moving with effort, but he seemed less labored now.

Vyrl continued to fight the other two healers. Kamoj felt his terror. Caught in his nightmare, he had no idea what was happening. The healers were trying to put him in restraints, using straps that had grown out of the bedframe much as the healer's belt had become a sling.

The man with the broken arm unhooked what remained of his belt. Kamoj recognized the tube it formed. A sleep gun.

"Be careful on the dose," the man in green warned him. "Perital reacts with the alcohol in his bloodstream."

"I calibrated it," the other man said. "And he's been off the rizz for days." He came closer, then leaned over Vyrl.

Kamoj clenched her fists in frustration. "Leave him be!" As the healer shot Vyrl with the tube, Kamoj said, "No! *Stop.*"

Suddenly she let herself go limp. Her legs buckled. The woman holding her tensed, worry emanating from her mind, fear that she had injured her delicate charge. The woman shifted her grip, relaxing for just an instant—and Kamoj tore out of her arms.

Kamoj ran to the bed and scrambled up next to Vyrl. The man with the broken arm swung around to her and the healers holding Vyrl jerked, alarm on their faces. In her side vision, Kamoj saw the woman she had escaped from lunge after her, then stop at the bed. But none of them touched her. She felt their concern; with her so close to Vyrl, they couldn't risk agitating him further or losing their grip, lest he hurt his own wife.

Kamoj brushed Vyrl's tangled hair off his forehead. She had no idea how to calm this stranger who stared at her with frantic eyes and no recognition. All she could think was to stroke his head and repeat, "It's all right," over and over.

He made a choked sound. Then his muscles went slack.

"Vyrl?" she asked. "Can you hear me?"

"Kamoj?" he whispered.

"It's me."

"Gods." His voice was low. "Is it over?"

"I think so." She swallowed, her hand on his forehead. Sweet Airys, she hadn't realized. Yes, she had known terrors haunted his sleep. But this went far beyond nightmares.

Moving with care, the two healers released Vyrl. Kamoj looked up to see them all standing by the bed, staring at her. She felt their astonishment like a tangible presence.

"What did you do?" the woman with yellow hair asked.

Kamoj took a breath, trying to quiet her hammering pulse. "I don't know."

Vyrl spoke tiredly. "Just leave. All of you. Except Kamoj."

"I'm sorry, Your Highness," the red-haired woman said. "But we have to monitor your condition."

"You don't need to be in here for that," Vyrl told her.

"I'm sorry." She looked as if she genuinely meant her words. It was also obvious none of them intended to leave.

Vyrl closed his eyes. "Where's Dazza?"

"Colonel Pacal is on her way," the man with the broken arm said. "She was in a meeting with General Ashman."

"Great," Vyrl muttered. "Now Ashman will confine me to Medical again."

The yellow-haired woman spoke. "Other options may exist."

"Other options?" Vyrl's voice blurred with sleep.

"Your wife seems to have an ameliorating effect."

"She's an angel . . ." Vyrl mumbled.

After a moment, Kamoj realized he had succumbed to the sleep that came out of the tube. She bowed her head over her unconscious husband, her temples aching. "I don't know what to do," she whispered to him.

"Governor Argali?"

She looked up at the man in green. "Yes?"

"Do you feel any effects of his convulsion?"

"Effects? Why?"

He had retrieved his palm-square and now had ghost images of Kamoj floating above it. "You're in a neural resonance with him. I've never seen one so large. Being near him alters the way your neurons fire. Whatever his were doing, it also affected yours."

"My head does hurt," she admitted.

He studied his palm-square. "It's odd. According to this, you're unconscious."

"I am?" That was quite a feat, to be unconscious while she was conscious.

His face relaxed into a smile. "It's your resonance with Prince Havyrl. His pattern is superimposed on yours. The closer you come to him, the more you affect him. It swamped his neural activity and stopped his convulsion."

"How is he?" a man asked, his voice deep and brisk.

Kamoj's attention snapped to the entrance of the room. Ashman stood in the archway with Dazza at his side. The general loomed over even the tall, rangy colonel. He spoke to the man in the green jumpsuit. "Corporal, have Medical send an air stretcher for Prince Havyrl."

"No!" Kamoj glared at Ashman. "Leave Vyrl alone."

All the healers stiffened, except Dazza, who seemed to hold back a smile. It occurred to Kamoj that she had just defied an order from the *Ascendant*'s commander. Having already committed herself, she plunged on, feeling as if she were jumping off a cliff. "It's better for him to stay here. It hurts him to be in that place, Medical, where they took him out of—of the coffin. It was the first place he saw. He can't stand to be there now because it reminds him of what happened in space. Let him stay here. I'll look after him."

To her unmitigated astonishment, Ashman's face turned

kind. "Young lady," he said, his voice no longer curt. "I've no doubt it would soothe even a raging demon to wake up with his head in your lap. But we can't endanger you."

"We hope you can help him," Dazza told her. "But we have to be careful. Think how he would feel if he injured you during a convulsion."

"If you thought he was dangerous," Kamoj said, "why did you let him come back here?"

"We had determined he wouldn't relapse this way." In a dry voice, the colonel added. "We were wrong."

"Dazza, please," she said. "Trust my judgment."

General Ashman shook his head. "I appreciate your concerns, Governor Argali. But we can't take such a risk based on the judgment of a child."

Kamoj's anger sparked. "Stop calling me that." A memory came to her, the Inquiry in Jax's tent, when she had been without recourse. Trapped. Bile rose in her throat, and a feeling she had no words to define, except that it *hurt*. She wanted to hit Ashman. That option not being available, she spoke in a cool voice. "I have led my province for years, and none of my people have faulted my maturity or judgment."

Ashman considered her. Then he glanced at Dazza. "Your opinion, Colonel?"

"Leave him here," Dazza said. "I'll stay with them."

Ashman pushed his hand across his short buzz of hair, and for the first time Kamoj realized he wasn't always certain of his choices either. "Very well, Colonel. Notify me of any change in his condition."

Dazza nodded. "Yes, sir."

After Ashman and the others left, Dazza came to stand by the bed. Sitting against the wall now, Kamoj lifted Vyrl's head into her lap. A sense of security washed through her; soothing Vyrl comforted her. Had it been anyone else, she would have resisted that response, knowing it was designed into her. But given that both she and Vyrl descended from peoples created to please others, a certain justice existed in their choosing to please each other instead. She gave to him of her own free will and that made all the difference.

Dazza was watching her. "I've never seen anyone speak that way to General Ashman. If any of us did, we could end up in the brig."

"Brig?" Kamoj asked.

"Prison."

Kamoj winced. "Will he send me there?"

"No, I don't think so." Dazza smiled. "I think Hamilton likes you."

"Hamilton?"

"General Ashman."

"Are you and he friends?"

"To an extent. Off duty."

Kamoj tried to fathom the maze of authority here. "You are his stagman?" Embarrassed, she amended, "Stagwoman."

Dazza didn't seem offended. "Essentially. I'm attached to the Medical sector of this habitat."

Each time Kamoj began to understand, they threw another new word at her. "What is a habitat?"

"Like a floating province." Dazza rubbed her eyes. "This ship is large enough to qualify as a space habitat. Right now I don't think Vyrl could handle anything smaller. The *Ascendant* has a huge crew. All those minds form a bulwark for him against the emptiness of space."

Kamoj began to understand. "Like Balumil and her people."

"Yes." Dazza covered her mouth, smothering a yawn. "A planet is even better."

Concern rippled over Kamoj. If Dazza went to sleep, would the other healers come and take Vyrl to *Medical*? "Will you have to go back to your—" She tried to remember the word Vyrl had used. "To your quarters? To sleep?"

"Not tonight." Dazza indicated a molded chair against one wall. "I can sleep here. Andorian will also be watching. We'll give Vyrl Perital if he has any more problems."

"Please don't." They obviously knew it upset Vyrl; otherwise, the healers wouldn't have held off before, at risk to their own safety. "When you drug him, it may help the physical problem, but it makes his emotions hurt inside."

Dazza spoke quietly. "Please understand, Kamoj. We have to keep a balance. Which is worse—sedating him or the risk of injury? We have to make that decision every time he has a convulsion."

"Can't you see this is destroying him?"

"I wish it could be different. But we're doing the best we can."

At the back of her mind, Kamoj had always assumed the Skolians had the answers. But they weren't omniscient, none of them, not even Ashman. For the first time, she realized Vyrl might never fully recover. If this mission failed, he would condemn himself, souring his life; if they succeeded, it could leave his mind crippled. Either way, he could pay a hard price to ensure the well-being of his people.

Like I do with Argali. Why did they have such unforgiving choices? Selfless or selfish—they had to decide: do for others at their own expense or do for themselves at the expense of others. They had refused the latter, but she felt no nobility in choosing the former, only regret for the joy it stole from their lives.

Kamoj wasn't sure what to expect in the Tactics Room, but she was becoming more accustomed to facing the unexpected after having been on the *Ascendant* a few days.

Antonyo brought her into a huge sphere. Vyrl's entire suite would have fit here, with room to spare. Had they been floating, she couldn't have told up from down. The walls glowed white. They gave an impression of depth, as if they were liquid light that went on without end. They felt solid, though.

She and Antonyo followed a walkway that circled the sphere. It did help define a direction, though from what she had seen, the crew could rearrange the ship's fixtures to suit any "up" or "down" they wanted. Across the chamber, Vyrl sat with Ashman, Dazza, and several uniformed strangers. The white disk of their table floated, and they each sat on a smaller floating disk. Kamoj still had trouble with the concept of a weightless or "microgravity" environment. How could people have weight when the furniture had none?

Then she realized she had misinterpreted what she saw. The furniture *did* have weight. A transparent column supported the table, curving out from the wall. The "disks" were chairs with transparent supports and backrests. She rubbed her eyes. Learning to judge what was and wasn't possible here was turning out to be harder than absorbing the wonders themselves.

As she and Antonyo reached the table, Vyrl and the others rose to their feet, standing on air. But no, a transparent disk even larger than the table served as a floor. It resembled glass, but gave like sponge when Kamoj stepped onto its surface.

Antonyo remained on the walkway, on guard. She suspected that on the *Ascendant* he stood more for Vyrl's honor than his protection: the ship itself acted as a huge bodyguard. Vyrl had told her that its brain was a great computer, an "Evolving Intelligence." It linked to all the smaller EIs, like Andorian; to many of the palm-squares, called "palmtops"; and to uncountable nanobots. Kamoj imagined the *Ascendant* as a living entity, one that knew and saw everything. She wanted to think of it with a personality too, but she suspected that came from her own need to envision it in a more human light.

She was glad to see Vyrl looked better today, less tired. As long as they stayed together at night, he slept reasonably well. His medical team monitored him at all times. The sentries were often EIs rather than people, to give her and Vyrl privacy, but it still wasn't the same as being alone. That she didn't feel ready to resume marital relations with her husband was moot now; they lay next to each other at night, too aware of the monitors to kiss, let alone make love. If thwarted passion could have powered space ships, she and Vyrl would have launched an entire fleet by now.

As a disk detached from the wall to form a chair, the other chairs moved, making space for the new one. Kamoj scratched her chin, bemused by all this active furniture. Everyone was still standing, apparently waiting for her to respond.

Vyrl's face changed, as if he had just remembered something. Then he sat down. Relieved by his attention to protocol, at least a protocol she knew, Kamoj nodded to him and started to take her own seat.

Then she remembered Ashman. What was proper here? A woman of authority always let her consort sit first, followed by the consorts of the other women in her presence, in order of rank. Ashman wasn't anyone's consort, but he outranked everyone. Perplexed, she turned to him. To her surprise, he was watching her with an intrigued expression. She gave him a formal nod, as one governor to another, and waited. He considered that, then settled into his chair.

Satisfied, Kamoj took her seat, followed by Dazza and the other officers. Ashman introduced the strangers. Their jobs seemed part of their titles: *Logistics*—an iron-gray woman; *Plans*—a man with fiery hair; *Operations*—a compact woman with a buzzed hair cut that shocked Kamoj; *Security*—a striking man with dark coloring; *Communications*—a short, wiry man who looked friendlier than the others; *Telops*—an elegant woman with gold hair piled on her head; and *Intelligence*—a homely woman whose gray eyes had a piercing intelligence.

Kamoj had never seen a woman like Operations. She had no idea what to think. A woman's hair was her glory. But maybe not for Skolians. This one seemed perfectly happy with almost none at all. Security looked the youngest of all the officers, and he was at least in his fifties. Communications, the shortest, was still tall compared to a Balumil man. Kamoj felt small and vulnerable here with her hair tumbling to her waist, wearing a blue dress with the Argali tight bodice, lace trim, flared skirt, and ruffled underskirt. Had she understood the nature of this meeting, she would have tried to present a more pragmatic appearance.

It helped that Vyrl also wore clothes native to his culture, a white shirt laced by thongs up the front, blue trousers, and dark blue knee-boots. Although in detail they differed a great deal from the garments of her people, they had an overall similarity. The jizate chain sparkled around his neck, a striking contrast to the somber uniforms of the others. The gold braid on Ashman's cuffs was the only adornment any of the officers displayed.

Vyrl's many aspects fascinated Kamoj. She had seen him as a Balumil noble, a farmer, a modern Skolian man, and now in his native clothes. She liked him best like this, masculine in a way she understood, yet different enough to be exotic. Regardless of how he dressed, though, he seemed completely natural, unaware of how attractive he looked. It made sense, given that he had spent his life in an isolated rural area, married to the same woman, rather than someplace where women were always pursuing him.

The fiery-haired officer called Plans was speaking. He described to Kamoj the ISC defenses that protected Lyshriol. The Allied Worlds of Earth had taken over those defenses, so now ISC found itself locked out of that stellar region by the very systems it had created to guard Vyrl's home world.

"We can't take the *Ascendant* into Lyshriol," Plans continued. "Prince Havyrl will travel in a racer with a drop-down JSO team."

"JSO?" Kamoj asked.

"Special operations," Plans said. "The J-Force."

"He means Jagernauts," Vyrl told her.

"Will I go with them?" Kamoj asked.

Logistics, the gray-haired woman, answered. "If you agree."

Vyrl spoke to Kamoj in a quiet voice. "You have a choice.

If you don't go, they can sedate me with Perital for that step of the mission."

She stared at him. "You *agreed* to that?"

He raked his hand through his hair. "We've come this far. If it makes it possible to complete the operation, I'll do it."

Kamoj could tell how much it took for him to make that offer. Still, she wasn't sure what to think. "Are you sure you need me?" She knew her lack of experience troubled them all.

Dazza answered. "In space, in a small ship, the sedation doesn't stop Prince Havyrl's convulsions. It just makes it easier for him to tolerate them." She glanced at Vyrl, as if to apologize for discussing his condition. To Kamoj, she said, "Regardless of whether or not he is unconscious, however, every time he has a convulsion, it strengthens the neural pathways that create that state, which makes his brain damage worse."

Brain damage. Although Kamoj had known Vyrl was hurt, those words brought it home with force. "Will the racer help protect him, like the *Ascendant?*"

Operations shook her head. "It's too small, only the size of a shuttle." Her voice had a burr to it, reminiscent of her hair—short and abrupt.

"The *Ascendant* would be impossible to hide," Dazza said. "Unfortunately, sending Vyrl in a racer leaves him vulnerable. Even with you there, he may still need the Perital."

Alarmed, Kamoj turned to him, remembering his convulsion in the metal bird on Balumil. "You can't risk it."

He gave her a reassuring grin. "I'll be fine."

Despite his claim, she felt his doubts. But he didn't want to reveal his unease. She picked up his other emotions too; he wasn't any more comfortable here than she was. Like Kamoj, he feared to appear provincial or emotional. For all his education and heredity, the *Ascendant*'s crew still saw him as rustic, perhaps even primitive.

"We're using the racer because it can get into Lyshriol fast," Plans was saying. "The less time it's at risk, the less chance of detection."

"If the Allied Worlds control Lyshriol, how can any ship get in?" Kamoj asked.

Intelligence, the woman with gray eyes, spoke. "We've developed a procedure."

When no one elaborated, Kamoj said, "But how?"

Security spoke in his rumbling voice. "Governor Argali, you don't need to know that information."

Kamoj frowned. "Do I need to know what will happen if we get caught?"

All he said was, "I'm sorry, ma'am."

His lack of emotion unsettled her. With his black eyes and dark skin, he resembled Akabal, an Argali spirit of the night and fertility. But Akabal was an affectionate, emotive soul, whereas the head of security projected implacable strength. Kamoj suspected that to ISC, her people seemed too demonstrative, full of unguarded emotions, governed by passion rather than reason.

Ashman had been listening with intent focus. Now he spoke. "Governor Argali, we aren't being arbitrary. The less we tell you about our operations, the less you can reveal if you're captured. However, be assured our relations with the Allied Worlds of Earth aren't hostile. If you become their prisoner, they should treat you well."

"Then our capture is possible?" she asked.

Ashman didn't hedge. "Yes."

At least he gave her the truth. "If they catch us—will they let us go?"

"I doubt it."

"Is that why you don't use the racer to bring out Vyrl's family? Because they might be caught?" Her unasked question hung in the air like an accusation: *Why didn't you send a racer for Vyrl?* It would have spared him the horror of his burial in space.

Telops, the statuesque woman with yellow hair, answered. "Certain components of the Lyshriol ODS require a Rhon psion."

"ODS?" Kamoj wondered if Ashman's people always talked in letters instead of words.

"Orbital Defense System," Logistics said.

"The Allied Worlds of Earth now control our ODS," Telops continued. "But they can't use its Rhon functions. Those constitute only a small fraction of the system, but it's a powerful fraction. That chink in the AWOE control offers us a way to drill a hole in the ODS, but only with the help of a Rhon psion. The Allieds have almost the entire Ruby Dynasty, who refuse to help. So the AWOE forces can't do anything with the Rhon functions.

Kamoj thought AWOE must mean Allied Worlds of Earth. "And now you have Vyrl," she said, aware of him at her side.

"Yes." Logistics leaned forward. "Governor Argali, the racer has a good chance of reaching Lyshriol. But you should know: you won't get out again if the operation doesn't succeed. If we had sent it in for Vyrl's family and failed to extract them, we would have played our hand and wasted our only advantage."

Intelligence scrutinized Kamoj with her keen gaze. "We also know of certain hidden installations on Lyshriol that a Rhon psion could use to contact the ODS."

"Can't Vyrl's family use them, then?" Kamoj asked.

Vyrl spoke in a cold voice. "We were never told about these 'certain hidden installations.' "

An awkward silence followed his words. Then Security said, "For your protection, Prince Havyrl. What your family doesn't know, they can't reveal."

Kamoj didn't like it. "So we could end up trapped on Lyshriol."

"I'm afraid so," Logistics said.

Ashman regarded her. "Are you willing to go?"

Kamoj knew if she stayed on the *Ascendant,* she could return to Balumil regardless of whether or not this mission succeeded. A part of her wanted to do just that. Her concern for Argali was always in her thoughts. But it would be a betrayal of Vyrl's trust. She had agreed to come with him; it was time now to follow through. Besides, she was curious to see Lyshriol.

"Yes," she said. "I'll go."

Approval washed out from Ashman's mind—and another emotion she hadn't expected; he wished he could keep her on the *Ascendant* so he could protect her. None of that showed on his face, though. He just said, "Tactics attend."

The chamber vibrated with a cool voice. "Attending."

"Begin simulation," Ashman said.

The lights went out—and they plunged into a void spangled with stars and dust. The abrupt transition rattled Kamoj. How did the Skolians take these wonders for granted?

Someone put a hand over hers. Vyrl. She curled her fingers around his, grateful for their solidity.

Plans spoke. "We've set up the simulation as if we're on the racer."

"This looks like the Hinterland Star Sector," Vyrl said.

"That is correct, Your Highness," Plans said.

Kamoj wondered if all Skolians were this formal with Vyrl. Did everyone have to call him "Your Highness"? He seemed used to it, though. That gave her insight into how he viewed Dazza. Kamoj had thought he didn't like her, but she realized now he allowed the colonel a familiarity he granted none of the others.

"What is Hinterland Sector?" Kamoj asked.

Logistics answered. "It encompasses several star systems on the edge of settled space."

"Including Lyshriol," Vyrl said.

Kamoj gazed at the jewel stars. "Which are your suns?"

"Do you see the two gold stars in the center?"

She did indeed. "They look like topazes."

His voice warmed. "The bigger star is Valdor. It means Bard. The smaller is Aldan, the Younger Brother."

Kamoj wasn't sure, but she thought the two stars were growing larger. "Valdor sounds like your name."

"It's the same root. Valdoria means 'The Dalvador Bard.' It was my father's hereditary title."

She squeezed his hand, feeling his sorrow.

Suddenly the stars leapt in size. "We've accelerated the racer's progress," Plans said, "The actual trip will take several hours."

Valdor and Aldan filled the chamber now. Geysers of fire leapt up from them like liquid fire, regal and magnificent in their deadly beauty. The stars whorled in hues of gold, marred in places with dark spots. Both were distorted, as if they were pulling on each other, the smaller more than the larger.

As the stars grew, they separated and moved apart, until they vanished. A sapphire appeared in the center of the void and swelled into a aquamarine ball wrapped in blue swirls.

"It's beautiful," Kamoj said. "What is it?"

"Lyshriol," Vyrl murmured. "My home."

Plans spoke. "Governor Argali, do you see the land mass in the Northern Hemisphere?"

"What is 'northern hemisphere?' " she asked.

"The top half of the planet," Plans said.

Their comments disoriented Kamoj. "Planets are disks. That's a ball."

A long silence greeted her response. Finally Communications spoke, his voice gentler than the others. "No, ma'am. Planets are balls."

"Oh." Kamoj winced. In Argali, she had been considered learned: good at arithmetic, skilled with finances, even able to understand some Iotaca. Among Vyrl's people she felt like a ship adrift among the North Sky Islands without an anchor.

Plans spoke again. "Do you see, in the upper half of the ball, a brown and green patch surrounded by blue?"

"Yes," she said. "I see it."

"That's the Rillia continent."

Lyshriol filled her view. Then her perception changed. Instead of the globe growing in size, it suddenly seemed as if they were rushing toward Rillia. The blue swirls resolved into huge cloud banks. When they dropped into the clouds, the chamber filled with fog. Kamoj kept expecting to feel wet, but she stayed dry. Nor did she smell or hear anything.

"Are clouds blue on most planets?" She would have thought not, but after her mistake with the shape of worlds, she hesitated to make assumptions.

"I used to think so when I was a boy." Amusement lightened Vyrl's voice. "But the color is rare. It comes from a chemical in the Lyshriol water similar to blue dye."

"Won't that make you sick?" Kamoj asked.

"It bothers some offworlders. Most need specialized nanomeds in their bodies to deal with it. You'll get them too. The dye is benign, but it can turn things blue."

"Like people?" The idea produced all sorts of images in Kamoj's mind, some of them quite entertaining.

Vyrl gave a soft laugh. "Not Lyshriol people. Our bodies produce chemicals that break down the dye. So do most plants and animals adapted for the planet. But it can have bizarre effects on people without that protection."

Kamoj could guess at least one human product it turned blue. For the sake of delicacy she didn't mention it.

They dropped out of the clouds, plunging toward mountains that looked oddly familiar. They slowed as they neared the peaks, until they were skimming over snow-capped tips. Then she recognized the range; these were the mountains in the panels of Vyrl's suite. They made her think of the backbone on a huge skeleton.

The simulation took them through the areas they would need to know for the mission. Kamoj listened and watched, always wondering if she would end up trapped on this strange world, with its alien sky and suns.

Kamoj made a decision: she would go to the Observation Bay. After the past few hours in the Tactics Room, she needed time to think.

To reach the Observation Bay, one opened a hatch in the

deck and climbed down a ladder. The bay formed a great transparent bowl with the ship above and the endless ocean of space all around. Vyrl had taken her there a few days ago, but she had wanted to leave almost as soon as they arrived. The shock had been too great: no floor, no walls, no ground, no sky, only gemhard stars and glowing interstellar dust in every direction.

Today Antonyo opened the hatch for her, but then he stepped aside, respecting her wish to climb the transparent ladder alone. Kamoj wanted to prove to herself she could face the bay without leaning on Vyrl or anyone else. She went halfway down the ladder and stopped, breathless with the view. All around her, stars glowed in colors far more intense than she had ever seen on Balumil. Great dust clouds frothed like radiant spumes in the abyss. The panorama had a terrible beauty, dark and yet also brilliant, a vista unlike any she had imagined.

Then Kamoj realized she wasn't alone. Two people stood across the bay on a clear shelf, facing away from her, their hands resting on a clear rail at waist height. She could see their faces in profile when they looked at each other. With no visible structure supporting them, they might have been standing in the nothingness of space itself.

Ashman and Vyrl.

Kamoj hesitated. Should she greet them or leave? Their voices carried to her despite their distance.

". . . if it doesn't work," Ashman was saying, "we'll end up fighting the Allieds. It could get ugly."

"Why don't you just say it, Hamilton?" Vyrl had his arms crossed. "You don't think I can do this."

General Ashman remained unruffled. "You aren't trained for this work. You and your wife are the type of people we're supposed to protect, not send into danger."

"We're not going to fight." Vyrl lowered his arms. "But you're right, I'm not comfortable with military operations. I'm not my brothers or my sister. I'm sorry if that disappoints you."

Ashman spoke quietly. "Your brother Kurj was the bed-rock of ISC, your brother Althor a worthy successor, your sister Soz a military genius. Did I hope you would be like them? Yes, certainly. Am I disappointed? For the sake of this mission, I suppose the answer is yes. But in the greater scheme of life? No." He regarded Vyrl steadily. "Without those of you who are our gentler side, civilization has no meaning. ISC exists in the large picture, the political back-drop. But that picture is nothing without the personal histo-ries of the people who create it. People like you. Human history is the collected stories of individuals: their hopes, dreams, achievements, passions, triumphs, tragedies. That defines what it means to be human—and what we, the sol-diers, dedicate our lives to protect."

Vyrl was silent for so long, Kamoj wondered if he would answer. Then he said, "Thank you." He sounded surprised.

The two men fell silent, watching the stars.

After awhile, Ashman said, "Colonel Pacal tells me you're sleeping better now."

Vyrl's posture eased. "Having Kamoj here helps. She's an angel."

"I'm not surprised her husband wanted her back."

Vyrl stiffened as if Ashman had struck him. "That abusive bastard wasn't her husband."

Ashman exhaled. "Her former betrothed, then."

"He ought to be in prison."

"He won't back down. He knows she's bluffing about go-ing to court." Ashman made a sharp motion with his hand, as if to throw away the scandal. "We don't need this. The media will excoriate you, especially after they see Ironbridge. He looks and sounds so damned noble. And here is Kamoj—sweet, lovely, innocent, valiantly trying to protect her de-fenseless world against marauding ISC. Wait until the holovid producers get ahold of it. And every drama needs its villain, Vyrl. Guess who wins the role."

Vyrl scowled. "The charges Ironbridge brought against me are a crock of sludge. He won't win."

"We don't know that. We can probably prove he forced her, but we can't prove you *didn't* unless she testifies. As for interfering with their culture, you're guilty. A court may go easy on you, given your position and the circumstances, but you could still be convicted." Ashman shook his head. "Your enemies will drag out the whole business into a flaming mess."

Vyrl stared at him. "What enemies? I'm a *farmer.*"

Ashman snorted. "Don't be naïve. You're also a Ruby prince. It doesn't matter that you ignore politics. There are those who would see your family stripped of power."

"Even if this mission succeeds?"

"Even then. The moment this goes to court, you've lost. Even if you're exonerated, the taint will follow you." Ashman pushed his hand across the bristle of his hair. "The Radiance War crippled ISC far more than we've revealed in public. If we go to war now with the Allieds, we may lose. We can't risk a crisis of confidence among our people. Their morale has already taken a beating. The last thing we need is to have the symbols they look to for courage—your family and ISC—dragged through the mire."

Dryly Vyrl said, "So I'm to save Lyshriol, stop a war, and be a paragon of virtue for several trillion people. Anything else you need while I'm at it? A few new galaxies?" He spread his hands. "Gods, Hamilton, I've given you everything I have, even my sanity. What more do you want?"

Ashman's voice quieted. "I'm sorry for what this has done to you. But what I want doesn't matter. None of us has a choice."

"We all have choices," Vyrl said wearily. "Unfortunately, most of them are hell."

When Kamoj climbed out of the Observation Bay, she saw Antonyo talking with Secondary Ko, one of Vyrl's bodyguards. As Kamoj went over to them, they both bowed. But then Antonyo smiled. At least he didn't treat her with the lonely distance everyone else used with Vyrl, and by extension with her now, too.

"Where would you like to go?" Antonyo asked.

"Can I see Dazza?" Kamoj asked.

"I'll check." He stepped a few paces away, then spoke into the "comm" on his wrist gauntlet.

"You look well today, Governor Argali," Secondary Ko said.

"Thank you." Kamoj was glad they had respected her wishes and quit calling her *Your Highness*. Whatever the state of "highness" entailed, she didn't feel she had it. Besides, if that state existed, she didn't want to attain it only because she married someone who already had it; she wanted to earn it through her own actions.

Antonyo came back to her. "Colonel Pacal can see you in her Sector Two Medical office."

They took their leave of Ko and walked down a corridor with copper walls, what Vyrl called "bulkheads," though they didn't look bulky to Kamoj. They soon reached a magrail station with a carriage waiting by its platform. Kamoj thought it was hilarious that they called these stagless carriages "magcars." On Balumil, mags were little creatures that crawled in the mud.

After she and Antonyo took their seats in a car, it shot along a tunnel. They watched the view on holoscreens, but only metal walls rushed by them. Kamoj rubbed her eyes. Metal. Dichromesh. Luminex. She wanted to walk in the mountains, feel rain on her face, shiver from the cold. The air here was always the same perfect, boring temperature.

Sector Two looked like every other sector: immaculate, bright, and hard. Antonyo took her through several offices, past robots and humans. The people sat at consoles, sheathed in silver meshes, caged in equipment, their eyes closed or covered by visors, their awareness elsewhere. To Kamoj they seemed part machine, melded with their creations. Did it make them more than they were before, the way plants grafted together could create a better crop; or less, like a great work of art that lost its vibrancy in starlight, its colors only visible as shades of gray? She only knew that it made her miss the forests of her home.

They found Dazza in a room cluttered with equipment. It all gleamed white, silver, or black, with odd angles and curves. Kamoj hadn't felt sick for days, since Dazza gave her the meds, but all this strangeness was making her queasy again. An odd place this, where you went to the healer and then got sick, rather than the reverse.

As Dazza stood up behind her console-desk, Antonyo saluted her. Then he left Kamoj alone with the doctor.

"My greetings." Dazza motioned her to a chair, an innocuous seat with plush cushions. Kamoj sank gratefully into it, glad Dazza had at least one piece of normal furniture.

The colonel settled into her own chair, with its panels, knobs, and projections. "What brings you here today?"

"I need advice," Kamoj said.

"Yes?"

"On Balumil, when you examined me . . ." She stopped, wishing she could avoid this. But she made herself go on. "You said you could prove Jax forced me."

Dazza became very still. "Yes. There wasn't any doubt."

"If I really do 'press charges,' will Jax go on trial? Will it get that far?"

"It's possible. It depends on Governor Ironbridge. And on you."

"On me? Why?"

Dazza folded her arms on the desk. "You have to decide what you want. To send Jax to prison? Or to bargain with him?"

Kamoj had no doubt on that score. "I want him to withdraw his charges against Vyrl and leave Argali alone."

"If he knew you weren't bluffing, he might bargain."

Kamoj's anxiety felt physical, a clamminess on her skin, a chill on her spine. She had never openly defied Jax. For years she had dealt with their alliance, finding a balance on the edge between protecting herself and protecting her people. Now she had to jump off that edge.

She took a breath. "I want to press charges. Can you help?"

Dazza spoke gently. "Yes. I can. I'll make you an appointment with the Imperial Counsel."

When Vyrl came into the suite, Kamoj was sitting on the divan, curled into a ball with the cushions molded around her. He sat next to her, and the divan rearranged itself, accommodating them both.

"I just heard from the Counsel." He sounded subdued.

"They told me they sent notice to Balumil, too."

Vyrl answered her unspoken question. "It means they notified Jax Ironbridge that you filed charges against him with the Imperial Court."

"Oh."

He tried to pull her into his arms, but she wouldn't unfold from her protective curl. She took his hand instead, holding it in a tight grip.

"Why did you change your mind?" he asked.

"What I feel about all this . . . it's small compared to what your people face." Her voice caught. "This business of responsibility—why must some people bear so very much more of it than others? How can one man shoulder the obligations of an empire? They want a god-hero and curse you when they discover you are a man instead."

"Ah, Kamoj," he murmured. "What did you hear?"

"You. And Ashman." She wiped away the moisture in her eyes. "They want too much from you. Too much for one person."

"But I'm not one person." He rubbed his thumb over her knuckles. "We're two. Together. I just wish you would do this for yourself, rather than me."

She answered softly. "For myself, I only wish I could forget."

Andorian suddenly spoke. "I'm sorry to interrupt."

Vyrl practically jumped off the couch. "What do you want?"

"You have a message from Plans," Andorian said, apologetic. "The racer is ready. It is time to leave for Lyshriol."

20

Lyshriol

Transition (A → L)

The racer streaked through Hinterland Sector, unseen and unheard, shrouded. The drop-down team consisted of eight Jagernauts, four men and four women, all in uniform. Several were in their seats, one working on his wrist gauntlet, three others intent on palmtops. The remaining Jagernauts floated in the cabin, checking their gear. Picotech packed their gauntlets, and their minds were linked into the racer's Evolving Intelligence brain. Kamoj wasn't sure how they "talked" to the skyship; only one of them sat sheathed in a control mesh, with its prongs plugged into his neck, spine, wrists, and ankles. The other Jagernauts made "wireless" links with the EI. She was curious to know more about their mysterious, silent communication.

Vyrl was also connected to the EI, with wireless devices the *Ascendant* doctors had put in his body. He sat next to Kamoj, his eyes closed as he mind-spoke with the ship. Either that, or he had fallen asleep.

"Vyrl?" she asked.

He blinked his eyes open. "Eh?"

"Can you hear the ship in your mind?"

"Some." He yawned. "Most of the time I don't notice the data flow between my internal nodes and the EI. It's almost on an unconscious level."

"But you can talk to it if you want?" When he nodded, she said, "It must be strange, to have a voice in your head."

"I never wanted this tech in my body." He rubbed his eyes. "But some of my siblings had extensive biomech systems. Althor told me once he would feel crippled without his enhancements."

The idea of such additions seemed intrusive to Kamoj, but she could also see the advantages. She imagined having a mental string with beads in her mind, to help her do arithmetic. It would certainly make bookkeeping less onerous.

The pilot's voice came into the air. "Prepare for inversion drop."

Kamoj sighed. Secondary Ko had "explained" inversion: *Add an imaginary component to your speed, so it becomes a complex number, and you can go around the light speed singularity, giving you access to superluminal speeds.* The taciturn Jagernaut had revealed this with flourish, as if it carried deep import. Well. Indeed. Kamoj had no clue what it meant. The "equations" Ko showed her looked like demented Argali vine patterns someone had drawn after smoking crushed ophine scales.

"So," Kamoj said dryly. "When we drop out of inversion, do we hit the floor?"

Vyrl smiled. "We're just returning to normal space." Leaning his head back, he closed his eyes. "It makes us easier to detect, so we have to be careful."

"On approach to the Lyshriol system," the pilot said.

Kamoj waited for the pressure that came whenever a ship left or reached a place. She felt nothing, though, aside from the nausea of her space sickness.

"Are we going to land?" she asked.

"Not yet," Vyrl said. "It takes a while to cross the system even when we're traveling close to light speed."

"You mean we're going almost as fast as the *Current?*"

"That's right."

Kamoj wasn't sure she believed him. "It doesn't feel like we're moving at all."

He opened his eyes. "We've dropped in and out of quasis twice in the past few minutes."

"Quasis?"

"Quantum stasis. It fixes the molecular wavefunction of the ship."

"Oh, well, I haven't had my molar cuticle wave-funted lately." When Vyrl laughed, she said, "What does "in and out of quasis" mean?"

"It keeps us from being crushed. You know how, when we go fast in a magcar, you feel pushed against the seat?"

Kamoj held back a smile, thinking of mag slugs. But she knew Vyrl meant the cars on the *Ascendant*. "They do have that effect."

"It's a lot stronger when we speed up or slow down in a star ship. We're dumping speed *fast*. The process would turn us into juice if we had no protection." He sat up straighter. "Quasis doesn't freeze us, it just makes it impossible for anything to change. We essentially turn into completely rigid objects. Not even our thoughts can change, which is why you don't notice the interlude."

Kamoj squinted at him. "And this is safe?"

"Safer than riding a greenglass stag."

That struck her as a good answer. "Will we pass other worlds on the way to yours?"

He shook his head. "Lyshriol is the only one the engineers put in this system." Anticipation touched his voice. "It's orbit is a circle and it has no axial tilt. That means every day is the same length and we have no seasons. The weather is almost always good." He paused. "Having two suns does complicate the tides and climate, though."

Kamoj found it hard to imagine. "It sounds so strange."

"I suppose. It's all I've ever known, though." He gave her a rueful smile. "To me, the seasons and diurnal variations on Balumil seem wild and violent."

"I'm not surprised." It astonished her that his people had chosen Balumil as a *close* match to his world. What wondrous differences must exist in the universe, that these Skolians considered Balumil and Lyshriol similar.

The Jagernauts continued to work, loading packs now. Kamoj became aware of pressure pushing her into her chair. She blanched, remembering Vyrl's words about "quasis." She hoped they weren't about to become juice.

"Prepare for landing," the pilot said.

As the Jagernauts meshed into their seats, the pressure grew stronger. Kamoj threw an alarmed glance at Vyrl. "What happened to the quasis?"

He didn't seem at all concerned. "We don't need it to land. Besides, landing involves too many changes in our surroundings. The ship doesn't alter during quasis, so if it comes out somewhere too different from where it went in, the discontinuous forces could tear it apart."

Kamoj made a *hmmph* sound. "I think you Skolians came up with all this business when you were in a bad mood from a stomachache."

Vyrl laughed. "Could be."

As the pressure increased, she fell silent. The Jagernauts sat in readiness, apparently unaffected, but Vyrl didn't look as if he felt much better than she did. Although his education made him seem experienced, she realized now that he had almost never traveled. She wasn't sure what it meant that he had attended university as a VR simulacrum, using the ultrafast communications provided by Ruby technology, but it had apparently let him study without ever leaving Lyshriol.

The racer finally landed. Like a finely tooled machine with eight parts, the Jagernauts prepared to disembark. A statuesque woman named Primary Stillmorn led the team. She stood as tall as Vyrl, with short red hair and a strong face. Like Secondary Ko, she had many muscles. Even though the female Jagernauts curved like women, they seemed masculine to Kamoj. She had expected them to scorn her as too soft. Instead, they treated her well. She felt their curiosity about her, and their courtesy in holding back their questions.

As they left the racer, cool air gusted over Kamoj's face. The onslaught of sights made her head reel. They were in a small valley, little more than a cup in the mountains. Beyond the area blown clear by their landing, light blue snow dusted the ground. Needles of rock bordered the barren pocket, scantily clad in snow. To the south, the mountains fell away in gentle slopes; to the north, large peaks jutted into the lavender sky, rising into the distance until they blurred into an ice-blue haze.

The two suns had risen half way to the zenith: Valdor and Aldan—the Bard and his Younger Brother. They shone with far less ferocity than Jul, who punctured the Balumil sky like a white-hot bead hammered into the heavens. Yet these suns were *huge*. Valdor looked like a gold coin. Aldan was a darker gold and about three quarters the size of his brother. Halfway in front Valdor, the smaller sun had a blurred look about its edges, like a halo. Sunlight streamed everywhere, gold and clear.

Kamoj flared the membranes in her nostrils. Rich and pure, the crystalline air had an astringent scent, as bracing as icy water. This high in the mountains she smelled no plants, or at least no fragrance she associated with any she knew, but she caught other scents, musky and faint, perhaps animals of some kind.

Tilting up his head, Vyrl closed his eyes. The wind played with his curls. His joy at coming home spread to Kamoj, an emotion as deep as the vibrant sky.

She and Vyrl had on hiking clothes and brown leather

jackets that flapped in the wind. Her outfit's web system kept her body at just the right temperature despite the chill air. She had expected the boots to fit like iron, but they flexed with her feet, easy and comfortable.

Vyrl opened his eyes. "What do you think?"

"It's beautiful." She gazed out across the panorama of mountains. "Terrifying, too."

"That's how I felt about Balumil at first."

She turned back to him. "And now?"

"Your world awes me, especially since I understand better what it takes to survive there."

Awe. It wasn't usually a word people used for a place they thought of as home. But it was a start. Perhaps someday he would love Balumil.

Stillmorn and her team spread out, checking the area. The pilot, an angular woman in the gray uniform of the Pharaoh's Army, remained with the racer. Kamoj and Vyrl stood to one side, trying to stay out of the way. Kamoj wished she had more to do.

"We will," Vyrl said. "Our role is different. They're here to protect us."

She glanced up at him. "You're doing that even more now."

"Doing what?"

"Listening to me think."

"I don't mean to be invasive. I'm still regaining my control."

She hesitated. "Will your mind ever heal?"

It was a moment before he answered. "Maybe not fully. But it's improving."

Stillmorn came over to them. "We're ready to go."

"Are you shrouded?" Vyrl asked.

The Primary nodded. "The jammers disguise our EM signatures and hide our augmentations. As far as we know, AWOE intel can't compensate for this new model. If their monitors pick us up, we should look like natives."

"AWOE intel?" Kamoj asked.

Vyrl squinted at her. "I think it means Military Intelligence for the forces of the Allied Worlds of Earth."

A smile touched Stillmorn's face. "That is correct, sir."

Although the Primary said nothing to her team, they suddenly finished their various tasks and came over, taking up positions around Vyrl and Kamoj. Kamoj's breath caught. Psions. From what she understood, the Jagernauts had much less telepathic strength than Vyrl. Nor could the neural enhancements in their brains boost their abilities too high without causing damage. But apparently it gave enough amplification to let the team link minds when they were this close together, so they could share brief thoughts among themselves if they had the training and sufficient concentration.

But that wasn't what surprised her the most. She had no link to the Jagernauts—yet she picked up a vague sense of their communication.

Can you hear them? she thought to Vyrl. Then she asked what she really wanted to know. *Can you hear me?*

A susurration came from his mind, like wind in a distant forest: *A bit, you more than them.* None of it seemed to faze him. Kamoj doubted she would ever have his casual acceptance of such marvels.

They walked to the southern edge of the valley. As they climbed its side, blue powder sifted around them. Kamoj smiled at the pretty snow. Compared to the ice-blizzards on Balumil, this was a benediction.

At the top of the valley, she paused between two crags. On the other side, after a short drop, a slope rolled down into the mountains. Cloaked in snow, it sparkled in the streaming sunlight. Jagged fingers of rock jutted up here and there. She drew in a breath, taking in the pure air and spectacular view.

Two Jagernauts were scouting ahead. With fluid grace, Vyrl jumped down to the slope, landing in snow up to his waist. Powder swirled around him. He headed down the slope with three Jagernauts, his boots kicking up blue eddies.

When Kamoj tried to jump, vertigo swept over her. The slope wasn't that steep. She should have no trouble hiking here. But she couldn't move. It wasn't that the scene bothered her: far from it. Lyshriol enchanted her. But the sky, snow, and suns, the needled mountains, the rich air—it all saturated her mind.

"Governor Argali," Stillmorn said. "Would you like the neural relaxant?"

Kamoj turned her head. The Primary had stopped on the other side of the rock needle. She was watching Kamoj with concern.

"Yes," Kamoj said, strained and tense. "Thank you."

Stillmorn took a tube from her jacket. Dazza had explained it when they ran tests on Kamoj; the relaxant would alter the level of certain chemicals in her brain to help her handle the overflow of sensory input.

Stillmorn leaned past the crag and pressed the tube against Kamoj's neck. Despite Dazza's assurances that the relaxant would cause no harm, Kamoj clutched the rock, half-expecting to topple over the edge of the valley. After several moments, though, tranquility spread over her. Lyshriol became manageable. Life was serene.

Vyrl had stopped down the slope and was looking up at them. Afraid he would come back and cosset her, Kamoj dropped over the edge. She lost her balance when she landed and sat down with a thump. She beamed as the snow puffed around her in a blue cloud.

Stillmorn jumped down next to her. As the Primary helped her stand, Kamoj gave her a beatific smile. Then she started down the slope, headed for Vyrl's home.

Stained-glass bubble forest.

It glowed in the distance, at the foothills of the Backbone Mountains. As they hiked nearer, Kamoj could make out separate trees. Flat bubbles in stained-glass hues floated around tubes, which in turn branched out from clusters of larger tubes, all of them as clear as tinted glass. The gem colors beguiled her.

They had left the snow behind. Now Vyrl strode through a field of slender, supple tubules that rippled around his knees with glimmering translucence. He started to run toward the forest, his jacket flapping open, his joy vivid in Kamoj's mind. As he passed the first tree, he plucked a "leaf" and twirled it through the air. The disk inflated and floated on the breezes like a red soap bubble, catching sparks of sunlight.

"Pretty," Stillmorn said.

"It truly is." Over the past few hours Kamoj had come to like the taciturn Primary who strode at her side, always present yet never intrusive.

They followed Vyrl and the other Jagernauts into the forest. The sunlight turned into jeweled colors as it slanted through the canopy. The bubble "leaves" were connected to the glassy pipes by slender stems made from the same translucent substance. Kamoj paused to touch a yellow leaf. It vibrated on its stalk, then delicately broke off and drifted into the air, swelling into a sphere. The bubble brushed another stalk and popped, spraying glitter all over Kamoj.

"Oh!" Laughing, she brushed off the sparkles.

They found the others in a small clearing filled with multi-hued shadows. A carpet of crumbled bubbles covered the ground, dusted by glitter they must have sprayed when they popped. Although the sparkling powder looked nothing like the fat seeds on Balumil, Vyrl had told her it played a similar role, spurring tubules to grow. Kamoj thought it resembled Balumil's scale dust more. But exposure to the glitter posed her no danger, whereas the scale dust could kill Vyrl.

He was kneeling on the ground. As he brushed away loam, Stillmorn knelt across from him and went to work on a computer in her wrist gauntlet. The other Jagernauts remained standing, some monitoring the area, others guarding Kamoj and Vyrl. The serenity of the forest soothed after the exhilarating hike down the mountains.

"I can't find it." Vyrl was digging in the loam now.

Stillmorn frowned at a display on her gauntlet. "I'm not registering anything either."

He sat back on his heels. "Are you sure this is the place?"

"Positive." She looked up. "Unless AWOE intel discovered the base and tampered with our security."

"How?" Vyrl asked. "I've lived here my entire life, and I never had any idea this forest sat on top of an ISC installation."

"But you had no reason to look. The Allied forces will have scanned this area thoroughly."

"Can they break our security?" Vyrl asked.

She ran another check on her gauntlet computer. "I wouldn't think so. But we can't be certain."

"Are you sure you've all the right codes?"

"Except for the Rhon codes. Only you have those."

He spread his hands out to his sides. "I can't use my mind to trigger a mechanism if I can't find the mechanism."

Kamoj had trouble concentrating on their words. The neural relaxant made her mind drift. She closed her eyes, listening to the forest. The pipes vibrated in the wind, producing musical tones. The chimes, the unfamiliar fragrances of the forest, and the murmuring voices blended together until she submerged into a trance.

"It's the resonance," she murmured.

"Governor?" Stillmorn asked.

"The resonance." Kamoj opened her eyes and gave Vyrl a dreamy smile. "Can't you feel it? This place amplifies our resonance." Her thoughts drifted on the wind. "I can find your ancient place."

"Ancient place?" Vyrl asked. "What do you mean?"

Kamoj knelt next to him. "It's old. Ancient. Alive."

Stillmorn froze, staring at her. "I'm afraid you're mistaken, Governor Argali."

Kamoj watched the play of red, blue, and violet light on Stillmorn's face. "It knows Vyrl is here. It . . . recognizes him." Turning to Vyrl, she took his hand. "But it can't reach you."

"Flaming hell," Stillmorn said.

Vyrl gave the Primary an appraising stare. "You know what she's talking about, don't you?"

"It's secured," she answered.

Vyrl scowled. "I *have* a need to know."

Stillmorn considered him. Then she said, "The base we're looking for is over five thousand years old. It dates from the Ruby Empire. It's small, only the one room we described to you. We've managed to modernize the telops chair you need for your work, but the other machines are long dead."

"It's not dead," Kamoj said. "It wants Vyrl."

Vyrl looked from Stillmorn to Kamoj. "I don't understand what you mean," he told Kamoj.

"It has waited many ages." As Kamoj became of aware of everyone listening to her, she began to lose her trance. "I'm not sure what it wants. I only caught impressions."

Stillmorn was scrutinizing her. "None of Prince Havyrl's family has ever experienced this. How can you?"

"I don't know. It's aware his family is here, though."

Vyrl frowned at the Primary. "Apparently that knowledge wasn't reciprocal for my family."

"Your half-brother Kurj knew," Stillmorn said. "Also your sister, when she became Imperator. And probably your brother Althor."

Kamoj felt Vyrl's conflicted emotions. He resented the ignorance that ISC pressed on his family, yet he also realized that his siblings who had commanded ISC were the only ones who truly needed to know. His mood flooded her, their resonance enhanced by whatever slumbered below the forest.

"What is the Imperator?" Kamoj asked.

"Commander in chief of the ISC forces," Vyrl said. "The Imperial Fleet, Pharaoh's Army, Jagernaut Force, and Advance Services Corps." His face had turned distant with his memories. "Some called my half-brother Kurj a military dictator, but I never saw him that way. Soz was brilliant, and Althor had a gift for strategy."

"Who is Imperator now?" Kamoj asked. She noticed that the Primary had gone as still as her name, as if she were trying to become invisible while they discussed the leaders she served.

"My brother Kelric," Vyrl said. "The Allieds were holding him, my parents, and Kurj's family on Earth. They let my parents return here for—" He swallowed. "For my father's death. Naaj Majda, General of the Pharaoh's Army, is acting as Imperator until Kelric can assume his duties."

Kamoj could guess what Vyrl meant by "assume his duties." He hoped his brother Kelric could someday escape Earth. Vyrl had claimed their titles were titular, but the more she heard about his family, the less it sounded that way.

Stillmorn continued to watch her closely. "Does your link to the base cause you pain?"

Kamoj shook her head. "No. That place is asleep."

"Can you wake it?" Vyrl asked.

"I don't think that's wise," Stillmorn said. "We have no idea what we might stir up. We can't risk this mission. We can investigate when it's over."

Vyrl didn't look thrilled, but he nodded. "Yes, of course."

Kamoj felt as if a dream were drifting away from them like scale dust on the wind. They might never have another chance to investigate. If they became prisoners, they couldn't let the AWOE forces know about the base. Although she had nothing against Earth, Vyrl had her undisputed loyalty.

Stillmorn went back to work on her gauntlet. "I'm still not getting any activity."

Vyrl started scooping out the loam again. "How far down is the safe door?"

"Too far to dig all the way. But you should have found the trigger by now." Suddenly she said, "Wait a minute!"

Vyrl straightened up. "Yes?"

"I caught something . . ." Tiny holos appeared above her gauntlet. "I'll be damned. It's *scared*." She grinned at Vyrl. "The EI brain that controls the trigger is hiding from us."

He blinked at her. "Why?"

"Let's see . . . All right. I have it." She studied the display. "It knows AWOE intel breached the ODS. So it hid. It didn't recognize us. I'm downloading your brain wave patterns— all right, try now."

A red tube rose out of the ground, much like the stems of the trees. Vyrl scooted closer, until he was kneeling over it. He placed his hands around the tube and gazed into its open end. Rose-hued sunlight reflected from its glassy surface onto his face.

So they waited. Kamoj had expected a more dramatic scene when Vyrl used the gifts that made his family unique among all humanity. Instead, they had a serene moment in a forest while he knelt in silence.

Suddenly the tube began to turn itself into the ground. As it disappeared, Vyrl raised his head, his face drawn. "We should move back." He stood up, his motions slow and heavy.

"Prince Havyrl?" Stillmorn rose to her feet, her attention focused on him. "Are you all right?"

"Yes. Fine, thank you."

Kamoj stood up as well. She felt Vyrl's headache as if it were her own. He wasn't ready to use his mind this way. He hadn't healed enough.

Vyrl gave her a tired smile. "You look like a vision, bathed in all the colors of the forest, with glitter in your hair."

"I wish you didn't have to do this," she said.

"It's all right. I just wish . . ."

He didn't finish, but she felt his craving. He wanted a drink. A strong one.

Then the ground collapsed.

The hole Vyrl had dug fell inward, revealing a well. Glinting loam dribbled from the sides, and three ladders descended into the hole.

Kamoj climbed down with two Jagernauts, one above and one below. Vyrl and the rest of the drop-down team used the other ladders. Sunshine sifted over them, and also loam, which the walls of the shaft seemed to absorb. Kamoj guessed that nanobots ferried away the dirt, though she wasn't sure if that insight came from her own mind or someone else.

The safe door filled the bottom of the well like a plug. They hung on their ladders above it while Stillmorn worked her gauntlet. Then the door slid to the side, retracting into the wall, and they continued down. After they were past the door, it closed, leaving them in darkness.

Blue light suddenly filled the well. Looking down, Kamoj saw that they still had a long ways to climb. Too far. Her grip on the ladder tightened.

They continued to the bottom, which was—the bottom of a well. Bare. Empty. A dead end. But Stillmorn went to work on her gauntlet again, and the wall beside Kamoj soon shimmered into an archway. A tunnel stretched beyond it, lit with blue light.

Kamoj walked with Vyrl down the tunnel. She had become so attuned to him that she even felt his tenuous mental link to the Jagernauts now. At the tunnel's end, Stillmorn opened another entrance—

And they walked into the impossible.

21

Stained Glass Slumber

Ancient Potential

Stillmorn had been right—in part. A single room did lie at the end of the tunnel.

Beyond it lay a city.

It extended in every direction, huge and dark, filled with shadows. Only dimly visible in the darkness, gigantic machines hulked in row after endless row as far as Kamoj could see.

"Flaming mother," Stillmorn said. "What the hell happened?"

They were standing in the entrance of a chamber about ten by ten paces. A white grid defined its walls, the well-spaced bars making squares almost as tall as a person. An ancient chair stood in the room's center, attended by modern machines. Beyond the chamber, a shadowed complex spread out, forever it seemed, too big to take in all at once.

Stillmorn entered the chamber, turning in a circle as she walked. "This room is all we knew about. The walls were solid. We went over this place with microbes even. We had no *hint* the rest existed."

Kamoj barely heard. Staring out at the city, she walked past Stillmorn. She was aware of the Primary turning to her, but she kept going. At the grid-wall, she ducked her head and stepped through a square. A wash of blue light from the tunnel softened the shadows.

The city pulled Kamoj, a call she couldn't hear, only feel. The floor was corrugated in places, smooth in others. She walked north, to the right, out onto a metal catwalk. It had chains for rails and a segmented floor, like the swinging bridges that stretched across crevices in the North Sky Islands, high above the thundering sea. But no water surged below this bridge.

An abyss opened beneath her. Towers rose from its shadowed depths, too large to comprehend. Just the rounded crown of the nearest looked bigger than the entire Quartz Palace. The slits of her pupils dilated, adjusting to the dark. She was a mote dwarfed by immensity. One misstep on this walkway and she would plummet into the chasm.

"Sweet Airys," Kamoj whispered.

"Governor Argali," a voice said.

Kamoj turned to find Stillmorn standing next to her. "It would be best to come on back now, ma'am," the Primary said.

"Of course." Kamoj caught her lower lip with her teeth, acutely aware of the emptiness below her.

The catwalk was too narrow for two people to walk abreast, so Kamoj followed Stillmorn. It was then that she saw the four Jagernauts standing at a retaining wall that bordered the chasm, their snouted guns up and aimed. One of them fired. A net shot across the chasm and caught the catwalk near Kamoj. With a start, she realized they had already fired several times. Webs stretched from the wall to the catwalk. Had she fallen, those nets would have caught her—but whether or not they would have held her weight was another question altogether, one she was glad not to answer.

Vyrl met them at the end of the bridge, as she stepped onto solid ground. Despite the lack of privacy, he pulled Kamoj into his arms. "Gods," he whispered against her hair. "Don't ever do that again."

She looked up at his strained face. "I don't know why I did. The city . . . it called me."

Stillmorn had stopped next to Vyrl. "Do you feel anything?"

"I'm not sure. Maybe a pressure on my mind?" He rubbed his temple. "Let's get to work, so we can get out of this place."

"You set up," Stillmorn said. "We'll secure the area."

Kamoj touched Vyrl's face, wishing she knew how to ease away the new lines around his eyes. He took her hand and kissed the palm. Then they returned to the grid-room, accompanied by three Jagernauts. The chair sat on a dais, washed in blue light. It reminded Kamoj of a throne. The massive armrests were two hand-spans wide, the back of the chair even thicker. The seat had a molded look, similar to the *Ascendant* couches that adjusted when a person sat on them. Panels, screens, projections, and jointed arms attended the chair, and she suspected more devices crammed its interior.

As Vyrl settled into the chair, lights came on within it, but they gave almost no illumination. In the shadows, his face had a brooding aspect, one heightened by his distant gaze, as if he were already leaving the conscious realm. He made Kamoj think of Ba Vitz, the Balumil god who ruled the skies and sat on a mica-stone throne high in the East Sky Mountains.

Stillmorn came up on the other side of the chair. "Shall we start?"

"Yes." Vyrl stared into the shadows. Kamoj didn't think he was looking at anything, at least not in this reality.

Stillmorn worked on her gauntlet computer, and lights moved within the chair like trains of firepuff flies swirling in the long Balumil evening. "Did you receive that?" she asked.

"I think so. You activated the D-four memory cells." Vyrl paused. "I'm patching into the computer web that ISC installed down here. It's difficult, though, without my having a hard link to this console. The data stream down here is noisy."

Stillmorn glanced up but didn't say the obvious, that Vyrl had refused to have hardjack sockets implanted in his body.

Kamoj was surprised he had let ISC put anything at all inside him.

He shifted his gaze to her. "I didn't. They implanted the biomech web without telling me, after they recovered the coffin from space."

"I'm sorry." What *else* had they done to him?

"Sorry?" He regarded her with a guarded expression. "Why? It's a superb system. State of the art."

Kamoj felt what lay beneath his words, how much he disliked the biomech. She said nothing, respecting his wish to keep his reaction private. In his position, she wouldn't have wanted to talk about it either, surrounded by Jagernauts with far more biomech in their bodies, augmentations they had freely chosen.

Vyrl brushed his fingers across her cheek, the shadow of a smile on his drawn face. Then he settled back in the chair and closed his eyes.

Stillmorn was working on her gauntlet. "Are you into the web system?"

"The one in this room," Vyrl said. "I haven't managed a link to the orbital defense system yet."

"Have you encountered anything unusual?" She glanced at Kamoj. "Anything like what Governor Argali detected earlier?"

"Not yet."

"Do you feel any strain?"

"No." Then Vyrl said, "Yes. My head aches."

The Primary spoke quietly. "Colonel Pacal gave me meds for your alcohol withdrawal. I can give you a dose."

"No." Vyrl rolled his shoulders as if to shed his tension. A few moments later he spoke. "There it is. Take a look."

Stillmorn frowned at the screen of her gauntlet computer. "I'm not reading anything. What did you find?"

"I opened a pathway to the ODS web. But it's full of Allied traps." He fell silent for awhile. Then he said, "I've found a Rhon back door."

"Can you go through?" Stillmorn asked.

"I think so. The Allieds haven't found the Rhon entrances. They don't know how to look for them." He sat for several minutes, still and silent, his eyes closed. Then: "All right. I'm in."

"Good work." The faint furrows on Stillmorn's forehead went away, which for the cool-headed Primary was a great display of relief. She glanced at Kamoj. "Governor Argali, you'll have to go now."

Kamoj nodded. They had discussed this on the *Ascendant*. Vyrl had the means to access the ODS and Stillmorn knew how to use the system. Until now, those two resources—means and knowledge—had been kept separate, for the sake of security. But only Vyrl could go beyond the Rhon doors. The time had come for Stillmorn to tell him what she knew. No reason existed, however, for Kamoj to listen.

As she withdrew from the room, two Jagernauts came with her, a man and a woman. She wished Antonyo was here; she felt more comfortable with him than these strangers. She hadn't realized how stiff she had become until her shoulders relaxed. It hurt to watch Vyrl in that chair, his mind dissociated, his resources drained, his body exhausted but craving the seductively ruinous drink.

She walked to the retaining wall and gazed into the chasm. Across the abyss, a tower rose from the depths. How far down did that monstrous structure go? She longed to search for answers, but whatever secrets slept here would have to wait.

Kamoj turned away. With her bodyguards, she walked past the chamber where Vyrl was working and went into a maze of pipes on the other side. They ran back into the shadows, glinting in the dim light like a forest, dark green, murky red, metallic blue, varying from columns wider than her body to tubes as slender as her wrist. She had to duck to keep from banging her head, then lift her feet over barriers. No dust showed anywhere, though this maze had been here far longer than modern civilization had existed. Perhaps like the nanobots in the Quartz Palace, invisible servants preserved this empty city long after its builders had vanished.

A Jagernaut was up ahead, monitoring the area. When he stopped to examine a pipe, Kamoj caught up to him. He bowed from the waist. "My honor at your company, Your Highness."

"My greetings." The formality made her self-conscious, but curiosity overcame her reticence. "Have you found out anything about this place?"

"A bit o'bit." He motioned at the pipes. "These beauts are over five thousand years old."

"What do they do?"

"Aye, now that's a question." He regarded her with green eyes. "Can't say I know, ma'am. Plumbing? Climate control? Seems primitive for a people who could move planets. But truth be told, the Ruby Empire was a mishmash o' high-tech and barbarism."

She hadn't expected that. "Even their machines?"

"Especially their machines." He waved his hands at the pipes. "What were our ancestors? Primitives, that's what, thousands o'years ago, carried away from Earth without the least warning. But on their new world, they made starships, eh? Well, I'll tell you how. They had some to work from, see, wrecks left by those folk who dumped them there. And the original crews o'those ships? What happened to them? Gods only know."

Kamoj smiled, charmed by his dialect. She recalled what Vyrl had told her. "I thought the Ruby Empire had technology so advanced no one can replicate it even now."

"S'truth we can't replicate it. I don't rightly know if 'advanced' is the word. It's *different*. They came at things from other angles."

She looked at the pipes going off in every direction. "I guess their logic made sense to them."

He laughed. "Aye, ma'am, we can hope so."

Kamoj knew he would answer her questions as long as she asked, even if it meant a reprimand from Stillmorn for neglecting his work. So she thanked him and moved on. After a ways, she stopped by a green pipe that rose up straight, then bent over and stretched off in a tangle of other pipes. Setting her hand on its cool surface, she closed her eyes and let her mind drift.

Deep.

Old.

Asleep.

Just as a ball held high in the air had the potential to fall, so mental energy surrounded her, waiting to let go.

Waiting.

A ball needed someone to release it. This sleeper sought its keys. Not her. Not Kamoj. Its plea rose in her mind from a level below conscious thought: *Bring him.*

Who are you? she asked.

So long have I waited. So long. . . . Bring him.

Do you mean Vyrl?

Ruby prince . . . The presence faded . . .

"—won't answer!" The man's voice broke her concentration.

Wait! she thought to the presence. *Come back.*

No answer.

"Governor Argali!" Someone was shaking her shoulders.

Kamoj opened her eyes. Her bodyguards were staring at her, and the man had his hands on her shoulders. Seeing Kamoj focus on his face, he exhaled and dropped his arms.

The woman had that inward expression Kamoj had come to recognize, the sign that the Jagernauts were mind-speaking. IR. Radio. Photons. Neutrinos. Kamoj didn't understand. She wished they would use their gauntlets, something she could *see*. Where lay the line between technology and telepathy? The two seemed so intertwined, she couldn't separate them.

"Please don't bother Primary Stillmorn," Kamoj said.

The woman looked apologetic. "I already notified her, ma'am."

"Are you all right, Governor Argali?" the man asked. "You seemed in a trance."

"It's this place," Kamoj said. "It's alive. It wants Vyrl, but it can't reach him."

"How do you know?" the woman asked.

"It's hard to describe. I only had a few seconds with it."

The man's forehead furrowed. "Governor, you were standing there for thirty minutes."

Kamoj stared at him. "No. Are you sure?"

"You told us to let you rest," he said.

"I did? I don't remember."

The woman spoke. "Primary Stillmorn wants us back in the console room. She and Prince Havyrl are finished. You need to tell her about this."

As they headed back, Kamoj looked around the maze. She knew its purpose now. It focused the presence that slept here. Whatever in her mind resonated with Vyrl somehow also resonated with this ancient entity.

But what did it want?

The ten of them filled the grid-room. Stillmorn leaned against a console and Vyrl sat in the chair, with Kamoj at his side. The Jagernauts stood posted around the grid walls, listening.

"If it's trying to reach me," Vyrl said, "it's failing."

Stillmorn studied Kamoj as if the Argali governor held secrets that Kamoj herself didn't know how to unlock. "Do you feel danger from it? Threat? Malice? Hostility?"

Kamoj shook her head. "Power, yes, but no threat. It serves the Ruby Dynasty, but no one has summoned it for ages."

"Serves how?" Vyrl asked.

Kamoj spread her arms. "I don't know."

"Will it try to stop Vyrl or you from leaving here?" Stillmorn asked.

"I don't think so," Kamoj said.

Stillmorn began to pace. "We'll report this to the *Ascendant*. But we can't stay here. If we delay, we could compromise the mission." She stopped and considered everyone in the room. "After we vacate this base, none of you are to mention what we found here. Understood?"

A murmur of assent answered her. Nor did Kamoj miss her implication. *Report to the* Ascendant. Even just minutes ago, that would have been impossible.

"You did it!" Kamoj said to Vyrl. "You got through."

He rested his elbow on the arm of the chair, leaning slightly toward her. "I've set up a link to the *Ascendant,* yes. However, it won't be easy to use."

That sounded like it defeated the purpose of all their work. "But wasn't the intent to set up an easy link?"

Stillmorn answered. "The *Ascendant* is too far outside this star system. With our signals going at light speed, it would take months for them to reach the ship, and they could easily be intercepted. That makes the process useless for our work here."

Dismayed, Kamoj said, "Then how can we talk to them?"

A hint of Vyrl's wicked grin came back. "With stowaways. We'll piggyback our messages onto signals destined for Allied starships, have the messages hide in the ship's comm system, and then have those systems transmit the messages to the *Ascendant* at the appropriate time."

Kamoj didn't see how that helped. "Then the Allieds will know everything."

"Not if we've set it up right," Stillmorn said. "We'll code and hide the messages. AWOE intel can't detect the process without a Rhon psion who is willing to cooperate with them. Even if they do figure out we're doing it, they can't stop us unless they completely cut off the Lyshriol system from the rest of their forces—which would mean the *Ascendant* could move in. If this works, everything we do from now on will be broadcast to the *Ascendant*."

It better work, Kamoj thought. Otherwise, they had sacrificed Vyrl's well-being for no reason.

"The *Ascendant* public relations office will decide how much of what we send to them, they will release to the news services," Vyrl said. "We won't know what's going on, though, because the *Ascendant* doesn't have any Rhon psions now either, so they have no way to send messages back to me."

Stillmorn looked around at them all. "I won't mislead you. If we can't get out these broadcasts, we have almost no chance of success. All we can do is give it our best shot."

Vyrl smiled tiredly. "Let's just hope that's the only shot fired."

"Would that the fates hear that wish, your highness." Stillmorn gestured to the entrance to the chamber as if inviting them to dinner. "Shall we?"

Vyrl rose to his feet. "Yes. Let's go to Dalvador."

Plains spread to the horizon in a rippling silver-green ocean. The grass consisted of tubules that were as sheer as slender glass straws, but as soft and as flexible as velvet. It came up to Vyrl's knees and Kamoj's thighs, slowing their trek through that vast, swaying ocean.

The grass chimed when breezes tickled it. Tiny bubbles nodded on the tips of the tubules. When Kamoj touched one, it detached and drifted into the air. Then it popped, releasing a pinch of silver glitter. As they hiked through the plains, they scattered bubbles everywhere, leaving a floating trail that glistened in the sunlight.

Vyrl's joy suffused Kamoj. Dalvador. His home. She had imagined soaring ruby towers, or a place of strange angles, or endless machines. Instead, plains surrounded them, their simplicity far more beautiful then her extravagant mind images.

He spread his arms wide. "I feel like a boy again."

Kamoj smiled. "Why do you say that?"

"I grew up here. My farmstead is in the south, but I ran in these plains when I was a boy." His mood quieted. "My father died in Dalvador, in our family home. That was my last sight of this place."

"I'm sorry," Kamoj murmured.

"He had a good life." Vyrl seemed less strained now than the other times he had spoken of his father. "He was ninety when he died. My brothers and sisters came from all over Rillia and Dalvador to say good-bye. They will still be at the house, I think." His grin flashed at her. "My brothers will envy me. I'll have to make sure they don't charm you away."

Kamoj pretended to give him a quelling look. "You're a sweet talker, Oh Exalted Prince Whats-It."

Vyrl laughed and draped his arm around her shoulders, pulling her so close that she thudded against his side and tripped in the grass.

A Jagernaut up ahead called back. "I see a building."

It rose out of the silvery plain, a round, white-washed tower with a blue turreted roof. Then Dalvador came into view.

For all her attempts to imagine Vyrl's home, Kamoj would never have expected this rustic village. Ah, but it was lovely. The turreted roofs were bright blue or purple, with upturned edges, like blossoms set upside down on round, white houses. The buildings clustered along lanes paved in blue cobblestones. Stained-glass gardens surrounded them, and bubbles floated through the village, popping now and then to spangle people with glitter. The dynasty that had founded one of the greatest interstellar empires ever known to humanity lived in a village that appeared, on the outside, even more primitive than Argali.

Vyrl took off, with a Jagernaut running on either side of him. As they neared the village, children dashed out to meet him. Wind tousled their hair and fluttered their clothes. Caught by the excitement, Kamoj sped after him. This close to Dalvador, the plains were cropped short, making it easier to run. The children scattered as she reached Vyrl. He grabbed her around the waist and swung her in a circle, making the children shriek with delight.

"Hai!" Kamoj gasped. "Put me down!"

Grinning, he set her on her feet. Youngsters ran around them and bedeviled the perplexed Jagernauts. The children seemed to know Vyrl. In fact, many of them *looked* like Vyrl, with tawny hair and well-formed features. A small girl threw her arms around his waist and burbled in an unfamiliar language. Another girl stared solemnly at Kamoj, her violet eyes large in her freckled face. Two boys collided with Vyrl and pummeled him with gusto.

Trying to hold them all in his arms, Vyrl looked over their heads at Kamoj. "Come to Dalvador with me and my great-grandchildren."

Seeing him so happy lightened her heart. "I would be honored."

Together they entered the town, surrounded by children and Jagernauts. As they walked through Dalvador, they collected adults: women in richly dyed dresses and skirts made from scarves that swirled around their knees, showing their legs, then hiding them; men who dressed as Vyrl had on the *Ascendant*, in trousers, bell-sleeved shirts, and knee-boots. Everyone called to everyone else. A girl skipped along playing a stained-glass pipe. It wasn't clear if all these people actually knew Vyrl or if they were just coming along for the excitement.

The immaculate streets and houses offered Kamoj the first indication that this village relied on a more advanced culture for its upkeep. It showed no sign of the dirt and disarray that, in her experience, came when thousands of people lived together.

Suddenly a voice cried out. A young woman was running down the lane toward them, her tawny curls streaming behind her body. As she came through the crowd, people stopped to watch. The Jagernauts stiffened, their hands dropping to the snouted guns on their belts. Just when it seemed the woman would barrel into Vyrl, she skidded to a stop and threw her arms around him. Tears were running down her face. He was crying too, hugging her as they both spoke at the same time.

Then more adults were there, crowding around Vyrl, tall men and women with violet eyes and lion's hair, some graying, some young, most in between, all talking at once, while Vyrl laughed and talked and embraced them.

Kamoj stepped back, giving them space. Even knowing he had a big family, she hadn't expected half the village to greet them. She thought of Maxard and Lyode, her only kin, and of Argali, the province she had left in the hopes of making herself a better leader for her people. Hai, but she missed them. She felt out of place here.

With no warning, Vyrl called her. Flustered, she came forward through the curious crowd. When she reached Vyrl, he drew her to his side and spoke to the others in their language. Everyone went silent. No one seemed to know how to take whatever he had just told them.

Then a woman with gray-streaked hair came forward and clasped Kamoj's hands. She spoke in Iotaca, or Iotic rather, her words softened by an ethereal chiming. "Welcome to Dalvador, wife of my father."

The others greeted Kamoj then, all at once, in Iotic and their own language, the women chiming, the men rumbling. Vyrl switched back and forth between the languages as if his words were melodic water flowing over polished stones.

They set off again, their procession even larger now. More people joined them, coming to celebrate despite having no relation to Vyrl. A second reed player joined the first, and the two girls ran together until they dissolved into laughter. So they all made their way uphill, past white houses and gardens. Bubbles floated around them, liberated from their stalks by children so they could suffer the indignity of being popped.

As they neared the tower, it resolved into one of four that marked the corners of a castle, though perhaps that was too grandiose a word for the picturesque house. Spires topped the towers, with pennants snapping in the breeze. The white-washed wings of the building had the same round shape and turreted roofs as those in the village. Windows sparkled all over the house, some frosted and textured, some stained glass, others clear. It gave Kamoj another hint that this village wasn't as rustic as it appeared; she doubted a culture that primitive could have produced such exquisite glasswork.

A wall of pale blue stone surrounded the castle. After many farewells, the villagers clustered in the fields outside the wall and formed festive groups, stirring up more of the beleaguered bubbles. Vyrl and Kamoj went on alone, to the open gate in the wall. In the courtyard beyond, another group waited. Unlike Dalvador's effusive citizens, these people simply stood. The contrast of their reserved silence with the ebullient villagers made Kamoj feel off-balance, unsure what to expect.

A man stood in front of the group. He was taller than Vyrl, with a leaner build. Wine-red hair brushed his shoulders and metallic lashes fringed his violet eyes. He resembled Vyrl, but his features had a wilder, edgy quality. A woman stood next to him, tall and calm, with yellow curls cascading down her back. She too resembled Vyrl, except her face was angelic, a word Kamoj would never have dreamed of applying to her husband. An even larger man stood on her other side, strong and broad-shouldered, his hair and features almost identical to the center man. His hand rested on the shoulder of a boy of about ten.

All so tall. Kamoj felt shorter by the moment. At least the woman on the other side of the center man was small. A cloud of black curls with metallic gold tips floated around her shoulders. Round and curved, she had a sweet, childlike face that belied the age of her gaze. Two men stood with her, shorter than the other men and slighter in build. One wore his hair in a cap of yellow curls; the other had a fey gaze and white-gold hair that brushed his shoulders.

Then, through the center of the group, a woman came forward.

She shimmered gold: eyes, hair, eyelashes, skin—all except the rosy blooms of her cheeks. A glorious mane of curls streamed around her body down to her hips, gold, copper, bronze, and every metallic hue between. Tall and statuesque, she had a radiant presence that made Kamoj's breath catch. Although her beauty reflected in the other two women, in her it was at full force. As youthful as she appeared, she had the gaze of someone who had seen more years than most people lived. An aura of power surrounded her.

Kamoj held back, letting Vyrl go on alone. He and the golden woman met in the courtyard. A tear ran down the woman's face. With quiet simplicity, she and Vyrl embraced. From the woman, Kamoj felt a profound joy; from Vyrl, a deep, abiding peace.

The others came forward then and clustered around Vyrl, hugging him or slapping his back. For all their outward reserve, their emotions spread out from their minds, just as it had with Vyrl's children and their families. These people loved one another, deeply and fully, with no conditions, no hesitations, and no doubts.

Turning to scan the courtyard, Vyrl caught sight of Kamoj and beckoned her forward. When she came to him, he took her hand. Then he spoke in Iotic to the golden woman. "I present Kamoj Quanta Argali, Governor of Argali in the Northern Lands of Balumil. My wife."

The woman watched Kamoj with an appraising gaze that turned her inside out, weighing the quality of her heart.

Then Vyrl turned to Kamoj. "I present to you Roca Skolia. My mother." Quietly he added, "The Ruby Pharaoh Presumptive of Imperial Skolia."

22

Ruby Dynasty

Multi-Particle Interactions

Kamoj stood in the arched entrance to the Hearth Room, in the shadows. Down the length of the room, Vyrl's family had gathered before the fireplace. The only light came from flames crackling in the hearth.

Roca, Vyrl's mother, sat in an armchair near the fire, in a blue sweater and leggings, her hair spread in a gold waterfall over the chair. Firelight bathed her face. Kamoj found it hard to believe Roca was well into her second century, fifty years older than Vyrl's father—who had died of old age.

According to Vyrl, the longevity of his family came from good heredity, good health care, and "cell repair" treatments that began before their birth. Apparently the nanomeds in their bodies could delay aging. His father had received the meds when he married Roca, but he had been an adult by then, which made the process less effective. It sobered Kamoj to realize that, even with similar treatments, she would age faster than her husband.

Vyrl's older brother, Del-Kurj, sat in an armchair across the hearth from his mother. It was Del-Kurj who had stood at the front of the family in the courtyard today. The golden-haired woman who had stood with him was Chaniece, his twin, younger by five minutes. Now she sat in a chair at his side. They leaned slightly toward each other, though Kamoj didn't think they realized it.

The man with white-gold hair was Shannon, Vyrl's younger brother. He sat in an armchair by Chaniece, dressed in green leggings and a green shirt laced with thongs, his lithe body poised as if he were ready to bolt. He seemed fey to Kamoj, with his pale face and silver eyes. When he leaned forward, his long hair fell across his ears, and their tips poked through the strands. Although Kamoj knew of myths about beings with pointed ears, she had never seen a real person with them. Until now. But if Shannon felt self-conscious about his differences, he showed no sign of it. She wasn't sure he noticed much at all.

Denric, the man with yellow curls, was the brother closest in age to Vyrl. He sat in a chair facing the fire. Instead of Dalvador clothes, he had on gray slacks and a gray sweater. Vyrl's sister Aniece, the small woman with black hair, had curled on a couch near her mother. Lord Rillia, her husband, relaxed next to her, his long legs stretched out, a mug of steaming wine in his hand. It amazed Kamoj that the hale, hearty Rillia was over eighty. He did have silver hair, though, and lines around his eyes. He carried the name of the district he governed, Rillia, which consisted of the Dalvador Plains and its villages, the Stained Glass Forest, the Backbone Mountains, and the extensive Rillian Vales beyond the Backbone.

Vyrl had told her that Del-Kurj's wine-red hair, Chaniece's yellow hair with lavender highlights, and everyone's violet eyes came from their Rillian heritage. But Vyrl's father had also had an ancestor from the Blue Mountain Dales, a cold region far to the north. His family was one of the few that could trace its lineage back to the ancient Dale Archers. Those traits expressed themselves in Shannon, with his silver eyes and smaller size. The height and metallic coloring on some of the others came from their mother, the Pharaoh Presumptive, an offworlder.

Right now Vyrl was sprawled on a couch facing the fire, his legs stretched across the blue stone floor. Like the rest of his family, he held a mug of mulled wine. When he took a swallow, Kamoj wanted to call out in protest. Why had he accepted it? They should never have offered him wine. But how could they know? The Vyrl they remembered hadn't even liked alcohol.

Primary Stillmorn was sitting on the other end of the couch from Vyrl. She had her booted feet planted wide and was resting her elbows on her knees, her hands folded around her mug. *She even sits like a man,* Kamoj thought. But maybe that was unfair. So what if women never sat that way in Argali? Stillmorn didn't come from Argali.

Kamoj wasn't sure about her ideas of masculine and feminine anymore. Vyrl wanted no one to know he danced because men here didn't do that. Yet to her, he embodied a masculine ideal. Her body reacted to him. It was lust, really, though the word embarrassed her. She smiled. If he became any more masculine, she would have to take him up to their bedroom right now.

The circle of his family made her feel closed out. Even her ability to sense Vyrl's moods had receded. After a quiet celebration this afternoon, he had shown Kamoj his childhood bedroom, and she had fallen asleep on the bed. Although it had been kind of them to let her rest, she had been uneasy when she awoke alone in the darkness. But now she felt like an intruder.

As she started to leave, Vyrl called, "Kamoj?"

She turned back, self-conscious. "My greetings."

"Come join us," he said.

Aware of everyone watching, she walked down the hall to the hearth. She wished she looked more presentable. Vyrl and Stillmorn had both changed into clean clothes. In her hiking gear, Kamoj felt she made a poor showing to her new in-laws.

Stillmorn moved to an armchair. As Kamoj sat with Vyrl, he put his arm around her shoulders. A spiced aroma came from his steaming drink. She looked at the wine, then up at him.

"It's fruit juice," he said. "I took it without the wine."

Relief flowed over Kamoj, physical in its intensity. She cupped his cheek in her palm, then remembered everyone watching and flushed. Lowering her hand, she turned to see Vyrl's mother studying her. Kamoj had no idea what Roca saw, but she feared she came up lacking.

At least Denric smiled at her. He seemed more relaxed with offworlders. Apparently he taught school on the world Sandstorm. He had a doctorate in literature, the only person in the immediate family besides Vyrl with an advanced degree. ISC had sent him back here during the war. Neither Chaniece nor Del-Kurj seemed hostile, but neither smiled at her either. Shannon looked through Kamoj as if he were gazing into some other reality.

Kamoj would never have guessed Aniece was almost Vyrl's age. Her husband, Lord Rillia, beamed at Kamoj, much as he did with Aniece. He remained reserved with everyone else, making Kamoj suspect his warmth toward her had more to do with how much she resembled the wife he obviously adored than with anything Kamoj had done. She wondered if anyone called him anything besides Rillia, the name of his province. She wasn't sure the Lyshriol people had provinces, though. Their government seemed rather informal.

"Did you sleep well?" Vyrl asked.

"Yes." Kamoj looked up at him—and he kissed her.

A throaty laugh came from his mother. "Vyrl, do you think you could let her go long enough to finish here?"

Vyrl lifted his head, then turned red as he realized what he had been doing. "Yes. Of course." He released Kamoj and took a long swallow of his mulled juice.

Rillia leaned back in his seat. "It is no wonder you've seemed distracted, with so charming a wife."

Del-Kurj considered Kamoj. "I'm surprised Hamilton Ashman sent you on a special operations assignment."

"Kamoj isn't the one he wanted off the mission." Vyrl said dryly. He glanced at his mother. "I don't understand how you tolerate him."

Roca regarded him with gold eyes. "He's a brilliant war leader, Vyrl. He also knows when to stop warring and look for other solutions."

"True," Vyrl said. "He's also insufferable."

Roca smiled—and it changed her face. No longer was she the sculpted goddess of intimidating perfection. Suddenly she showed an open warmth that Kamoj suspected she reserved only for her family. "You and Hamilton are opposites," Roca said. "He's logic, organization, precision, analysis. You're art, light, emotion, fire. It's no wonder the two of you conflict."

"He's a retentive pain," Vyrl grumbled.

Del-Kurj leaned forward. "That 'pain' set up this whole mission and smuggled you back in here. You might try to remember that."

Vyrl scowled. "Back off, Del."

"Boys," Roca said.

Vyrl gave her an exasperated look. "Mother, I stopped being a boy fifty years ago."

Chaniece smiled at her brother. "It's a hopeless cause, Vyrl. She'll never forget we were her babies."

"Ah, well." Roca sat relaxed in her chair, the hint of a smile on her lips. Kamoj felt her pride in her family, her love for the dynasty she had birthed. It flowed around them in a deep, powerful current.

Vyrl had obviously told none of them what happened in the coffin. It gave Kamoj an insight into her husband: for all that he resented Ashman, he understood the general's reasons. Watching Roca, she had no doubt that if Vyrl revealed the truth, Ashman would soon have no rank at all. *No wonder I can't feel his moods.* Vyrl had blanketed his thoughts to protect Ashman. So Kamoj imagined a blanket over hers as well.

Roca was going over the plan they had discussed earlier, before Kamoj slept. "We should leave at dawn. If we each take different villages, we can cover more area. It won't be long, though, before the Allieds know something is going on."

"If all goes well," Stillmorn said, "our media team will be broadcasting by then. If anyone tries to stop us, all settled space will know. That's almost three trillion people."

Denric leaned one elbow on the arm of his chair. "It would be more effective if Vyrl could speak himself at more locations. He's the one who took the risks. It makes him look the hero. That will strengthen his arguments."

Del-Kurj snorted. "Vyrl, a hero?"

"Go dance on it, Del," Vyrl said.

"That's your misgendered forte," Del-Kurj told him.

"Del, what's wrong?" Roca asked. "You're wound as tight as a coil."

He just shook his head. It was Chaniece who answered. "The Allieds want him to go to Earth with them."

Stillmorn stiffened. "Have they threatened force?"

Del-Kurj gave a dry smile. "Something more effective."

"They like his singing," Chaniece said. "Mac Tyler insists he will make Del 'wealthy and famous, like star busters.' Whatever that means."

"They call that noise you make *singing?*" Vyrl asked.

Del-Kurj regarded him with a cool gaze. "Better than dancing."

"Oh, stop, you two," Aniece said.

Roca spoke to Del-Kurj. "You don't find this offer strange?"

"I see nothing strange about people wanting to hear me sing."

"I do," Vyrl muttered.

"I've no doubt you would be a success," Roca told Del-Kurj. "You're a far better vocalist than the singers I've heard their soldiers listening to. That isn't the point. Think about why they're offering this now."

"Yes, the timing is obvious. And no, I'm not stupid enough to let them divide us." Del-Kurj glanced at Vyrl. "Regardless of what our 'better educated' members imply."

"I've never called you uneducated," Vyrl said.

"It's an old trick," Lord Rillia said. "Divide your enemy and destroy their morale. Then you've won half the battle."

Stillmorn spoke. "Which makes it *our* strongest weapon. We need to turn public opinion in favor of our cause."

Roca considered Vyrl. "Your marriage will help."

He tensed. "Why do you say that?"

"I'm surprised you need to ask." Rillia smiled at Kamoj. "You've a beautiful young wife, a love match made in the depths of your grief over the losses in your family. Very romantic. Very heroic. Good publicity."

"I prefer to keep our private life out of this," Vyrl said.

"Why?" Roca asked. "What happened?"

"Nothing happened," Vyrl said.

"Nothing?"

He shifted on the couch. "Nothing we need discuss."

His mother refused to be put off. "Are you sure?"

Vyrl was silent for awhile. Then he said, "I prefer Kamoj not be pushed into this. She's been hurt already."

Although Kamoj appreciated Vyrl's concern, she could see that she needed to speak. She regarded Roca. "When Vyrl and I married, a leader among my people took exception. He and I had been promised. He annulled my merger with Vyrl and signed my name to a new contract. It caused a battle. Governor Ironbridge, my former betrothed, has since filed suit against Vyrl with your civil authorities."

Denric stared at his brother. "What have you been doing?"

Roca had gone very still. "What are the charges against you?" she asked Vyrl.

He spoke in a tight voice. "Assault and coercion against Kamoj, and abuse of her people's cultural sovereignty. Essentially he claims I raped both Kamoj and her culture."

Roca stiffened. "I find that hard to believe."

"The charges are lies," Kamoj said.

"Then this Ironbridge will lose his case." Roca's tone suggested Ironbridge would lose a great deal more if she had any say in the matter.

"It doesn't make any difference," Vyrl said. "If he goes to court, it will be a disaster regardless of the outcome. And he might win on the sovereignty charge."

Rillia leaned forward. "If this becomes public, it could destroy what we're trying to do."

Denric, the teacher who had lived offworld, said, "News of a scandal involving our family will reach everywhere. How can we portray the Allieds as abusing the cultural sovereignty of Lyshriol, with our family as the injured party, when Vyrl is accused of the same elsewhere? Gods, Vyrl, it's even worse. You're here with Kamoj. It could look as if you brought her against her will."

"I'm aware of how it looks," Vyrl said tightly.

"The case may never go to trial," Stillmorn said.

"What's to stop it?" Roca asked.

"I brought charges against Jax Ironbridge," Kamoj said. "I will withdraw them only if he withdraws his against Vyrl." Just saying the words felt like a crime, breaking an unwritten law she and Jax had forged over the years.

"Charges for what?" Roca asked.

"Mother." Vyrl spoke softly. "Let her be."

Kamoj glanced at him. "It's all right. They should know."

"You're sure?" he asked.

She nodded, far less sure than she tried to project, but knowing this had to be done. Turning to Roca, she made herself speak. "The charges against Jax are kidnapping, blackmail, aggravated assault, and rape."

"Gods," Roca said. "Are those true?"

Kamoj swallowed. "Yes, ma'am."

"We have proof," Stillmorn said.

Roca spoke quietly to Kamoj. "Then please accept my deepest apologies that your introduction to my family caused you such pain."

A murmur of agreement came from the others. Then Del-Kurj said, "Vyrl, I can't see how anyone could believe those charges against you. You may be an interminable pain, but you're a singularly decent one."

Vyrl squinted at him. "I'm not sure if I've just been insulted or complimented."

Chaniece's lips quirked up. "From Del, that's a compliment."

"He's right," Aniece told Vyrl. "It isn't like you to be involved with the law."

After a pause, Vyrl said, "When people grieve, they don't act like themselves."

Softly Roca said, "No. They don't."

No one else spoke. Kamoj felt their grief, like a deep, still sea. She wished Vyrl could share everything with his family and have their comfort. But she understood his reasons for silence. His family had to trust Ashman now.

"What I don't understand," Roca said, "is why Hamilton didn't hush up this matter."

Denric spoke in a wry voice. "Are you suggesting that ISC block the due process of law?"

"What law?" Roca demanded. "Those charges are slander. Hamilton should have prevented them from being filed. Barring that, he should have stopped anyone from prosecuting the case."

Vyrl answered tiredly. "What you're suggesting isn't legal." He held up his hand when she started to speak. "Before you debate points of legality with me, you should know that he did try to hush it up."

"What stopped him?" Roca asked.

"Me. It was either that or Kamoj's life."

Roca exhaled. "What a mess."

Stillmorn spoke. "After the civil authorities had the case, we did what we could to delay the proceedings. But every time we pushed, people asked questions. We couldn't risk the secrecy of this operation."

"So what you're telling me," Roca said, "is that we don't even know if the case has gone public."

"That's correct, ma'am," Stillmorn said. "General Ashman advised us to assume it hadn't. Our link with the *Ascendant* is one way, so we won't know for certain until this is over."

For the first time, Shannon spoke. "Unless she wakes that which slumbers."

Everyone blinked at him. Kamoj suspected some of them had forgotten he was listening. From what she understood, he had run away at sixteen and lived in the Blue Mountain Dales most of his life. Although the rift with his family had long ago healed, she had a feeling that his extended separations made him an enigma to them.

Finally Denric said, "The what?"

"She listens to the sleeper," Shannon said.

"What do you mean?" Aniece asked.

Shannon regarded Vyrl. "It would speak to any of us. But it wants you." He indicated Kamoj. "Because of her. She resonates. The ancient code in her genes recognizes what we've lost. Through her, it can find you."

Del-Kurj snorted. "Shannon, you're even more hallucinogenic than usual tonight."

Shannon glanced at him. "I have never used hallucinogens. Unless you can make this same claim, which most assuredly you can't, I suggest you leave off with the insults."

Del-Kurj stiffened but said nothing. Kamoj didn't think the others were really angry at him. She felt Stillmorn's tension more; how could Shannon know what they had found under the Stained Glass forest?

"It's been an exhausting day," Stillmorn said. "Maybe we should retire, so we can start early tomorrow."

In other words, Kamoj thought, *you want to question Shannon in private.* They had plenty of time before they had to retire. When she had awoken tonight, the sunset had been in the sky. Vyrl said night and day were the same length here, so that gave them almost thirty hours to dawn, assuming Lyshriol had sixty hour days.

But why should it? So much else here was different, she didn't see why nights should have the same length as on Balimul. Maybe Stillmorn's comment made more sense than she realized.

Roca considered the Primary. Her gaze flicked to Kamoj, then to Vyrl. Then she turned to Shannon. "What wants to speak to us?"

"The sleeper," Shannon said.

"What sleeper?"

"Below the world."

"Shannon." Her voice softened, ameliorating her rebuke. "That makes no sense."

"Does he ever?" Del-Kurj asked. When Shannon raised his eyebrows, Del-Kurj said, "Well, you *aren't* making sense."

"That which sleeps under the world," Shannon said. "I don't know how else to say it."

"You think someone is sleeping under the ground?" Rillia asked. "And he wants to talk to Vyrl and Kamoj?"

"No." Shannon's gaze turned distant again. "Don't you feel it? All around us. Sleeping." He focused on Kamoj. "You almost woke it today."

"I'm sorry," she said. "I don't know what you mean."

"That was tactful," Del-Kurj said. "Better than, 'Vyrl, are all your brothers this crazy?' "

"Del." Chaniece laid her hand on his arm. "Enough."

To Kamoj's surprise, his face relaxed. He set his hand over hers for a moment, then sat back in his chair.

Roca sipped her spiced wine. "Shannon, are you saying that you felt Kamoj wake someone today?"

"Or something," Shannon said.

Roca looked at Kamoj. "Did you?"

"I don't understand what you mean." Kamoj wished Stillmorn would let her talk about it. She disliked being evasive.

Roca turned her piercing intelligence on Stillmorn. "Did she?"

The Primary met her gaze. "I don't know, ma'am."

"My pardon, Grandfather." The unexpected voice came from the back of the room.

They all turned. One of Vyrl's grandsons, a teenager with tawny hair, stood in the entrance arch.

"Yes?" Vyrl asked. "What is it, Gari?"

"An officer from the Allied command post is here," Gari said. "He brought an escort of soldiers." Apprehension spilled into his voice. "They wish to speak to Lady Roca."

Vyrl swore, rising to his feet. "They must have found out we're here."

23

Sundered

Projection Operator

Stillmorn stood up. "It's unlikely. If they had detected us or found the racer, they wouldn't have given any warning." She turned to Roca. "But we should hide."

Rising, Roca motioned toward a discreet archway by the hearth. "From the alcove there, you can hear what they have to say."

"We can't risk being trapped," Stillmorn said. "We may need to leave the house."

"The alcove has a door to the basement," Roca said. "It leads to tunnels that go under the village."

"I can show you," Vyrl said. "I played down there when I was a boy."

Four Jagernauts took form out of the shadows, giving Kamoj a start. She hadn't even realized they were there. They went with her, Vyrl, and Stillmorn into the dark alcove. As Vyrl knelt and pulled aside a rug, Kamoj spoke in a low voice to the Primary. "Where are the other Jagernauts?"

"In the house. Keeping watch." Satisfaction showed on her face. "They'll melt away like mist in the hot sun if any Earth soldiers come near."

Vyrl lifted a door in the floor, revealing a square hole. A ladder extended down into darkness. As they climbed into the cool shadows, one after the other, they heard boots thud in the Hearth Room. Voices carried to them.

"Our honor at your presence, Pharaoh Roca." The man spoke in accented Iotic with formal cadences.

Kamoj, Vyrl, and the Jagernauts gathered at the base of the ladder, listening.

Roca answered in cool tones. "I am not yet Pharaoh, Colonel Shipper. Until we verify my sister's death, I remain Pharaoh Presumptive." In a deceptively soft voice she added, "Or perhaps you suggest my sister is already dead?"

Kamoj winced.

"Please accept my apology if I gave offense," the man said. "I honor both you and your sister, the Pharaoh Dyhianna." His voice had just the right amount of deference blended with authority to indicate he meant to show respect but knew he controlled the situation. He had no wish to offend Vyrl's mother. But he knew who stood as prisoner and who as jailer.

"Lord Rillia, you also honor us." Shipper's phrases had the sound of ritual and established protocol.

"Indeed." Rillia sounded singularly unhonored.

"What brings you to my home?" Roca asked.

Parchment rustled. It puzzled Kamoj. The offworlders had palmtops, consoles, even devices in their bodies to make records. Why would they need a codex? This had a sound of ritual, though, like the contract scroll in the marriage ceremony on Balumil.

"Is this a joke?" Roca asked.

"No, ma'am," Shipper said.

"My answer is no." Roca's voice could have chilled ice.

"Ma'am, I'm sorry." Colonel Shipper sounded uncomfortable. "But you have no choice."

"Choice?" Aniece asked. "What is going on?"

"They want to take Del-Kurj and me to Earth," Roca said.

"Like hell," Del-Kurj exploded. "What is wrong with you people? Our father is only a few months in his grave."

"We're moving you somewhere safer," Shipper said.

An unfamiliar woman spoke, apparently another AWOE official. "We have people to pack your belongings, Your Highness."

"I'm not leaving," Roca repeated.

"Nor I," Del-Kurj said.

Shipper exhaled. "Please don't make us use force."

Primary Stillmorn formed the words *Draw it out* with her lips. Kamoj felt a pressure against her mind, as if the Primary were trying to send that message to Roca and the others.

"None of us are going anywhere," Lord Rillia said. "If you use force, you will be violating your own laws."

"Precedent exists," Shipper said, "for the transfer of dignitaries in custody, when necessary to ensure their protection."

"Protection against whom?" Del-Kurj asked. "You're the ones holding us prisoner."

"We won't let you take them," Rillia said.

"If any of you interfere," the AWOE woman replied, "we will use restraint."

"Attack us in our own home, is that it?" Denric asked.

Shipper spoke quietly. "Professor Valdoria, we have no wish to hurt any of your family. But the fact of our orders remains. The ship leaves for Earth in an hour."

"We're in mourning," Denric said, which struck Kamoj as a rather odd statement, given that everyone already knew.

In the darkness here, Primary Stillmorn glanced at a Jagernaut and he nodded. Kamoj understood then. They were trying to record the conversation. If this scene made it into the news broadcasts, it could be effective.

"What will you do if we refuse to go?" Roca asked. "Shoot us?"

The woman answered. "If we must, Your Highness. The sedatives won't harm you."

"You can't do this," Del-Kurj said.

"I'm afraid we can," Shipper answered.

"You'll have to shoot us all." Aniece's sweet voice made her sound vulnerable.

"No," Roca said. "I don't want any of you, my family, hurt by these people."

Shipper spoke quickly. "Your Highness, please be assured, we have no wish to hurt anyone."

"Why now?" Roca asked. "It has only been a few months since my husband's death."

The AWOE woman spoke. "We recorded a disturbance in Dalvador this afternoon that involved your family."

Roca made an incredulous sound. "You're taking Del-Kurj and me from our loved ones and our home because my grandchildren had a festival?"

"I'm deeply sorry, ma'am," she said. "But those are our orders."

"You can't take Del!" Chaniece said. "What about the children?"

Kamoj blinked. Children? What children?

Del-Kurj's voice softened. "Take care of them, Chani. I will say good-bye before we leave."

Kamoj hadn't realized Del-Kurj had children. Or perhaps they were Chaniece's. In either case, if he could get away long enough for his farewells, the Jagernauts might be able to slip him a message from ISC to the family members on Earth.

"I'm afraid you won't have time to speak with anyone," Shipper said. "I'm sorry."

Stillmorn mouthed the word *damn*.

The conversation continued in low, courteous tones that did nothing to disguise its nature as a battle. But the conclusion had been set the moment the occupying forces entered the house.

In the end Roca and Del-Kurj left with them.

"They must know something," Vyrl said. They were all standing by the hearth now. The Jagernauts stayed back, discreet and silent.

Stillmorn shook her head. "If they suspected our presence, they would have searched the house more thoroughly."

Kamoj rubbed her arms, feeling cold. She hadn't realized anyone had searched the house.

Stillmorn spoke to a Jagernaut standing near them. "How did your recordings come out?"

"We have a good audio record," he said. "We're working on visual. But they have jammers all over the house. We're trying to filter out the noise."

Stillmorn nodded, then turned to Vyrl. "If we get a good record, that scene will play right into our plans."

"At what price?" He glanced at Chaniece. She had slumped on the couch with her arms wrapped around her torso.

Shannon sat next to her. "Del will be all right."

Chaniece stared into the fire. "Being separated . . . it's like being cut in two."

Aniece sat on her other side. "We'll stay with you and the children. It will be all right."

Kamoj felt Chaniece's desolation. She and Del-Kurj were twins. Rhon twins. Two parts of one mind. Chaniece apparently also cared for Del's children, or else he helped with hers. Had one of them lost a spouse? Kamoj thought of the broad-shouldered youth and the young boy in the courtyard. Their resemblance to Del-Kurj was unmistakable.

Sorrow settled over Kamoj like a cloak. She had never witnessed the toll exacted by war when the battles were over. People like Vyrl and Chaniece paid the price without ever lifting a weapon.

The wall sconces held lamps molded like flames. They shed dim light over the stone hall in the second story of the Valdoria ancestral home. Kamoj padded along in bare feet. The lacy white robe Aniece had given her swirled around her calves. She had luxuriated in the bathing room, which had plumbing even better than the wonders Vyrl's people had put in Quartz Palace. Now she was returning to Vyrl's suite, the one where he had slept in his boyhood.

A soft crying came from a hall on her right. She hesitated. As a newcomer, she didn't want to intrude. But the crying tugged at her heart. She followed it to an alcove like the one where they had hidden earlier tonight while soldiers tramped through the house. Kamoj peered into the shadows. She could make out the silhouette of a person sitting across the alcove. It sounded like a child sobbing, but the shape belonged to an adult.

"Can I help?" she asked.

The crying cut off. After a pause, a man spoke, his voice deep and rumbling, like Del-Kurj's but without the rough edge. "Who is that?"

"It's Kamoj. Vyrl's wife."

"The lady that looks like Aunt Aniece?"

Kamoj hesitated. He had an adult's voice but he spoke like a child. "Yes. That's right."

"All right. You can come in."

Kamoj entered the alcove. The shadow resolved into the well-built young man she had seen in the courtyard. She sat next to him on the bench. "Are you missing Del-Kurj?"

He nodded with sincerity. "Hoshpa never goes."

"Hoshpa?"

"Father."

"Del-Kurj is your father?"

"Yes." He rubbed his palm over his cheek. "Don't tell that I was crying, please. I don't want Hoshma to worry."

"Hoshma? Your mother?"

"Yes."

"I didn't realize your father's wife was in the house."

"Wife?" He sounded confused. "What?"

Kamoj feared she had made an embarrassing mistake. No one had claimed that Del-Kurj married the woman who bore his children. "Your mother?"

"You met her."

"I did?"

"In the Hearth Room."

Who could have been Del-Kurj's mistress? Kamoj saw only one candidate. Never in a hundred Long Years would she have guessed. "You mean Primary Stillmorn?"

"Who?"

"The woman in the uniform."

"No. Not the Jagernaut."

Suddenly she understood. "Sweet Airys."

"What did you say?"

Kamoj took a breath. "Chaniece is your mother."

"My Hoshma. Yes."

Kamoj had a good guess now as to why the man sounded like a child. After all her years working with the Argali greenglass stags and does, she knew the problems inbreeding could cause.

"I'm sorry your father had to leave," she said.

"Delson?" a boy asked from the archway. "Are you here?"

"Yes." The man, apparently Delson, smiled in the dark. "Come meet Uncle Vyrl's new wife."

The ten-year-old boy that Kamoj had seen in the courtyard came into the alcove, exuding suspicion. "You aren't supposed to bother Delson," he told her, his tone accusing.

"She's nice, Jaqui," Delson said.

Jaqui sat between them. The light leaking in from the dim

lamps was enough to show her his expression. Protective. He didn't want her to hurt Delson.

Kamoj softened her voice. "Are you two brothers, Jaqui?"

The boy said nothing.

"You look a lot alike," she said.

Jaqui considered her. Then he seemed to come to a decision. "The war killed Uncle Kelric twenty years ago. Well, they thought it did. He wasn't really dead. But no one knew. Grandmother and grandfather couldn't make any more Rhon psions. So the Assembly said mother and father had to have us."

Kamoj stared at him. She hadn't really understood, until now, what Vyrl had meant when he said the Imperial Assembly pressured his family to reproduce. She wanted to say, *They had no right.* But her anger wouldn't help them. She spoke gently. "I'm sorry your father had to leave."

"They've always wanted him to go," Jaqui said.

"Do you know why?"

"He's the oldest here now that Grandfather is dead." Jaqui stopped, and Kamoj felt his ache for the loss of the grandfather he loved. "Uncle Eldrin is the oldest of our uncles, but he's a prisoner someplace. Uncle Althor was next oldest—" His voice caught. "But the war killed him. Hoshpa is next. That makes him important."

"Uncle Vyrl will fix the problems, won't he?" Delson asked.

"I hope so," Kamoj murmured. So much needed fixing. She didn't see how Vyrl's family would ever heal from all the wounds left by this war.

"I have a chip," Delson suddenly said. "It says I have to go to bed."

"A chip?" Kamoj asked. "What do you mean?"

"A computer implant," Jaqui explained. "It helps him think."

"I can add up to six now," Delson told her.

"That's very good," Kamoj said. He made her heart ache.

If he was this slow with his intelligence augmented, what would his life have been without modern technology? Someone ought to strangle the Imperial Assembly.

"Someday I'll learn to subtract," Delson said with pride.

"I'm sure you will," Kamoj said.

Delson beamed at her. "I like you."

"Del?" Chaniece's voice came from the archway. "Is Jaqui with you?"

"I'm here, Hoshma." The younger boy went to his mother. "We were talking to Uncle Vyrl's wife."

Chaniece regarded Kamoj with a long, appraising stare. Then she spoke to her sons, tender but firm. "Come now. You must go to sleep."

"Not tired," Delson protested.

"I know," Chaniece said. "But you must come."

"Don't want to."

"Come now," she repeated, her voice soft.

Delson sighed. Then he stood up, towering over them all.

Kamoj went with the children. She and Chaniece walked down the hall together, but neither of them spoke. When they reached the main hall, Chaniece turned to her. "Thank you. For comforting them."

Kamoj managed a smile. "They're nice boys."

"Yes." Pain edged her voice. "My beautiful sons." Then she went on, taking her children down the hall.

The spacious bedroom was dark. Vyrl had fallen asleep in the big canopied bed. Kamoj shivered as she padded across the stone floor. The woven rug by the bed warmed her feet. She climbed in and rolled against Vyrl, seeking his heat. Half-asleep, he pulled her into his arms. He moved his hands on her body with the drowsy confidence of a husband who had forgotten his wife feared making love to him.

Kamoj tried to relax. *It's time,* she thought. And indeed, as Vyrl deepened the kiss, her mind blurred into the haze that came over her when they made love. He pulled off her nightrobe and gave it a toss. It fluttered ghostlike through the air, to land somewhere out of sight on the floor. They sent his nightshirt after it. Then she and Vyrl embraced, her skin soft against his muscular planes.

But when he rolled her onto her back, Kamoj froze, hit with a sudden memory of Jax holding her down.

Vyrl lifted his head. "Kamoj?" He was more awake now.

She laid her palm against his chest, unable to speak. The painful words would be trespassers here, in their bed. Instead she tried to open her mind, to let him know that she wanted him, but felt suffocated.

Vyrl brushed his fingertips across her cheek. Then he rolled onto his back and drew her against his side. Without his weight on top of her body, her sense of being trapped faded. Violet moonlight slanted through windows across the room. It silvered his hair where it spread across the pillows and turned his eyes into large, dark pools.

"There is a poem in the Northern Lands," she said. "As Akabal, spirit of the night, sends his starlit hair across the sky, unmatched in his splendor, thus so do you, my love, come to me in the sweet, sensual hours of his reign."

Vyrl smiled drowsily. "Thank you."

He caressed her with an experienced touch, giving her the time she needed. As she relaxed, he pulled her on top of his body and kissed her as if she were a treasure to him.

So they finally came together, and filled the hollowed places in their hearts with tenderness.

24

Dawn

Airy Rainbow

Light slanted across Kamoj. Groggy, she rubbed her eyes. Surely she couldn't have slept an entire night. She pushed back the quilt and climbed out of bed, leaving Vyrl snoring on his stomach. She moved pillows to shade his eyes so the sunlight wouldn't disturb him.

After rescuing her robe from the floor, she pulled it on and went to the window seat, a recessed alcove with tall windows. A bench strewn with cushions circled the recess. Curling on the cushions, she gazed out at the view. Vyrl's home was a never-ending marvel.

Dawn had turned the sky violet. The Dalvador Plains stretched out in a bubble-tipped sea. In the north, the Backbone Mountains rose up in needled peaks, stark against the heavens. In the east, the suns were halfway above the horizon, the smaller orb eclipsing the larger, both of them huge and molten, edging the world in crimson, circled by haloes.

The serenity of the landscape comforted Kamoj. Breezes rippled the plains, and shadows stretched across the land, alternating with long rays of light. The suns had already moved higher above the horizon. Another wonder. Jul never came up this fast.

"It's beautiful, yes?" Vyrl said.

With a start, Kamoj looked around. In his blue robe, he

looked exotic, similar enough to a Balumil man to make her that much more aware of the differences. He sat behind her and gathered her into his arms, with her back against his front.

Content, she turned back to the sunrise. "It's lovely. But so fast. What happened to the rest of the night?"

"The days here are only twenty-eight hours."

"And the night?"

"I meant all of it, both day and night."

She smiled. "You're teasing me."

"It's true. The engineers set it up this way."

Such a strange choice. "Why twenty-eight?"

"Probably because it fits natural human cycles of sleep."

"Is that the length of the day on Earth?"

"Actually, no. That's twenty-four hours." Vyrl shifted her in his arms, settling her more comfortably, his legs stretched out on either side of her along the wide bench. "For some reason humans tend to prefer a longer day than the one on the planet where we evolved."

Kamoj had a hard time imagining a twenty-eight hour day as "long." "Are these suns like those that shine on Earth?"

"Earth only has one. It's brighter than these two."

"These are kind. Jul will blind you."

Vyrl nuzzled her hair. "It's a much hotter, bigger star."

"Jul?" She laughed. "No, it is small."

He tangled his fingers in her curls. "That's because you're farther away. If Balumil were as close to Jul as we are to Valdor and Aldan, Jul would look fifteen times bigger." He slid his hands down her arms and spoke in a low voice. "It would make Balumil far too hot for humans."

"Hmmm." Kamoj leaned back into him. "I like hot."

Mischief tickled his voice. "Now that I'm done doubling the population of Dalvador, maybe I could repopulate Argali. What do you think?"

"Pah!" She elbowed him in the ribs. "I think you have an ego as big as those suns out there."

Laughing, Vyrl rocked her. "Ah, Kamoj, I do love you."

Her contentment deepened. "And I you, my skylion."

"I'm afraid we can't stay up here, though."

"Are you worried? About speaking to your people?"

"I feel like a fraud. I'm no hero. What if we go through all this only to find out my name has been spoken across the stars as a monster?" He swallowed. "I don't think I could bear it. The worst of it is, part of what Ironbridge claims is true."

"How can you say such a thing?"

"I did interfere in your culture."

"I'm glad you did."

Softly he said, "You said otherwise at the Inquiry."

Kamoj had no answer. She had recovered enough to realize that the conclusions she had come to that morning, before the Inquiry, were made under duress, the combined effects of starvation, exposure, pain, and fear for her life, as well as sexual and physical abuse. But she feared that if she looked too closely at those memories, she would still condemn herself for turning to Vyrl. Nothing had changed for Argali, and now she better understood the cost to the Skolians. Jax's vengeance against Vyrl threatened to destroy both the man she loved and his hopes to free his own people.

Yet for all that, she couldn't regret her choice to stay with Vyrl. She had begun to see new ways to help Argali. As for Jax, she found it better to lock her doubts away than to face truths that hurt too much to remember.

"Kamoj, get angry." Pain ached in his voice. "Shout! Tell me I'm a damn fool idiot. Stop holding it all inside."

"I don't want to shout."

"Repressing it won't make it go away."

She shifted her weight. "You sound like this man, Jak Tager, on the *Ascendant*."

"Gods. Shoot me, then."

Her mouth quirked in a smile. "I most certainly will not." She thought of the soft-spoken healer. "Don't you like him?"

"Actually, yes, I do. I just don't like the way he always wants me to talk to him."

Kamoj made a *hmmph* sound. "He does that to me, too. Why does he like to talk so much?"

"He's a psychiatrist. A healer who treats emotions."

"My emotions have no illness."

In a gentle voice, he asked, "Even after Jax?"

She remained silent.

"If this goes to trial, you will have to speak."

"I know." The thought made her want to wither. How could she reveal to strangers what had happened? "Maybe Jax will withdraw his charges."

"I hope so."

Kamoj sighed. Jax had called her bluff, so she had made it real. Could she take the result? The answer didn't matter so much as what Jax believed. He knew her well. If he didn't think she could handle the trial, he wouldn't back down.

"Even if you don't testify," Vyrl said, "our lawyers won't back off now that you've withdrawn your objection to their seeking prosecution."

"If I don't testify, can your ISC win?"

"I think so, at least on some charges."

"But not as many as if I do speak?"

Vyrl stroked her hair. "It doesn't matter." He motioned to the sky. "It's like the dawn. No matter what happens, life always renews itself."

She tried to smile, but even the beauty of the burgeoning day couldn't warm the chill inside.

It does matter. That was what made it so hard.

In the clear light of early morning, the courtyard bustled with people and animals. The commotion had a subdued quality, not only due to the early hour, but also because everyone knew the Earth forces might soon come ask what they were up to.

Breezes tugged at Kamoj as she entered the yard. Aniece

had given her an outrageous dress. It had slits in the swirling skirt, slits in the belled sleeves, laces up the bodice, laces up the back, laces everywhere, pulling it tight about her torso. The flared blue skirt fluttered around her knees. It was lovely, but much too sexy, and would have mortified her, except all the other young women dressed the same way. The men looked at them, yes, but none seemed outraged by the dresses. It had never occurred to her that clothes considered seductive in one culture might be normal in another. Styles rarely changed in the Northern Lands.

Animals stamped and huffed in the courtyard. *Lyrine.* Denric, the professor, had told her that on most worlds settled by the Ruby Empire, the colonists had "engineered" similar animals to carry humans. Balumil had greenglass stags; Lyshriol had lyrine. Kamoj thought it very sensible of those ancients to make sure they had animals to ride if their machines failed.

She didn't see how Denric could call the animals "similar," though. The lyrine were pretty, yes, but odd. They had only four legs and no scales. Long, silky fur covered their bodies. The big ones had violet coats; the smaller ones had blue or lavender. Their silver eyes gleamed with a liquid quality, and their snouts had four nostrils, two on each side of the head. They also had two horns, the larger above the smaller. Made from a clear material that splintered light, the horns sparkled with rainbows. Their hooves were the same material, and struck sparks of color when the animals stamped.

People filled the courtyard. They loaded brightly painted carts, tended lyrine, and spoke among themselves. No robots appeared anywhere. From what Kamoj gathered, the Lyshrioli didn't resist offworld machines, they just kept their use discreet. Technology had turned their hard lives into an idyll, but they wanted Lyshriol's simple beauty to remain untouched.

Five women in red robes stood by the house, surveying the

scene. Intrigued, Kamoj waited for them to do something. One left her post and moved through the courtyard. People bowed as she passed, and she nodded, then went on, walking and watching. Kamoj wondered what she was doing.

A husky man came up to Kamoj, leading a lyrine with a blue bridle. Its silver-white fur shaded into blue on its legs, and its delicate build made it look ethereal. When the animal huffed at Kamoj, she stepped back, startled.

The man spoke to Kamoj in Trillian, the language of Vyrl's people.

Kamoj spread her hands. "I don't understand."

He rubbed the animal's neck, and it made pleased rumbling noises, all the while watching Kamoj. Then the man nudged it closer. Unsure what he wanted, Kamoj laid her palm against the lyrine's neck. The man made an encouraging sound, and the lyrine rumbled again. When she scratched its neck, its contented noises deepened.

"Do you like her?" Vyrl asked.

Kamoj turned to find him watching. "I've never seen such a lovely animal."

"She's yours."

"Mine? What do you mean?"

"To ride." He came forward and scratched the animal's neck, evoking more appreciative rumbles. "You can ride with me until you learn."

Kamoj wasn't certain she had heard correctly. "Women ride by themselves here?"

"Well, yes. Of course."

"We don't on Balumil. It is considered unfeminine."

Vyrl frowned. "That's absurd."

"No more absurd than telling a gifted artist he mustn't dance because men don't do that."

He considered her. "Do you really like it? The dancing, I mean."

"Oh, yes. It's spectacular!" Her voice took on a throaty burr. "Very nice."

Vyrl grinned. "If you keep looking at me like that, we'll have to go discuss this idea of repopulating Argali."

She ran her finger down the front of his shirt. "Just discuss?"

Laughing, he drew her into an embrace. They stood kissing in the middle of the courtyard. Kamoj felt amusement from the people around them, but everyone continued with their work as if they didn't notice.

After awhile, Vyrl lifted his head. "I would like you to meet Mercury."

"Mercury is a name?"

"Yes. Well actually, it's an element. A liquid metal." He caught a blowing lock of her hair. "We'll both ride him until you can ride by yourself."

"He is your lyrine?"

Vyrl considered the question. "No. He owns himself. But he lets me ride him."

"Like Graypoint."

"Yes, I suppose so. I never thought of it that way."

"That's why they come to you," she said. Vyrl didn't try to own anyone or anything, neither his wife nor the animals that gave him their trust.

He took her across the courtyard, past the bustle, to a man struggling to hold the bridle of a huge lyrine. Its violet coat was tipped by silver, and sunlight sparkled through its horns in a dazzle of rainbows. The lyrine stamped and pulled on the bridle, then bared its teeth at the man.

"Hai!" Vyrl called as they came up.

The lyrine turned toward Vyrl. It stopped snarling but kept moving, tramping back and forth. With obvious relief, its handler gave Vyrl the reins.

"You don't like that, hmmm?" Vyrl murmured to the lyrine. "I'm sorry. I didn't know they were trying to put on the bridle." He kept talking, his voice soft, until the animal quieted.

Vyrl glanced at Kamoj. "This is Mercury."

"He's gorgeous." The lyrine looked unreal to her, born of someplace too exotic for humans.

"Come meet him," Vyrl said.

Kamoj approached, then stopped one step away, as she would with a new greenglass. A stag would have spent a long time studying her, first with one eye, then with the other. This animal widened his nostrils, smelling the air, much as Kamoj did when she wanted to catch a scent. Then he thrust his nose against her shoulder and pushed her away.

Kamoj laughed. "What do you think?" she asked Mercury. "I smell strange?"

He gave her a silvery stare. Moving with care, she stepped closer. When he didn't object, she scratched his neck. His fur fell over her hand in silky curls.

"Beautiful lyrine," she crooned. "You know that, don't you? I'll bet everyone wants to ride you. Only you don't let them."

A deep rumble came from his chest. Suddenly he pulled away from her and pushed his nose against Vyrl's shoulder, almost knocking him over.

"Hey!" Vyrl caught his balance. "Careful."

"He likes me," Kamoj said smugly. Except then Mercury shoved his nose against her shoulder too, pushing her into a woman carrying a basket of food.

"Ah!" Mortified, Kamoj made apologies in Iotaca. Although the woman obviously didn't understand, she smiled before hurrying on her way.

Laughing, Vyrl said, "He's playing." He took Mercury's bridle and beckoned to the man who had been holding it before. The fellow came over, regarding the lyrine with a wary gaze. Then he cupped his hands together. Vyrl put his foot in the cup and swung onto Mercury with mesmerizing grace.

The man turned to Kamoj, offering his hands. Feeling clumsy compared to Vyrl, she set her foot in his hold. With help from him and Vyrl, she got onto Mercury, straddling the lyrine in front of her husband.

Mercury went stock still under them, like a statue of ice. Vyrl began talking in Trillian, his voice a soothing river of sound. Mercury shook his head, then went still again. Vyrl continued talking, holding the reins loosely, his arms around Kamoj. She scratched the lyrine's neck in the place he liked.

After several moments, Mercury took a grudging step. He paused again, his stance tense. Then he began to move more naturally, as he tested the new weight. Vyrl pulled Kamoj back against his chest, holding the reins in one hand.

It pleased Kamoj that this stunning animal would agree to let her ride with Vyrl. She felt only a soft blanket under her legs, though. "I should have some trousers. Riding this way will rub my skin raw."

"Women here do it all the time." Vyrl said.

"But I never have." Although she enjoyed the freedom the dress gave her, she didn't want problems that might slow them down later. "I should have a change of clothes."

"All right." Vyrl called to a woman in the courtyard. She bobbed her head, then handed her armload of fabric to another woman and headed for the house. At the door she bowed to the women in the long robes. Then she disappeared into the castle.

"Who are those women in red robes?" Kamoj asked.

Vyrl was scratching Mercury's neck. "They're Memories."

Memories? "Of what?"

"Of everything." He coaxed Mercury to the entrance of the courtyard with careful but firm tugs on the reins. "The Lyshrioli people have no written language. Before my mother came, they didn't even have the concept."

Kamoj stiffened. "Lyshriol is like Balumil, then? An experiment to breed people?"

"An experiment, yes, but not like Balumil." His words sounded too light for the origins of his people to be as dark as hers. "It's strange, really. The Ruby Empire apparently intended this colony as a binary computer analog. Why binary? Not all computers use it. The experiment has fallen apart over the millennia, but pieces of it remain." He indicated the red-robed women. "Those women you see in red robes have almost perfect memories. It comes from a genetic trait engineered into our ancestors. They store knowledge. It's what they're doing now. Memorizing this event."

"It's a useful talent if you don't read or write."

"It does help. But it's odd, too." Vyrl brought Mercury to a stop at the gate. "People here act like bits. Zero and one. That's why you rarely see singles, why children marry so young. And bits don't read and write. They're *part* of the process." He thought for a moment. "Asking someone here to read is like asking a book to read. My father was never able to learn and some of my siblings have problems with it. Del-Kurj struggled with it for years and finally gave up."

"Is that why he resents you?"

Vyrl fell silent. After awhile he said, "I'm not sure. He's much better at math than me. We think in octal or hexideci-mal rather than base twenty like you do in Argali. It's probably because of the hands and feet. Eight fingers, eight toes. Del can do octal arithmetic like a wizard."

Eight. So it *was* natural. At first Kamoj had thought that Lord Rillia, Del-Kurj, Chaniece, and Shannon had deformed hands. But everyone else she saw here had them too. Instead of four fingers and a thumb, they had two sets of opposing fingers, a total of four digits, all as thick as thumbs. A hinge down the center of their hands let them fold their palms together, so they could hold and manipulate objects.

Vyrl had five-fingered hands, inherited from his mother. He had been born with vestigial thumbs, so the doctors reconstructed them. Kamoj had never known such variations existed among humans. She wondered if she and Vyrl could have children.

"It's all so different," she said. But she liked Lyshriol, especially after the metallic landscape of the *Ascendant*.

Vyrl spoke thoughtfully. "Maybe if we knew the purpose,

it would make more sense. The records were lost over the centuries, after Lyshriol became isolated and its technology failed."

A call came from behind them. Vyrl glanced back, then guided Mercury to the side, letting a woman ride out the gate on a blue lyrine. She carried a pole with a pennant snapping at its end. Vyrl urged Mercury after her, riding into the streets of Dalvador. Looking back, Kamoj saw a procession forming behind them, people riding and walking, and lyrine pulling the colorful carts. Vyrl's descendants were everywhere. Denric, Shannon, Aniece, and Rillia all rode with retinues. Chaniece stood in the courtyard with her sons, the wind blowing her long hair around her body as she waved to the procession.

So they left, a simple group from a rural village, hoping to change interstellar history.

25

Migration

Propagator

They galloped through an ocean of grass, the lyrine flowing like liquid silver across the plains. The procession separated into five groups, with Vyrl, Denric, Shannon, Aniece, and Lord Rillia as their leaders. Vyrl's group consisted of Stillmorn and the drop-down team, several villagers on lyrine, and four more bringing two carts with supplies and gifts.

The Jagernauts rode with Vyrl and Kamoj, but far enough away to give them the illusion of privacy. Just as the Jagernauts on Balumil had easily adapted to greenglass stags, so these took to the lyrine. Apparently they had "neural enhancements" specific to such tasks. The enhancements affected both their brains and the modifications in their bodies that augmented their ability to move. So they rode the lyrine as if they had done so for years.

Kamoj sat on Mercury, exhilarated by the wind, with Vyrl solid behind her, his muscular arms around her waist. As they raced across the plains, the suns rose in the sky, though they never reached the zenith overhead. In the morning Aldan had been in front of Valdor, but by midday he had moved to the side and no longer eclipsed his elder sibling. They were also both distorted into eggs, Aldan more than Valdor.

A shout rang out, coming from Vyrl's pennant bearer up ahead. She wheeled her lyrine around and repeated her call. *Rishollinia.* Then she took off again, speeding onward.

Turreted roofs rose out of the plains, blue, violet, rose, and gold, like overturned blossoms on this world that had no flowers, only stained-glass bubbles. The village looked like Dalvador on a small scale. Curious children came to watch them approach. Vyrl slowed Mercury to a stately lope, and the lyrine shook his head, his wild energy calmed by the day's ride.

Adults gathered at the edge of the hamlet as the pennant bearer rode up to them. The Jagernauts arrived next, suitably impressive in their black uniforms, astride their huge lyrine, with Vyrl and Kamoj in their midst. The Rishollinia people swirled around them and waved stained-glass stems, releasing bubbles into the air. The orbs floated and popped over Vyrl and Kamoj, until Kamoj had multi-hued glitter all over her hair and dress.

Vyrl spoke to the villagers in Trillian. Although Kamoj didn't understand him, she loved the language. Lyshrioli voices were chimes, their conversations music. Vyrl swung off Mercury, then helped her down. People gathered around, curious but subdued. It was a quieter parade than his entrance into Dalvador. Here, awe tinged their welcome.

So they entered Rishollinia, Vyrl leading Mercury as they walked. Tall and broad-shouldered, he looked like the golden leader that everyone believed him to be, except Vyrl himself.

The meeting hall was a large, white-washed building. Inside, it consisted of one big room with scalloped sides. Vyrl used no stage or podium; he just went to one end. The people closest to him sat on cushions; behind them, the listeners used stools made from stained-glass tubes; and behind them the people stood. Others filled the balcony that formed an arcade around the interior, and more overflowed into the night outside, where they listened to speakers set up by the Jagernauts. Although the ISC machines seemed to intrigue the villagers, they showed no surprise at the devices.

Kamoj sat with Primary Stillmorn on stools in a corner behind Vyrl. Stillmorn offered to translate for her.

"You speak Trillian?" That surprised Kamoj, though she wasn't sure why. Perhaps because the rustic life here seemed so far removed from the starswept universe of ISC.

"We all do." Stillmorn indicated the Jagernauts dispersed throughout the crowd. "It's a requirement for any bodyguard of the Valdoria family." She tapped her head. "I've a biochip with the language, to help."

Vyrl was sitting on the floor, talking with some people. As he rose to his feet, the crowd quieted. After a final cough from the back, silence descended. Then Vyrl spoke. His resonant voice carried throughout the hall, aided by acoustics and amplifiers. Kamoj closed her eyes, letting his words roll over her. He had a strong baritone, accented with a vibrato even when he spoke Iotic. Now, in his native language, it became more pronounced and turned his words into music.

He spoke of his family, creating a luminous image of the people he loved. His audience beamed with approval. Then he spoke of his father's death, and those of his siblings, and the mood in the hall turned to sorrow. Vyrl described the Radiance War, the desperate combat where armies used weapons as powerful as a sun, and great ships rode the seas of space, turning the heavens into battle fields. The dismay of his listeners filled the room until Kamoj felt it as her own.

Then he told them how the Allied Worlds of Earth had come to protect his family during the fury of that terrible war, how they added their strength to the ISC guardians around Lyshriol. The mood in the meeting hall eased, but not much. Everyone knew that protection had taken an unwelcome turn.

Finally he spoke of the war's end, how the two giants, Skolia and the Traders, battered their armies against each other until they collapsed. The Allied Worlds of Earth stepped into the void—and wrested Lyshriol away from the people who had protected this idyllic world for so many decades.

Yet through it all, Vyrl described the Allied Worlds with respect. Skolia had no quarrel with Earth. They would rather have called the Allieds friends, these peoples from the world that had birthed humanity. But when he came to know how the Allied Worlds treated his family, his words darkened. Earth betrayed them. His audience listened and their anger became tangible.

As Stillmorn translated for Kamoj, she explained the context of Vyrl's words. On Lyshriol, his family were legends. His mother was called a golden goddess from the stars. Vyrl's father had been a leader among the Lyshrioli, known for his wisdom, his love of Dalvador, and his spectacular singing voice. Together he and Roca raised towering sons and beautiful daughters, some of whom went to the stars and became legends themselves, others who stayed on Lyshriol, loved and honored by the people. The fairy tale caught Kamoj, until she forgot the reality they faced and believed in the dream Vyrl created.

After the meeting ended, people came up to talk with Vyrl or gathered in groups to discuss his speech. Listening to them, Kamoj realized that his idealistic dreams felt real because he believed them. Despite the harsh realities of politics, war, and death, and for all the tensions within his family, he truly saw them, and his life on Lyshriol, in the golden glow he evoked for his listeners.

The next morning, Vyrl spoke with the Bard and the Memory of Rishollinia. The Bard served as the village's judiciary and recorded its history in ballads; the Memory carried out the executive duties and remembered. Kamoj realized then that the hereditary title of Dalvador Bard, which passed from father to son in Vyrl's family, referred to more than singing. It was the closest these people had to a governor for the Dalvador region, which included the village itself and the smaller hamlets scattered throughout the Dalvador Plains.

Each village had its own Bard, a man chosen for his singing ability and leadership. They all answered to the Dalvador Bard, who in turn answered to Lord Rillia. Kamoj was amused to learn that Aniece's husband didn't use his real title, the Rillia Bard, because he couldn't sing. Dalvador Bard and Rillia Bard were hereditary titles, so Lord Rillia had the unenviable job of recording the history of his people in a voice no one wanted to hear. However, he compensated by being an inspired and enlightened leader.

Vyrl's people seemed to have even less interest in hierarchy than her own. Memories and Bards were the closest they had to formalized government. Memories inherited their gift, but it didn't always run true and could appear in unexpected places. A girl who manifested the trait could choose to study at a Memory House. To Kamoj, it sounded similar to the way Airysphere Prism had trained to become a priestess at the Spectral Temple in Argali.

In the morning, Vyrl's group rode on to tiny Hollindale, a hamlet of only three hundred people. From there, they went to Jalidor. Over the next few days, they visited Morillei, teeming Aquinal, Kelridor, Starlo Vale, and finally the distant Whisperton.

Then they started back.

On the day they left Whisperton, almost the entire town

gathered in the rolling hills outside the village. Six hundred people waited to walk with them. Only about sixty remained in the village: the elderly and sick, as well as guards to protect the houses and businesses. When Kamoj saw so many people waiting to follow Vyrl, moisture gathered in her eyes.

They set off in the crystalline morning, their pace through the plains slowed now, with six hundred people. It wasn't long before blue and silver birds were streaking above them, fliers with the AWOE insignia. Rumors filtered back to Kamoj and Vyrl; AWOE officials were landing to question people about the procession.

And the people answered: *We're migrating.*

It took all day to return to Starlo Vale. Sitting in front of Vyrl on Mercury, Kamoj felt his tension. Would they find any Starlo citizens waiting for them? Whisperton had joined the migration, but if Vyrl couldn't inspire solid support from a good portion of the other villages, they probably couldn't achieve their goal.

As they started up the rolling hill that crested above Starlo, Vyrl motioned at the sky. "Look." In the distance, silver and blue fliers were circling above the plains.

A rumbling vibrated in Kamoj's ears and grew louder as they rode on. It came from the direction of Starlo, but the village remained hidden behind the long hill. The first wave of Whisperton's people swept to the top—and a shout went up. As Kamoj and Vyrl reached the crest, Vyrl reined Mercury to a stop. A large village lay below them, Starlo Vale, four thousand strong.

Almost the entire four thousand had come to meet them.

People milled, ran, bustled, and called to one another in the plains below. As more Whisperton citizens surged over the hill, pouring around Kamoj and Vyrl, AWOE fliers roared above them in an ever-changing pattern, monitoring the commotion. Sitting astride Mercury, Vyrl and Kamoj gazed over a sea of people, while more people flowed past them in waves.

Vyrl leaned his head against hers so she could hear him

above the thunder of so many voices. "They came." His voice caught. "For my family. They *came*."

"Hai, Vyrl," she said. "That they did."

They camped in the plains outside Starlo Vale, beneath the stars, nearly five thousand strong. In the morning, they resumed their journey. The migration spread out now in a great column as long as Starlo itself, with Vyrl and Kamoj riding near the front.

They reached Kelridor at noon—and found two thousand more waiting. By now the silver fliers were their constant companions. As the migration approached Aquinal, people came pouring out to meet them, running through the grass, calling to friends and relatives in their swelling ranks. Rather than one village, Aquinal consisted of many small hamlets gathered together, an archipelago in the ocean of the plains. Their total population rivaled that of Dalvador, the largest Plains village. Word soon reached them; nine thousand Aquinal citizens had heeded Vyrl's call.

Their procession swelled to sixteen thousand. It spread across the plains, headed to Dalvador—and the tiny starport where the occupying forces had made their on-planet headquarters.

The Jagernauts recorded everything. They sent their messages into the heavens, never knowing what—if anything— escaped the cordon of silence imposed on Lyshriol. They worked in shifts, some recording, the others protecting Vyrl from the thousands of people who wanted to talk to him. A flier shadowed his position all the time, winging in the sky. Although Kamoj still often sat with him on Mercury, she sometimes rode her own lyrine now.

Late that afternoon, a flier landed. As the silver bird settled down, people flowed away in all directions, forming a huge circle around the craft. Then they waited.

Riding on Mercury, Vyrl tightened his arms around Kamoj. "This is it."

"It will work out," she said, hoping that were true.

The crowds parted to let Vyrl ride to the flier. A retinue surrounded him: Stillmorn, the Jagernauts, and the Bards and Memories from the towns in the migration. They stopped about twenty paces away from the flier. Its hatch swung open and four people jumped out, two men and two women.

Vyrl spoke to Kamoj in a low voice. "The man on the right is Colonel Shipper."

She studied the colonel. Crisp in his uniform, he had a stocky build, average height, gray hair, a square jaw, and a look of intelligence. So this was the officer who had taken away Roca and Del-Kurj. On behalf of her husband and his splintered family, she immediately disliked the colonel.

The four AWOE officers waited quietly. Kamoj was growing more and more sensitized to everyone around her as her neural pathways became attuned to those in Vyrl's brain. Shipper and his people appeared calm, but she felt their fear. She had to admit, it took courage to face sixteen thousand people.

Yes, the flier had weapons, but in this situation it could be a disaster to use them. If the *Ascendant* was receiving the Jagernauts' signals, then all settled space would witness whatever the AWOE forces did here. The sum total of humanity numbered nearly three trillion, spread out on thousands of worlds. An exhausted humanity. Even in the best times, seeing a defenseless people attacked would incite anger. Now, in the aftermath of the Radiance War, it would be diplomatic suicide for the Allied Worlds.

Vyrl swung off Mercury and helped Kamoj down. Then their group regarded Colonel Shipper's group, each trying to judge when the other would start walking. Both moved at almost the same moment. Shipper came with his three officers; Vyrl came with Kamoj, Stillmorn, and another Jagernaut. The other Jagernauts continued to record the proceedings, with devices built into their bodies and uniforms.

It had surprised Kamoj when they asked her to accompany Vyrl, until Stillmorn explained. With Kamoj and Vyrl's minds in resonance, ISC didn't want to hamper Vyrl by separating them at crucial times like this.

The two groups met halfway between the flier and the crowds of the migration. "Prince Havyrl," Shipper said. "My honor at your presence." He looked more disconcerted than honored.

"My greetings," Vyrl said cautiously.

"You've a lot of people here," Shipper said.

"I do."

"What do you plan on doing with them?"

"We're going to Dalvador."

"Why?"

"To wait."

"For what?"

"Your forces to leave."

Shipper stared at him. "You can't be serious."

Vyrl looked serene. "We are indeed."

"How will all these people fit in Dalvador?" Shipper asked. "What will they eat? Where will they sleep? What if the weather turns bad? This is truly reckless. I must insist you disband."

"Why?" Vyrl asked. "We've done nothing wrong. The people have brought food. Tents. Supplies."

Shipper started to respond, then glanced at the Jagernauts. That one look told Kamoj more than anything he had said. The colonel was acutely aware his words were being recorded, which she doubted would be true if the broadcasts weren't making it off Lyshriol.

Vyrl, she thought, with force. *I think the Jagernauts are getting through.*

He glanced at her and his optimism surged, though he showed no outward sign.

The colonel indicated the Jagernauts. "The presence of ISC officers here is a violation of the Iceland Treaty between your people and mine. They haven't been cleared with our authorities."

Vyrl frowned. "This is a Skolian world. We don't have to clear our officers with your authorities."

"Lyshriol is under our protection. We're trying to keep the peace." Shipper glanced at the Jagernauts, then paused for effect. "Our presence here is neither arbitrary nor hostile. Would you drag humanity into war after bitter war, Prince Havyrl, as the Ruby and Qox Dynasties throw world-slagging armies against each other, until the human race again vanishes from the stars, as it did five thousand years ago? We must act in the best interest of *all* humanity. If preventing the Ruby Dynasty from rebuilding its bellicose power base will preserve this peace we've paid so dearly to achieve, then that is what we will do."

That was certainly dramatic, Kamoj thought dryly. She felt Vyrl's anger. She suspected that one reason General Ashman questioned Vyrl's ability to carry out this mission was because Shipper's people were almost certainly making their own records. If Vyrl lost his cool here the way he had in the Inquiry, it could do a lot of damage.

Then Vyrl took a breath. "A pretty speech, Colonel. You make it easy to forget how much Earth stands to gain from imprisoning us. Control my family and you have access to an empire." He stopped for his own carefully timed pause. "Conquerors rewrite history. Perhaps your history of the Radiance War will even 'forget' how your military refused to hear the desperate pleas of my people for help against the Traders, or your refusal to believe the atrocities they committed against us."

Shipper frowned, but before he could respond, Vyrl continued. "Colonel, I know the truth. You of Earth let the Traders woo you into aiding them in their crimes against human decency. You could have *prevented* the Radiance War by heeding our cries. But you watched while we died. Now you step into the chaos. In the false guise of protectors, you come to our home, a defenseless world, and imprison us. Exile us. Separate us in the worst hours of our grief." He let his voice rumble. "How does this make you of Earth any different from the Traders?"

Shipper scowled at him. It didn't surprise Kamoj. From what she had seen of the Skolians, she doubted that ISC made "desperate pleas" to anyone, let alone the Allied Worlds, which Skolia dwarfed in population, resources, and wealth. If the Traders were like Jax Ironbridge multiplied many times over, then Vyrl's comparison of Earth to the Trader Empire was outrageous. Kamoj had a sense that the Allied Worlds were gentle compared to the Skolians and Traders. They wanted to protect themselves. She could tell Shipper genuinely believed the universe would be better off if Vyrl's family didn't have free run of the place.

Yet she also felt the truths in Vyrl's speech. Earth *did* have a great deal to gain by imprisoning the Ruby Dynasty. They *had* turned a disbelieving ear to ISC, letting Trader propaganda fool them. The AWOE forces *were* violating the spirit of the Iceland Treaty. No easy answers existed here. Like the Inquiry on Balumil, this situation tangled the truth in complexities—but on an interstellar scale.

Vyrl and Shipper continued to parry, but they were only repeating their arguments in new ways, each trying to sound eloquent while making the other look bad. They finished their meeting without coming to a resolution; they had been making speeches more for the listeners who would receive these broadcasts than for each other. All the while, Kamoj felt a growing sense of presence from the sheer mass of the humanity around them, which continued onward even as Vyrl and Shipper spoke.

No, that presence didn't come from the migration.

But yes, it did.

She wasn't sure. The collective minds of so many people in one place were acting as a lens, magnifying and focusing something else—

A presence that had slept for eons beneath the world.

* * *

The shadow appeared as the migration flowed from Aquinal toward Morillei. Kamoj was riding her own lyrine now, which she had named Harmonic after the Spherical Harmonic wraiths from the Spectral Temple in Argali. Looking west, she saw a huge shadow moving across the plains. It made no sense. Only a few puffs of blue cloud floated in the lavender sky, and those were drifting the other way.

Then suddenly Kamoj realized what she was seeing. People. Hundreds of people. They were headed toward the migration, coming on with the same steady patience as those who already walked in the column.

Vyrl rode up alongside her. "They're from Silverdell."

"That's one of the cities we didn't have time to visit, isn't it?"

He grinned at her. "Yes. Aquinal sent messengers. Word is spreading."

Silverdell was the first. As more villages joined them over the next few days, the migration swelled. At the village of Morillei, they picked up three thousand more. The column spread out across the plains, twenty-five thousand strong. Each village organized itself. The Bards and Memories assigned jobs to volunteers: keep the townsfolk moving in an orderly fashion, ensure supplies were distributed, see that everyone had shelter when they camped, and give aid where needed.

In the east, the gleaming Silverdell River wound across the plains. Teams were already setting up crossing sites. They hoped to confine the damage of fording the river to a small region, lest they turn the Silverdell into a giant marsh. Other teams worked on irrigation channels, which they would extend from the Silverdell, also from the Tyrole, Jalidor, and Taquinaire Rivers, bringing water to quench the thirst of the multitudes.

On a bright afternoon, Kamoj and Vyrl rode their lyrine up a long hill that rolled through the plains like a great ocean swell. At the top, they gazed over the migration. It astonished Kamoj, not only for its sheer size, but also for the affable nature of the people. They came for the adventure, yes, but mostly for love of Vyrl's family. She felt as if she were witnessing a miracle, an entire population working together for a goal that had no advantage to individuals, but instead benefitted a higher ideal. A good people and a good leader could work wonders. But Jax could destroy all this, in vengeance, if he destroyed Vyrl.

Kamoj looked at her husband. "I'll testify."

He turned, his hair blowing across his face. "Testify?" He pushed back his curls. "You mean, for these people?"

"No. For you. Against Jax." Somehow, though, that wasn't what she meant either, or not all of it. A part of her heart was flying free after years of being trapped. "It is for me also. All my life I've done for others. For Argali, Jax, you." Her voice softened. "To see you happy means the world to me. I give to you in joy, as I do for Argali. But I cannot live my life through others. I must do it for myself as well."

His expression reminded her of Dazza, when a patient began to heal. He took her hand and said, simply, "Yes."

So they started down the hill, headed onward.

Eight hundred people joined them in Jalidor. On the way to Hollindale, Kamoj rode in front of Vyrl, on Mercury. "I hope the *Ascendant* is receiving the broadcasts of all this."

"I'm still connected to the orbital web." Vyrl leaned closer, so she could hear him over the rumble of the migration. "My links are diffuse, given the distances involved, but I would know if anyone had cut them. And they haven't. That's no guarantee our signals are getting out, but it's a good sign."

She laid her head back against his shoulder. "Colonel Shipper wants to stop us. Can they turn back so many people?"

"They could spray the plains with sleep gas. They've probably held off because it would look appalling on a broadcast to have tens of thousands of people dropping to the ground. Also, it's hard to know the side effects on an untested population of altered humans like this. That's true for most methods they might use, like sonic vibrations or airborne nanomeds."

"Do you think that's enough to keep them from doing it?"

"I can't say." He considered. "The stakes are high, maybe even the control of an interstellar civilization. It might drive them to extreme measures."

Kamoj sighed. "I wish we knew what was going on out there."

Vyrl blew out a gust of air. "I also."

They slept on the plains, surrounded by thirty thousand people. Instead of using their tent, tonight Kamoj and Vyrl lay outside, in a nest of blankets, gazing at the star-washed sky. A gibbous lavender moon glowed overhead and a blue crescent hung near the horizon.

"How many moons does Lyshriol have?" Kamoj asked.

"Two." Vyrl spoke with drowsy langour. "All two. Everything. Suns. Moons. Lyrine horns. Eight fingers per hand, two sets of two opposing fingers. Eight toes, two sets of two toes on two feet."

Kamoj tickled his leg with her foot. "You've ten very healthy toes, husband."

"That's from my mother." Vyrl yawned. "The Lyshrioli are a binary people. This whole migration is like a big flow-chart. Maybe that's why it's working. Give us a good flow-chart to follow and we're happy."

"These words make sense?"

He laughed sleepily. "A flowchart is a diagram of how a computer program works."

"Why would the first colonists here make themselves into a human computer?

"Gods only know." Vyrl was quiet for a while. Just when she thought he had fallen asleep, he said, "We think of computers as machines. The Ruby ancients considered them an extension of human thought into other universes. They lumped physics, abstract theorems, and mysticism into one discipline. That's why we have trouble understanding their technology."

Kamoj turned his words around in her mind, as if she were viewing scales that changed their color patterns depending on how the light hit them. "The people on Lyshriol must be part of a bigger creation."

Vyrl nodded, his eyes closed, his head next to hers on the blanket. "Maybe the city you found has clues that will tell us more about the purpose of that creation."

"I'm not so sure." Kamoj considered. "I think your people and that city are two parts of a whole. For one part to tell about the other would be like a book reading itself."

Vyrl opened his eyes to look at her. "You know, that would make sense with what we know about Ruby tech. Maybe to understand all this, we need someone from outside Lyshriol to look at the whole of it. Someone to read the book. No one has been able to because, without that city, we didn't have all the pages."

His response startled Kamoj, though it took her a moment to figure out why. She had contradicted him—and he had agreed. Had she done similar with Jax, he would have scorned her insight. He might have later repeated the idea, if he thought it had merit, but he would have phrased it as his own. Jax felt that her accomplishments diminished him if they came at what he called "his expense." Vyrl didn't seem to care.

Encouraged, she said, "Your brother Shannon is closer to it. He felt the city stirring before he knew it existed."

"Shannon has always been different." Vyrl pulled her into his arms. "He looks like a Dale Archer from the Blue Mountains. They've stayed isolated for thousands of years. We Rillians are a much bigger population, and we've experienced more genetic drift, nothing huge, but apparently enough to cut us off from whatever in us resonated with that buried city. As a throwback to the Archers, Shannon may be closer to what it needs."

Kamoj thought about it. "If Lyshriol is a book, then perhaps he has some of the missing pages."

He laughed softly. "An interesting concept." Then he added, "You are my missing pages, sweet Kamoj."

She touched his cheek. "As you are for me."

After that they lay together, content in the moonlight. Her mind drifted, submerged into the great, sleeping migration around them.

Sleeping . . . for millennia . . . until she answered its call . . .

The people of Rishollinia came out to meet them, streaming across the plains. The column had picked up most of Hollindale's three hundred residents, plus thousands more from hamlets Vyrl hadn't visited, more flowing in each day as the news spread. They had enjoyed ideal weather, breezy days and warm nights, but now blue clouds scudded across the sky and a darker line edged the southern horizon. Kamoj hoped the storm held off until they reached Dalvador; if it hit now, it could be a disaster.

She rode Harmonic today, always with a Jagernaut as her shadow. People surrounded her; they rode, walked, pulled carts, laughed, grumbled, and trudged onward. Guided by herders, livestock lumbered along, animals with more bulk than grace. Carts rolled by laden with food, though Kamoj had no idea what kind; it all looked like bubbles to her. A boy strode by and waved to her. When a group of children dashed in front of Harmonic, yelling and laughing, the lyrine froze in protest. Kamoj scratched her neck until she started forward again.

The column veered south, flowing past Rishollinia at a safe distance. Silver fliers patrolled their progress, always aloft above them now. The clouds on the horizon steadily grew larger.

The flux and flow of people opened enough for Kamoj to see three specks flying across the plains toward the migration.

As they drew nearer, they resolved into riders on lyrine. She lost sight of them as the crowds blocked her view. Curious, she urged Harmonic forward. After a few minutes, she glimpsed Vyrl up ahead with the riders, two women and a man, their hair wildly tousled. The clouds on the horizon continued to swell.

As Kamoj rode up beside Vyrl, he turned to her. He didn't seem able to speak. The three riders gazed at her with open curiosity, their faces flushed.

Kamoj's apprehension surged. "What is it? What happened?"

Vyrl indicated the horizon where fog stretched across the plains. "Look." His voice caught. "Gods, Kamoj, *look*."

Troubled now, she studied the cloud banks. "Do you think it will slow us down? We've had such good weather until now."

"Weather?" Vyrl asked. "What do you mean?"

Kamoj wasn't sure how to interpret his mood. He didn't seem upset so much as stunned. She looked again—and then she understood.

That great dark band in the south wasn't fog.

It was people.

Vyrl's brother Denric brought over twenty thousand. They stretched along the southern horizon, a wave of humanity sweeping across the Plains. The migration swelled to sixty thousand people.

The day they came into view of Dalvador, they sighted another fog bank of humanity on the eastern horizon. Vyrl's dark-haired sister, Aniece, rode at the front, flanked on one side by her pennant bearer, a powerful man on a violet lyrine, and on the other by a red-robed Memory from Graymarch, the largest city in the northern plains. Twenty-five thousand Lyshrioli came with her.

However, they saw no sign of Lord Rillia or Shannon, who had both gone north, over the Backbone Mountains. Rillia had headed to the Vales in the northwest, the densely populated regions central to his realm. Shannon went much farther north, into the cold Blue Mountains where the Dale Archers lived, their numbers unknown, possibly a few thousand, maybe less.

The people of Dalvador flooded out to them, swelling their ranks by ten thousand. Vyrl's kin came by to greet him in a constant stream. The migration had reached one hundred thousand now, a sea of people. For all that the spectacle thrilled Kamoj, who had never even imagined so many together in one place, it also unsettled her. They had trampled the Dalvador Plains as far as she could look in every direction. Vyrl assured her the grass would grow back. But it would be months at the least, probably longer.

The column didn't stop at Dalvador, but continued on to the starport, a ten-minute walk. Compared to the great shipyards Vyrl had described to Kamoj, this was minuscule. The cluster of white-washed buildings resembled a tiny Dalvador hamlet. The airfield was big enough for maybe ten shuttles. None sat there now.

The Bards had already assigned people to help maintain order. As the migration poured around the starport, monitors moved through the crowds, talking, organizing, and calming, as well as preventing enthusiastic youths from overrunning the fragile buildings. No one came out to meet them, of course. The port had long been evacuated. Kamoj doubted she would have stayed around either, if one hundred thousand people had come to visit.

Today she rode with Vyrl on Mercury. Kamoj felt him struggle with the craving for rum that still sometimes hit him. When she tried to project thoughts of comfort, he murmured and pulled her back against himself, his arms around her waist.

A roar thundered overhead, louder than the usual fliers. With a start, she looked up to see the ISC racer arrowing south, gold and black in the sky, a stark contrast to the silver and blue Allied fliers.

Vyrl pulled Mercury up beside Primary Stillmorn, who sat astride a lyrine. "What's she doing?" he asked, indicating the racer.

"Keeping watch for us." Stillmorn shaded her eyes with her hand, watching the racer as it dwindled to a speck. "Not much point in hiding it now. And we wanted AWOE intel to know your people have ISC backup." She went to work on her gauntlet.

Although Kamoj had become more accustomed to *Ascendant* devices, it startled her when the pilot's voice came out of a mesh in the gauntlet. Stillmorn spoke to the pilot in another language, then glanced at Vyrl. "Your brother-in-law is bringing a group over the mountains. They should be here tomorrow. We're less sure about your brother Shannon."

"He probably had trouble convincing the Dale Archers," Vyrl said. "They never come into Rillia."

"So what do we do now?" Kamoj asked.

"Now," Stillmorn said, "we wait."

Kamoj, Vyrl, and Denric were at dinner inside Vyrl's tent when Stillmorn came for them. "It's Lord Rillia!" Her face was flushed from running. "Their front riders are already in camp. Your sister Aniece went to meet them."

As they jumped up from the table, Vyrl asked the question they all wanted to know. "How many?"

Excitement surged in Stillmorn's normally unruffled voice. "They say he's bringing more than three quarters of the population from the Rillian Vales." Stillmorn grinned at him. "Sir, it's *huge.*"

Denric glanced in the direction of the mountains. "I hope they haven't destroyed the Stained Glass Forest."

"The racer made sure they bypassed it," Stillmorn said. "The mountain crossing took a beating, but apparently they've proceeded in a orderly fashion." Dryly she added, "I wish the cadets I train would operate with such organization."

Vyrl motioned at the sky, where the AWOE aircraft droned above the camp. "My people aren't used to seeing them, not all the time this way. It's probably sobering enough to discourage the wilder festivals."

Stillmorn gave him a look of satisfaction. "However they did it—they're coming."

The Vales migration poured into Dalvador throughout the night—eighty thousand strong. They came on, wave after wave, hour after hour, with carts, lyrine, livestock, and supplies all thundering across the land. The night turned into a festival, as the peoples of the Plains and Vales mingled, curious, wary, and intrigued by one another.

Near dawn, Shannon arrived with the Dale Archers, far more than anyone had expected, or even knew existed, twenty thousand, rank upon rank of the mysterious, elusive nomads. In an eerie contrast to the Vales migration, they came in the predawn light, utterly silent, fey archers with white-gold hair astride ethereal silver lyrine. Shannon rode at the head of the column, his uncanny resemblance to them living proof of his Dale ancestry.

So they gathered, two hundred thousand people, almost the entire human population on Lyshriol. As the two suns rose above the horizon and turned the sky crimson, the unarmed natives of a primitive world in the hinterlands of settled space commenced their siege against humanity's greatest remaining interstellar power.

26

The Sea of Hope

External Forces

Come to me.

Kamoj turned over under the quilt . . .

Come to me.

Ancient and deep, an unnamed power . . . Focused through the lens formed by the collected minds spread across the plains, it reached out to her, trying to awake . . .

Kamoj opened her eyes. Turning on her back, she gazed at the top of the tent. A globe drifted there, casting a dim glow that left most of the tent in shadow. She felt restless, disquieted by the remnants of her vague dream. Vyrl was lying on his side facing away from her.

She brushed her hand up his arm. "Vyrl?"

He stirred, then settled back to sleep.

She put her arm around his waist. "Wake up, sleepy lion."

"Kamoj," he mumbled. "I'm tired." He rolled over to face her. "I'm almost seventy, young wife. You have to let me rest." Then he went back to sleep.

Kamoj sighed. She contemplated life for awhile, or at least how boring it was to lie awake when everyone else slept. Then she slid out of bed. Cold air hit her with a shock, and she scrambled into her warmest clothes, her hiking outfit and jacket from the *Ascendant*.

Wind gusted across her face as she stepped outside. The blue crescent moon had moved up the sky, telling of the late hour. The camps slumbered now, their fires gone to embers. A child cried and a mother soothed it. Somewhere a lyrine snorted.

The weight of so many minds pressed on Kamoj, but when she put distance between Vyrl and herself, the pressure eased. She wandered among the camps. After the arrival of the Archers this morning, everyone had spent the day setting up tent villages. Tomorrow, they would organize irrigation, hunting, and planting teams. It gave Kamoj a sense of satisfaction. The Allieds expected the siege to fail from lack of necessities, but they hadn't witnessed the Lyshrioli tenacity she had seen on the journey here.

She sat on an abandoned crate and pulled her jacket tight, letting it warm her with its "picoweb climate controls," whatever that meant.

"My greetings, Lady Kamoj."

She turned with a start. A lithe figure stood in the shadow of a nearby tent. "Shannon?"

"May I sit with you?" he asked.

"Yes. Certainly." She slid over for him. The crate was plenty big enough for several people, but moving around helped her deal with the shyness she felt around Shannon.

He sat on the end of the crate, watching her with his distant gaze.

"Did you have trouble sleeping too?" she asked.

"Yes." The blue moonlight turned his shoulder-length hair silver. She wondered if he had any awareness of his ethereal beauty. He had a luminous aspect, almost as if he were made from the moonglow instead of flesh and blood.

For awhile they sat in silence. Then Shannon said, "It's reaching for you."

"It?"

"The sleeper."

Kamoj wished she could talk to him about what they had found. "I don't know what you mean."

"You do." His voice was a distant breeze rippling over

musical pipes. "Otherwise Primary Stillmorn would never have questioned me so intently that night we talked."

So Stillmorn *had* talked to him in private. It didn't surprise her. "I'm not allowed to discuss it."

"Why?"

"I'm not sure."

"ISC security." Now he sounded like dry leaves.

"I think so."

He looked off toward the Stained Glass Forest. "During the thousands of years that my people have lived here, since the fall of the Ruby Empire, our gene pool has shifted."

"Gene pool?" She had never heard of such body of water.

"Our hereditary traits." He turned back to her, his cool face unexpectedly warmed with a smile. "I suppose that's a simplification. Better that, though, than a dull soliloquy on deoxyribonucleic acid."

His words startled her. He came across as so uncanny she tended to forget that, until the age of sixteen, he had received the same education as Vyrl. She thought of what Vyrl had told her. "You mean the Rillians have changed more than the Archers."

"Yes. I've more in common with the Archers than the rest of my family, but it's not enough. Your people must be closer. But your minds aren't strong enough, not like a Ruby psion." His silvered gaze seemed to see inside of her. "Perhaps only you, in your resonance with Vyrl, can wake it." With soft-spoken calm, he added, "I think it is a Lock, Lady Kamoj."

A Lock? "I don't know what you mean."

"You know that our family powers the ancient Ruby machines?"

"Vyrl told me. He said they help you survive."

"Yes. We call them Locks. Our family, the Ruby Dynasty, are their Keys." His words seemed to ripple. "After five hundred years of searching, throughout hundreds of planets, my people have found only three Locks. The Traders captured one in the last war."

"And you think we found another?"

"I'm not sure. This is different. How, I cannot say." Moonglow shone around him in a silver-blue nimbus. "It is lost to us, unless we stir it from its slumber. Can you?"

"I don't know how." Kamoj wished she had a better answer to give him.

His voice drifted like wind through a field. "Please don't give up." He rose to his feet. "Sleep well, my new sister."

Then he vanished into the shadows.

The flier landed in the morning, an AWOE insignia gleaming in blue on its side. Vyrl, Kamoj, Rillia, and Stillmorn walked out to meet it, guarded by Jagernauts.

A dark-haired woman in a blue uniform jumped down from the hatch. She greeted them with formal phrases of respect and introduced herself as Major Jenski.

Vyrl watched her warily. "Have you come to tell us your forces are leaving?"

"I've come to speak for your people," she said.

He scowled. "You, speak for them?"

Jenski motioned at the sea of humanity spread across the plains. "These people trust you. They've followed you on a hopeless quest that can only fail. You disrupt their lives. Prince Havyrl, be reasonable. Be kind. Let them go home."

"Don't patronize us," Vyrl said. "We aren't children who need to be sent home."

"You're only causing harm," Jenski said.

"We stay until you leave."

"We will not leave," she told him. "Not if you stay here a hundred years."

"Jenski believes what she said," Kamoj said as the four of them walked back to the encampment. "She really thinks we're hurting them."

"What if she's right?" Vyrl gazed out at the migration. "What if all I've achieved is to create hardship for my people?"

"They're trying to demoralize you," Lord Rillia said. "Don't let them undermine your confidence."

Stillmorn snorted. "So they don't like us here. Tough."

Vyrl smiled at the Primary. "I should turn you loose on the next AWOE officer who comes down."

Stillmorn gave him a wicked grin. "It would be my honor to serve you, Your Highness."

Vyrl laughed, his posture relaxing. But as they walked, Kamoj felt his fatigue. Even though he knew what the Allieds were trying to do, it didn't make him impervious to their efforts.

On day three of the siege, the Bards and Memories set up a government for the encamped migration. Over the next few days, each village elected representatives to a Large Council, which then chose a much smaller Senior Council. Vyrl, his siblings, Lord Rillia, and Primary Stillmorn also sat on the Senior Council.

Farmers set up areas for crops, in case the siege outlasted their supplies. Others built corrals for livestock and worked on irrigation canals, aided by a Jagernaut with a degree in civil engineering. Major Jenski came back to spar with Vyrl again. Then she asked to meet the Senior Council. They spent an hour inside the port having the same debate as before, with the same result, both sides refusing to give.

One night AWOE commandos came down and tried to deactivate the Jagernauts. With their augmented speed and strength, AI-enhanced intellects, computer-driven reflexes, and internal hydraulics, the Jagernauts made difficult targets; besides which, in the midst of so many people, the commandos found it impossible to remain covert. Gleeful Lyshrioli went after them, with no idea of the damage the AWOE team could have done had they chosen to fight back. Kamoj saw a group of giggling young women pin down one soldier and try to remove his uniform, making impressed noises over his well-built physique. From his embarrassed response, she suspected that dealing with females intent on mischief wasn't a well-studied part of his training.

In the end, rather than risk harming anyone, the team withdrew to their racer and flew off. After that, Stillmorn stepped up security. Throughout it all, the Jagernauts made recordings and sent them to the *Ascendant*.

On the twentieth day, Major Jenski asked to talk with Vyrl and his siblings. Kamoj, Rillia, and Stillmorn joined them, and of course the Jagernauts. They met in one of the port lounges, a white-washed room with blue chairs. After the usual twaddle about how everyone was honored to be in everyone else's presence, Jenski got down to business.

"You're cut off," the major said. "We've stopped your transmissions."

Lord Rillia shrugged. "Of course you make this claim. You can't expect us to believe you."

Jenski kept her focus on Vyrl. "Did you think we wouldn't find your entry into our webs, Prince Havyrl? We tracked you down. The game's over. You can't send signals out any more."

Vyrl gave her an unimpressed look. "You're bluffing. I'd know if you had cut me off."

"I don't need to bluff." Jenski rattled off a series of numbers. "Sound familiar?"

"So you know a few memory locations in the ISC web." Vyrl moved his hand in dismissal. "It means nothing."

Kamoj didn't like it. With so many Ruby telepaths around her, she had become a lens focusing their perceptions. It made her hyperaware of everyone's emotions. Jenski exuded confidence. Vyrl knew. His brothers and sisters knew. Stillmorn knew. Jenski wasn't bluffing. And regardless of what Vyrl claimed, Jenski had shaken him with her list of numbers. Beneath his display of noncholance, he was worried. Public opinion was the *only* weapon they had here. If they lost that, they had nothing.

"Prince Havyrl." Jenski put on a *let's be reasonable* tone.

"Why put your people through all this when it serves no purpose? Let them go home."

It was Denric, the teacher, who answered. "You should realize by now that this argument won't work. If you're really so concerned, tell your superiors to withdraw."

Jenski responded with the usual platitudes. The moods of Vyrl and his siblings swirled around Kamoj, doubt mixed with distrust. As empaths, they felt Jenski's confidence. The major *knew* AWOE intel had succeeded in blocking Vyrl's link.

And yet . . . something didn't fit. Kamoj couldn't define it, but she felt a *glitch*.

She closed her eyes. When she concentrated, a stir came at the edges of her conscious mind.

Resonance.

The presence buried under the forest drowsed in her mind, half awake. Drawing on the heightened awareness it gave her, she resonated with the Ruby psions in the room, especially Vyrl. Then she focused on Jenski.

Tampering.

Someone had tampered with Jenski's brain? No, not exactly. Jenski had a strangeness about her. What? Deception. Yes. That was it. But how?

Kamoj opened her eyes. Denric was talking about the legalities, or lack thereof, in the AWOE occupation. The others listened, deferring to his knowledge of offworld judiciary.

"This is being covered by our governments," Jenski pointed out. "It's pointless here—"

"You're tricked," Kamoj said.

Jenski stopped, obviously startled by an interruption from the group's silent member. "Governor?"

"Your mind." Kamoj studied her, so caught in what she had discovered that she lost her reticence about speaking. "You've a trick in your mind. It changes your brain. It makes you appear confident when you aren't."

Jenski rubbed her chin. "Governor Argali, my people have no Kyle sciences."

"I don't know what Kyle sciences means," Kamoj said. "But I know you have a trick in your mind."

"Kyle science is a branch of neuroscience," Denric said.

"It's the study of telepaths," Vyrl told her.

Chaniece turned to Kamoj, the intensity of her violet-eyed gaze a reminder of her twin, the absent Del-Kurj. "What do you mean, 'tricked?' "

"Major Jenski has a glitch in her mind. It makes her thoughts seem like other thoughts." Kamoj concentrated on Jenski. "You seem confident, but it's false."

Jenski gave her a wry smile. "I wish we had the ability to do such a thing. But I'm afraid you've imagined it."

Kamoj scowled. "I have not."

Neither Vyrl nor his siblings spoke. Their emotions flowed over Kamoj. How could she pick up what remained hidden from them? She had nowhere near their mental strength, and they detected no tricks in Jenski's mind. However, if they admitted they believed Jenski, they lost ground in this battle of wills.

But they feared Jenski told the truth.

"I didn't detect any deception," Vyrl said. Now that Jenski had left, they sat more easily, relaxed in the blue chairs.

"She knows you're all Ruby psions," Kamoj said. "She was projecting for all of you. She didn't worry as much about me."

Leaning his elbow on the arm of his chair, Denric rested his chin on his hand. "The Allieds can claim all they want that they have no Kyle sciences, but I don't believe it for a second. I may not have picked up any tricks, but I sure as hell could tell she had protections in her mind."

"They were terrible, though," the dark-haired Aniece said, curled in her chair.

"You were supposed to think that," Kamoj said. "To distract you from the tricks."

"How can you know this?" Chaniece asked.

Kamoj hesitated. If she revealed what had enhanced her resonance with Vyrl, she was violating ISC security. She glanced at Stillmorn, and the Primary returned her gaze with an inflexible stare. So all Kamoj said was, "When I'm near Vyrl, we resonate. It increases my ability as an empath."

"I've heard it can happen that way," Aniece said. "But isn't it rare?"

"Very rare." Vyrl smiled. "But real."

"So." Lord Rillia considered Kamoj. "You think this soldier from the sky bluffs?"

"Yes. I do."

Vyrl looked around at the others. "I say we stick to our plans."

After some discussion, they agreed. Kamoj just hoped she was right about Major Jenski. If not, she had just sentenced two hundred thousand people to a useless seige. They might see it as an adventure now, but this migration would soon take its toll.

On night twenty-one of the siege, the people of Aquinal had a festival. All the adjoining villages soon joined in. By the time the Large Council sent in patrols, rowdy groups of inebriated youths had knocked over tents, trampled fledgling crops, and in general enlivened the camps far more than anyone needed.

On day twenty-two, Aquinal cleaned up the mess.

On day twenty-four, more villages had festivals, but this time they stayed reasonably well-behaved. Kamoj had never known such a playful people. Yes, the camp authorities had to keep watch on the impromptu celebrations. But the merriment tickled her.

On day twenty-five, a woman from the Vales gave birth to a baby girl. On day twenty-seven, Vyrl performed a marriage for a couple from Tarlaire, in his capacity as Dalvador Bard, now that he was the eldest Valdoria male on Lyshriol. On day thirty-two, a farmer from Morillei stabbed a merchant from Jalidor during a fight. They recovered, but Lord Rillia fined them both.

On day thirty-five, Silverdell had a dance. Kamoj whirled with the other women in the moonlight, caught in the joy of motion and music. The men stood along the sidelines, enjoying the show and clapping for the twirling women. Kamoj felt how much Vyrl wanted to join in. She wished they could dance together. But he showed no outward sign of his interest.

On day thirty-eight, Colonel Shipper showed up.

"You have only one option." Shipper stood in the port lounge, his body rigid as he stared at Vyrl across the separating expanse of a table. "You are in violation of civil property module eight-B in the Iceland Treaty. You must disband."

Vyrl was standing as well, facing off with Shipper like a greenglass stag defending his territory. Kamoj, Stillmorn, and Denric remained in their seats, listening with growing dismay.

"*We're* in violation of the Iceland Treaty?" Vyrl demanded. "*You* people violated it the moment you refused to release my family."

"That is for our governments to decide." Shipper pointed toward a view-screen that showed the encampment. "What happens here, however, bears directly on us. You're endangering the lives and property of our people and yours, and interfering with our ability to meet obligations specified by a treaty that your leaders—and your family—signed."

"That's a crock," Vyrl said. "This is our port, our land, and our planet. So get the *hell* out."

Shipper hit the table with his fist. "Disperse the camps, Valdoria. Or we'll do it for you." With that, he strode to the door, followed by his officers and bodyguards, and swept out of the building.

In the ensuing silence, Vyrl stared at the door. Then he sat down. "Damn."

Stillmorn gave him a dour look. "I've heard you be more tactful."

Denric leaned forward. "What he claims about the Iceland Treaty will never hold in court."

"It doesn't matter." Stillmorn rubbed her eyes. "They've created a reason to use in defense of whatever they plan next. It will probably go into broadcasts they've been producing to counter ours. I'll give you odds to beat the season that they'll portray themselves as protecting the people here against supposedly fanatic behavior by Vyrl."

"Then we have to speed up the preparations we've been making," Denric said. "Teach more people how to defend themselves."

"Against what?" Kamoj asked.

"That's the problem," Stillmorn said tiredly. "We don't know."

The AWOE forces came in the night, when most everyone slept.

Fliers hummed overhead, spraying sleep gas. Stillmorn's team had taught as many people as they could how to protect themselves against gas, acoustics, and brilliant light. Those people taught others, and they others, until knowledge spread in waves across the sea of humanity. But it was impossible to prepare two hundred thousand in time. Tens of thousands went to sleep normally that night—and stayed that way. AWOE shuttles landed, bringing soldiers, who proceeded to load sleepers onto the aircraft.

Kamoj and Vyrl worked all night with hand-picked teams, urging people to resist. For protection against the gas, they wore masks, shimmer sheaths, dampened cloths—whatever they could put together. Crowds of Lyshrioli harassed AWOE soldiers, climbed on their shuttles, got in the way, shouted a lot, and generally made a nuisance of themselves. They were especially effective, as well as zestfully melodramatic, when they knew Jagernauts were recording them.

The struggle went on throughout the next day and the one after that. Fliers sprayed and soldiers loaded. The ISC racer pilot reported that the shuttles were taking people home and leaving them in the care of those who had remained behind. By the end of day thirty-nine, the Allieds had removed well over half of the encamped migration.

Tired and disheartened, Kamoj finally forced herself to admit the truth: they were losing. Earth would win after all.

Standing next to Vyrl with her hair bedraggled, her face flushed, and her gas mask dangling from her hand, Kamoj watched as villagers from Rishollinia and Jalidor rode past them, calling out greetings, *entering* the camp. They were bringing new supplies and livestock, with fresh lyrine pulling carts.

A tear ran down Kamoj's face. "They're coming back."

Vyrl grinned in exhausted triumph. "That they are."

On day forty, the first villagers returned to the camp after having been lifted out by the AWOE forces. The trickle of people soon turned into a river. It had become even more a matter of principle now: they did *not* like being sent home when they were having the biggest wind-singing, foot-stomping festival in known history.

They poured into the tent-nation, their numbers surging as the day passed. As fast as shuttles ferried people out, other people returned. The inflow soon swamped the outflow. The AWOE forces had too few shuttles both to lift people out and to stop the ones they had already sent home from coming back.

On day forty-five, the Allieds gave up. It was either that or take more drastic measures, which no one wanted, particularly with all settled space watching the spectacle. That night, festivals sprang up everywhere, with dancing, singing, laughing, and couples sneaking off for privacy.

Kamoj stood with Vyrl on the edge of a campfire, listening as people told stories. When the group broke out bottles of a vintage wine, Vyrl turned to Kamoj. "Let's go."

She nodded, understanding. So they returned to their tent

and had their own festival. Within a nest of blankets, they moved together, langorous at first, then with more heat. Vyrl tried things she would have never imagined on her own. Kamoj struggled valiantly not to giggle or make noises, lest someone happen by the tent and hear. She felt both her own sensations and Vyrl's as well, until it all merged into a blissful haze. Afterward she and Vyrl lay still, content, their limbs tangled in the mess of blankets, their hearts beating together.

On day forty-six, the healers tended people for side effects of the gas, and also for aftereffects of having too much fun the night before. Vyrl and Lord Rillia met with the Memories to make a Lyshriol-style record of the migration. Kamoj helped the Bards set up activities for children. Stillmorn carried out an emergency cesarean section on a lyrine mare and delivered a blue colt. Shannon and the Dale Archers ranged far out in the plains, seeking game for cook pots.

Thus they continued their siege.

Carrying an armful of cloth bolts, Kamoj walked behind a row of tents. Camp sounds surrounded her: people talking, cooking, working; animals rumbling and huffing; children playing. She finally had a few moments of privacy here, except for the ever-present Jagernaut at her side.

With a sigh, she sat on a barrel, resting the bolts in her lap. The suns beat down on her bare head, heating her hair until she wanted to cut it off. She felt tired, with a mild nausea. The lavender sky bothered her today, not because she didn't like it, but just on principle, because she was worn out and homesick. She missed Argali. Had Vyrl felt this way on her world? She understood his melancholy even more now.

A scratching came from behind Kamoj. She looked around but saw nothing. But that was wrong. Where was the Jagernaut? It took her only seconds to realize she should go for help.

By then it was too late.

* * *

Colonel Shipper sat in the pilot's chair of the shuttle, with control panels arrayed around him. Another officer was in the copilot's seat. Soldiers filled the other seats, which faced inward. Gazing at them implacably, Kamoj sat between two giant soldiers. They had webbed her wrists to the arm rests of her chair so she wouldn't scratch anyone else. A medic was still treating the gashes on one fellow's cheek and arm. Kamoj felt a surge of remorse for gouging him so deeply, then reminded herself that he deserved it for helping spirit her up here into "orbit."

Although Shipper spoke to the air, Kamoj had gathered that a device in this shuttle sent his words to the port on Lyshriol. "Make no mistake about it," the colonel was saying. "If you want to see her again, you will stop your transmissions."

Vyrl's voice came out of the air. "This is blackmail."

"I don't plan to argue semantics with you, Prince Havyrl. If you want her back, meet our terms."

Don't do it, Kamoj thought.

"I want to talk to her," Vyrl said. "For all I know, you've concocted this entire story."

"And you have your wife?" Shipper asked.

Silence. Then Vyrl said, "How do I know you haven't harmed her? If you really do have her."

"You have the medical reports we sent. She's fine. How would we have those if she wasn't here?"

"How do I know you'll let her go?" Anger edged Vyrl's voice. "You people have already split up my family. What's to stop you from taking her away after you get what you want?"

"You can join her," Shipper said. "We will send you both somewhere safe."

"That's *it?* 'Do what we want and we'll let you become our prisoner?'"

"You're already in our custody," Shipper pointed out. "This would let you stay with your wife."

Vyrl spoke quietly. "The answer is no."

"Good," Kamoj said, though she knew Vyrl couldn't hear. The soldiers guarding her looked uncomfortable. Lines of fatigue creased Shipper's forehead and he had lost weight.

"Disperse your people," the colonel repeated.

"Go to hell," Vyrl said.

"Then we'll take Governor Argali to Earth."

"I realize that." Vyrl took a breath. "Gods, man, can't you see how close your people and mine are to open hostilities? Do this and we may end up in a war."

"We do what we must, Prince Havyrl." Shipper rubbed his eyes. "Sometimes we have to pick the lesser of two evils."

Kamoj understood that situation only all too well.

"Please tell my wife I'm sorry," Vyrl said.

"You don't need to apologize," Kamoj murmured. When Shipper glanced back at her, she gave him an angelic smile.

Shipper turned forward again. "Close comm link."

The shuttle computer sent farewell messages to the Dalvador port. Primary Stillmorn answered rather than Vyrl.

"Link closed," the computer finally said.

The officer in the copilot's seat spoke. "The media will pulverize us for this one."

"Only if they find out." Shipper glanced at him. "Any sign in the broadcasts that Stillmorn's people have sent recordings of this incident?"

"None, sir."

Shipper expelled a breath. "That means Valdoria isn't certain what to do. He may come around."

He better not, Kamoj thought.

"She's been crying," Shipper told Vyrl. "She wants to see you."

"Vyrl!" Kamoj yelled across the cabin. "He's ly—" Her voice cut off when a soldier put his hand over her mouth. She bit his finger, chomping down *hard*.

"*Ah!*" The soldier jerked, his face creasing with pain.

Vyrl was speaking again, and from the strain in his words,

Kamoj doubted he had heard her shout. "For my wife, I have the deepest regret over what has happened." His voice hardened. "As for you, Shipper, I hope you rot in a bilker's bordello."

Then he cut the link.

"She's pregnant," Shipper said.

Kamoj stared at him. *Pregnant?* She opened her mouth to shout again, to tell Vyrl that they had given her no tests to find out such a thing. The soldier with the bandaged hand reached for her, tensing as if he could already feel her teeth. Knowing he would stop her yell before she could get out anything useful, and that Vyrl didn't seem to hear her anyway, Kamoj took pity on the injured soldier and closed her mouth.

"I don't believe you," Vyrl said.

"Have you ever read the book of Genesis?" Shipper asked. "I believe the phrase is 'Be fruitful and multiply.' You seem to be a remarkably pious man."

Kamoj felt certain then that Vyrl would blow up. She could almost hear Stillmorn cautioning him to restraint.

After a long silence, Vyrl said, "Shipper, as soon as we send out recordings of what you've done, taking my wife this way, every person on every planet and habitat in settled space will know. They'll destroy you."

Shipper raked his hand over his hair. Kamoj felt how much he hated the situation. But she also felt his resolve; he believed in the need for these measures. "Then you will never see your wife again, nor your son. Is it really worth that to you?"

Vyrl had no answer.

The colonel sat in silence, with only lights from his controls illuminating in the cabin. Unable to sleep, Kamoj watched him. Finally she said, "He will never give in."

Shipper swiveled his chair around and watched her with

quiet concern. "Doesn't it bother you, that he's willing to leave you?"

She answered without hesitation. "No." In truth, the idea of being in custody without Vyrl, never able to return to her people and province, shook her at a deep level. But she would hate it even more if Vyrl gave into them.

Shipper spoke quietly. "You are a remarkable young woman, Governor Argali."

She hadn't expected that. Since she had no polite reply, she remained silent.

The copilot spoke. "What are your orders, sir?"

"Reopen the link."

Kamoj listened wearily while the copilot and someone in the port down on the planet went through the rigmarole of arranging for Shipper to talk to Vyrl.

Finally Stillmorn came on the comm. In a cold voice she said, "You may speak with His Highness now."

"My honor at your presence, Prince Havyrl," Shipper said.

"Forget the protocol." Vyrl sounded exhausted.

"Have you sent a broadcast of our conversations to the *Ascendant?*" Shipper asked.

"We've a transmission ready to go," Vyrl said. "We were preparing to transmit."

Shipper took a breath. "Don't do it."

"You can't stop us," Vyrl said.

"Even if I send back Governor Argali?"

A long silence followed his words. Kamoj had no doubt Vyrl was arguing with Stillmorn. If Vyrl cut a deal with Shipper, they lost a great advantage in their siege; the news broadcasts would excoriate the Allieds for this maneuver.

Vyrl came back on. "All right, Colonel. Release my wife and we won't send this out."

Shipper leaned back in his chair and closed his eyes. "You have a deal."

* * *

After the shuttle landed, Shipper escorted Kamoj out into a ruddy evening. Sunset flamed along the horizon, limning the blue clouds with pink, gold, and purple, making banners across the sky.

Vyrl was waiting with Stillmorn and the drop-down team, including the Jagernaut that the commandos had overcome when they took Kamoj. Her bodyguard was a welcome sight; she had feared they killed him.

Shipper and his people stood around Kamoj, staring across the tarmac at Vyrl's group. She had no doubt they were all about to embark on another wave of interminable formalities. She was fed up with the whole business. Without waiting for either group to make contact, she took off, walking across the field toward Vyrl.

Kamoj *felt* Shipper's people tense behind her, as if the air tightened. In front of her, across the tarmac, Stillmorn and the Jagernauts reached for the guns on their hips.

Vyrl strode toward Kamoj, his jacket flapping in the wind. They met between the two groups. As they embraced, their relief fountained, their emotions so intertwined that Kamoj wasn't sure what came from her and what from Vyrl. Holding him, she closed her eyes, so glad to be back she wanted to laugh, then to cry.

When they separated, Vyrl took hold of her shoulders and gazed down at her face. "Kamoj, I am truly, truly sorry—"

"No." She put her fingers over his lips, stopping his apology. "I would have been furious if you had given in to them."

He pulled her back into his arms and spoke against her hair. "It's good to see you."

"Me too, for you." The words hardly began to express how she felt. Softly she said, "You gave him your word. You must keep it."

"I will." He raised his head to look over hers.

Turning, she saw Shipper about ten paces away, with his officers. The colonel looked out at the endless camps of people sprawled over the Dalvador Plains. Then he turned to Vyrl and said, simply, "Without a shot."

With that cryptic remark, he and his officers returned to the shuttle. Silhouetted against a fluorescent red sunset, it rose into the sky, higher and higher, until it dwindled to no more than a black dot. Then it vanished altogether.

A new shuttle arrived in the morning. It descended as the suns rose over the horizon. Ablaze with the dawn's crystalline light, it caught the first rays of Valdor as he raised his great gold orb above the horizon.

This shuttle glittered gold and black. *Ascendant* colors.

After the ship landed, an oval opening shimmered in its hull, so different from the solid hatches on AWOE shuttles.

Then General Ashman stepped onto the soil of Lyshriol.

27

Ruby Rebirth

Glory

Kamoj was aware of the camps behind them and the crowd clustered along the landing field, all waiting to find out what this latest development meant. How did an ISC general come here—as a free man or a prisoner?

Vyrl and Kamoj crossed the field together. A Jagernaut was standing in the hatchway of the shuttle. Antonyo Lopezani. A call of welcome came to Kamoj's lips, but she held back, unsure what they faced with Ashman.

The gold trim on the general's cuffs glinted in the light slanting across the field from the suns, which were halfway above the horizon, Valdor partially eclipsing Aldan. Ashman came toward them and they met half way to the shuttle. For a moment the three of them simply looked at one another. Then a truly astonishing event took place. Ashman grinned, and at Vyrl of all people.

"You did it," Ashman said.

Vyrl stared at him. "Are you saying they *left?*"

Ashman's gratification was almost hidden by his granite countenance, but Kamoj saw and felt it despite his rock-solid control. "The AWOE occupation has withdrawn."

Kamoj didn't know whether to shout or cry. Down here, with no way to judge the effect of their efforts, it had never seemed fully real. Vyrl spoke as if he thought this moment was about to crack and crumble away. "Just to make sure—you're saying Earth returned this system to us?"

Ashman nodded, actually looking pleased for once. "That, Prince Havyrl, is exactly what I'm saying."

Vyrl's grin flashed. Then he spun around to the throngs that crowded around the field, including his family. Raising his hands over his head, he shouted "We did it! They're gone! *We won!*"

For a moment the tableau of people remained frozen. Then Denric broke into a run. More of Vyrl's family followed, with the Jagernauts, then the Bards and Memories. Shouts went up within the gathered crowd.

People soon surrounded Vyrl and Kamoj. Voices flowed and sparked, first incredulous, then jubilant. Kamoj couldn't catch it all; people were speaking in both Trillian and Iotic, many at once, excited and flushed. It didn't matter. Their elation poured out in a bracing flood.

A realization came to her. If the occupying forces had left, then so had the danger that those forces might find the buried city. Vyrl's distant ancestors, their names and histories lost in the collapse of their vanished empire, had birthed whatever slept there. Now it was theirs again, neither to own nor serve, but a part of them, intertwined within their existence.

The robots were building a stage in front of the main starport building. Antonyo stood with Kamoj in the shadow of a wall, watching. Kamoj had space sickness again, though it had been a day since Shipper's people took her up in the shuttle.

"Lyshriol has been the top story everywhere," Antonyo was saying. "It spread like a fire."

"How did the citizens of the Allied Worlds take it?" Kamoj asked.

He beamed, his dark eyes alight. "Outrage, mostly, but *not* against us. The Allied Worlds have always seen themselves as the kinder aspect of humanity. *Everyone* sees them that way, including we and the Traders. They *loathed* having their forces cast in the role of villains."

She smiled. "And your people? How did they respond?"

His expression warmed. "They are your people, also."

Kamoj let that soak in. Of course. She was Skolian. She had trouble thinking of herself that way. "Our people."

"The outcry was incredible." Antonyo motioned at the sky. "The debate exploded. Ethical issues, freedom, war, peace, cultural sovereignty—it's all come up, not just for Lyshriol, but for all of us. We and the Traders have fought for centuries, but nothing as extensive, or destructive, as the Radiance War. What happened here was a miracle. To see these gentle people embark on a mission of peace, one that seemed so hopeless, and then *succeed*—" He took a breath. "It's like new air blowing across the world."

Kamoj gazed out at the tent-nation. Distant sounds of celebration drifted to her. She wished they had a tangible way to show these people what their efforts had achieved, more than just the word of ISC that they had accomplished their goal.

Denric was walking toward them, his yellow curls tossing

in the breeze. She felt more comfortable with him than with Vyrl's other kin, in part because he wasn't big, at least not compared to the others. He also had a brightness Kamoj liked. She could see why he would make a good teacher; children would respond to his tender nature and the glow of his personality. Was it happiness he exuded? Joy in life? All she knew was that she liked to be around him.

It impressed her that a man with such privilege, wealth, status, high connections, and academic credentials would devote his life to disadvantaged children. A widower of several years, Denric apparently lived alone in a modest home on the minimal salary he earned as a teacher. He had taken the position on Sandstorm, a world where furious dust storms whipped across the deserts in its equatorial regions, the only part of the planet fit for human settlement.

Denric nodded to her as he joined them. "Vyrl will speak soon." He indicated the ground near the stage, where the Valdorias were deep in conversation with Ashman and another ISC officer.

"Who is the woman with General Ashman?" Kamoj asked.

"A media tech. They're setting things up so everyone can hear the speeches." Denric considered her. "Are you sure you won't stand with Vyrl when he speaks?"

Kamoj felt his puzzlement. They had all noticed Vyrl's refusal to touch alcohol and his silence about what had happened after he left Lyshriol. They were empaths. They knew something was wrong, even though Vyrl and Kamoj veiled their minds.

She chose an answer that was true, but also guarded their privacy. "We still don't know what Jax Ironbridge is going to do. I would feel awkward appearing in public."

Denric watched her with an empathic compassion that she suspected made him a gifted teacher. She averted her gaze from his kindness, gazing into the encampment. A few tents away, a girl was lining a pit with stones, probably for a cooking fire. "I don't want the ugliness of what happened with Jax to taint Vyrl now," Kamoj said.

Denric spoke gently. "Are you sure that's what holds you back, Kamoj? Please don't let it taint *your* heart."

Is that what I'm doing? She ached inside when she thought of Jax.

Kamoj looked to where Vyrl stood with his siblings. The picture they made could have been the scrolled images on a codex drawn for art instead of words: Aniece and Lord Rillia in purple velvet, as befitted their titles; Shannon in his green tunic and leggings, an exotic Dale Archer; Chaniece graceful and statuesque, her hair swept up on her head in a classical roll, with golden tendrils framing her face; her sons at her side, the towering Delson resting his hand on the shoulder of ten-year-old Jaqui, who kept watch on his older brother, as if to protect him from the world. Ashman had withdrawn into the shadow of a building with his bodyguards—Ashman, unseen and unheard, the unrelenting power that had made this possible, but only at great price, a shadow king moving pieces on a game board.

Denric raised his hand in a gesture of invitation to Kamoj. "Come stand with us."

She took a breath. *Good-bye, Jax.*

Then she went with Denric to join her new family.

The media tech sent a flock of voice globes out over the camps. The spheres glimmered and swooped, which enticed children to chase them. Whenever the children made a capture, the snared globe would whir with protest until they let it go. Then it spun off, its primitive EI brain obviously trying to find a balance between staying high enough to escape the indignity of becoming a toy but low enough so people could hear its transmissions.

Vyrl and Kamoj stood on the stage with a globe whirring above their heads. His siblings made a semicircle around them, with the ever-present Jagernauts serving as their guards.

And Vyrl spoke.

The globe picked up his words and sent them to the globes humming over the camps, giving his speech to the entire tent-nation, his voice a work of art in his native language. Although Kamoj didn't understand the words, she knew he was telling his people how they had overcome the might of an interstellar civilization. His listeners cheered and whistled their approval. Still, Kamoj wished they had more tangible evidence to offer that their world was once more their own.

Then she knew.

Closing her eyes, she let the sounds of Vyrl's speech roll over her. The minds of his listeners below merged into a luminous wash of thought. She drew on that radiance, focusing it like a lens.

Kamoj opened her eyes. She was so tuned to Vyrl now that she could almost understand him, not because she had learned more Trillian in the past few seconds, but because their minds touched at a subconscious level.

Then she reached—and opened herself to the presence beneath the Stained Glass Forest.

Awake!

It came as a *burgeoning,* like tender shoots unfolding in the warmth of a Balumil spring, after their seeds had lain dormant for years, protected from the storms and ices of winter.

Vyrl finished his speech. Then he simply stood, staring out at the sea of people. Kamoj realized he was listening, not with his ears but with his mind. He gazed toward the Stained Glass Forest, which was visible only as a sparkle in the distant foothills of the Backbone Mountains.

The presence continued to unfold, its awakening felt rather than heard in their thoughts. Like new shoots of grain lifting their heads, swaying in the wind, rippling, growing, full with life—so the sleeper awoke.

Come to us, Kamoj thought.

The people in the tent-nation shifted and rustled, waiting for Vyrl to continue. Children ran, cooks tended fires, and women polished stalks of bubble-glass. Wind gusted, stronger this time. Vyrl took Kamoj's hand as they looked out over the human ocean that lapped up against the stage and spread as far as they could see. The wind rose again, tossing Kamoj's hair around her body.

When the rumbling began, Kamoj thought she must be hearing a machine within the port, its engine hushed by the walls. Then she realized it was distance rather than walls that muted the thunder. She looked around, first at the sky, then back at the landing field, to see if another craft had appeared. But no, the skies were clear and only General Ashman's shuttle sat on the field.

The rumbling deepened, coming from . . . where? The mountains? Under the plains? People in the camps had stopped their chores and were also turning as they tried to locate the source of the sound. Many waved at the spheres, laughing with delight at the spinning carriers of voices and now apparently rumbles as well. At first Kamoj also thought the orbs produced the sound. Then her resonance with Vyrl vibrated, like a plucked string, and she felt the rumbling on a deeper level—

A level otherwise known only to Vyrl and his Rhon siblings.

The wind sang across the plains. It tore off a youth's cap and sent it sailing into a livestock pen; it flapped pennants on the larger tents and the cloths hanging in their entrances; it bedeviled the voice globes, which spun ever faster in the rushing currents, reflecting sunlight with sparks of color.

The rumbling swelled, coming from the distant Stained Glass Forest, maybe even the mountains, but here too, under them, throughout the plains. A small girl cried out and ran to her mother. Shouts came from the camps as the wind knocked over tent supports, shook the fledgling crops, and whipped water in the irrigation canals. People looked toward the stage as if for an explanation, unease rippling into their joy. Kamoj caught their streamers of thought; they feared an earthquake.

"It's all right," Vyrl said. The globes sent his words to everyone, carried above the wind, a swirl of reassurance that came from thousands of spinning messengers. "Everything is fine."

Kamoj said, "See your heritage, beautiful Lyshrioli." The globe above them changed hue, matching its colors to her higher voice, turning almost transparent, like a diamond, as it translated her words and sent them into the windy sunshine.

The air began to glisten. The effect resembled the shimmer curtains Vyrl's people used to protect themselves on Balumil, but these rippled through the air in waves of light, throwing sparks of color like the horns of a lyrine. They spread across the land and air, filling the world with radiance.

Yet almost no one behaved as if they saw the luminance. A few people gazed around, their faces puzzled. A small child laughed, waving her hands through a ripple of color. But most looked as if they were only listening to the sounds they assumed came from the orbs. Vyrl and his Rhon siblings had a far different reaction, seeing what no one else witnessed—except Kamoj. Waves of emotion rolled out from them: wonder, apprehension, awe.

Then the Dalvador Plains began to sing.

It swelled from the ground, deep and beautiful, resonating with a powerful vibrato like the voices of Lyshrioli men, sparkling with melodic bells like the Lyshrioli women. The resplendent sound twined in and around the gales that blew across the plains, until it was impossible to tell where the singing left off and the wind began. It made Kamoj think of spring in Argali, when the first vine-roses opened their buds in Jul's cool blue light.

The ground began to ripple. Circles undulated across the plains like the waves created when a pebble dropped into a lake, spreading in rings, except here it was as if a thousand hands dropped a thousand pebbles into the sea of the Dalvador Plains.

Cries of *earthquake!* came from the camps as the moving ground shook tents, set livestock stamping, knocked over urns, and splashed water out of cisterns. Linked so closely with Vyrl now, Kamoj understood the Trillian word. She felt a tremor of doubt. Had she made a mistake in calling forth the ancient city?

Vyrl turned to her, his mind becoming even more tuned to hers, through the awakening presence. "It's all right." Light glazed his eyes with the colors of the Stained Glass Forest. "It's a miracle."

Then the ground opened.

It happened in thousands of places, all the way to the Backbone Mountains, and to the east, west, and south, in spaces cleared by the traveling ripples, so neither person nor animal fell. The ground parted in fissures and holes, yet the tent-nation behaved as if the effect was invisible. A few people backed away, looking confused or uncertain, rubbing their eyes, shaking their heads. No one else seemed to see anything at all.

Stained-glass towers arose from the ground, otherworldly phantasms more air and light than matter. They glowed with color and released clouds of iridescent bubbles. In thousands of places across the Dalvador Plains, they reached up, delicate, airy, and luminous. Sunlight streamed through them and emerged in sprays of rainbow color. All across the land, a city of towers formed, so ethereal it might float away on the wind. The sparkling air flashed while the earth poured forth its haunting song. It filled Kamoj with both joy and sorrow, glorious beyond words.

It seemed only moments before the towers began to dim, blurring into ripples in the air. The openings in the plains faded as well, until she realized the ground had never split. It was illusion. The wind calmed and the singing became distant, withdrawing to the mountains. Soon the spirit towers and glistening light were no more than echoes, like the reflection of an aurora. The afterimage faded, leaving behind only luminous morning sunlight.

Then the plains were as they had been, with only toppled tents and upturned urns to give reality to what they had witnessed. The ghost city may have been only light, but the music, wind, and rippling ground had all been real.

Taking her hand, Vyrl spoke for her only. "Could that be where we came from?" His eyes had a distant, sunrise quality. "Was that the image of a vanished city built by our ancestors five thousand years ago?"

Kamoj knew that of all the thousands of people here, only Vyrl and his Rhon siblings had seen the images of light or realized the music didn't come from the spheres. She spoke softly. "The city under the Stained Glass Forest gave that to your family as a gift. For bringing back the Ruby Dynasty."

Vyrl pulled her into his arms, unheeding of the tent-nation watching them. "You gave me the gift, Kamoj."

28

Resolution

Complete State

General Ashman placed the gold-striped ribbon around Kamoj's neck. A medallion hung on its end, a platinum triangle inscribed with a ruby circle. Centered within the circle and triangle, the gold silhouette of an exploding sun burst past their boundaries.

"With the authority vested in me by Imperial Space Command," Ashman said, "I present to you, Kamoj Quanta Argali, the Imperial Medal."

They stood in front of the fireplace in the Hearth Room, Vyrl and his family grouped to one side. Ranks of Jagernauts and ISC officers filled the room, including Stillmorn and her team, and Antonyo, whom Kamoj had requested be allowed to attend the ceremony. They applauded after Ashman finished.

Kamoj spoke to Ashman in a low voice that only he could hear. "I don't deserve this."

He answered quietly. "Heroism comes in many forms. Courage, valor, and integrity don't have to announce themselves with flash or trumpets. Yours is of that quiet kind, and you have honored us with it."

Kamoj held the medallion, her knuckles pressed against her heart, unable to express how much his words meant to her. She glanced at Vyrl, who had a similar medallion around his neck, and he smiled, his gaze filled with affection.

They said good-bye to Vyrl's family in the courtyard. He hugged his children, grandchildren, and all the greats, and his sisters and brothers, tears running down his face. Several members of the family were still in custody on Earth: Vyrl's mother, Roca, the Pharaoh Presumptive; his brother Del-Kurj, the twin of Chaniece; Vyrl's youngest brother, Kelric, the Imperator; Kelric's wife; and Ami and Kurjson, the widow and young son of the former Imperator. The withdrawal of the AWOE forces from Lyshriol had been as far as ISC had been able to push the matter with Earth.

But the rest of Vyrl's kin came today. At first they were all talking at once, the yard filled with lyrical, chiming voices. The commotion slowly faded, as each waited turn to bid him farewell. Kamoj stood back, giving them room, smiling if they came to her, taking their hands or embracing them if they offered, but not pushing herself into their family sphere. She felt their conflicted emotions; although many of them liked her, they resented her taking Vyrl away from Lyshriol.

As empaths with shared kinship, their emotions filled the courtyard. The intensity was too much to endure for long. They soon left the house and walked through Dalvador, the children running and playing, the adults more subdued. As always, the Jagernauts shadowed them. At the edge of town, they said their final farewells.

Vyrl, Kamoj, Aniece, and Lord Rillia walked by themselves across the trampled ground to the starport. It had been five days since the occupying forces had withdrawn. Camps were still scattered across the plains, but many of the people had returned home.

As far as the public knew, and even most of ISC, the spheres had broadcast the glorious music everyone heard. ISC put out the story that their media specialist produced the music. A few people claimed to have seen shimmering ghosts of a great city, but they had little credence offworld. The Lyshrioli believed Vyrl had commanded the ground to move in an expression of triumph. ISC called the "earthquake" a coincidence and let the tabloid holovids claim Ashman's people caused it as a display of power.

Only the Ruby Dynasty, General Ashman, and a few other officers knew the truth, that the music and earthquake had come from the awakening city. No one but the Rhon and Kamoj had witnessed the full extent of the spectacular illusions, and Kamoj suspected that even her vision paled next to what Vyrl and his siblings had seen.

Now Aniece walked with Kamoj across the plain. Small in size, round and curved, with her cascade of dark hair, youthful face, and fluttering blue dress, she could have been Kamoj's sister by blood rather than marriage. She spoke in her musical voice. "I'm glad we had the chance to meet."

"I too," Kamoj said.

Aniece looked to where her husband walked with her brother up ahead. Vyrl was a little taller than Rillia, broader in the shoulders, with tawny curls rather than silver hair. But both men had a similar quality in their posture, an assurance that came with self-confidence.

"You make him happy," Aniece said. "I am glad. He has been so lonely since—" She paused. "These many years."

"Since his wife died?"

"He told you?"

Kamoj nodded. "He must have loved her greatly."

"Ai. He did." Mischief flashed on Aniece's face. "He was always in love, that one. What did he want, ever since he was a boy? A girl in his arms, a farm bursting with life, and many children." Her voice turned thoughtful. "It may be hereditary. Before my mother came here, the Lyshrioli had a high infant mortality. No medical system, inbred populations, and inconsistent prenatal care—it all made their lives a struggle. Only those who bore many children saw their lines continue."

Kamoj understood all too well. "It sounds like Argali."

"Vyrl says this, too." Aniece indicated the people working on the irrigation canals and reseeding the plains. "After my mother married my father, Lyshriol became a world with high status. It doesn't look much different on the outside. The advances are the kind you can't see: medical care, sanitary improvements, education, those sort."

Hope glimmered in Kamoj's heart. Lyshriol had given her a more positive view of the Skolians. "Perhaps Vyrl and I can do the same for my people. I so wish to see Argali prosper, but without losing what makes it unique."

"Talk to Vyrl," Aniece said. "He will want to help."

"Do babies die so much here now?"

"Rarely. We've clinics in the villages that offer the best care Skolian medicine can provide."

Kamoj smiled. "But the urge to have large families remains."

Aniece laughed, her voice like the bubbling of a musical creek. When Vyrl and Rillia glanced back, Aniece waved her hand at them. "Go back to your man talk," she admonished. Vyrl grinned and Rillia raised his eyebrows. But they turned around again.

Aniece spoke to Kamoj in a confidential tone. "My brother, he has always had the urge toward large families."

Kamoj blushed, thinking about how diligently she and Vyrl were working toward that goal. The urge wasn't only his.

"You must bring him back to visit us often," Aniece said.

"I will." Kamoj hesitated. "I hope Shannon will be all right with the city." None of them knew yet what secrets that enigmatic presence hid beneath the Stained Glass Forest, or how it had called with such power to the Ruby Dynasty while hiding its wondrous display from everyone else. It had sent Vyrl's family a message unlike any other ever known in recorded history. *How?* ISC hadn't even believed such a mental link was possible, except perhaps among Rhon psions. But this was a *city.* It could offer Vyrl's people great wonders, answers to the mysteries of their origins, perhaps even entry into other universes—if only they could solve its riddles.

Without Kamoj as a conduit, most of Vyrl's family still couldn't reach the presence even after it awoke. But Shannon, the fey, mystical son, could hear its call now—and unlike Kamoj, he could link to the city with the full power of a Rhon mind. It made him invaluable to ISC, perhaps to all human civilization. To solve the city's mysteries would probably take years, decades, maybe even longer. But in Shannon, they had a key now to unlock those secrets.

"So strange," Aniece murmured, "that it took a visitor from another world to summon what had always lain beneath our lands, unknown to us." She regarded Kamoj. "It pleases me, I fear, for selfish reasons."

Kamoj tilted her head. "Why do you say that?"

"This will bring Shannon back to us. He has been so distant, far away in the Dales. After Althor's death—" She sighed. "He and our brother Althor were close. They were as different as two people can be, but they loved each other. When Althor died, Shannon withdrew even more. But now he will live here in Dalvador again, to work with ISC on the city." Pensive now, she looked toward the Blue Mountain Dales. "I've so missed Shannon. He is closest to my age of all our siblings."

Kamoj felt again the depth of affection among the family of empaths. It flowed almost below conscious thought. "I'm glad it worked out."

"Kamoj—" Aniece drew her to a stop. "Be gentle with Vyrl's dreams."

"Always." Kamoj wondered what she meant.

"If he surprises you with his artistic gifts . . ."

Ah. Now Kamoj understood. "Men dance all the time among my people. No one finds it strange at all."

Aniece looked startled, obviously unprepared for such an open, accepting acknowledgement of Vyrl's forbidden art. She took Kamoj's hands. "May you both have the best in life."

"And you also." Kamoj swallowed, still hardly able to believe the miracle, that she had this new family.

Sometime, somewhere, Kamoj had stopped fearing space. The view of that jeweled vastness outside the *Ascendant* filled her with wonder now, rather than bewilderment.

Her apprehension today, as she entered the Observation Bay, had no connection to the view. Vyrl had respected her wishes and let her go alone, though he had first tried to change her mind. Antonyo waited outside while she climbed down the ladder. She knew a security team was monitoring the bay, but she wanted to face this on her own, by herself, without help.

The man she had come to meet stood across the bay on

the transparent ledge, with his back to her. Tall and well-formed, with broad shoulders and narrow hips, he made a striking figure against the panorama of stars. He wore black diskmail, a violet shirt, black trousers, and black knee boots with silver fur. His hands rested on the clear railing as he stared out at the panorama, its fire and jeweled luminance, the birth of stars against the forever black of space.

Kamoj walked along the pathway that crossed the bay. She knew the moment Jax realized he was no longer alone. His shoulders tensed, but he continued to gaze at space. Even when she stepped up on the ledge next to him, he didn't turn.

So they stood.

After awhile he spoke in a subdued voice. "How could I ever compete with this?" He finally looked at her, his eyes dark. "It is no wonder you prefer Lionstar."

"It has nothing to do with this."

"Of course not." Jax waved his hand at the view. "To have this at his beckoning—" He shook his head. "Try as I did, I never imagined the full extent of it. I am not surprised that he seduced you with this. But I am disappointed. I had thought you put more value into your promises." His words grated. "I had thought better of you, Kamoj."

I won't let you twist my emotions with guilt anymore. She spoke in a low voice. "What you did was wrong. Trying to blame me won't change that." Her anger surged, threatening to overwhelm the calm exterior she wanted to present. "You had no right force me, to starve, to hurt—to—" She was losing her fight to keep her voice steady. "You had no right."

He met her gaze. "I had every right. You made me do it."

"No one makes you to treat the person you're supposed to love as if you hate them." A tear ran down her face. She clenched her fists, angry at herself for revealing how much he had hurt her. "If you had tried kindness instead of cruelty, I would have stayed with you no matter what Vyrl offered."

As had happened so often before, Jax switched, going from harsh to tender in a heartbeat. "Kamoj, don't cry. I'm sorry I hurt you." He brushed the back of his hand along her cheek. "I could never have used that knife."

"Don't." She pushed his hand away.

"I couldn't bear losing you, our dreams, our hopes—all gone to conquerors who disrupted our lives as if they were swatting aside a firepuff fly." He took a deep breath. "Do you think I love you less because I made desperate choices? If you do, you're wrong. I've never felt this way about another person."

She tried to shield her heart against her memories of the lifetime they had known each other. "It's too late. The damage is done."

"I still love you. Come back to me."

"Jax, don't," she whispered.

"I won't hurt you again."

"Until the next time you lose your temper? I could never go back to that."

"Kamoj—"

"No!" Then she said, *"No."*

His voice hardened. "Will you feel the same when your so-called hero goes on trial? When you must tell your most private moments to strangers?" His gaze bored into her. "Have you ever seen a hero scorned? It isn't pretty. Public approval one day, scathing contempt the next. Tarnish spreads fast." He waved his hand as if to dismiss the *Ascendant.* "General Ashman thought bringing me here to witness what happened on Lyshriol would dissuade me from pursuing legal action."

Kamoj swallowed. "And it hasn't?"

"No. But you can stop it."

"I'm not coming back to you." She steeled herself against the surging, complicated emotions he stirred in her. "If that means I have to testify to strangers, I will do it."

A muscle in his cheek twitched. "Think of it. Billions listening with avid interest to your most humiliating secrets. What happened in your bed. With whom. For how long. In excruciating detail. Is that what you want?"

She stared at him. "Is it what *you* want? If you drag this out, you will go down, too."

"I've a lot less to lose than your Ruby prince."

"Is your pride and self-respect worth so little to you?"

"You won't be able to go through with it," he said tightly. "You're not strong enough."

"I am."

His fists clenched. "I know you better than that."

"What are you going to do? Hit me?"

He stared down at his hands as if he were just seeing them. Then he relaxed his fists. "Of course I'm not going to hit you."

"Let it go, Jax. Please. If not for me, then for yourself." She willed him to relent. "General Ashman said the Skolians want to deal with you as a leader of our people. This is your chance to achieve *your* dreams. You would travel offworld, represent Balumil in the Imperial Assembly, learn so much. Do you think that will happen if you drag this into the courtroom? Will you give all that up for revenge against Vyrl?"

For a long time he stared at her. Then he looked out at the stars. In a distant voice he said, "An astonishingly beautiful view."

She understood what he left unspoken. "It could be yours."

"Ah, Kamoj, you know me too well."

She waited in silence, afraid to say the wrong thing. Ashman had provided Jax with an out, a way to back off from this public trial without losing face. Jax wouldn't let up in his claims against her on Balumil, particularly that she must return his dowry as he specified. But that would stay in the Northern Lands, and having Vyrl at her side would help. What mattered now was that Jax not take this offworld, turning it from a discreet matter into an interstellar catastrophe.

Finally he said, "I will consider what you have said."

This far from other psions, her ability to sense moods faded some—but even so, she still caught his response. He wanted her, not only to spite Vyrl or because it gave him Argali. He also wanted her for herself. She wasn't sure he even knew how to define love, but what he felt was real. She didn't know where to put this knowledge of him, that he could love her and yet cause such pain.

Jax lifted his hand to touch his hair—and she flinched. He stopped, then lowered his arm. Incredibly, tears showed in his eyes. "I do hope you have happiness. Who knows? Maybe someday I will see you in the Imperial Assembly." Quietly he added, "But not, I think, in an Imperial courtroom."

Relief flooded her, so intense it almost hurt. She said, simply, "Thank you," and wondered if any two words could encompass the depth of what she felt.

He spoke softly. "Farewell, beautiful rose."

A tear ran down her cheek, for all the pain. "Farewell, Jax."

Epilogue

The Rose Pool

Asymptotic State

Kamoj awoke into darkness. She lay in bed, listening to sounds of the Argali night that drifted through the window: the cooing of a green-tailed quetzal, distant wind in the trees, a trilling warble-angel. She was home.

Water splashed in the bathing room. Curious, she slipped out of bed and padded into the chamber. Vyrl was swimming laps in the pool. Moonlight poured through the stained-glass window across the chamber, reminding her of Lyshriol, filling the room with gem colors. The radiance reflected off the water and made patterns on the tiled walls.

Kamoj was struck again by his athletic grace. She recalled his question so long ago, that morning after he had gone riding in the village: *it is accepted for men to dance here?* Such a simple matter, one so small compared to what he had given up, but at least it was a gift she could offer in return for his leaving his home to live on Balumil.

She imagined him at the harvest festivals, swinging her around in the central square of the village, everyone whirling beneath the aurora. No more cowl and cloak, no more metal mask. Perhaps he would always have to sheath his body in a shimmer, but once her people knew the good man beneath it all, they would accept his differences.

Kamoj placed her hand on her abdomen. Dazza had given them the news yesterday, the reason why Kamoj had space sickness now, even when she wasn't in space. Shipper had been right, after all. The future held such promise for she and Vyrl—and the child within her. The Argali heir. Vyrl's child.

As Kamoj knelt by the pool, Vyrl swam over to her.

"We have skylions in the mountains," she told him. With mischief, she added, "I've heard it said they don't like getting wet," and gave him a hearty splash.

He caught her hand. "Ah, but nothing is so beautiful as a rose covered with dew." Then he yanked her into the pool.

She thrashed to the surface, spluttering. "Hai!"

He grinned. "I get clumsy sometimes."

"Clumsy, hah!" She splashed him again, then took off like an ottermock, arrowing under his body as she blew bubbles at him.

They played in the pool for a while, and held each other as they drifted around the fountain, passing in and out of the moonlight. When they nudged against the stairs, they settled on a step, their bodies submerged in the water.

So they sat in each other's healing embrace.

Author's Note: Quantum Dreams

One pleasure in writing science fiction is extrapolating ideas from science and mathematics into the realm of "What if?" We can also turn those ideas into allegories. *The Quantum Rose* plays with quantum scattering theory, an elegant mathematical formalism that is its own art form.

In a typical scattering process, a beam of particles hits a target and scatters off in every direction. To start with a simplified model, imagine that two billiard balls collide and bounce away. Such a process is *elastic scattering*. Now suppose that when the balls collide, they squash, stick together, orbit each other for a while, or otherwise undergo some change. Eventually the balls will separate, but when they do, they are no longer the same as before the collision. This is *inelastic scattering*.

Similarly, in quantum scattering, particles in the beam collide with those in the target. If two particles join to form a single bigger particle, they are in a *bound state*. For example, when an electron and a proton socialize, they make a hydrogen atom, which consists of the electron bound to the proton. A bound system can have only certain energies—anything between those is forbidden. In our macroscopic world it would be roughly equivalent to saying your car could go at ten, twenty, or thirty miles an hour, but never at, say, twenty-two. In other words, energy is *quantized*. We don't notice because the differences in the allowed energies are too tiny to detect in our everyday lives.

Suppose particles 1 and 2 form a bound state. We'll call it (1,2). Then particle 3 collides with them. If the energy of 3 is low, it will simply bounce off (1,2) without causing any changes. However, if particle 3 has enough energy, it might excite (1,2) into a higher bound state and lose some of its own energy. When that happens, we say a new *channel* has opened.

Now imagine that we zap a sample of (1,2) particles with a beam of 3 particles. Some 3 particles have enough energy to excite a (1,2) and some don't, so both types of collision take place. Often the elastic and inelastic channels interact, changing how the 3 particles influence the (1,2) particles. When such processes can affect each other, they are *coupled*.

Suppose 1 and 3 can also form a bound state, (1,3). If 3 has enough energy, it could barrel in, nab particle 1, and take off again, leaving 2 as a free particle cruising the continuum. This is a *rearrangement channel*. A (2,3) channel might also exist. If 3 has even *more* energy, then when it whams into the (1,2) pair, it may break them apart, making 1, 2, and 3 all fly off by themselves.

Chapter subtitles:

1. First Scattering Channel
2. Incoming Wave
3. Second Scattering Channel
4. Scattering Kernel
5. Vibrational Coupling
6. Metastable State (1,2)
7. Perturbations

In *The Quantum Rose,* Kamoj, Vyrl, and Jax play the parts of particles 1, 2, and 3 respectively. The Chapter 1 subtitle, *First Scattering Channel,* refers to Kamoj and Jax together, with Vyrl in the role of a free particle. Soon, however, Vyrl and Kamoj form a pair (a new channel) and Jax is on his own (free particle). A free particle doesn't have quantized energy levels, so it can take on any energy, similar to how a normal car can have any speed. Because such a particle has a continuous range of allowed energies, we say it is in a *continuum*.

The *kernel* is a mathematical quantity used to figure out how a colliding system will behave given certain information, such as how the particles act when they aren't bumping into one another. The character Dazza Pacal plays the role of a "kernel" for interactions among Kamoj, Vyrl, and Jax.

Perturbation theory can offer insight into how a complicated system will behave based on what we know about simpler systems. We split the problem into two parts: a known simple system and the perturbations that disturb it. Such a process only approximates the true behavior, so it works best if the perturbations are small compared to the overall interactions. The Ironbridge archers in Chapter 7 have a significant effect on Vyrl and Kamoj, but it isn't enough to tear apart the two lovers. They perturb rather than rearrange.

8. Phase Shift
9. Resonance
10. Rearrangement
11. Metastable State (1,3)
12. Three-Particle State

Quantum theory uses *wavefunctions* to describe matter. Why? On a microscopic scale, particles often behave like waves: they oscillate, have wavelengths, interfere and diffract, aren't solid, and don't have discontinuous edges. We see matter as solid because the wavelengths are too tiny to detect. So are particles *really* waves? Quantum theory is a model rather than Absolute Truth. However, it is a remarkably successful model, which means it probably gives a reasonable picture.

The incoming particles come into the target as a collimated beam. After they scatter, they zip off in all directions. In quantum terms, we say a *plane wave* is incident on the target, and it scatters into outgoing *spherical waves*. Imagine swells in an ocean or lake. Plane waves are like swells rolling in straight lines. Spherical waves are more like the ripples you get if you drop a rock into a still pond, except in three dimensions rather than two.

Far from the target, the incoming and outgoing waves have an important difference: a shift in phase. The *phase* is where the peaks of a wave are located relative to those of other waves. If we drop two rocks into a pond, one after the other, the ripples from the second lag behind those from the first. So the ripples from the second rock are shifted in phase relative to those of the first. Similarly, after waves scatter off a target, their phase is shifted relative to the incoming wave. If we determine the shifts in the various scattered waves (also known as *partial waves*), it reveals a great deal about the scattering process. In Chapter 8, Vyrl undergoes a major "phase shift" due to his interaction with Kamoj: he finally talks about what happened in the coffin and so begins to heal.

A rearrangement happens when Jax takes Kamoj. They then form a "bound state." But Vyrl is still very much involved. Both times that Kamoj, Vyrl, and Jax come together in an Inquiry, they play the role of a (1,2,3) state—a decidedly unstable one!

The 3 particle normally has too much energy to stick with (1,2). To form a (1,2,3) particle, it must give up some of that energy to another particle, say 2, enough so 3 stays put, but not so much that 2 flies off. The 3 + (1,2) state has the same energy as (1,2,3). However, the (1,2,3) state is almost bound. Since both states exist simultaneously, we say (1,2,3) is a *metastable* state within the 3 + (1,2) continuum. Similarly, particle 2 might join (1,3) to form the (1,2,3) state, which means (1,2,3) is also metastable in the continuum of 2 + (1,3).

If the binding of 3 to 1 has no effect on how 2 binds to 1, then (1,2,3) can last forever; it has an *infinite lifetime*. However, in scattering processes 2 and 3 can interact, so 2 may give 3 back its energy and send it away (or vice versa). In such cases, (1,2,3) is metastable and has a *finite lifetime*. The (Kamoj, Vyrl, Jax) state isn't likely to last long, given the strong interactions between Vyrl and Jax.

States (1,2), (1,3), and (2,3) can also be metastable, or else disturbances (perturbations) in their environment might break them apart if their binding is weak. A *resonance* is the big increase in the probability that free particles will stay together when their energy is near that of a metastable state. Sharp resonances correspond to metastable states with long lifetimes. Kamoj has separate resonances with both Vyrl and Jax; the (1,2) and (1,3) states each have different lifetimes. Their "scattering processes" are all coupled; the interaction between Vyrl and Jax destabilizes any pairing that Kamoj makes with either of them in the presence of other.

13. Capture Amplitude
14. Steepest Descent
15. Three Particle Scattering
16. Predissociation
17. Transition (B $\Rightarrow$ A)

A *capture amplitude* gives the probability that, in a three-body interaction, one particle will capture another in a metastable state. The larger the amplitude's magnitude, the greater the capture probability. In Chapter 13, and indeed throughout much of the book, the amplitude serves as a metaphor for Jax's attitude about his pairing with Kamoj.

Steepest descent is a method used to determine the long-range form of scattered wavefunctions at distances far from the target. The technique relies on *saddle-point integration*. Suppose we put a marble in the center of the saddle. The marble is in an unstable equilibrium on top of the "hill" formed by the saddle; it sits happily in place until we nudge it to either side, at which time it rolls off its perch. However, if we nudge it forward or backward, it goes *up* the saddle, either toward the horn or in the opposite direction. So it is in a valley where it wants to stay. In other words, the marble is simultaneously at the top of a hill and the bottom of a valley. The past of steepest descent from that curve gives the best solution to the problem.

During the final Inquiry in *The Quantum Rose,* Kamoj is on a saddle-point of sorts. What is her path of steepest descent from that point? The choices she makes at the Inquiry will determine whether, in the long run, she ends up with Vyrl or Jax.

Predissociation happens when a metastable state leaks into its embedded continuum, letting the particles go free (it's called predissociation in molecular physics, the *Auger effect* in atomic physics, and *internal conversion* in nuclear/atomic physics.) The (Kamoj, Vyrl, Jax) state corresponds to a resonance with a short lifetime; after the Inquiry, the state predissociates into (Kamoj, Vyrl) + Jax. Nor does it stop there: Vyrl soon "predissociates" from Kamoj, leaving her at a lower energy while he goes off into space. So for a time all three "particles" are free. Not that any of them are happy about it; apparently quantum mechanics has its own lonely hearts club!

We use scattering wavefunctions to calculate *transition elements,* which give the probability that particles will make a transition from one state to another. In Chapter 18, Kamoj undergoes a major transition—she leaves Balumil. To figure out the likelihood of a successful transition, we need the wave function behavior for our allegorical particles.

How do we figure out a wavefunction? Despite all the hype surrounding quantum theory, it actually consists of little more than solving Schrödinger's equation (over and over and over . . .). If we use Y for the wavefunction, then Schrödinger's equation is: $HY = EY$, where E is the energy of the particles and $\mathbf{H}$ is the *hamiltonian*. $\mathbf{H}$ determines the behavior of the wavefunction.

Although $\mathbf{H}$ is a complicated mathematical expression, it has a simple interpretation: the energy E. It is the sum of the kinetic energy (the system's energy of motion) and the potential energy that describes all interactions among and within the particles. The potential energy (or just "potential") can vary dramatically from system to system. In *The Quantum Rose,* the potential serves as a metaphor for the psychological processes that motivate Kamoj, Vyrl, and Jax.

For an actual experiment, we don't know what happens during the scattering process until we collect the scattered particles in a detector and take a look at them. We need to measure the amounts of the various products that scatter from the target. The trip Kamoj and Vyrl take on the *Ascendant* corresponds to products traveling outward in spherical waves, and their visit to Lyshriol corresponds to the detection and measurement of their final state. In a sense, Kamoj and Vyrl take the measure of their experiences, trying to understand and come to terms with what happened on Balumil.

The *propagator,* or *Green's function,* acts as a kernel in many scattering equations. It propagates a wavefunction from start to finish. When we measure the products of that process, those products also interact with whatever measures them, which means new potentials are now affecting their behavior, requiring new kernels to describe their wavefunctions. In other words, the scattering process couples to the measurement process, and making measurements alters the state of the products. However, it is often a good approximation to describe the scattering and measurement as separate. Also, in a careful experiment, the measurements should leave the products intact.

Kamoj and Vyrl go to Lyshriol as a "final product": (1,2) + 3, where Jax (the 3 particle) has gone off in a different direction. Although the events on Balumil affect how Kamoj and Vyrl behave on Lyshriol, those experiences are independent enough to be "approximated" as separate processes. The migration becomes the measurement, though the "measuring" here concerns the resolution of Vyrl and Kamoj's psychological state. As Vyrl and Kamoj "propagate" the migration from start to finish, they are also resolving for themselves how their experiences on Balumil changed them.

Particles eventually reach an *asymptotic,* or final, state. Technically, they don't attain it until they are an infinite distance from the target. However, they usually become essentially asymptotic soon after they leave the scattering center. So it is with Kamoj and Vyrl. They may never be completely free of Jax's influence or the trauma of Vyrl's experiences, but they have a good chance of healing.

The story has other scattering metaphors I'll leave for the reader to discover. A few hints: Volterra integrals, classical scattering, projection operators, and spherical harmonics. The Glories, Airy rainbows, sun dragons, and other details in the Spectral Temple connect to glorious effects caused by light scattering. One aside: the dragon of light that snakes down the Argali temple is based on an actual style of architecture from the Maya Indians.

One thing I noticed with writing this book: scattering terminology is rather provocative. In using it for research, I hadn't noticed much. The imagery becomes more vivid when translated into human behavior: we capture particles, make bound states, define dominant wavefunctions, split degenerate levels, and control particle beams. We apply forces to most everything. Systems we can't define in such terms we call chaotic.

I've heard debates that such terminology has its roots in gender roles defined by our cultures. If physicists had mostly been women, would we have come up with different terms? Probably, at least to some extent. But I've also wondered if our terminology reflects an instinctual need to attain control over a universe that for most of human history was a capricious mystery, a thing of seeming magic that tossed humanity around like driftwood on the sea.

However, we also have free particles unhampered by bound quantization. The theme of humans having a basic need to seek freedom is one I've explored in an arc of stories: *The Last Hawk, Ascendant Sun, The Quantum Rose, The Phoenix Code,* and the *Analog* novellas, "Aurora in Four Voices" and "A Roll of the Dice." As soon as a "bound state" exists for humans, it highlights the "free state." How (or if) humans seek freedom depends on their situation, just as particle interactions depend on the potentials that affect their behavior.

Some of those stories also deal with male-female role reversal, since the roles of women in many cultures have been confining even when that confinement wasn't physical. Although the obvious role-reversals garner the most attention (such as the husband harems in *The Last Hawk*), for me it was the subtler reversals that served to highlight inequities we tend to take for granted, such as patterns of dialogue that indicate assumptions of dominance rather than, say, cooperative problem solving.

Braided into those explorations is another theme that has always intrigued me: immersion into different cultures. All the above stories, and also *The Veiled Web,* involve a character plunged into another culture. In a sense, those characters become anthropologists trying to understand their new life. In fact, the main character in "A Roll of the Dice" *is* an anthropologist, a graduate student doing doctoral work on the planet from *The Last Hawk*.

So this arc of stories deals with two themes: how humans seek freedom and how coming to appreciate cultural differences may help make the world more peaceful. The idea of understanding the "other" is, I think, a major aspect of science fiction. We look at what is different—the alien—and in doing so, perhaps better understand ourselves.

Characters and Family History

Boldface names refer to the Rhon. All members of the Rhon within the Ruby Dynasty use Skolia as a last name. The Selei name indicates the direct line of the Ruby Pharaoh. Children of **Roca** and **Eldrinson** take Valdoria as a third name. The "del" prefix means "in honor of" (it is capitalized if the person honored was a Triad member). Names are based on world-building systems drawn from Mayan, North Africa, and Indian (India) cultures.

= marriage

Lahaylia Selei (Ruby Pharaoh: deceased) = **Jarac** (Imperator: deceased)

Lahaylia and **Jarac** founded the modern-day Ruby Dynasty. **Lahaylia** was created in the Rhon genetic project. Her lineage traced back to the ancient Ruby Dynasty that founded the Ruby Empire. **Lahaylia** and **Jarac** had two daughters, **Dyhianna Selei** and **Roca**.

Dyhianna (Dehya) Selei = (1) William Seth Rockworth III (separated)
= (2) **Eldrin Jarac Valdoria**.

Dehya is the Ruby Pharaoh. She married William Seth Rockworth III as part of the Iceland Treaty between the Skolian Imperialate and Allied Worlds of Earth. They had no children and later separated. The dissolution of their marriage would have negated the treaty, so neither the Allieds nor the Imperialate recognized Seth's divorce. Both Seth and Dehya eventually remarried anyway. *Spherical Harmonic* tells the story of what happened to Dehya after the Radiance War. She and Eldrin have two children, Taquinil Selei and Althor Vyan Selei.

Althor Vyan Selei = 'Akushtina (Tina) Santis Pulivok

The story of Althor and Tina appears in *Catch the Lightning*. Althor Vyan Selei was named after his uncle/cousin, Althor Izam-Na Valdoria.

Roca = (1) Tokaba Ryestar (deceased)
     = (2) Darr Hammerjack (divorced)
     = (3) Eldrinson Althor Valdoria

Roca and Tokaba had one child, Kurj (Imperator and former Jagernaut), who married Ami when he was about a century old. They had a son named Kurjson.

Although no records exist of Eldrinson's lineage, it is believed he also descends from the ancient Ruby Dynasty. He and Roca have ten children:

Eldrin (Dryni) Jarac (bard, consort to Ruby Pharaoh, warrior)
Althor Izam-Na (engineer, Jagernaut, Imperial Heir)
Del-Kurj (Del) (singer, warrior, twin to Chaniece)
Chaniece Roca (runs Valdoria family household, twin to Del-Kurj)
Havyrl (Vyrl) Torcellei (farmer, doctorate in agriculture)
Sauscony (Soz) Lahaylia (military scientist, Jagernaut, Imperator)
Denric Windward (teacher, doctorate in literature)

Shannon Eirlei (Blue Dale archer)
Aniece Dyhianna (accountant, Rillian queen)
Kelricson (Kelric) Garlin (mathematician, Jagernaut, Imperator)

Eldrin appears in *The Radiant Seas* and *Spherical Harmonic*.

Althor Izam-Na = (1) Coop and Vaz
            = (2) Cirrus

Coop and Vaz have a daughter, with Althor as co-father. Althor and Cirrus have a son. Althor also has a daughter, Eristia, with Syreen Leiro. After his two years of interrogation by the Traders, Althor lost many memories, including those of his marriage with Coop and Vaz. Althor and Coop appear in *The Radiant Seas*. The novelette "Soul of Light" tells the story of how Althor and Vaz met Coop. ("Soul of Light" appears in the erotica anthology *Sextopia,* from Circlet Press.) Vaz and Coop also appear in *Spherical Harmonic*.

Havyrl (Vyrl) Torcellei = Lilliara (Lilly) (deceased)
                    = Kamoj Quanta Argali

The story of Vyrl and Kamoj is *The Quantum Rose.* An early version of the first half was serialized in *Analog,* May 1999–July/August 1999.

Sauscony (Soz) Lahaylia = (1) Jato Stormson (divorced)
                    = (2) Hypron Luminar (deceased)
                    = (3) Jaibriol Qox (aka Jaibriol II)

The story of how Soz and Jato met appears in the novella, "Aurora in Four Voices" (*Analog,* December 1998). Soz and Jaibriol's stories appear in *Primary Inversion* and *The Radiant Seas.* They have four children, all of whom use Qox-Skolia as their last name. Jaibriol III, Rocalisa, Vitar, and del-Kelric.

Aniece = Lord Rillia

Lord Rillia rules Rillia, which consists of the extensive Rillian Vales, the Dalvador Plains, the Backbone Mountains, and the Stained Glass Forest.

Kelricson (Kelric) Garlin = (1) Corey Majda (deceased)
= (2) Deha Dahl (deceased)
= (3) Rashiva Haka (Calani trade)
= (4) Savina Miesa (deceased)
= (5) Avtac Varz (Calani trade)
= (6) Ixpar Karn (closure)
= (7) Jeejon

Kelric's stories are told in *The Last Hawk, Ascendant Sun,* the novella "A Roll of the Dice" (*Analog,* July/August 2000), and the novelette "Light and Shadow" (*Analog,* April 1994). Kelric and Rashiva have one son, Jimorla (Jimi) Haka, who becomes a renown Calani. Kelric and Savina have one daughter, Rohka Miesa Varz, who becomes the Ministry Successor in line to rule the Twelve Estates on Coba.

Time Line

circa 4000 B.C.	Group of humans moved from Earth to Raylicon
circa 3600 B.C.	Ruby Dynasty begins
circa 3100 B.C.	Raylicans launch first interstellar flights; rise of Ruby Empire
circa 2900 B.C.	Ruby Empire begins decline
circa 2800 B.C.	Last interstellar flights; Ruby Empire collapses . . .
circa 1300 A.D.	Raylicans begin attempts to regain lost knowledge and colonies
1843	Raylicans regain interstellar flight
1871	Aristos found Eubian Concord (aka Trader Empire)
1881	Lahaylia Selei born
1904	Lahaylia Selei founds Skolian Imperialate
2005	Jarac born
2111	Lahaylia Selei marries Jarac
2119	Dyhianna Selei born
2122	Earth achieves interstellar flight
2132	Earth founds Allied Worlds
2144	Roca born
2169	Kurj born
2203	Roca marries Eldrinson Althor Valdoria
2204	Eldrin Valdoria born; Jarac dies; Kurj becomes Imperator; Lahaylia dies

2206	Althor Izam-Na Valdoria born
2207	Del-Kurj and Chaniece Roca Valdoria born
2209	Havyrl (Vyrl) Torcellei Valdoria born
2210	Sauscony (Soz) Lahaylia Valdoria born
2211	Denric Winward Valdoria born
2213	Shannon Eirlei Valdoria born
2215	Aniece Dyhianna Valdoria born
2219	Kelricson (Kelric) Garlin Valdoria born
2237	Jaibriol II born
2240	Soz meets Jato Stormson ("Aurora in Four Voices")
2241	Kelric marries Admiral Corey Majda
2243	Corey is assassinated ("Light and Shadow")
2258	Kelric crashes on Coba (*The Last Hawk*)
early 2259	Soz meets Jaibriol (*Primary Inversion*)
late 2259	Soz and Jaibriol go into exile (*The Radiant Seas*)
2260	Jaibriol III born (aka Jaibriol Qox Skolia)
2263	Rocalisa Qox Skolia born
2268	Vitar Qox Skolia born
2273	del-Kelric Qox Skolia born
2274	Radiance War begins (also called Domino War)
2276	Traders capture Eldrin; Radiance War ends
2277–8	Kelric returns home (*Ascendant Sun*) Dehya coalesces (*Spherical Harmonic* Kamoj Argali meets Vyrl (*The Quantum Rose*)
2279	Althor Vyan Selei born
2287	Jeremiah Coltman trapped on Coba ("A Roll of the Dice")
2328	Althor Vyan Selei meets Tina Santis Pulivok (*Catch the Lightning*)

About the Author

Catherine Asaro grew up near Berkeley, California. She earned her Ph.D. in Chemical Physics and her M.A. in Physics, both from Harvard, and a B.S. with Highest Honors in Chemistry from UCLA. Among the places she has done research are the University of Toronto, the Max Planck Institut für Astrophysik in Germany, and the Harvard-Smithsonian Center for Astrophysics. She currently runs Molecudyne Research and lives in Maryland with her husband and daughter. A former ballet and jazz dancer, she founded the Mainly Jazz Dance program at Harvard and now teaches at the Caryl Maxwell Classical Ballet, home to the Ellicott City Ballet Guild.

She has also written *Primary Inversion, Catch the Lightning, The Last Hawk, The Radiant Seas, The Quantum Rose,* and *Ascendant Sun,* all part of the Skolian Saga, and *The Veiled Web* and *The Phoenix Code,* near-future science fiction thrillers. Her work has been nominated for both the Hugo and the Nebula, and has won numerous awards, including the *Analog* Readers Poll (the AnLab), the Homer, and the Sapphire Award. Her short fiction has appeared in *Analog* and anthologies. She can be reached by email at asaro@sff.net and on the Web at http://www.sff.net/people/asaro/. If you would like to receive email updates on Catherine's releases, please send email.